Goldine Serafin

Her body was the product of growth-inducing drugs and Nazi master-race experiments. Hers were six feet, two inches of incredible beauty—and even more incredible athletic promise. . . .

GOING FOR GOLD

The words had been implanted in Goldine's mind through years of psychological conditioning: electric shocks, brainwashing. By now, the very syllables gave her a thrill no man could ever provide. . . .

GOING FOR GOLD

Her Amazon body was primed to do it—to win those three Olympic medals for the team of scientists and businessmen who owned her.

GOING FOR GOLD

She had to win. Had to. At any price.

At any price at all!

ELLIOTT KASTNER and DANNY O'DONOVAN
in Association with
AVCO-Embassy Pictures Corp.
present
A Joseph Sargent Film
"GOLDEN GIRL"

Starring
JAMES COBURN

Also starring (in alphabetical order)
LESLIE CARON
ROBERT CULP
HARRY GUARDINO
CURT JURGENS
JOHN NEWCOMBE
JESSICA WALTER
and introducing
SUSAN ANTON
as "GOLDEN GIRL"

Screenplay by John Kohn
From the Novel by Peter Lear
Executive Producer Elliott Kastner
Produced by Danny O'Donovan
Directed by Joseph Sargent

Goldengirl

Peter Lear

BALLANTINE BOOKS • NEW YORK

Copyright © 1977 by Peter Lovesey

Cover photograph copyright © 1979 by Goldengirl, Inc.

All rights reserved. Published in the United States by Ballantine Books, a division of Random House, Inc., New York, and
simultaneously in Canada by Random House of Canada, Limited, Toronto, Canada.

Library of Congress Catalog Card Number: 76-56312

ISBN 0-345-28320-1

This edition published by arrangement with
Doubleday & Company, Inc.

Manufactured in the United States of America

First Ballantine Books Edition: February 1979
Second Printing: June 1979

First Canadian Printing: March 1979

Goldengirl

[1]

A girl in a white vest and gold satin shorts stood alone in a narrow corridor thirty meters in length. Across the floor in front of her was a thin metal strip with two small terminals at the left end. Behind it, a set of starting blocks. Ahead, a rubber mat, flush with the floor. The wall at the end of the corridor was padded.

"Na Mesta."

The instruction in Russian came from behind a glass observation panel to her rear. She advanced to the blocks and got into the hunched position for the crouch start, with her fingertips splayed on the metal strip.

"Gotovo."

She raised her buttocks and leaned forward, distributing her weight on a tripod formed by the front foot and two hands. The only movements were the pulsing of her temple and a strand of blond hair that slipped from her left shoulder.

The crack of a shot.

The girl screamed in pain, cannoned from the blocks and crashed heavily on the mat.

"I got a reading of point seventeen," the voice indifferently announced from behind the panel, speaking now in an American West Coast accent. "You're not going anyplace this way. On your feet and try again. When your reaction is down to point fifteen, you'll beat the electric shock. But if you come away slower, by Jesus, I'll step up the impulse."

The girl was still prostrate on the mat. Her back gave a series of small tremors.

1

"Action, Goldengirl!" the voice ordered. "You're going to make point fifteen before we finish this session, and point fourteen tomorrow. It's a fact of life that good gun response is essential to a top-line sprinter."

She got up slowly, biting her lip. She went back behind the starting line without looking up toward the observation panel. Her eyes were moist.

"I tell you, chick," said the voice, "by the time you get to Moscow you'll be out of those blocks like hot cowshit."

At one-thirty on the afternoon of Thursday, June 12, 1980, a classic cream-and-maroon Mercedes SSK swept out of Alameda Street, Los Angeles, and slotted into one of the eight lanes of the Santa Monica Freeway. The upright lines of the SSK, conspicuous in the procession of streamlined sedans, were those of the 1933 model. But between the chrome flex exhaust tubes projecting from the hood throbbed a Chevrolet V-8 engine, for this was a modern "derivative," a Brooks Stevens Series III Excalibur. As it approached Santa Monica, its owner, Jack Dryden, of the Dryden Merchandising empire, registered that he was about to join the Pacific Coast Highway by pulling open his shirt. A whiff of sea on the gasoline fumes endorsed his feeling of release.

Traffic four lanes wide still snaked ahead, tires zipping over the antiskid grooves, radios tuned to local stations for news of diversions and delays beamed from the Sigalert helicopters patrolling overhead. But at intervals from this point on, there were stretches of sea and shore unscarred by gas signs and hamburger stands.

At six, if California 1 was clear, he would order a Rob Roy at Dick Armitage's tennis ranch two hundred miles up the coast at Cambria Pines.

The trip to Cambria wasn't to improve his forehand. Armitage, the 1979 U.S. champion, stood high in the organization's list of clients. He had phoned early on

Wednesday morning. Between the French Championships and Wimbledon there was a nine-day interval, and he had flown in on Tuesday night. Unlike most players on the circuit, Armitage took the first plane back to California when there were intervals between tournaments. This time he would need to work on a faulty return of service which had put him out at the semifinal stage in Paris.

"But this isn't about that," he had told Dryden. "I called to tell you I might be able to send some business your way. Could you possibly get out here for the weekend, Jack? You keep busy, I know, but I figure this might be worth the trip. I'd rather not discuss it now, if you understand me. How about checking in for dinner Thursday night and making it a long weekend? It's time you saw the ranch, anyway."

"I'll clear my calendar," Dryden had promised.

He reckoned Armitage would introduce him to some young player with ambitions on the professional circuit who was looking for an agent. He would go through the repertoire of his strokes on court, and Dryden from the sidelines would nod politely and agree to act for him. With upward of twenty agencies scouting for clients, a tip from the U.S. champion couldn't be ignored. Now that tennis ranches were firmly established up and down America as the places where anyone with Grand Slam ambitions learned to use a racket, the pros in residence were well placed to study form.

He wasn't likely to forget that Armitage himself had joined the list from John Gardiner's prestigious Camelback ranch in Arizona. Back in 1975, Ken Rosewall was the professional there. One baking afternoon that August, Dryden had taken a call which resulted in a helicopter flight over the mountains. To his eye, Armitage had looked no different from the dozen other willowy youngsters hammering shots at each other across the nets. Assured the boy would make it when he had grown some shoulders, he had taken him on.

That first season in 1976, Armitage wasn't even among the national seedings. It had been difficult to squeeze one thousand dollars from the Dunlop people for using their racket. Now they were glad to pay two hundred thousand dollars.

So once again he was off prospecting. And because he had struck gold with Armitage it didn't mean he was shouting Eureka this time. He would agree to add the boy to his list provided he didn't hold up banks or do something sponsors wouldn't care for, but he had been in the business long enough to know how many talented teenagers discover tennis isn't the whole of their lives.

Still, he didn't pass up a chance like this. Not in tennis. It was the number-one growth sport, bigger even than golf. In 1970, ten million Americans had played the game; in 1979, close to forty million. The industry was grossing in the region of two billion dollars. Sponsors were paying in excess of fifty thousand dollars a minute for commercial spots in nationally networked tournament matches. With that amount of money changing hands, agents were zeroing in on anyone who could hold a service game.

Whatever the outcome of the present trip, it would be interesting to look over the ranch his enterprise had helped build. For Cambria was financed before Armitage had clinched the 1979 championship at Forest Hills. Each endorsement, every consultancy fee, was won in the teeth of competition from Sports Headliners, International Management, and the others big enough to have a second line of clients. Dryden Merchandising had done well for Dick Armitage. From descriptions, the ranch relegated to the status of an ancient monument the wooden clubhouse reeking of rubber shoes and egg-and-cress sandwiches where Dryden had once enrolled for Saturday afternoon one-setters in England. The brochure Armitage had sent him when Cambria opened spoke of luxury casas, with four bedrooms, casitas, with two massage rooms, saunas, a gourmet

4

restaurant, swimming pool, and, almost superfluously, ten grass courts and five hard.

It sounded like an ideal place to take a girl. The conspicuous gap in Dryden's itinerary was the one beside him in the passenger seat. Thirty-two, with features that projected virility even from the pages of *Business Week,* with reddish-brown hair and a mustache more brown than red, he generally had no trouble arranging company for weekends. Apart from his southern English diphthongs, which he had tried to moderate until he found they worked better than alcohol in advancing a relationship, his principal asset was the deceiving blueness of his eyes, so pale that they seemed incapable of distinguishing anything so sordid as the main chance. He dressed to fortify the illusion, in discreetly patterned shirts and gray lightweight suits.

But this time there was the empty seat. After receiving the invitation, he had looked at his schedule for the rest of the week and rapidly telescoped three days into one and a half, but left no time for making social arrangements. He was happy to leave his personal secretary to make the adjustments on his calendar, arrange a service for his car, order a pair of new shirts—but not a female companion. Not even in California. He flicked a wistful eye over the talent making for the beach at Malibu.

No chance. He wasn't going to hazard his reputation by arriving with a pickup. He silenced the CBS news and lit a Winston. Christ, if he couldn't survive one weekend without a woman . . .

His former headmaster in England, a man more gifted in sarcasm than educating boys, had neatly encapsulated his school career in the words "Dryden Found Wanting" on his final report card. Within two years of that, he had a diploma in marketing, a controlling interest in three pop groups, and any girl he liked in Oxford. At twenty, he was negotiating film contracts from an office in Jermyn Street. Before the merchandising boom happened, he opened his agency, and cornered the London market. As the pace quickened in the seventies, he got a foothold in New York, and then shrewdly moved the center of his business to Los Angeles, where the biggest American agencies only had subsidiaries. By 1977, the Dryden machine was humming in Paris, Rome and Tokyo. As backups, he had eleven companies dedicated to managing, promoting and insuring the sixty-three celebrities in his clientele. They included superstars of TV, cinema, fashion and music as well as sports. Now, in 1980, he had a pre-tax turnover exceeding twenty million dollars.

Going past Carpinteria Beach, he had the agreeable thought that Armitage's rising star on the tennis scene could be a girl. Half a mile on, he shook his head and stubbed out the cigarette. There was something about women tennis players.

He filled up at Santa Barbara and bought four packs of cigarettes. At Gaviota, he followed U.S. 101 inland, since he had no reason to take the more spectacular route through the flower fields.

The coast came into view again soon after five. Pismo Beach. He was making good time.

Before six, he saw the first streamers of Spanish moss suspended over California 1 from the pine forest beyond the small dairy-farming center of Cambria. According to the brochure, there was a left turn soon.

A white notice confirmed it. No modest plaque hammered to a tree, but a thing the size of a billboard. THE DICK ARMITAGE TENNIS RANCH. TRY THE CHAMP'S WAY. HALF MILE LEFT.

He swung the Excalibur onto a descending road so thickly overhung that he needed headlights. The tires purred over pine needles. Past a firebreak, left again, another notice, trees dusty brown where the light never penetrated, and then the scene opened up like curtains parting.

The ranch lay below at the edge of the forest. Red-tiled roofs jutted among conifers. An arc of buildings sited at contrasting levels and angles, with obvious respect for the landscape. In the center, the tennis courts, smooth-surfaced like the piece of sea claimed by a fishing village.

Dick Armitage was at the gate as he drove up, unfamiliar in a floral Hawaiian shirt and black denim slacks. He made a movement that identified him as assuredly as an all-white outfit, raking his left hand through the length of his sun-bleached hair. On court, it would have drawn a rapturous murmur from his teenage following.

"You should carry a racket," Dryden called out. "You're not one bit like the guy on the cover of *Tennis World*."

"No more than you resemble the owner of that Third Reich automobile," Armitage responded, grinning. "The mustache is all wrong. I'm glad you made it, Jack. If I may get in, I'll show you where we've located you."

Dryden liked the ranch just as well in close-up. No gingerbread. The entire layout functional, yet visually pleasing.

He was housed in a casita overlooking the swimming pool. White-washed walls, rush carpets, original abstracts, the smell of pinewood furniture. "How do you persuade your guests to leave?" he asked.

Armitage saluted the compliment with a smile that put creases in the places the sun hadn't tanned. "The cocktail lounge is there, beyond the pool. Look me up when you're ready."

Dryden carried his case upstairs, decided which of the two bedrooms he would use, washed, took a green Shan-su shirt from its wrappings and slipped it on, picked up a pack of cigarettes and made for the lounge.

"Seems quiet," he commented to Armitage as the whisky in the cocktail supplanted the chill of that first, long sip. He didn't mean to offend, but he would have expected more guests to congregate there before dinner. Someone in a blazer who looked like staff was drinking Schlitz, and there was a couple with glasses of sherry in the bench seats behind the door.

"I discouraged reservations this weekend," Armitage explained. "The few you'll see around are residents, more or-less."

"You want to work on your strokes in private before Wimbledon?"

"Unkind!" said Armitage. "Okay, I wasn't putting it together in Paris, but I caught Raul on top of his form. He just *can't* serve like that two championships in a row. Sure, I'll be doing some homework, but there's another reason for clearing the place."

"The reason I'm here?"

"Check," admitted Armitage, peering into his beer. His conversation, like his tennis, progressed in phases, with intervals between points. He resumed: "I invited you here to meet—look, Jack, you've helped me a lot. That Dunlop contract a year or two back. Gave me security, a hedge against a sudden loss of form. You know?"

"I took my commission," Dryden reminded him, curious why Armitage thought it was necessary to express gratitude. He wasn't in the business from altruism, and he thought his clients understood that. "I don't suppose Dunlop are sorry about it, either. It was a long shot, but on target. They aren't all, and the trade understands that. There's no such thing as a stone-cold certainty. The days when Dunlop, Slazenger and Spalding waited for the seedings to be announced before they drew up endorsement contracts are history, Dick. Or legend. With so much going on in the game now—the Grand Prix, WCT, team tennis, the Federation Cup—they can't afford to stand aside. There's a fortune invested in tennis just now, enough for any young player of promise to take a cut."

Armitage nodded solemnly, but ignored the cue. "How's the auto-racing scene? I notice Jim Hansenburg won the Monaco Grand Prix last month. He's a Dryden man, isn't he?"

"Hansenburg? Yes, he's on the books," said Dryden indifferently.

"And what your golfers are raking in between them I wouldn't like to guess."

"It keeps me in cigarettes, Dick." He wasn't used to having his organization analyzed by clients.

"You must be one hell of a smoker." Armitage planted a sinewy forearm between them on the table and leaned over it confidentially. "Now tell me this. What happens when those guys hang up their clubs or whatever? They've been around a long time."

"Since Nicklaus was king," Dryden confirmed, beginning to see where this was heading. "Careful—this is a sensitive area. When a top-liner retires, there's a draft. You feel it no matter how big your agency is. It just happens that I have three or four on my list who could pack it in anytime." He poked his finger at Armitage's chest. "Not you. I'm counting on tennis to keep me solvent. If I could find another Dick Armitage, I'd throw my sleeping tablets away." He wasn't sure why he was doing this. It was more from habit than necessity. He just wanted to bring Armitage to the point.

"You've specialized in golf and auto racing. Would you want a bigger stake in other sports?"

"If you mean tennis—" Dryden began.

"How about track?"

"Track?" Armitage might as well have mentioned medieval jousting. "Did you say track?"

"You know, running—how do you say?—athletics?"

"There's no money in it, whatever you call it," Dryden flatly said. "It's an amateur sport. Olympic Games. The honor of taking part and all that crap. Yes, there's a small professional side, I grant you, but not enough to make it a merchandising proposition. It's on a par with circuses."

Armitage wasn't so easily put down. "A gold medalist has been known to make a few bucks in endorsements," he persisted. "Remember Mark Spitz?"

"He was a swimmer. All right, anyone who hits the headlines at the Olympics can generate some dollars if he turns professional immediately after, but that's one jackpot in a whole career. Spitz won *seven* gold medals. That was great news in 1972, but now who wants to know? The first commercial contract an Olympic athlete signs effectively destroys him as a newsmaker. He's a declining market. Just compare that with *your* game, where you have big-money tournaments all year round. Golf, Grand Prix, all the professional sports are repeatedly reinforcing the big names. It's hard work, but it makes sense commercially. Now tell me, Dick, how many of the 1976 gold medalists in track do you remember?"

Armitage nodded. "But you'll admit that the Olympics is a fantastic sales vehicle? The TV coverage alone."

"That's it, is it?" said Dryden. "You read the piece in *Newsweek* about the price the networks are charging advertisers for a spot in the telecasts from Moscow. It's crazy, isn't it? Two hundred grand a minute. I know sport moves the product, but with that sort of money involved, somebody could get his fingers burnt."

"You're saying you wouldn't care to get involved in the Olympics?" The champion looked as if he was two sets down.

Dryden hesitated. From the way Armitage was pressing the subject of track athletics, he was to some degree committed. To persist with the argument that track was not a commercial proposition would lead to embarrassment if there was some promising pole vaulter scheduled to join them for dinner. It would be crazy to damage his standing with the biggest star in tennis. This required a change of emphasis.

"I'll put it this way, Dick. One year in every four

you find a lot of men in my profession buzzing round the track meets offering the moon to anyone likely to make it to the Olympics. They say nothing is formalized till after an athlete has won a gold medal, but the speed at which those contracts are drawn up beats anything on the track. They're ready for signature before the band is through 'The Star-Spangled Banner.' Next day your gold medalist announces to the world that he owes his success to breakfast cereal, soft drinks and button-down shirts. Two weeks after, he's a forgotten man. Okay, that's exaggeration, but you follow me. Organizations like mine have tended to keep a little aloof from that. It seems slightly undignified to tag breathlessly around after quarter-milers. We keep it under review, naturally." He left it at that. To give more at this stage would be too obviously inconsistent. It was there for Armitage to pick up if he liked.

"I guess so. Same again, Jack?" Armitage beckoned the bartender. "Say, that Mercedes of yours is really something. Custom-built, is it?"

They discussed the elegance of nineteen-thirties automobile design, tacitly agreeing to a short adjournment of the main debate. But it wasn't long till dinner. Armitage couldn't leave the thing unresolved. Dryden, totally unenthusiastic about dabbling in track, was ready to compromise at least to the extent of sitting at the table with an athlete. There he would be on familiar ground, so to speak. Most of his business was conducted over meals. Without being too obvious about it, he ought to be capable of raising enough difficulties to smother the project. He gave details of the Excalibur's performance, pausing tactfully at intervals.

Armitage wasn't oversubtle at this game. "It was a great period, the thirties. There was hardship, I know, but fabulous things were going on in most areas of life. Take sports. Have you ever thought what a killing you could have made as agent to giants like Babe Ruth, Joe Louis, Fred Perry. Hey, and that's forgetting Jesse Owens. Now, *there* was a guy with merchandising po-

11

tential. What was it—four golds at the Berlin Olympics? You could have done Jesse a good turn if you'd been around in thirty-six, eh, Jack?"

Dryden avoided answering directly. "The best they could think of was matching him with racehorses and having him do a turn at the Globetrotters' games."

Armitage lobbed it back. "What if some genius like Owens showed up in America this year and goldrushed the Olympics? You'd be interested in handling the commercial rights, wouldn't you?"

"No agent would pass up a commission like that," said Dryden, and added with a wink, "Level with me, Dick. Do you have the grandson of Jesse Owens staying here?"

Armitage grinned. "Don't rush me, Jack." The awkwardness between them was lifting. "I want to fill you in a little before we get around to identities. Suppose, for example, I told you that my athlete *is* completely unknown to the public."

Dryden smiled back. "That's not a good selling point, Dick. You have me a little disappointed there."

"It could be an advantage if we really go over big at the Olympics," Armitage pointed out. *"Unknown American on Moscow Medal Spree."*

"I like that," said Dryden generously. "I begin to think you should try journalism, Dick. One detail still gives me a little trouble. How does our completely unknown athlete get selected for the U.S. Olympic team?"

The whimsical trend in the conversation was relaxing Armitage. "I can understand your problem there," he told Dryden. "Being unfamiliar with track in the States—up to now, that is—you wouldn't know our selection system. It's beautifully simple, actually. We have our U.S. Olympic Trials a month before the Games, and the first three in each event make the team. No argument, no comeback. If the worldrecord holder has muscle problems and finishes fourth, that's too bad. It saves a lot of hassle, though. Do you see it now? If our unknown can make the first three, that's the ticket to Moscow."

Dryden leaned back in his chair with an air of satisfaction. "Nice." He smiled for fully five seconds before allowing the puzzled look to steal across his features again. "There is another area of difficulty. The Trials. How does an inexperienced athlete get up there at the finish with fellows professionally coached in all the finer points?"

"Ah." Armitage held up a finger in acknowledgement. "I mentioned that our athlete was unknown. I didn't say inexperienced. There's a difference. You see, she's had expert coaching."

"*She?* We're talking about a *girl?*" Dryden's surprise cut clean through the irony that was cushioning the conversation.

Armitage began speaking rapidly. "We are. A good-looker. Blond. A natural for the admen, Jack. More important than that, a fantastic runner. Sure, I know everyone says American sports are male-oriented, and they are. But women do make it to the top, and don't tell me America doesn't need a sports goddess when there's one in my own sport earning bloody near as much as I am. That's in prize money. What she picks up in endorsements I wouldn't mind having." He glanced at his watch. "Look, I want to tell you about this, Jack. Two years back, I was having terrible hamstring trouble, remember? I did the rounds of the hospitals and was near despair. Finally I was recommended to a physiologist in Bakersfield, a qualified physician who earned his bread lecturing at the California Institute of Human Science. I was told he sometimes treated sports injuries and had a lot of success with muscle injuries. He fixed it for me, and I've had no twinges since. Doc Serafin, a great guy."

"I remember," said Dryden. "You were full of admiration for him."

"You bet. Well, you know how it is, you get talking in physiotherapy? I mentioned one afternoon that I

was doing some work to foster tennis at college level
—you know, my UCLA project? We soon got around
to talking about girls and the poor facilities they have
in college compared with guys. He said the system was
loaded against women in sports, and I had to agree.
Then he started to tell me about this seventeen-year-
old girl he knew with an incredible talent for track.
Left to herself, she'd most likely lose interest in the
sport. Doc Serafin had a plan to set her up in a secret
training camp with a team of top-line coaches. He
reckoned that in two years she could make the Olympics. He was forming a group of businessmen—a consortium—to sponsor her. They each put up a few
grand, and if she won, they'd recoup it with interest."

"From merchandising revenue, I suppose," said
Dryden. "And you joined the consortium?"

"I went to see her run a private trial in Bakersfield
first, and that convinced me she was blue chip."

"How much?"

Armitage frowned. "I'm not reading you."

"The stake. What did you hand over to Serafin?"

"Fifty grand."

Dryden closed his eyes.

"The physiotherapy was almost worth that," said
Armitage in justification. "I won two-sixty plus that
season, if you recollect."

"Sometimes I think I do you guys no good at all,
keeping you in pocket money like that," said Dryden.
"Tell me, this secrecy bit—did Dr. Serafin explain why
that was necessary?"

"Mainly to achieve a dramatic impact. If the girl
had spent this two years in competition around the
world, she'd be marked down as Olympic favorite by
now. Believe me, Jack, she's that good. It wouldn't
surprise anyone when she took the gold. But this way
she'll be a sensation. The all-American blonde who
appears from nowhere to beat the world in the Lenin
Stadium. The Golden Girl of the West. You've got
to admit it has great possibilities."

"What's Serafin's angle—political?" asked Dryden.

"Christ no," answered Armitage. "You mean he wants to put one over on the Soviets? No, I can't go along with that. He's just a regular American with an interest in sports who wants to see a talented girl get her chance in the Olympics. That's *my* reading, anyway. You'll be able to judge for yourself. He's coming to dinner. I think you'll find him a one hundred per cent genuine guy."

"I'll let you know," said Dryden, unimpressed. "Do I meet the girl as well?"

Armitage hesitated. He took a long sip of beer. "Well, no. That is, not this trip. He's bringing a film instead. I haven't seen it myself yet." He gave an embarrassed laugh. "It'll make a change from the late-night movie. And there is another guest. One of the backers, a guy named Gino Valenti. He's in pharmaceuticals in a big way."

"Valenti. I know the name," said Dryden. "From his profit margin, he can afford to lose a few grand."

Armitage looked injured. "You don't sound too impressed."

Dryden picked up his glass and gently rotated the last of his drink. "Don't worry, Dick. I won't upset your guests. But if you want to know, this whole thing sounds to me like a con."

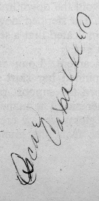

[2]

A speck above the pine forest flashed brilliantly, touched by sunlight.

"That's him!" At the window of the cocktail lounge, Dick Armitage was triumphant. "I told you I could count on him."

Undeniably an aircraft was coming their way, defined against a pink cirrus formation. The engine note carried to them, telegraphing its type by its flat pitch. It dipped low, skimming the conifers. Glasses rattled in the lounge as the sound intensified.

Armitage went out to meet his guest.

The helicopter passed overhead, a Jet Ranger 206A executive model, a white five-seater. The pilot banked as he spotted the concrete tennis court Armitage had cleared for the landing. The Jet Ranger hovered, descended and touched down.

Dryden from the lounge watched for his first view of the man who had relieved Armitage of fifty thousand dollars. The door swung open and a slight, silver-haired figure emerged, dipping to avoid the downthrust of air from the still-whirring rotor. He stepped down spryly, shook Armitage's hand and indicated that a second person was at the cabin door. A girl.

She was laughing at her predicament. Long red hair whipped her face while she pinned her skirt to her knees with one hand and gripped the support rail with the other. Armitage went to her aid. The maneuver was complicated by her shoes, glossy yellow creations with a heel Dryden could see from the lounge

16

was not styled for balancing on a bar two inches in width, but she got down without mishap.

If this was the wonder runner, she threatened a revolution in track, for she was generously curved and scarcely five feet tall in her elevated shoes.

The three moved briskly out of the rotor's unsocial orbit, leaving one of Armitage's staff collecting hand luggage from the pilot. They passed out of sight behind the projecting bay of the restaurant, the girl still laughing, more careless of her wind-blown hair than Armitage, who had clamped his to the back of his neck.

On returning to the lounge, he told Dryden the party was complete. "Gino Valenti's car was moving up the drive as I left Doc Serafin unpacking. They'll join us very soon."

"The girl?" inquired Dryden.

"An unscheduled bonus. Her name is Melody Fryer. Some chick."

"She's not by any chance the Olympic hope?"

Armitage gave a broad grin. "You've got to be kidding. The sport she's built for doesn't need spiked shoes. Not for my taste, anyhow. No, the Doc informs me Melody is his personal assistant, and in case, like me, you jump to conclusions, I can tell you they asked to be accommodated in separate casitas."

As it was past eight when the party finally assembled, they took their drinks to the dining table. The restaurant, empty now, but with seating for a hundred or more, was partitioned with white lattice screens. Circular tables of wrought iron, also painted white, suggested a period theme reinforced by photomurals of tennis action between women in bonnets and flounced skirts, and mutton-chopped partners in straw hats and long flannels.

Armitage steered his guests around a small water garden with fountain and lilypads. "I thought we'd use the table at the end. The large lady with the winning smile is May Sutton, the first U.S. girl to take the

Wimbledon title. She came from California and she was just eighteen years old when she won in 1905. I'm told she had a devastating forehand drive."

Dr. Serafin put on bifocals to examine the blowup. "The photographic evidence, so far as it goes, confirms what you say. This garment she is wearing has padded shoulders, of course, but the biacromial measurement must still have been formidable. I'll sit with my back to her, if you don't mind. Melody, would you take the place on my right?"

Dryden drew back the chair for Melody.

"You just *have* to be English," she told him, smiling over her shoulder as she sat down. She had disciplined the wayward hair, but it was too fine to lie still against the silk grosgrain of her dress. The movement of her head caused some to slip around her throat. She flicked it off her breasts without glancing down. There was no need to draw attention to them.

"Crazy about sports, you mean?" said Dryden. "Yes, it won't bother me facing Miss Sutton's forehand through dinner if I can sit here." He took the place beside her, shaking open the napkin with a decisive action.

She smiled without looking at him as she started unwrapping hers. Her arms were pale against the classic blackness of the dress, cut straight across the bodice, with shoestring shoulder straps.

The other guest, Valenti, seated himself by Dryden's right and made it clear from the outset that he expected conversation irrespective of Miss Fryer's claims. "So you're the super salesman. What is it—merchandising agent?"

"That's what I put on my tax forms," Dryden said, "but it's an area of employment that's variously described. Some of my colleagues are sensitive about the word "agent." They prefer to be known as managers or consultants. It doesn't trouble me."

"All this fancy labeling," said Valenti. "I'm in pharmaceuticals and I don't give a damn if you call

me a dope peddler so long as you buy my products."
Plenty did, if appearance was any guide. Valenti's
suit had the Brooks Brothers finish, and the several
rings on his hands indicated a predilection for rubies.
They weren't paste. "Myself, I don't have much time
for PR. I handle the production side and hire guys
like you to do the selling. When Dr. Serafin invited
me to join the consortium, I told him straight I'd be a
sleeping partner. I wouldn't interfere—just put up a
few grand as an investment. And you can't say I
haven't kept to it, eh, Doc? But when I heard they
were figuring on hiring a—what do you call yourself?
—I thought I'd like to know who was getting into bed
with us. You run that Brooks Stevens job I saw outside, do you?" He stabbed a glittering finger in the
general direction of Dryden's car.

"That's mine, yes," said Dryden, and to make it
clear he didn't expect a one-way interrogation over
dinner, asked, "What do *you* drive?"

"Nothing," said Valenti. "I have a chauffeur. We
used the Cadillac this trip. Here's the menu. What are
you ordering? Myself, I'm starting with prawns in
aspic."

"In case it influences your choice, we have nothing
strenuous planned for the rest of the evening," Armitage told his guests. "A film and, I believe, a progress
report from Dr. Serafin."

Serafin gave a nod in confirmation. Unlike Valenti,
he seemed indifferent to the impression he made, offering no remarks to the table at large, but speaking
quietly at intervals to Armitage on his left. Slimly
built, with the deep-set eyes and angular cheekbones
of a Slavonic cast of face, his hair silver, thinning and
neatly barbered, he made an unlikely—and therefore
potentially successful—con man. His bow tie was the
worst that could be held against him.

Dryden waited for Melody to complete her examination of the menu and asked her, "Is this a commercially made film we're going to see?"

She leaned his way, ambushing him with cleavage and Clinique. "You're too inquisitive. I'm not allowed to say. He doesn't want us to talk about the project over dinner. He's anxious that you should see the film first." So close that their shoulders touched, she added, "We're not too expert on the promotional side. That's where *you* come in—hopefully." She moved away as the waiter approached to change the cutlery for Dryden's *hors d'oeuvre*. "Say, could you really play Miss Sutton's forehand?"

The meal—Dryden had crab salad and escalopes of veal Valentino—could not be faulted, but the conversation never developed beyond trivialities. Serafin was unable or unwilling at this stage to commit himself to anything touching on their presence at the ranch, and the others took their cue from him. Dryden divided his attentions between topping up Melody's glass with *Pouilly-Fuissé* in the hope that it might give more substance to her conversation—it didn't—and reaching the conclusion, as he listened to Valenti's hard-headed rundown on the problems facing the U.S. economy, that if Serafin *had* conned him, he was a very skillful operator.

In all the talk of capital improvement and rising stocks, it seemed impertinent to mention coffee, but Armitage eventually slipped in a suggestion that they ask for it to be served in the screening room, and received almost total support.

The room they moved into was designed with the care evident elsewhere. It had a dual purpose, Armitage explained; although known as the screening room, it was more often used as a lounge. The low, velvet-upholstered easy chairs could be drawn together in rows to seat as many as eighty on a wet afternoon when play was impossible on the courts. He had a film library of most of the classic championship matches since the Smith-Nastase Wimbledon final of 1972. Once a film was running, an audience wouldn't shift until championship point was played, whatever the weather did, so in the planning he hadn't under-estimated the comfort factor.

For the screening of Dr. Serafin's film, five chairs were grouped behind a glass-topped coffee table. Dryden lingered by the door till he saw where Valenti was heading, and then moved toward the chair at the opposite end. He happened to notice that Serafin motioned Melody to the seat beside him. She gave her long skirt a twitch and slanted her legs his way, taking the cigarette he offered. "Do you suppose smoking is a forbidden activity on a tennis ranch?" she asked as she held her face toward the flame.

Dryden shook his head. "The place was built on prize money put up by the American Tobacco Company. The only objection I can think of is that these are Winstons. Keep the brand name under your finger like this and we might not be thrown out."

She looked quite serious and then laughed. "That's a cute idea. I'll pour you a coffee, then I can tap you for another illicit Winston with a clear conscience. Black or white? I'm sure it's here for us to help ourselves."

"Black, if you please. I'm still a little muzzy from the Dow Jones Index." But it was easier talking to Melody without Valenti at his other elbow. She was undoubtedly put there to soften him up for the hard sell, but she was doing it sweetly.

Dick Armitage handed coffee to his other guests, and asked Serafin if he wished to say a few words to introduce the film.

"No. It speaks for itself."

So he gave a signal, and a large screen slowly unfurled on the facing wall. Apparently by the same mechanism, blinds descended at the windows.

A projector whirred, and the gray surface of the screen changed to dazzling gold.

Yellow of various intensities is often described as gold, but true gold has a translucent quality that sets it apart.

For up to ten seconds the screen and the faces of the watchers were radiant with this unique color. Then the gold began to merge into an ocher shade, and Dryden became aware that he was watching the effect of pure sunlight on a close-up of softly tanned human flesh. As a suggestion of pink tinged the surface, the gold shimmered again on myriad tiny hairs, giving it the texture of silk.

A girl's stomach.

From the top left of the screen, as the camera zoomed out, a neatly formed navel came into frame, confirming Dryden's supposition. He felt like applauding, the camera-work was so effective.

Across the screen appeared the single word GOLD-ENGIRL.

The dead-still white lettering emphasized the delicate movement of the skin.

There were no credits. The camera stayed with its subject, the just perceptible movement of the navel toward the center of the screen confirming that the shot was moving outward. At the base of the screen, the sunlight discovered a concentration of flaxen down which slowly intensified in thickness and profusion until a triangular mound of fine gold hair was defined.

A warning signal sounded in Dryden's mind. There was nobody sharper than Dick Armitage in tennis, but off court he wasn't noted for his powers of discrimination. What was on the screen didn't look like an athlete training for the Olympics. It was more like the intro to a blue film. Professionally made, he conceded, but no different in kind from the skinflicks men with an eye to a fast buck had been purveying since the days of the brothers Lumière. He was no prude. While Goldengirl stayed on the screen he was as ready as the next man to enjoy her visible assets. But let anyone suggest the Dryden Agency might promote them, and he was going to sound off like Lincoln on human rights.

She was fully in frame, a tall, proud and undeniably

beautiful creature, motionless against a blue background, the breeze carrying wisps of her long, blond hair round her body and against the underside of her breast, affirming its roundness. The filming was obviously done at a high altitude, for the blue was as much mountain as sky.

By degrees, the camera angle shifted to the girl's left. It meant filming directly into the sun, so that her profile was cast into a dramatic silhouette edged with gold, reminiscent of the opening sequence of Leni Riefenstahl's *Olympia,* the celebrated documentary of the Nazi-staged Olympic Games of 1936. The shot into the sun is such a cliché of commercials that Dryden ought to have been squirming in his seat, but this unhurried treatment seemed to have rediscovered the heroic quality of Riefenstahl's film.

It was odd he didn't recognize the girl. One of his mental recreations was naming the girls in TV commercials. He reckoned he knew the face of every blonde, brunette and redhead modeling for ads across the country, if he couldn't always recall the name. Names weren't so important. The same girls used half a dozen different ones, and got all the work they could from knitting patterns to nude shots, so anyone with a stake in the advertising business needed to be able to spot them. It didn't please a company chairman to open a girlie mag and see a full frontal of the same girl who sedulously applied his brand of vapor rub to her wheezing husband's chest each night on all the major networks. It went completely against good merchandising practice, and it was Dryden's job to see it didn't happen; his nightmare that it might.

Goldengirl wasn't in any of the agency catalogues, he was certain. It was not a face you could forget. There was an elegance to it, a dignity in repose, a marvelous tragic quality about the eyes and mouth that film men would have pawned their Oscars to get under contract.

As he watched the camera's movement around her,

he marveled that a girl so stunning had been ignored
by the media. He half-expected some blemish to appear in shot and account for it, scar tissue or a grotesque birthmark.

She was flawless.

The camera had panned completely around her to
the position of the opening shot and was zooming in
again for a repeat of the close-up, with the navel trav-
eling across the screen like a scarab traversing the des-
ert. When it reached the point where the title had
been superimposed before, it stopped.

Expecting a cut to one of the standard postures in
the erotic repertoire, Dryden was unprepared, to say
the least, when a set of tabulated statistics appeared
against the gold background.

GOLDENGIRL WILL BE 19 YEARS OF AGE ON JUNE 6, 1980

weight	74.0Kg	163lb.
stature	1882mm	6'2"
shoulder (biacromial diameter)	390mm	1'3¼"
hip (bi-iliac diameter)	296mm	11¼"
bicep circumference	263mm	10¼"
thigh	579mm	1'10½"
calf	373mm	1'2¼"
endomorphy	20	
mesomorphy	60	
ectomorphy	20	
somatotype	262	

The shot moved out, dissolving into a second sequence which made it clear, if the statistics had not,
how tall she was. Till now, there had been nothing in
frame to compare her with. Here she was indoors, in a
gym, and she was not alone. Beside her, at the level of
her shoulder, stood a man in a white coat holding a
pen: Dr. Serafin.

His voice came over on the soundtrack, Dryden's
first opportunity of hearing it in more than a few terse

words. The accent was American, with a trace of central Europe in the clipping of consonants.

"I want to invite you to look carefully at this young woman, for as well as being singularly attractive, she is one of the most interesting subjects physiologically who has ever appeared on film. This begins to become apparent if we examine her by means of radiography."

A full-length X-ray was superimposed on the screen, so that the doctor appeared to be standing beside the girl one moment, her skeleton the next.

"You will see that although she is remarkably tall for a woman at one meter eighty-eight, and one would expect to somatotype her as an ectomorph according to the Sheldon classification,* her upper development is unquestionably in the mesomorph range. Notice particularly the width of the shoulders and thorax. The facility of a larger-than-average rib cage allows, of course, for increased lung capacity. An individual's aerobic capacity, which we define as the maximum amount of oxygen that can be absorbed, transported and used per minute of sustained work, depends on the size of the lungs and heart, the amount and hemoglobin content of the blood, and the mass of muscle tissue. If we now examine the muscular formation"— the skeleton dissolved into the more pleasing image of Goldengirl fully fleshed—"we see that she possesses the well-muscled thighs and calves of women many centimeters shorter in height. The traditional criteria of beauty in women—the relative sizes of bust, waist and hips—are, I would say, in a pleasing ratio, while the back and buttocks—if you would kindly turn round, my dear—have the classic appearance"—he made parabolas in the air with his pen—"of the female form."

---

* William Sheldon in 1940 devised the system of "somatotyping," identifying physique by reference to three extremes of body shape, endomorph (essentially rotund), mesomorph (broad-shouldered and well-muscled), and ectomorph (essentially lean).

Dryden took a check on the rest of the audience. Valenti was biting the end of an unlighted cigar, and Armitage was leaning forward, with his chin supported by his right fist. Melody blew a small cloud of smoke at the screen.

"It is a well-documented fact," Dr. Serafin continued, "that during the last hundred years there has been a tendency for children to reach the age of puberty earlier, grow taller and develop better physiques than their forebears. The trend in linear growth is about one centimeter per decade in the United States and Western Europe. Of course, I am speaking of the average. Already you will find some girls as tall as this one—taller, indeed. You are most unlikely to find one with a comparable physical capacity, and I speak with an experience of forty years of anthropometry. If the trend I described continues, we may expect our idealized woman of the twenty-first century to look like this, with the physiological advantages, the deeper chest, greater lung power, stronger cardiovascular system and muscular development to match her stature. Turn around, my dear. In short, this girl is eugenically thirty or forty years ahead of her time. And that, as you shall shortly see, has some interesting implications."

The film cut to a shot of the girl in a gold leotard —they knew how to implant their message—standing beside a set of weights.

"These are training weights of forty kilos normally used by male athletes," explained the doctor. "She will now give a short demonstration of her agility. This is not in any sense a test of her strength. I should merely like you to observe the fluidity and ease of her movements."

She crouched at the weight and completed the power-clean movement with smooth control, repeating it nine times, followed by similar repetitions of bicep curls, half squats and bench presses.

"Her pulse rate, if I took it," said Dr. Serafin when

the girl had finished and stood breathing deeply but evenly at his side, "would have increased to over one hundred and fifty beats per minute during this exercise, but will return to its normal fifty within two minutes. I have undertaken an extensive program of tests and measurements with her over many months, using as a basis statistical data obtained from the Stanford Physical Performance Research Laboratory, the Harvard Physical Fitness Index, the Soviet GTO Mass Fitness Program and the Freiburg Institute of West Germany, and I am able to tell you with authority that this young woman's performances place her in the top two or three per cent of women, irrespective of age, in each of the tests." Dr. Serafin made a dismissive gesture with his hand. "But physiological data are of consequence only to physiologists. An electrocardiograph is capable of exciting me, but I cannot expect it to stir the imaginations of men and woman at large. No, there are other tests of physical capacity. rather less precise than the measurements we carry out in the laboratory, but sufficiently validated by mass participation over many years to establish criteria. I refer, of course, to popular sports. Measurable sports. In particular, track and field athletics. Here we have a mass of evidence of the ultimate achievements of men and women in a number of physical activities. Sports journals are filled each year with details of thousands of athletic performances from all over the world.

"Certain athletic activities hold no interest for our present inquiry. Jumping and throwing, for example, now require sophisticated techniques that have raised the standard of performance, but destroyed the purity of the events as simple physiological measures. It takes at least three years of intensive coaching and training to bring a high jumper to the limit of his potential, and anyone who has observed a—what is the expression? —Fosbury Flop cannot conceivably classify it as a useful physiological test.

"Fortunately, there are still events in which the ac-

27

tivity is relatively unencumbered by coaching techniques, of which running over short distances is the obvious example. Yes, you may rightly point out that the start of a sprint race is a technical trick with some influence on the total performance, and I concede that. I am also aware that coaching manuals are filled with complicated information on details of stride length, knee lift, posture and so on, but I put it to you that running at the fastest speed of which one is capable is really a basic and natural exercise. In the last fifty years, the world record for one hundred meters for men has been improved by less than half a second, and that may be due as much to advances in shoe design and track surfaces as to coaching techniques."

Here the film returned to an outdoor setting. Dr. Serafin was standing beside a stretch of running track, drawing the hair back from his forehead against a slight breeze.

"So it is instructive," he resumed, "to see what our eugenically precocious young woman can achieve as a runner. I should tell you here that at no time in her life has she taken part in competitive athletics. You will not find her name in any of those voluminous statistical manuals. First, let us see her running freely, without regard to any athletic event, simply enjoying the experience of moving at speed."

Goldengirl was wearing a tracksuit in this shot, a white singlet and the predictable gold silk shorts, but she was barefoot. She was running easily and evenly along the track, her hair springing on her shoulders. Her movement gave the exciting impression of power in reserve, long legs stretching over the track, arms swinging effortlessly in the same rhythm. Whatever Serafin was trying to prove, this girl in motion was superb, an expression of physical well-being that lifted the spirit like the opening bars of a great concerto.

Then Dryden felt his right foot press against the carpet in a reflex movement, as if stepping on the accelerator of his SSK. The girl was powering herself to a faster rate, smooth and controlled as automatic transmission, her hair rippling behind her in a shock of gold, arms pumping in piston-rod precision, legs consuming the track. The background was a blur as the camera panned with her burst of speed for perhaps five seconds, when she slipped into a slower gear and trotted up to Dr. Serafin's side.

The interesting thing was that in spite of the assurance that this was a run for pure enjoyment, the girl's face gave no hint of elation, even of satisfaction. She looked, as she had through the film, detached and devoid of emotion of any sort.

The doctor was speaking again: "Now that she has warmed up, let us invite her to run one hundred meters. Put on your spikes for this, my dear. I shall start her from this end of the track and she will be electronically timed as she passes the line at the end of the straight." He paused for Goldengirl to lace up her spikes. "Are you ready now? Then go to the center lane and wait for my instructions." He picked up a starting pistol from which a lead trailed. "On your mark."

She approached the starting line and got into the crouch position. Without starting blocks she was handicapped already.

"Set."

She raised her hips and leaned forward over her fingers, her arms not straight as was usual, but bent slightly at the elbows, bearing the weight of her trunk, ready to use their strength to produce a more powerful impetus.

The gun cracked, and she was in motion, her body angled unusually low to the track for the first thirty meters or more. The transition from photographic stillness to rapid sprinting was dramatic, but less thrilling to Dryden than the surge of acceleration in her first free run. Yet the crispness of her running, even without opposition to measure her by, was demonstrated beyond question. Here was a marvelous athletic talent.

She crossed the line, eased down, stopped, put her hands on her knees and drew breath, repaying the oxygen debt she had incurred.

Dr. Serafin appeared in shot again. "The electronic timing gives us eleven point seventeen seconds. If achieved in competition, that would rank her in the top half-dozen women sprinters of the world this year. It is right to mention that this film was made at an altitude of six thousand feet and that the thinner air is advantageous to sprinters. Against that, one might set the absence of starting blocks and, of course, competition. If I state that in Mexico City in 1968, at an altitude of seventy-five hundred feet, Miss Wyomia Tyus, of the United States, set the Olympic Record at exactly eleven seconds, it puts this time in perspective.

"Allow me to conclude with a simple mathematical observation. If you study the heights of the world's leading twenty-five women sprinters, you will find that the average is one hundred seventy-two point three centimeters, almost sixteen centimeters less than the young woman you have just seen. Now, it is a fact that the maximum force a muscle can produce is proportional to its cross-sectional area. If, as I contend, her muscularity is in direct proportion to her height, and the ratio between the average height and hers is called r, then the ratio between any two corresponding areas of muscle will be r^2, as will the maximum forces those muscles can produce. The ratio between our young woman's height and the average is one point zero nine to one; the ratio of muscular strength is correspondingly one point nineteen to one. In other words, she is nine per cent taller than the average of the world's best, and her muscular strength is greater by as much as nineteen per cent." Serafin spread out his hands. "You may begin to understand why we have called her Goldengirl."

The film concluded with a repeat of the sequence of the girl's first, untimed run, but in slow motion, so that the minutiae of each stride, the ripple of thigh muscles, the hair's fluidic rise and fall, took on their own fascination.

As he watched, Dryden reflected wryly on his assumption after the first few frames that he was watching a skinflick. The notion that these people were going to invite him to promote porn had leaped so readily to mind that it had taken more than a minute of the unseductive Dr. Serafin to shift it. Now, as the film purred through its remaining footage, it was confirmed as a product launch. Dick Armitage's story had held up: there was actually an unknown girl who appeared to run like a dream. How she measured up to Olympic standards it was impossible to tell. There was only Serafin's word that she had covered one hundred meters in whatever he had said. It could still be an elaborate con. Camera-work can make diamonds out of drops of water.

For the present, it didn't matter whether Serafin was on the level. Armitage believed he was. Valenti believed it, too. They had backed Goldengirl and they wanted to squeeze the maximum from their investment. This was not the moment to raise doubts about her. He would have to discuss his possible involvement on the basis that Goldengirl was just as brilliant as the film suggested. He could still provide a plausible argument for refusing the commission.

There were four sportsmen on the Dryden books in the superstar bracket—Dick Armitage, Jim Hansenburg, the world champion racing driver, and the two golfers, Marler and Patrick, who between them in 1979 had wrapped up the PGA, the Piccadilly World Match Play, the U.S. Open, and the Masters. Now that they were walking corporations with their own investment managers and tax consultants, people looked at their success and assumed every clean-living kid with muscles could do as well. The plain fact was that merchandising opportunities didn't arise for people in sports till circumstances contrived to put them in a situation which held the world by its short hairs in front of the TV screens.

For a track and field athlete, there was only one route to Madison Avenue, and that, in 1980, was via Moscow. But these days even an Olympic gold medal didn't get your face on a cereal box. You had to beat the world in storybook style—falling flat on your face, getting up and *still* winning. Goldengirl—with no competitive experience—had it all to do.

And Dryden had to spell this out to the people who were behind the girl. When they had put so much already into the sales pitch, they weren't going to take kindly to being told they didn't have a marketable commodity.

It was a prospect that came uncomfortably closer when the film ran out, the screen ascended smoothly out of sight, and Dr. Serafin turned his chair to face them, a propitious smile on his lips.

[3]

"I begin with an apology. It was discourteous of me to decline Mr. Armitage's invitation to preface the film with a few words." Without amplification, Serafin's voice sounded thin, an unequal substitute for the soundtrack. He must have decided a less assertive approach was now appropriate. "In planning this evening, I was concerned to ensure that Goldengirl made her own impact, without any preamble from me, so I left the explanations, such as they are, till now. I also apologize for bringing you here on such short notice, without specific indications of the purpose of this get-together. You are extremely active in your different spheres, I know, and I am appreciative that you rearranged your schedules to respond in this way to my invitation. The reason for the lack of advance information will, I assure you, be made clear before very long, but I do not regard a justification as an apology, and I make that now. I believe you will find the rest of this weekend both instructive and profitable." On the last word he paused, smiling. "Comfortable, too." He was feeling his way. It was obvious an interval was necessary to subdue the images and sounds of the film. "Melody, I wonder if you could arrange for another jug of coffee? I am sure it would be welcome."

Armitage started from his chair. "I'll fix that."

Serafin put up his hand. "You've done enough, Dick. Miss Fryer may not look it, but she is an old-fashioned girl who has no objection on principle to fetching coffee for four men, do you, my dear? She is perfectly capable of persuading one of your staff to make it for her. I would prefer that we aren't interrupted by waiters."

Melody said nothing, but the swing of her bottom as she carried the tray to the door suggested she wasn't downcast.

Serafin resumed: "Gentlemen, you are entitled to know a little more about me and my personal involvement in the project we are here to discuss. You would find, if you were sufficiently interested to look me up in the technical and scientific directories publishers unendingly produce, that my name is William Serafin, I was born in Salzburg in 1920, and I have a medical degree from the University of Geneva and a Ph.D. from Yale. I specialize in the field of physiology, and I am a Fellow of the American Academy of Physical Education. Until 1978, I was Professor of Anthropometry at the California Institute of Human Science. I still live in Bakersfield, where I amuse myself trying to keep up with the latest developments in my field of study. You may think it appropriate here to exchange biographical data all round. Dick Armitage need say nothing, he is so familiar from our TV screens. But Mr. Valenti, although yours, too, is a household name, I am sure we should all be interested to know—"

—who we're getting into bed with, thought Dryden.

Valenti drew on his cigar, his brown eyes darting at this unexpected development. "What do I say? I'm in pharmaceuticals. Always have been. Inherited the business from my father back in sixty-four. I have an interest in sports, which is why I'm here. Just from the sidelines—don't get me wrong. I do ten pushups each morning, and that's plenty. I'd like to buy a basketball franchise, but do you see Jack Kent Cooke selling out? So I speculate in other sports, and here I am. Forty-two, just for the record, and I live off Wilshire Boulevard—the Beverly Hills end. Over to you, Dryden."

"If you would oblige us," Serafin unctuously added.

After Valenti, he was determined to keep it short. "I'm from England, as you've gathered. Been in business all my working life, exclusively on the entrepreneurial side. Formed my own agency in London, specializing in negotiating contracts for big-name sports stars. It prospered, but the real opportunities were over here, so I transferred to New York in seventy-three. Since then, I've moved the head office to Los Angeles, and opened branches in several other cities around the world. My clients are principally golfers, Grand Prix drivers and tennis players. No track stars."

"Is that a fun remark?" asked Valenti. "Is it like a joke? You're our big-wheel agent and you don't know about track?"

"Skip it, Gino," said Armitage. "He didn't know tennis till I joined him. Jack's just the best damned agent in America. That's why he's here."

Before Valenti could answer, Serafin added, "Mr. Dryden is as much a byword in his particular profession as you gentlemen are in yours. He is here this weekend because I consider it timely to bring him in on our discussions." He was articulating his words with an emphasis that made it clear he intended to lead those discussions. "Well, gentlemen. None of you had seen the film before. I am naturally interested to have your first impressions."

"The girl looks good," declared Armitage.

"Runs good, too," said Valenti, with a sneer. "What's your opinion, Dryden? Would you say we've got a Grand Prix winner there, or should we try her in the U.S. Open?"

"Knock it off, Gino," warned Armitage.

"Leave this to me," said Serafin. "Gentlemen, if this consortium is to operate successfully, it has to be on a basis of mutual respect. Personal insinuations of the kind we have been hearing are intolerable, and as your chairman I emphasize now that I shall not hesitate to cut short the meeting if necessary and abandon consultation altogether."

35

Valenti leaned forward and stretched out a mollifying hand. "Don't give yourself ulcers, Doc. It's my style. There's no sense getting disturbed about things I say. You asked me if I liked the film. Sure, I did. That's a twenty-four-carat dame. No argument. What do you say, Dryden?"

Drawn into committing himself, he commented, "Yes, I was impressed. I don't pretend to be an authority on track"—he glanced Valenti's way—"but I've seen my share on the TV networks, and I reckon I can spot a runner with class. The sprinting in the film was a revelation. I'd like to see what your Goldengirl could do against other runners."

Instead of picking up the last point as criticism, Serafin was delighted by it. "So should I, Mr. Dryden —and we shall! I intend to come to that presently, but first I see Miss Fryer approaching."

"Mission accomplished, too," said Valenti, exuding bonhomie. "Mine's black without, Melody."

He was the last to be served. The coffee was in tall Troika mugs instead of the porcelain cups they had used after dinner. Whether it was the coffee, or Melody's return, the tension had lifted when Serafin resumed.

"I propose to tell you a story which until this evening has been unknown in its entirety to anyone but myself. In all our interests, I must insist that you never repeat it. Do not worry; it will not incriminate you. I am not a breaker of laws, nor do I ask others to be.

"It takes us back more than forty years, to prewar Nazi Germany. Dick, who majored in physical education at Berkeley, would tell you that there is a strong tradition of organized gymnastics in Germany which can be traced back at least to the beginning of the nineteeth century, the era of Johann Guts Muths and Ludwig Jahn. It was a movement that spread irresistibly through Germany and much of Europe, taking in other forms of sport as they developed. Even the First World War was not allowed to halt its progress. One of the few lasting achievements of the Weimar Republic of the postwar period was its provision of sports facilities and clubs on a scale unparalleled anywhere else in the world—facilities the Third Reich is often incorrectly credited with having provided.

"From the beginning of what he termed his *Kampf,* Adolf Hitler saw that the emphasis on physical improvement in Germany was a perfect vehicle for his ambitions. The strike force of the Nazi party, the Storm Troopers, or SA, was originally formed as a gymnastic and sports association as early as 1921. One of Hitler's first actions on coming to power in 1933 was to appoint SA Group Leader von Tschammer und Osten *Reichssportsführer,* with instructions to dissolve all sports associations regarded as left wing and unite the remainder in a single organization, the *Reichsbund für Leibesübungen.* At the same time, Baldur von Schirach was performing a similar exercise with the youth organizations, welding them into the Hitler Youth Movement. The young people of Germany were to embody that crude philosophy of racial elitism culled from the Nietzschean notion of the superman and given its expression in Alfred Rosenburg's *Myth of the Twentieth Century.*"

"The superiority of the Aryan race," said Valenti, not missing a chance to reinstate himself.

"Exactly," said Serafin. "The theory that a flaxen-haired, blue-eyed people had carried the torch of civilization since primitive times and survived in Germany to found another great culture under Hitler's leadership, a state that would become more noble even than Aryan Greece. It was a theory that conveniently placed a high priority on sports and physical development, so that the Germans were able to continue to practice their gymnastics and outdoor pursuits, but in Nazi-oriented organizations. The Youth Movement grew to a membership of almost eight million. From the age of six in the *Deutsches Jungvolk,* and from fourteen in the Hitler Youth, the young people took part in a strenuous program of boxing, wrestling, gymnastics, camping and soldiering that occupied their time out of school. Much of it was, of course, competitive, which appealed to the German temperament and provided a massive pyramid of achievement. The children who emerged as the finest physical specimens were taken out of the normal schools, the *Gymnasien*, and placed in special schools, *Nationalpolitischeerziehungsanstalten*, which even Germans found too much of a mouthful and contracted to *Napolas*. They were equipped with outstanding facilities for every kind of physical development, and usually situated beside a lake. There, these selected few were trained, physically and politically, to become the elite of Germany, the future torchbearers of the Third Reich.

"It happened that one of these children was a girl, a pretty child of conspicuous athletic ability, who came to a *Napola* in Lower Saxony that took girls from the *Bund Deutscher Mädel,* the female branch of the Youth Movement. Let's call her Gretchen. Even in the hand-picked community of the *Napola,* Gretchen showed up as a superb all-round athlete, and one morning in 1935, when she was seventeen, she was summoned to the director's office and told that she was to join a squad of women gymnasts training for possible selection for the Olympic Games. You may imagine her excitement. The 1936 Olympic Games were scheduled for Berlin and were to be a Nazi showpiece, Hitler's opportunity to demonstrate to the world the achievements of the Third Reich and the brilliance of his Aryan athletes.

"The story of those Games has been told often enough, gentlemen. Let us concentrate simply on Gretchen. She was duly selected to be one of the eight women who represented Germany in the Combined Exercises team event. There were no individual gymnastic contests for women in the Olympic Games at that time, or she would probably have competed in more than one event. But gymnastics was the parade sport of the Games for the Germans, their traditional ideal of sport, and every seat was sold months ahead for the program in the Dietrich Eckart Stadium, specially built in a wooded ravine at the edge of the Olympic complex. As it was, Germany's gymnasts dominated those Games in the men's and women's events, and Gretchen won a gold medal. She could not have done more for her *Führer*." Dr. Serafin paused, glancing down at his fingernails. The room was silent. If there had been any question earlier who was in control, it no longer applied.

"But there was one service more that was required of her. As a product of the *Napola* and an Olympic champion, she was a flower of German womanhood, the female equivalent of one of the SS. Had she been a man, there is no doubt that she would have graduated to one of the *Ordensburgen,* in which selected members of the SS received further indoctrination. Her name was certainly in the card-index system of RuSHA, the SS Race and Resettlement Bureau, for one afternoon soon after the outbreak of the war she was visited by two members of the SS. They reminded her of the benefits the Reich had bestowed on her and of her obligations as one of the *Frauenschaft*. Then they spoke to her of the commission the *Führer* had given Heinrich Himmler, the leader of the SS, to make facilities for RuSHA-approved racially pure unmarried women to bear children by similarly approved members of the SS."

"The human stud farms?" said Valenti.

"Yes. The infamous *Lebensborn*. In setting up this 'Fount of Life' association, Himmler had issued a notice to all SS officers reminding them of their duty to set an example to all Germans by rearing a healthy family of at least four children. Those unable to perform this obligation were to sponsor 'racially and hereditarily worthwhile children' instead, and *Lebensborn* would provide for them. The evidence eventually provided by the Nuremburg Trials established conclusively that 'valuable and racially pure men' performed as so-called 'conception assistants' in the service of the state."

"And that's what happened to Gretchen?" said Armitage.

"She was driven the following weekend to a hotel in Bavaria," said Serafin, "where she was introduced to her 'assistant,' a captain in the SS. Being a well-brought-up daughter of the Reich, she made no objection to what took place. As it happened, she found him reassuringly considerate and charming. They spent two nights together. During the day they skied and took meals together like any honeymoon couple. She learned that he was a former international sportsman, an expert in each of the five events comprising the modern pentathlon. She never met him again, but she heard that he was killed in the bombing of Dresden. In August 1940, she returned to Bavaria, to one of the *Lebensborn*'s thirteen maternity homes, at Hochland, and there gave birth to a daughter. She elected to bring the child up herself. Money was provided by the *Reichsführung* of the SS for the child's upkeep until shortly before the end of the war. The little girl's name was Trudi.

"It was hard for Gretchen bringing up the child without a father's help in postwar Berlin, as you may imagine. She worked in a street market, helping on a fruit stall, and her health suffered each winter. Sometimes, when she was feeling at her lowest, she would take out the gold medal from its case and draw some kind of inner strength from it. Fortunately, Trudi was a robust child, and seemed, if anything, to thrive better without the sponsorship of the SS. Being so prone to bronchial troubles herself, Gretchen formed the idea of saving enough money to make a new life in California, where the milder climate would be kinder to her health. In 1953, she contracted pleurisy and permanently damaged one of her lungs. That made up her mind; she sold her apartment and left

40

Germany for good. They came here and rented a place in Santa Barbara. For several years her health improved, but in the winter of 1959, the pleurisy returned. This time she was not strong enough to pull through. She was forty-one when she died.

"So Trudi was left without family in Santa Barbara. By now, she was eighteen and a capable young woman, able to fend for herself. She got a job as a stewardess with TWA and took an apartment of her own near Los Angeles International Airport. She did not lack cash, clothes or boyfriends. During her childhood, her mother had often talked to her of the two cherished events of her life—the gold medal at the Olympics and the weekend in Bavaria with her SS captain. When Trudi saw that the Olympic Games were to be held in Rome in 1960, she decided to make the trip, to watch the gymnastics, almost in tribute to the mother whose gold medal had so unfailingly raised her spirits when she took it out to look at it in the dark years of the forties and fifties. As a TWA employee, Trudi got a free flight to Rome.

"The gymnastic team event in 1960 was dominated by the Russians. There was no storybook victory for Germany, I'm afraid. But something else happened which in some ways had a certain logic to it, but in others was quite remarkable.

"The gymnastics took place in the evenings in the historic Terme di Caracalla, a former Roman bath. One evening Trudi found herself sitting next to a group of young Americans watching the beam exercises. They were cheering a little Czech girl named Eva Bosakova, who was performing so brilliantly that she looked to be snatching the gold medal from the Russians, and so preventing a clean sweep in the women's events. When the result was announced, and Bosakova was declared the winner, the young man sitting next to Trudi jumped up in excitement and tipped half a bag of popcorn into her lap. As so often happens in such incidents, it started a friendship between them. He told her that he and his companions were members of the U.S. track team, and he presented her with a ticket for the next day's events in the stadium.

"I have never discovered whether the young American became a medal winner in the event, because Trudi concealed his identity from the one person with whom she discussed these things. I do know that when his competition was over and the team manager no longer checked his movements around the Olympic Village from hour to hour, he met Trudi and they went out together, discovering the beauties of Rome. I am speculating now, but I imagine that to Trudi, who had so often heard her mother speak with pride about that short weekend in Bavaria with the handsome sportsman chosen by the Reich as her *Leibhaber*, the friendship with an Olympic athlete must have seemed intensely romantic. And it may be that when she gave herself to him in her hotel bedroom, she was exhilarated by the knowledge that she, too, was privileged to enjoy the embrace of a superman.

"Whether she made a conscious decision to conceive his child, I do not know. I can only say with certainty that she was not ignorant about birth control. As a schoolgirl in Germany and in the States, she would have received a comprehensive sex education, and her mother would certainly have talked to her about the methods in use."

"But she had a child, I guess," said Armitage.

"Goldengirl?" said Valenti.

"She was born in the Norwalk State Hospital, Los Ángeles, on June 6, 1961," Serafin said in confirmation.

"When did you first hear of her?" Dryden asked. Determined still to have no part in promoting the girl, he had found himself becoming increasingly interested in Serafin's narrative. A question or two didn't commit him to anything.

The doctor leaned back in his chair, pausing, Dryden suspected, not to recollect the date—because the

details of the story had come so readily to his lips—
but to take the measure of the interest it had evoked.
"In 1964," he answered. "I mentioned earlier that I
studied in Vienna. I was engaged in a research project there during 1963, on the influence of heredity
on human physique. I set myself the task of comparing
the skeletal proportions of one generation of females
with their offspring at maturity. To achieve this, I had
to locate accurate data obtained about twenty-five
years previously, trace the progeny of the women concerned and measure them. I decided to use the data
obtained by the medical team at the Berlin Olympics
in 1936. Perhaps you recall the sequence in the official
film of the Games when hundreds of women gymnasts
were shown moving in perfect co-ordination in a display in the stadium. With their customary attention to
detail, the Germans recorded the measurements of
two hundred of those women. I estimated that I might
be successful in tracing about half this number, of
whom perhaps a third might have given birth to daugh-
ters. I needed more to achieve a statistically valid
sample, and to my great good fortune, I also found
anthropometrical data for each of the forty-two
women in the official German team. The fact that they
had achieved distinction by representing their country
was likely to prove helpful in the process of contacting
them and their children. Actually, I found twenty-
nine of them, which wasn't bad after twenty-seven
years, including World War II.

"One of those I did not meet, of course, was
Gretchen, who had died four years previously. However, I succeeded in tracing five of her teammates
from that successful octet who won the gold medal
for combined gymnastics. One of them had been a
close friend of Gretchen's, actually attending the same
Napola in Lower Saxony. They had corresponded right
through the war and for some years after. She it was
who told me of Gretchen's pride in being selected to
participate in the Nazi eugenics program, and of the

birth of Trudi. After Gretchen emigrated to the States she lost touch with her, except that she received a Christmas card one year bearing a Santa Barbara postmark, but no address. It amused me that one of the group I called 'my 242 *Frauen*' had found her way to my own state, to a place, in fact, less than two hours' drive from my home in Bakersfield. Unfortunately the research grant didn't stretch to transatlantic trips, so I had to put a small cross beside Gretchen's name on my list.

"I didn't forget her, however. The story intrigued me. After all, there can't be many women about who will admit to having served the Third Reich in the way she did. After I had presented my thesis, I took a little time off to check the story. In the university library at Vienna, I found a sports almanac listing the names of all Germans who had competed internationally in scores of different sports in the prewar years. I looked for the names of men who had competed in the modern pentathlon. There were twenty-three listed as full internationals between the years 1924 and 1936, which I considered the likeliest span that would include Gretchen's SS captain. With a list of those names I traveled to Berlin, to the American sector, where the SS records captured at the end of the war were still held. In the document depository there, I explained the purpose of my mission—although I will admit that I gave the impression that the information was vital to my thesis.

"They were extremely helpful. Some of the records had been destroyed by the SS in the last hours before the Allied occupation, but I was able to consult a catalogue of the names of officers, and compare them with my list of pentathletes. Eventually, I had eliminated every name but two: a Manfred Schmidt and a Wolfgang Meyer. Either or both could have been pure coincidence; the names are really quite common in Germany, and the SS catalogue was like a telephone directory. Schmidt was listed as a captain, Meyer a colonel. I was permitted to examine the dossiers for both, including the RuSHA R-card, on which assess-ments of physique, racial origin and personality are recorded. Schmidt's I put aside after scanning it quickly; if I can recollect it now, he was born in 1918, whereas *my* Manfred Schmidt had competed for Germany against Sweden in 1934, which would have made him only sixteen at the time—practically impossible in an event requiring such versatility. But as soon as I opened Meyer's file I noticed that he was born in 1910 and had died before the war's end, on a date of considerable significance: February 14, 1945." Serafin stopped, raising his eyebrows for some reaction from his listeners.

"St. Valentine's day?" Valenti thoughtfully suggested.

"True—a fact that had not occurred to me," said Serafin, without enthusiasm. "It lends a certain irony to the story, if that is what you had in mind. No, gentlemen, February 14, 1945, was the date of the British RAF bombing which devastated the city of Dresden, killing at least thirty-five thousand people, among them, if what Gretchen had heard was true, her SS captain. Wolfgang Meyer had attained the rank of colonel, but it was quite possible that in the five years since that weekend in Bavaria he had been promoted to colonel. So I studied the document with gathering excitement, and there, below his personal data and photograph, was the detail that confirmed the story I had heard: Gretchen's name, and beside it the date: November 12, 1939. In different writing someone had added another date, August 10, 1940, and the letter "W," for *Weib,* the German word for female.

"I looked at Colonel Meyer's picture with interest. He was very close to the Aryan ideal—fair-haired, with a high forehead, light eye-brows and strong features, a sufficiently handsome face to impress any girl meeting him for the first time. I could almost have understood Gretchen's hero worship of the man if I had not also noticed the names of five other women on the R-card, with dates beside them. It seems the colonel sired three female children and two males to the glory of the Third Reich. One copulation had been unproductive; even the SS could not guarantee total success in such activities. I felt only revulsion when I looked at the photograph again.

"After my thesis was accepted by the university in the spring of 1964, I returned to the States. There was a tremendous backlog to attend to in my work, as you will appreciate, quite apart from the claims of my wife, who was a doctor and had been busy enough in my absence, but had a right to some of my time now I was home. One way and another, it wasn't until midsummer that I got around to thinking about Gretchen and her daughter again. The story still intrigued me, though, and one afternoon in August, I drove to Santa Barbara and tried to trace them. I began by looking for the name in the phone book. It wasn't there, so I tried the Chamber of Commerce in East Carrillo Street, where they produced a directory of the kind used for mailing sales literature. Again I drew a blank. I went to the City Library, where they got out an electoral roll for me to look at, but still no luck. That night as I drove home along the Cuyama Valley, I resolved to forget the whole thing."

"But you didn't, eh, Doc?" said Valenti with a knowing dip of the head.

"It was pure chance that brought the issue to life again," said Serafin. "Two months went by, and one Sunday evening in October, while my wife was watching something that didn't interest me on TV, I was thumbing absently through an old copy of *Time*. A feature about the safety standards of bathing beaches caught my attention. I don't know why—the subject wouldn't interest me nine times out of ten. Well, this piece drew attention to the havoc a freak wave can sometimes cause on an apparently safe beach. In particular, it mentioned an incident the previous May on

46

Huntington State Beach, Los Angeles. On a placid Saturday afternoon when the surfers were complaining that the sea was too calm to ride, a huge breaker rose up from the sea in seconds and ripped along the beach, carrying numerous bathers, including children, out of their depth in its undertow. The lifeguards did their best, but five people lost their lives, including a young airline stewardess who had gone to the rescue of her two-year-old daughter. The lifeguards picked the child up, but the mother was drowned."

"Trudi?" said Dryden.

Serafin nodded. "I recognized the surname, you see. I had spent so long looking for it in those lists in Santa Barbara that it leaped out of the page at me. Next morning I went to the Los Angeles *Times* building, looked up the file, and got the whole story. It gave Trudi's address and age and the year of her arrival in California, and there couldn't be any doubt that this was Gretchen's daughter. I visited the apartment Trudi had occupied, and spoke to the young married woman living next door, who had formed a friendship with her. From her, I learned about the death of Gretchen, the affair in Rome and the way Trudi had brought up her child, giving up her job with TWA until the little girl was old enough to attend a day nursery. It was a story that moved me deeply, and I felt I couldn't leave it there. I asked for the name of the children's home where the child was being cared for, and next afternoon I drove out there with my wife. It was a place called Tamarisk Lodge, just north of Ventura.

"The matron-in-charge listened to us sympathetically and agreed to let us see the child with others in the playroom. That, gentlemen, was when I first saw Goldengirl, three years old, tragically orphaned, standing alone, half hidden behind a curtain, hugging a grimy rag doll dressed in the costume of a Bavarian peasant girl.

"In reply to my inquiries, the matron told us that

the child appeared to be adjusting as well as you could expect in such a case. It seemed likely that she would soon be adopted. In fact, a couple had practically arranged an adoption that had just fallen through on account of some drinking misdemeanor of the husband's that had come to light. The adoption authorities are very careful about such things. Well, after a few minutes the matron picked up the child and brought her over to us. You may imagine the interest with which I looked at her, this representative of the generation succeeding the ones I had studied for my thesis. Moreover, nobody—not even my wife—knew, as I did, each link in the remarkable chain of circumstances that had contributed to that little girl's genetic profile. Let me make it unequivocally clear that I am opposed to the idea of selective procreation. That is not my notion of eugenics, gentlemen. But when events had contrived to produce a child whose lineal origins were as distinguished as Goldengirl's, I would have been a poor physiologist if I had not taken an interest in her.

"I could see at once that she had inherited an excellent physique. I would have put her skeletal age—the indicator of physiological maturity in children most commonly used—at four or five months beyond her chronological age, and that, in a child of under four years, is a significant discrepancy. Her muscularity, too, was well-developed. It crossed my mind that the members of the SS who arranged Gretchen's weekend in Bavaria all those years before would have looked with approval at this young recipient of the precious Aryan genes.

"Before we got home that night, my wife said she knew the directions my thoughts were taking, though I had given no hint of them to her. She, for her part, had been charmed by the little girl and shed some private tears for her. We were childless ourselves and I was in my mid-forties, but we talked over the idea of adoption. She was quite prepared to give up her

48

medical career, so I knew that this was no whim on her part. The more we discussed it, the more obvious it seemed. In the morning I went to the authorities and got the papers to fill in. Adoption isn't easy to arrange, particularly if you have set your hearts on a certain child, but my wife was very well known locally as a doctor, and I think what the Bakersfield people said must have carried some weight with the adoption agency in Los Angeles. Early in 1965, the formalities were completed, and Trudi's child became ours."

Dr. Serafin looked keenly at his listeners, as if gauging their reaction to this development in his narrative.

One, at least, hoped his private thoughts were not written too plainly on his face. It seemed to Dryden that Serafin had acquired the child primarily as an extension of his researches. He might be misjudging the man, but everything he had said so far about his adopted daughter sounded more clinical than paternal.

[4]

"YOU will have noticed that I have not mentioned the child's name yet," said Serafin, looking steadily at Dryden. "I shall explain why. It was an unusual one for a girl: Dean." He spelled it. "To tell you the truth, neither my wife nor I particularly liked it. Whatever Trudi's reason was for choosing it—wasn't there a Hollywood cult hero of that name young people of the fifties revered?—we accepted that it would have been psychologically damaging to change it when the child became ours. But after a year, before she started her formal education, we embellished it a little by calling her Goldine, which she liked."

"I like it, too," Valenti announced. "Sounds zippy—Goldine the Goldengirl. Can't you just see that on the newsstands?"

"That was not a factor we took into consideration," Dr. Serafin flatly replied. "She led the life of any other girl of school age in residential Bakersfield."

Dryden frowned slightly. "Didn't the school discover her ability in sports? You said in the film she has never competed with other girls."

"Correct," said Serafin with a sharp glance. "If you listened carefully, I said she was of school age, not that she attended school. We arranged for her to be tutored at home."

"Why was that?"

"Because we wanted to be quite certain she had the best opportunities possible for mental and physical development. As people in our profession do, we had

50

ideas on nutrition, exercise and so on, from which Goldine could derive only a partial benefit if she attended school. At home, we were able to ensure that her diet had the correct balance and that the physical demands made upon her matched her capabilities. She was a gifted child, you see. Gifted, I mean, in physical respects. But like the child of very high intelligence, the athletically precocious child needs a form of education that makes demands, presents challenges. The physical education provided in schools for children of her age would have been unsuitable. She would have become bored and very likely put on excess weight."

Dryden felt increasingly hostile to Serafin's rationale, but he couched his next question as blandly as he was able. "Did you give any consideration to her social development?"

Serafin said without altering his expression, "Do I detect a note of censure, Mr. Dryden? Yes, we took steps to see that she met other children of her own age. She attended ballet classes regularly from the age of six. She also went swimming—not at the beaches, which might have been traumatic—but at the municipal swimming pools. I believe she made a number of friends there. I don't think you would regard her as socially deprived, would you, Melody?"

"Deprived?" Melody's eyebrows peaked. "No way."

"Thank you," said Serafin. "My account is now reaching the point where some of those present enter the picture, you see. Up to the age of sixteen, Goldine had the upbringing I have briefly described. Two years ago, the situation was complicated by certain differences between my wife and me—they didn't concern Goldine, except in their upshot, which was that we separated. My wife now lives in Jamaica, but the details are unimportant here. At about the same time, I arranged for Goldine to run some private time trials on the Bakersfield College track. I had monitored her progress since she was a small child, but her running that evening was truly as you described it earlier, Mr. Dryden. In a word, a revelation. It was evident to me that with the advice of a first-class coach and proper training facilities, she was capable in a year or two of representing this country at the Olympics. There was even the possibility of emulating her grandmother and winning a gold medal.

"I would be guilty of deception if I gave you the impression that this was the moment I first regarded Goldine as a potential Olympic champion. The idea had germinated in my brain many years earlier, but what parent has not at some time pictured his child as a concert pianist, a brilliant attorney or a President of the United States? We learn to curb these ambitions, do we not? To load them onto our children would be monstrous. But when a child in adolescence reveals a prodigious talent, an undeniable potentiality to do great things, then I think the parent has a moral obligation to do everything in his power to foster that talent.

"Allow me to mention an example. Exactly fifty years ago in Fort Worth, Texas, a girl of sixteen saw a running track for the first time in her life. Like Goldine, she was a second-generation American, the daughter of Norwegian immigrants. Her mother had been a brilliant skater and skier. The child, who had the unprepossessing name of Mildred Didrikson, had inherited some of that facility for sports. Her father recognized the talent, and encouraged her by fitting out what was in effect a private gymnasium in their backyard, complete with weight-lifting apparatus: a broomstick with flatirons fastened at the ends. Primitive, but effective, and, for 1930, enlightened. The girl had several brothers, and she benefited from joining in their games, often outplaying them, in fact. Her ability at baseball was so outstanding that she acquired the nickname of 'The Babe,' after the celebrated 'Babe' Ruth. When she came to that running track, she took to the sport at once, astonishing the coaches there.

"Within two years, Babe Didrikson was the outstanding girl athlete of America. In the Texas State Championships, she entered all ten events and won eight, finishing second in the others. At eighteen, she was nominated for three events in the Olympics, held here in 1932 at the Los Angeles Coliseum. With her first throw in the javelin she beat the world record, but tore a ligament in her shoulder. Despite that, she qualified for the final of the hurdles and won that, again in world-record time. That left her third event: the high jump. For this, she had spent many months mastering the technique of the Western Roll. The competition developed into a duel between the Babe and another American girl who used the conventional scissors style. They tied at a height that beat the world record, but the rules in force stated that a jump-off must take place to get an outright winner. The bar was raised by another three quarters of an inch, but both girls failed their three attempts. The judges lowered the bar by half an inch and told the girls to try again. It was still almost an inch and a half above the official world record, and with both girls obviously tired it seemed a pointless exercise, but to everyone's relief and astonishment the other girl got over on her first try. That seemed to have settled the matter. It meant that the Babe had to clear the bar with her next jump, or take the silver medal. She was possibly the only person in the Coliseum who hadn't written off her chance. She took a long look at the bar, gritted her teeth, ran smoothly forward and got over. Stalemate. Then one of the judges ruled that with her Western Roll style she had contravened the rules by 'diving,' so she was placed second. Even so, she had every right to go down in Olympic history as the first 'golden girl' of the Games."

Valenti released a long sigh and shook his head

sadly. "Today that kid could have made a million—easy."

"Actually, she did turn professional," said Serafin. "An advertisement appeared before the end of the year linking her name with the latest Dodge automobile. Ruthrauff and Ryan acted as her agents, and she appeared for a few weeks in vaudeville at the Palace Theater, Chicago, for a fee of twenty-five hundred dollars, doing an Eddie Cantor imitation and demonstrating running on a treadmill. I gather that a sports star can make a little more than that these days in a more dignified manner, Mr. Dryden."

He nodded. If he didn't come up with the obvious example, someone else would. "Mark Spitz, the swimming star of the seventy-two Olympics, is said to have scooped up something in excess of five million dollars."

Valenti gave a jump in his seat.

"Do you see the point of the story?" Serafin asked, a missionary gleam behind his gold frames. "Given the proper encouragement, a girl can beat the world."

"And make at least ten million," added Valenti, no slouch in speculative mathematics.

"We'll come to that at the proper time," Serafin told him with pedagogic stiffness. "The position as I saw it in 1978 was that Goldine deserved a chance to fulfill her potential as a runner. But these days you need training resources more sophisticated than flatirons. An all-weather running surface, a fully fitted gymnasium and, of course, a knowledgeable coach. And research has shown that training at high altitude markedly improves athletic performance. For reasons I shall explain, I had decided to keep Goldine's ability secret for as long as possible. But my personal savings were not sufficient to provide the facilities she needed."

"That's how the rest of us came in," Armitage told Dryden.

"Yes, indeed," said Serafin with a slight smile. "I was fortunate in knowing Dick through my work. He

54

was referred to me when he sustained a hamstring injury. I occasionally treat patients privately, to keep myself from becoming too much of a theoretician. Somehow we got around to talking about women in sports, and I spoke in general terms about Goldine and my hopes of providing her with a high-altitude training camp. I mentioned the idea of approaching possible sponsors, and Dick was enthusiastic to be included. So I made soundings among other acquaintances, putting my project as a commercial proposition —I couldn't ask people to finance us without some return on their investment. Mr. Valenti was one of those who agreed to form a consortium dedicated to making Goldine the golden girl of the next Olympics.

"Between us, we put up more than two hundred and fifty thousand dollars as an initial outlay. I purchased a strip of land in the Sierras, six thousand feet above sea level, and had the camp built there to the consortium's specifications in the most stringent secrecy—the contractors thought we were setting it up for a challenger for the heavyweight boxing title—at a cost of one hundred and fifty thousand dollars. The total outlay will be in excess of half a million."

Dryden looked at the ceiling.

"Should still leave a modest profit margin," said Valenti. "We aim to clear at least ten million. That's where *you* come in, buster."

Four pairs of eyes fastened on Dryden. He gave a hollow laugh. "Ten million!"

"You just told us yourself Spitz made five," said Valenti. "That was back in seventy-two."

"Spitz won seven gold medals," Dryden pointed out.

"For swimming," said Valenti. "That's peanuts. Track's the thing in the Olympics."

Dryden drew a long breath. These people had sunk money into the project already. They weren't going to like what he had to tell them. "Look, she's a stunning girl. A marvelous runner. But she won't turn ten million bucks by winning the Olympic one hundred meters."

Serafin held up his forefinger. "But if she won the one hundred meters, the two hundred meters and the four hundred meters?"

Dryden chuckled and shook his head. "That's crazy! We're really into fantasy now. Why not throw in the marathon while you're at it?"

Serafin said without any display of irritation, "Not crazy, Mr. Dryden. Have you ever heard of Fanny Blankers-Koen?"

"Sure I have. The one they called the Flying Dutchwoman."

"In the 1948 Olympics she won one hundred, the two hundred and the hurdles, and picked up a fourth gold medal in the relay."

"Come now, that was over thirty years ago," said Dryden. "Women's track was a picnic. There were no Russians in the Olympics, no Germans. Two rounds of heats and you were in the final. We're talking about 1980. One hundred and forty nations chasing medals. There are women in East Germany who have trained for one event in these Games since they were ten years old. No disrespect to Fanny B., but the era of the all-round woman athlete went out with knee-length running shorts. I hate to say it, but you've spent too much time reading sports histories. In 1980, it's pure fantasy."

Serafin remained as cool as he had throughout his narrative. "Very well. Since that is your opinion, let's stay in the realm of fantasy for just a moment. I would like the benefit of your expert knowledge, Mr. Dryden. Suppose the miracle happened: that Goldine went to the Olympics and won those three events. I do not need to remind you where they are taking place. An unknown American blonde of stunning appearance—to use your word—strikes gold three times in the Moscow Stadium, watched by the largest TV audience in the history of the world. If you *knew* that

56

was going to happen and were acting as her agent, and had a campaign ready to trigger into action the moment she stepped off the victory rostrum, what would you expect to raise in merchandising revenue?"

Dryden shrugged. "Okay. It would be high. But I don't deal in daydreams, Dr. Serafin."

"Ten million? Twenty?"

"Possibly. Listen, she'd have to run at least ten races of world-class standard inside five days. No girl could stand up to it. They test for drugs, you know."

"Nobody mentioned drugs," said Serafin in a shocked tone. "There's nothing irregular in what we are proposing."

"You wouldn't find me in a dope racket," declared Valenti.

Dryden smiled at this from the pharmaceutical king.

"Mr. Dryden, this is all new to you," said Serafin with an indulgent air. "The rest of us have lived with the idea for two years, and longer. It will take time for you to appreciate the planning in this project and the possibilities it opens up. That is why I suggested an extended weekend for our meeting."

"Point taken," said Dryden. "I'm not going to walk out on you. This might not be my idea of a few days away from it all, but I'm here at Dick's invitation and I don't upset my top-earning clients. There's one more thing I ought to say about the kind of money you people seem to be counting on. Even if you pulled it off somehow, and the girl won her three gold medals, that wouldn't be an automatic guarantee of ten or twenty million bucks. Let's remember that we're dealing with a human being, not just a marketable commodity. The turnover is governed by the girl herself, her personality, appearance—"

"No problem," cut in Valenti. "Remember Trixie Schuba, the Olympic figure skater? She took the gold in Sapporo. That kid was great on compulsory figures, but her free skating didn't look good on account of her size. Someone said she had the grace of a camel.

That could be a handicap in an ice show. Ice Follies signed her up just the same. So they have this golden girl with a figure problem. What do they do? They send her off to Arizona for a course on the Elizabeth Arden fat farm. She comes back glamorized and takes the star spot in the show."

"So how does that affect Goldengirl?" asked Armitage. "Her figure looked okay to me."

"I'm telling you this is a commercial sell like any other," said Valenti. "Package your product right, and you turn a profit."

"Possibly," said Serafin, with an embarrassed cough. "I don't think we should necessarily put it in those terms, but the principle is broadly true."

"All right," said Dryden, "let's stay with skating, because that's where the biggest money has been made by American girls. I can tell you another story about the Ice Follies. In 1968 they signed up Peggy Fleming, the darling of the Grenoble Olympics. She became a legend in the merchandising business, a TV personality with a name that was selling everything from pantyhose to refrigerators ten years after the Olympics. Now, by 1972, another girl was coming up for the Olympics: Janet Lynn. She was actually the favorite for the title Trixie Schuba won. Unhappily, she took a tumble in the free skating and only made the bronze. But Janet had a lot going for her. She was pretty and she pleased the crowds. That's star quality. Ice Follies gave her a one-and-a-half-million-dollar contract. It made her the highest paid woman athlete in the world. Everyone said they had another Peggy Fleming."

"Okay, so what went wrong?" asked Valenti.

"Janet didn't draw the audiences like Peggy. She didn't fit the golden-girl image so well. It's difficult to pin it down, but for one thing she was deeply religious. It was said she made herself unpopular with the other girls in the ice show by preaching at them between numbers. For another thing, she had a spell of poor health—"

"Save it," drawled Valenti. "We get the drift. But that's one out of how many?"

"More than you'd think," Dryden answered. "A girl puts years of dedication and personal sacrifice into winning a gold medal. This may surprise you, but some of them have difficulty adapting to a different way of life, even when that means a huge financial step-up. A few actually turn the big money down to devote themselves to some fresh cause. Jeannette Altwegg worked with orphans. Tenley Albright took up surgery. Janet Lynn often said she would be happier as a missionary. I think you ought to be aware that there can be problems of adjustment."

Serafin had remained silent while the dialogue had developed between Dryden and Valenti. Now he broke in with a quick laugh that seemed to originate high in his palate. "Mr. Dryden, excuse my mirth. I do assure you we are not investing half a million dollars on this project in total ignorance. Of course there could be personality problems, but a little intelligent planning can go a long way to overcome them. Goldengirl is most unlikely to make the injudicious gesture you describe, though we are aware of the possibility. It is one of many psychological syndromes that could arise in a project as ambitious as this. Believe me, we are working on them, and with expert advice."

"We hired a shrink," Valenti explained.

"Indeed," Serafin went on, ignoring this, "the contribution of psychology is quite fundamental to our planning. Although my own experience is all in the field of physiology, I do not underrate the influence of the brain on physical performance. Despite all one hears about football players 'psyching up' before a match, the psychology of athletics is little understood. A neglected area. You will sometimes find one chapter in a training manual devoted to jargon about motivation and mental attitudes, but the advice is about as relevant to modern track and field as cold baths and regular walks. The truth is that we are in the television age. Track, like every other sport, is so contrived that the competition is intense, the difference between winner and loser minimal. Without the uncertainty, there would be no drama, no audience participation."

"No televised track, no sponsors, no sport," chanted Dryden. "So far I'm with you."

"Therefore everything is arranged to ensure that no competitor secures a large advantage over his rivals," Serafin continued. "As soon as anyone breaks a record, his technique is filmed and analyzed by coaches the world over, his training methods are published in the technical journals, he tours the world demonstrating his form. Soon, of course, one of his imitators defeats him. The smaller the margin of victory the better. There are electronic timers, photo-finish cameras, and TV playbacks to allocate the glory."

"Isn't this technology, rather than psychology?" queried Dryden.

"The upshot is psychological," answered Serafin. "You see, it leads to a plateau of achievement. Athletes' aspirations are actually *limited* by the process. They lack the vision to innovate, and it is easy to understand why, when there is so much pressure to conform. They are inhibited by what they read, what their coaches tell them and what their fellow athletes do."

"If it's based on the best knowledge available, how can that be bad?" asked Dryden.

"I'll give you an illustration," said Serafin. "I am sure you remember the impact made by the Kenyan athletes, Keino, Temu and the others, in the sixties. They really fired the public imagination, didn't they? I wish I had a dollar for every dissertation I have read on the emergence of the African distance runner. Yet actually it started about ten years earlier, with two athletes whose names nobody remembers now, but whose achievement was in some ways more remarkable than all the gold medals won by Keino and his generation. I think it was in 1954 that Kenya decided to send two Kisii tribesmen to Vancouver to run the distance events in the British Commonwealth Games. Up to that time they had always confined their participation to the so-called explosive events: the sprints and jumps. It was widely believed that black athletes were physiologically unable to compete with whites over long distances. Well, these two changed all that. On the way to Vancouver they broke their flight in London and competed in the British Championships. The British at that time were among the strongest distance-running nations in the world, but that didn't daunt the Kenyans. The first of them, Chepkwony, running barefoot, set the pace from the start in the six miles, and refused to be overtaken until midway through, when he had to stop for the excusable reason that he had dislocated his knee. That was no discouragement to his countryman Maiyoro in the three miles. He set off in precisely the same style, but faster, so fast that he soon held a fifty-yard lead over some of the world's finest distance runners. Everyone assumed he would collapse after a few laps, but he didn't. It took a new world record to beat him."

"What happened in Vancouver?" Armitage asked.

"They both ran creditably, but allowed others to dictate the tactics. Maiyoro finished fourth in his event, Chepkwony seventh. The point of real significance is that they had arrived on the international scene without any preconceptions about top-class distance running. They simply ran to win, at whatever pace was necessary to keep their chances alive. And they matched the world's elite, athletes brought to a peak of fitness by years of expert coaching, intensive training and regular competition. When, inevitably, they were pressed for the secret of their training, they confounded everyone by stating that they ran only three days a week, and then just three-to-five miles. Compare that with the hundred miles a week almost obligatory among European and American distance runners!"

"Didn't altitude have something to do with it?" asked Dryden, remembering a piece he had read in a Sunday supplement. "They probably lived in the area of Mount Kenya."

Serafin didn't seem impressed. "It's true that training is improved in quality if it is done in thinner air. Putting it simply, the heart and lungs have to work harder to provide oxygen for the muscles. Understandably, the coaches fastened on to this as the explanation for the Kenyans' brilliant running on such a modest training mileage. Since that time, extensive research has confirmed the value of high-altitude training, but emphatically not to the degree that fifteen miles a week at six thousand feet is equivalent to one hundred miles at sea level. No, Mr. Dryden, altitude is far from being the complete answer."

"*Now* we're round to psychology."

A thin smile confirmed it. "You see it, then? The Kenyans were able to run so well because they knew nothing about the technicalities of track or the big reputations of the men they were taking on. They treated their running as a straight competitive challenge, as simple as two boys racing each other to the candy store. You see, there is a danger of too much specialization in track. Athletes believe that by competing with top-class opposition, they will raise their standard, and that is probably true, but they only raise it to the level of the opposition, or slightly higher. By constantly competing with others of a similar standard, they undergo a conditioning process. Running a mile means lapping the track at a certain speed. They believe their training is bringing them to the limit of their physical potential, but really it isn't. Otherwise, how can two Africans, untrained by our definition, stay in contention with them?"

"You're saying regular competition limits an athlete's aspirations?"

"Precisely," said Serafin. "If Goldengirl had joined a track club she would be no worse and not much better than scores of other girls with a talent for running who have rivaled each other on the track since kindergarten. To achieve what we have in mind she has to set her sights much higher. By deliberately keeping her out of track meets we have avoided the pitfall of mediocrity."

"Haven't you denied her something else?" said Dryden. "I thought track was all about tactics and competitive experience."

Serafin made an equivocal sideways movement with his head. "One balances these things, Mr. Dryden. Tactics are unimportant in the sprint events. Quite simply, one girl generates more speed than the others. Experience of competition, I grant you, is not so easily dismissed. The stress of lining up for a genuine race cannot be simulated on the training track. But if she is short on meet experience, what has she gained? Like the Kenyans, she is unconstrained in her approach to running, she has been spared the harassment of being known to the press and public, and she is capable when the time is right of delivering a devastating blow at the morale of her more famous rivals." He brought his hands together. "I could say more about our training methods, but others are better qualified to explain them. Let me tell you instead how we propose utilizing the next two days. Tomorrow, if you are agreeable, we shall airlift you to the Sierra training camp, where you will meet Goldengirl and the other members of our team. They will work through the scheduled events of the training program, and I think you will find answers graphically provided to the questions you might otherwise put to me this evening. We shall spend the night in the mountains, and then on Saturday there is a small meet in San Diego, where you will have the opportunity of seeing Goldengirl's first appearance before the public. We cannot keep her under wraps forever. She has to produce times good enough to qualify her for the American Olympic Trials in Oregon next month."

"Looks as if I came the right weekend," said Dryden brightly.

"You don't think that's pure chance?" said Serafin, insensitive to Dryden's irony. "We want you to have the opportunity of making up your mind about the project."

"Thanks. When do you want my decision?"

"By Sunday at the latest."

"And if I turn you down?"

Serafin stood up. "Shall we adjourn to the bar for a nightcap?"

In the cocktail lounge the party split. Melody Fryer stood at Dryden's elbow with her back to the others, excluding them. He ordered her a crème de menthe.

"You know why he didn't answer your question?" she said. "About what happens if you don't accept the commission? It doesn't arise. He's a positive thinker. He knows you're smart, or you wouldn't have the clients you do."

"I could be smart enough to see snags," said Dryden.

She lifted her shoulders a fraction. "What can you lose? He isn't asking for funds. You only do your bit if Goldengirl gets to be a merchandising proposition."

"It isn't quite so simple. For a job as big as this you make plans, stake something out. There are any number of commercial tie-ins I can think of, but it takes more than three renderings of the Star-Spangled Banner to get them under way."

She held the drink so high that a patch of green danced on her throat. "Explain."

"Okay. Let's say you're in cosmetics. The Miss Melody range. Perfumes, soaps, creams, the lot."

"That's nice."

"I approach you with a suggestion."

"It's getting better," she said, raising an eyebrow.

"To launch a new line. I tell you about this girl who

just won three events in the Olympics. I'm suggesting you have a Goldengirl promotion. A triple gold seal on every product she endorses. With heavy advertising, you could move a lot of perfume."

"Gallons. Niagara isn't in it," Melody said.

"We draw up a contract. You call in your admen and your market researchers and your design boys. It's a big launch, so you want to get it right. But a campaign on this scale takes weeks, months, to set up. While your artists are creating beautiful packages, the public are forgetting about the Olympics. It's all in the timing, you see? As this is a one-time thing, the launch wants to be reasonably soon after she hits the headlines, otherwise you've lost the impact."

"So it means selling the idea in advance," said Melody. "That's no problem. To be realistic, we can't keep this secret after the Olympic team is chosen."

Dryden smiled into his glass. "To be realistic, it's a secret nobody's going to believe."

She leaned toward him, chiding him with an exaggerated pout. "Come, Jack Dryden! You must have *some* commercial contacts who'll take your word that this is for real. If you believe in it yourself, you can convince anyone." She flicked her eyes over him speculatively. "I figure you should know a little about the art of persuasion."

He gave her a level look. "Thanks. I'm saving it for Dr. Serafin."

She shook her head. "You won't shake him, lover boy. Haven't you noticed? He's got a fixation. You're the guy he needs for this operation, so you're hired. Right now he could give you a rundown on every working part of your organization. He knows your clients, your contracts, your turnover, item by item. He knows exactly where the consortium can exert muscle if it needs to. Take my advice. You have two ways of handling this. You can take the job on his terms. Or you can move out of here tonight, sell out

65

your business and get the hell out of America." She smiled and moved a strand of hair off her forehead. "I hope you won't. I could use a little conversation now and then."

[5]

A lake several miles wide ended the symmetry of cabbages, olives and alfalfa. The Jet Ranger's engine sounded a higher note, and a herringbone pattern was churned on the water twenty feet below. Ahead ranged the National Forest, where the westerlies of California are wrung dry by the towering Sierras. No more cabbages, railroad junctions, elevators, silver refrigeration plants. The San Joaquin Valley lay behind them.

Dryden, seated at the rear of the cockpit next to Valenti, leaned forward, trying to orient himself. They were cruising at 120 over sequoias and Douglas firs, following the course of a river through a precipitous gorge, the helicopter's shadow picked out on the dead-still foliage. Soon they were compelled to rise almost vertically up the face of a cataract to the mirror surfaces of a glacial lake.

There the pilot left the river route. Dryden sat back. Without a contour map it was impossible to follow the Jet Ranger's tangential progress into the mountains, except that the direction was generally northward. Somewhere ahead was Mount Whitney, over 14,400 feet in height, the tallest point in the state. Through the windshield each peak looked like Everest.

They had taken off from Cambria at one, after an early lunch. Dick Armitage had seen them off, excusing himself from the trip to put in some practice for Wimbledon. He had tried to explain the conflict he felt on account of his obligations as host. Dryden had cynically

67

counted the seats in the Jet Ranger. Armitage had never been scheduled to join them.

For Dryden, the decision to join the flight was practical. Not because of what Melody had said, which revealed more about the kind of books she read than anything else, but because the showdown with the consortium had to wait. This required a cool approach. If he went along with them, looked at what they had to show him, and turned the project down from an informed standpoint, it would cause the least difficulty all round.

They must have traveled forty minutes among the peaks when Melody, on Valenti's left, pointed ahead, along a narrow valley, to the first sign of habitation in miles, a filiform column of blue smoke rising perhaps a hundred feet before dispersing in the thin air. The pilot took them low in that direction over the conifers.

A clearing appeared, about two hundred yards square. At the rear end a number of timber buildings were sited, some two-storied and large enough to have a communal function. The entire compound was surrounded by a tall fence. The open ground beyond the buildings formed a generous landing area. A second helicopter, a small Sikorsky, was already down there. Making a steep approach, the pilot dropped the collective-pitch lever to its bottom step and closed the throttle. The time as they touched down was 2:50 P.M.

A shaft of cold air ripped into the cabin.

"Coffee first, I suggest," said Serafin. "We'll take it in the staff lounge."

The exit from the Jet Ranger gave Melody another chance to wobble on the footrail. Dryden turned to help her down. He was rewarded with a gentle nudge from her bosom. "Altitude six thousand feet," she murmured. "You have to make allowances."

"Did you hear me complain?" said Dryden.

Serafin had turned to wait for them. He was rubbing his hands, not because it was cool. "This place has a regenerating effect on me," he told them. "I think of it as my retreat."

The references to Nazi Germany the evening before must have made a strong impact. There flashed into Dryden's mind a picture he had once seen of Hitler with guests at his "Eagle's Nest" in the Bavarian Alps.

Serafin led them across the compound to one of the larger cabins. From the Gold Rush exterior, it should have had a wood floor, bare tables and oil lamps.

Not, at any rate, a black mohair carpet.

The place was laid out like a Beverly Hills mansion. Two studio couches formed an angle containing a low, ceramic-tiled table and a Zenith 27-inch TV. The facing wall was taken up by a black Japanese shelf unit incorporating a stereo system and cocktail bar. In a recess to the left was a pool table. Playmates of the Month, in individually lit gilt frames, exhibited their charms at intervals along the silk-vinyl-covered walls. Most agreeably of all, it was heated. From where, it was difficult to tell. Perhaps below the floor.

Melody was at his shoulder. "With cream?"

"Thanks."

"Make mine black," said Valenti, in case he was not asked.

The coffee was waiting on a hotplate, fresh enough to underline the precision of the schedule.

"You like it?" said Serafin, seating himself near Dryden. "We decided a few comforts were justifiable with staff working up here for weeks on end. I expect you wonder about the power supply. We have our own generating plant working on gasoline. You need heat at this altitude, even in midsummer."

"That's for sure," chimed in Melody, handing him a mug of coffee. "I couldn't survive without my electric blanket."

"You'd find a way," Valenti dryly informed her.

Before she could produce an adequate reply, the door behind them opened.

"Ah, Peter," said Serafin. "Do come and meet our

guests. Peter Klugman is Goldengirl's principal coach," he told Dryden.

The newcomer approached at a brisk step, heavy on the carpet. He was wearing a Cornell blazer with gray flannels pressed to a razor crease. Large in build, he manifested fastidiousness in a series of precisely defined lines—hair parting, sideburns, blazer edging, the diagonal stripes on his tie, and the set of his mouth.

"Peter D. Klugman," he said unnecessarily as he gripped Dryden's hand.

"Peter was a track coach on the last U.S. Olympic team," said Serafin.

"Sprints and relays," Klugman confirmed.

"You're a Cornell man, I see," said Dryden.

"That's so. Class of sixty-five. I was captain of track."

"He should have made the Olympic team," said Melody, linking her arm in Klugman's. "Tell Mr. Dryden about your bad luck, Pete."

Klugman made a show of reluctance by shaking his head, then went on to say, "I was an AAU finalist three years in a row. In sixty-eight I was clocking forty-four regular, but I turned my ankle in the heats of the final Olympic Tryout. Achilles tendon. Zapped me. That was the year the U.S. took gold, silver and bronze in Mexico City."

"Tough," said Valenti without a trace of sympathy. "So you got into coaching." He held out a hand to Klugman. "Myself, I'm in pharmaceuticals. Gino Valenti."

Before the rundown could begin on the U.S. drug industry, Serafin left them, saying he had arrangements to make. He would leave them in Miss Fryer's capable hands.

Valenti took over. "Sit down," he told the coach. "Tell us how Goldengirl is making out. Get Mr. Klugman a coffee, Melody, and top mine up while you're about it. What do you say, Klugman? Are you satisfied with the kid?"

"She's still mobile," said Klugman guardedly.

Valenti wasn't settling for that. "Let's lay it out, shall we? Does she have the gold-medal look? That's what Dryden here needs to know. Serafin gives a great account of her pedigree, but you're the guy in the know. What it comes down to is, Can she run good?"

"She ought to hold up," said Klugman.

"Christ, she'd better!" rapped out Valenti. "I got seventy-five grand on this already."

"Cool it," cautioned Melody. "If Pete says she'll hold up, that's fine. He isn't given to exaggeration."

"You can check her out yourself at San Diego tomorrow," Klugman pointed out.

"You bet I will," said Valenti. "I like a pretty story as well as the next guy, but on the day it's the fastest dame who grabs the gold."

"Don't underrate the story line," Melody said, handing Valenti his coffee. "Goldengirl won't make it big just by running fast. You need an angle, don't you, Mr. Dryden?"

He was glad the point had come up. It gave him the chance to sow doubts which could usefully surface later. "You're so right. The news value of a good piece of running is practically nil. Okay, she's a pretty girl, and that helps a little. She does something extraordinary—wins three gold medals. Great, but in twenty-four hours that story is dead unless something is there to sustain it."

"A backup," said Melody with a pointed smile at Valenti.

"Okay, okay, so Serafin pitches in with his line on Goldengirl's background," said Valenti. "In-depth analysis. Grandmother with her gold medal. Mother's tragic accident. Great copy. They'll love it."

"I hope you're right," said Dryden. "What counts commercially, of course, is that the story matches up to the American dream. You don't want adverse publicity. To be frank, I'm not completely confident of the value of Goldengirl's story in promotional terms."

"Her unmarried mother, you mean?" Melody inquired.

Valenti laughed derisively. "That's immaterial," he crooned. "These days people don't give a monkey's whether your parents did it legitimate. That couldn't hurt Goldengirl." He turned to Dryden. "What's bugging you, then?"

"I wouldn't say anything is," answered Dryden. "Remember, I haven't joined you yet. If I did, I might suggest you drop the Nazi grandparents out of the story. The girl can't be held responsible for them, I know, and the war's been over thirty-five years, but it's still a sensitive topic. If you're creating a Goldengirl image, they're better forgotten." He might have added a suspicion that Serafin's interest in the Third Reich was not confined to physiology. For the present, he kept this to himself.

"Fine, we can ax the grandmother," said Valenti. "It's still one hell of a story. The kid from the orphanage: there won't be a dry eye in America when that's released. Kleenex should pay us a percentage. You don't think so? Okay, Dryden, you're the professional here. How would you package Goldengirl?"

"Unlike you, I've yet to be convinced she *is* golden," he reminded them. "No doubt you have the advantage of me, Mr. Valenti, coming into the consortium at the start, but since we're talking in commercial terms, I like to be sure of the product before I push it."

"Fools' gold, eh?" said Valenti, lighting a cigar. "Maybe you got a point. Personally, I've seen enough of Serafin to say he's no con."

"I'm impressed by him too," said Dryden. "But it won't be Dr. Serafin out there with the pick of the world's runners in the Moscow Stadium. With due respect to Mr. Klugman here, I don't see how all the coaching the girl can stand will see her through two rounds of heats, a semifinal and a final in three separate events. Has she seen the program, do you suppose?"

72

"It's pinned up in the gym," Klugman said stiffly. "Give us some credit for intelligence. I have a little experience of the Olympics myself, and I promise you Goldengirl is under no illusions. She knows exactly what she has to do."

"That's if she gets there," said Dryden, talking more than he intended. "She'll have to make the U.S. team first, and to do that she has to get to the Olympic Trial. Am I right? She has to qualify for an invitation to that first."

"Tomorrow," said Klugman tersely.

"Should be fascinating," said Melody, breaking the tension. "Her public debut! It's crazy when you think about it. Here we are two months before the Olympics, and nobody's heard of the girl."

"There's nothing crazy in it," Valenti told her. "It has to do with the image. She's the chick who comes from nowhere to win the Olympics. If she'd been running world-class races all year, the press would be homing in by now. And once they saw this complex, and learned who was backing it, we'd have no chance at all of putting her across as the wide-eyed California blonde who discovers overnight that she can run. Dryden calls it the American dream; I call it the Yukon syndrome. Mud today, gold tomorrow. People want to believe it: fine, we've got an angle."

"Just so long as the story holds up," said Dryden, tossing in a last uncertainty. "I'll be interested to see if Dr. Serafin can keep the press out of this place after Goldengirl makes the Olympic team—provided she does."

"He'll take care of that," said Klugman, with infinite faith in his employer.

After that, the conversation dwindled in the cigar smoke. Dryden strolled across the room to look at a relic of gold-mining days, a framed Notice of Claim fastened to the door. It didn't match the rest of the decor: possibly it had a superstitious value, or maybe someone in the camp had a sharp sense of humor. They would need something to sustain them up here. Melody was right. It was crazy, a fantasy. Nobody would believe that a girl totally unknown in June could pull off a triple in the Olympics in August. If she was Atlanta herself, there was still so much that could go wrong—sudden illness, a pulled muscle, a tumble on the track—that only a super-optimist would back her. Armitage and Valenti obviously had money to fool with. Dryden was being asked to stake something more valuable: the reputation of his business. Setting up a promotion on the scale Serafin had in mind meant selling the idea in advance to people whose confidence he had nurtured for years. If Goldengirl fell flat on her face exhausted before she ever got to Moscow, they weren't going to shake their heads and say it was a long shot that missed, but never mind; they were going to transfer their accounts to an agency they could trust. To go in with the consortium made as much sense as backing the fellow who posted the Notice of Claim.

Yet, mosquito-like, there soared and swooped on the edge of rationality the knowledge that if Goldengirl did pull it off, he would have passed up the biggest return in merchandising history.

A phone bleeped. Melody picked it up. "Okay, I'll bring them over. Gentlemen," she announced, "you're invited to the conference room, where the next phase of the program is about to take place. Would you come with me?"

"Anywhere you say, baby," said Valenti.

Melody led them outside and across the compound to a two-storied building. They mounted an open staircase to the upper floor.

"Nice to get some fresh air," Klugman commented, pausing at the top.

"Ain't you fit?" said Valenti, flicking his Panatella as he marched past.

In layout the room resembled a small university lecture theater, with twelve rows of tiered seats facing a demonstration table. The front was cluttered with

TV cameras and sets of arc lights, all focused on three empty seats behind the table. Loudspeakers were suspended from the ceiling at various points.

Someone Dryden had not seen before welcomed each of them solemnly as they entered: a man of forty or so with the unusual combination of a tall frame and oriental features. Behind thick, black-framed spectacles, his eyes had the spark of high intelligence.

"This is Dr. Lee, gentlemen," Melody explained. "He is an associate of Dr. Serafin's who specializes in psychology."

"The resident shrink," murmured Valenti.

Dr. Lee nodded affably and said in perfect English, "At your service whenever you have need of one, Mr. Valenti. Gentlemen, this afternoon you are to observe one of the simulated press conferences we hold from time to time to acquaint Miss Serafin, or Goldengirl as we call her, with the conditions she is likely to experience not only at the Olympic Games, but before, when her nomination for three events becomes public knowledge."

"Conditioning," Valenti declared in his authoritative style.

"A term I would prefer not to use," Dr. Lee mildly retorted. "It is implacably associated in popular ideas of psychology with Pavlov's experiments on dogs. What we are trying to achieve here brings us, I assure you, significantly further in learning theory than that. We have progressed some way beyond B. F. Skinner, whose work postdates Pavlov's by more than half a century. But I must not be drawn into lecturing you, gentlemen. We are here for another purpose. As you must have gathered from Dr. Serafin's account of Goldengirl's childhood and adolescence, she has led a relatively sheltered existence up to now, and to expose her unprepared to the pressure of Olympic competition and all that goes with it could have a disturbing, not to say disastrous, effect.

75

"The history of the Olympics is littered with the names of brilliant athletes built up before the Games as favorites who visibly wilted under the stress. I have in mind the case of Vera Nikolic, the Yugoslav girl who set a world record for eight hundred meters before the 1968 Olympics. She went to Mexico City as such a hot favorite that her country had a postage stamp bearing her picture ready to issue the day after her triumph. And what happened? In the semifinal she pulled up in the first lap and ran off the track—not from any physical injury, but acute psychological stress. Before the day was through, she tried to commit suicide by jumping off a bridge. That is the sort of thing that makes us so wary of revealing Goldengirl's talent prematurely. And it is my task to ensure that she can withstand the pressures when she can no longer be insulated from them."

Dryden liked Lee's style of delivery. It conveyed authority without recourse to psychological jargon. He was not condescending. He put over his ideas lucidly, taking account of his listeners. His voice helped, it was sensitively pitched, a relief after Serafin's almost toneless enunciation. The interest of the group was made clear when they moved with him, unprompted, slowly up the tiered floor as he continued speaking.

"So I am responsible for the preparation she has undergone to tune her mentally for what is to come. You will appreciate that press-simulation sessions are just one element in a pretty sophisticated program. So much of what is involved in being an Olympic athlete in 1980 is concerned with the personality that I hope Mr. Klugman will not object if I claim that my contribution is at least as vital as his. Because of our special circumstances, Goldengirl has to be initiated into quite basic situations that could promote stress. Take her first competitive appearance at the Metro Club Meet tomorrow. I have had to prepare her mentally for what could be quite an ordeal: the pre-meet buildup, dressing-room nerves, the atmosphere in the

76

arena and the tension of waiting between heats and finals of her three events. That's just the brief for San Diego. Magnify it all to the scale of the Olympics, throw in the mounting interest of the media, the journey to Moscow, a partisan crowd, sex tests, dope tests, Soviet officialdom, life in the Olympic Village, and you have some idea why I am employed here full time.

"What you will presently see is not staged for your benefit, gentlemen. It is the scheduled phase of her program. Her preparation for tomorrow is complete. As a diversion we turn to something she will enjoy. We make a mental leap of several weeks, and simulate her appearance before the press after her third victory in Moscow. Sessions like this are built into the program at regular intervals. We are great respecters of the influence of the media, you see. She needs to know how to acquit herself at a press conference, project her personality with charm but without conceit, answer questions without hesitation or evasion, and handle that difficult or unexpected one that always arises."

The monumental presumption in all this didn't seem to bother Lee. Like everyone else in this place, he was sold on those three gold medals.

The party had reached the back of the room and grouped around one end of a wood-encased electronic unit some twelve feet in length. A young man wearing earphones was staring shyly at one of the two blank TV monitors at the opposite end.

"With our facilities," Lee went on, "we cannot physically reproduce the conference room the Russians will use in Moscow. That seats upward of a thousand correspondents. We have had to improvise. The lighting is arranged with a twofold objective: to subject Goldengirl to the glare of TV arc lights, and to create the impression from where she sits that the room is much larger than it is. From the front, you can't see beyond the first three rows of seats, so they could stretch back indefinitely. And, of course, the audio system is graduated in a way that supports the effect. This device"—

he flattened his palm on the polished wood surface of the unit—"contains a bank of over five hundred questions. We recorded many at actual press conferences at major meets like last year's Pan-American Games, but the majority have had to be individually styled for Goldengirl. The computer mechanism is capable of working in three different ways. First, it can ask her questions totally at random. Second, if we want to regulate the level of difficulty, it will select them by reference to a grading system. And the third mode of operation is sequential, so that she can be asked a series of questions exploring a particular theme in depth. I'm sure Dave Robb, our media resource expert"—he extended his hand to the young man in earphones—"would dismiss this piece of wizardry as a simple electronic aid. It is only one of a number of ingenious gadgets he has constructed to assist Project Goldengirl. Dave actually had a lot to do with the technical side of the Goldengirl film. He fixed the audio system in the lounge too."

Probably bugged the place while he was at it, Dryden thought. He stepped forward to examine the control panel. It was surprisingly uncomplicated. Two rows of six squares under glass. Presumably they responded to finger controls. He had seen parking-lot checkouts with more intimidating controls.

"Without going into unnecessary detail," Dr. Lee went on, "there are six tapes bearing the questions graded in order of difficulty. If I touch this square on the left"—he demonstrated—"it should throw out a simple question."

"Do you use weights in your training?" a voice lower down the room asked the empty seats at the front.

"And this should produce a more demanding one." Dr. Lee touched the square on the right of the top row.

"Do you consider yourself completely feminine?" a different voice barked from the opposite side.

"The square at bottom left," Dr. Lee went on, "stops the tapes at random, like a fruit machine, and whichever one has a question closest in line is activated. Three seconds after Goldengirl's response, the process repeats itself. It can go on indefinitely, and it is actually closer to the reality of a press conference than our questions in sequence, which we activate by means of the override controls, the remaining four squares in the second row. In addition, we have a few refinements controlled from Dave's end of the console. We can phase in interruptions, simultaneous voices from different sides of the room, audience reaction in the form of laughter or hostile comment—in fact, any situation, apart from a maniac gunman, that a press conference could possibly produce.

"The obvious thing now is to let you see Goldengirl down there batting. And if any of you would care to put questions of your own to her during the session, please do so—it will add to the realism. I would only wish to make one point about the phrasing of questions. Everything in Goldengirl's conditioning—I've used the word, Mr. Valenti—is based on the premise that she will achieve the objective of three gold medals. Failure —even partial success—is not a concept she would understand. So it would not be constructive, for example, to ask her why she was beaten in one of her three events. Put challenging questions to her by all means —she is capable of coping with them—but kindly base them on an assumption of success. After all, that's the purpose of the project." He spoke into a grille beside the console. "Ready to begin, William." Turning to the others, he explained, "Dr. Serafin will be at Goldengirl's side. The press like nothing better than a proud parent beside the winner, if only for the photo session. The other place will be vacant this afternoon. It will normally be occupied by the IOC Press Chief. I should be glad if you would take your seats now—anywhere you please in the room. Do not be alarmed by our flash effects as they come in. We like to get as close to the real thing as conditions allow."

Dryden found an end seat toward the back. Just before the lights went out, Melody squeezed past into the next seat. Then from a dozen loudspeakers started the mix of world-weary and high-powered conversation characteristic of press gatherings everywhere—an uncanny effect when all that was visible from where Dryden sat was the glimmer of Valenti's cigar two rows down.

The arc lights at the front came on again. It was obvious that anyone in their glare could not have seen far into the empty auditorium.

"Ladies and gentlemen," a more insistent voice came through the hubbub. "Triple Olympic champion Miss Goldine Serafin is here with her father, Dr. William Serafin, to meet the press."

To the promised flash effects, some cries of "Here she is!" and a scatter of applause, they entered from the right, pausing as a volley of flashlight signaled the photo session. Goldengirl was wearing the white tracksuit of the U.S. Olympic team, with lettering picked out in red. It was the authentic team uniform; Dryden had seen it in a trade journal not three weeks previously. Detail was meticulous in this operation; from Goldengirl's neck three ribbons were suspended, each bearing a gold medal.

"She's cute," Melody remarked in his left ear. "Maybe too near the ceiling for perfection, though?"

He made no response, held by the ritual under the lights. He had learned to sit through advertising presentations and promotional launches fixing his undistracted eye on the product through displays of leg and bosom calculated to the last millimeter to impress, but he could not remember an occasion when the product itself was in desirable female form. That produced an unexpected consequence. He had looked at Goldengirl naked almost pore by pore through the camera lens, read her statistics, seen her in motion, heard her history, and still missed the thing her living presence hammered into his perception.

Her sexuality.

Dress it up in euphemisms, say she upped the pulse rate, sent the adrenalin racing, blew the mind. What it came down to was the simple, animal ability to arouse that sets one girl apart from a million others.

He could think of more seductive outfits than a U.S. sweatsuit, but Goldengirl didn't need them. It radiated from her as she blinked at the flashbulbs. No matter that she was six inches taller than Serafin, two or three taller than Dryden himself. The attraction wasn't a matter of statistics, though she was beautifully proportioned. Nor was it in the cast of her features, or he would have made his discovery during the film. Then he could study her objectively; it was out of the question now.

A remark Melody made helped him account for it. "She believes those medals are for real, you know."

She obviously did. Whether Dr. Lee's methods followed Pavlov, Skinner or Svengali, they worked. Goldengirl was vibrant with success. She moved with the conviction that she had conquered the world.

In a frenzy of flashbulbs, Serafin ushered her to the center seat. By degrees the volume of sound reduced to a level where a voice—Lee's—could announce: "First, on behalf of the Organizing Committee and the world press, congratulations, Miss Serafin, on your unique achievement. Before I invite questions, is there anything you would wish to say in the way of a statement?"

She smiled. Not once in the film had she done that. "This is a novel experience for me, and I'm not sure what you would have me tell you, but if you'll be patient with me, ladies and gentlemen, I'll do the best I can." The excitement came over in her voice. Her accent placed her as a Californian, but a tremulous note gave an unintended emphasis to certain syllables.

"Let's have the first question, then, from the *Pravda* representative."

A solemn voice said, "Congratulations, Miss Serafin, from the people of the Soviet Union. Did you believe it possible before the Games that you could achieve the distinction of winning three gold medals?"

She nodded emphatically. "You have to be confident. In some ways I can't believe it's happened, it's all been so quick for me, but I came to Moscow to win, yes, if that doesn't sound too conceited. Oh, and thanks for the congratulations."

"Jane Thomas, *Woman's World*," another loudspeaker announced. "How does it feel to be the greatest woman athlete in the world?"

"That's nice to hear," answered Goldine, "but it's just a little sweeping. You ought to save that accolade for the girl who wins the pentathlon tomorrow. Running, hurdling, high jump, long jump, shot put: that's the test of a great athlete. I can run fast—period. How does it feel? Like champagne, I guess. I don't drink liquor at all, but I guess it feels like this."

"Tell us about your preparation, Goldine."

"Which was the most difficult medal to win?" came a second voice over the first.

"I'll take the second question first. The four hunded was the tough one. They're all sprints, and that's the longest. As for preparation, I trained seven days a week, with plenty of practice starting, some work on technique—stride, knee lift, pickup and so on—but generally aiming at speed without strain. You're going to ask me next how many hours a day, and the answer is that it varied. Some days it might be just an hour on the track, some as much as four. I feel my extensors tighten up, and I think, hmm, it's time to shower."

"Doesn't all this training mean sacrifices?"

She raised her eyebrows. "Sacrifices? Like not going out with guys? There are still some hours left in the day for that. You can't do trackwork after dark, but other things aren't impossible." She paused, waiting for the laughter to die in the loudspeakers. "Like reading books and listening to music."

"Do you have a current boyfriend, Goldine?"

"Is that a proposition?" More laughter. "I have all the dates I can cope with. There's a point I'd like to emphasize. Track isn't all sacrifice and sweat. It can be a social opportunity as well. I don't know how things are coming along here, but in the States the men in track outnumber us by five to one, and that's one area where I'm not pressing for equality."

"Jim Poindexter. *Sports Illustrated.* I believe you're six foot two, Goldine. Would you say your height gives you an unfair advantage over other girls?"

"If that's a reference to the previous question, I admit I can spot a good-looking guy at fifty yards, yes. Seriously, it's definitely an advantage in running to have a certain type of physique. Whether mine's more efficient for the job, I couldn't say. Remember I weigh a little more than other girls, so there's more of me to move, so to speak. How am I doing? Am I talking too much? There seem to be plenty of you with questions."

"You're doing fine," said Lee. "If I can structure the questioning a little, there are still a number of people with things to ask about your achievements in the stadium."

"Jerry Fisher, *Track and Field News.* I'd be interested to know who you regarded as your greatest rivals."

"The answer to that is that every girl was a potential rival. You see, I hadn't raced against anyone except the U.S. girls before."

"Did you study the form of other girls, Miss Serafin?"

"I don't mind Goldine, if you like to be informal. Well, I knew the times other girls had clocked, but I didn't consciously put names to them. In sprints, you don't have to study other girls' tactics. We all go like crazy for the tape."

"Is it correct to say that you remained aloof from

the other girls on the training track?" Dr. Lee's finger had apparently moved to the right-hand end of the console.

"I can understand how it could seem that way," answered Goldine evenly. "They know each other, you see, from frequent track meets in capitals across the world. I'm really very new to track. I hadn't done anything till June this year, so the girls just didn't know me. I didn't freeze anyone off, but it's not in my nature either to force a friendship on people."

"What goes through your mind as you run?"

"How it feels, I guess. Whether I'm going smoothly. I sometimes offer up a prayer that I can still burn the last fifty yards."

"How did you feel as you stood on the victory rostrum?"

"Proud. Pleased for the American people. It really gets you here when you see your country's flag being raised."

"Why didn't you run for America in the relay teams?" That was a nasty follow-up.

She didn't falter. "I know my limitations. There's a technique to be learned in baton-changing that I simply haven't acquired. In the short time I've had in competitive running it seemed best to concentrate on individual events. I made that clear to the U.S. Olympic Committee just as soon as I qualified for the team."

"Why didn't you compete before this year? Did you know you were so superior, you had no need?"

"I didn't know that at all. I'm nineteen years old, and this is my first season in track. The coaches tell me it couldn't happen in any other event to get to the Olympics so soon, but sprinting is natural. Sure, I've run before, and I knew I could inject a little speed when I wanted, but I never tried it on a track. I was more interested in swimming. My mother died in a drowning accident when I was a small girl, and I guess

I wanted to make sure I could hold myself up in the water."

"Didn't you do any running in high school?"

"If I may put in a word here," said Dr. Serafin. "My wife and I adopted Goldine when she was four, in the tragic circumstances she has mentioned. At that time, our major consideration was that she should begin to identify with her new home and family. We judged it right to have her educated in the environment we wanted her to accept. I still believe this was the right thing to do, but it may be that later, if she had gone into the state school system, her potential as an athlete would have come to light before this year. Once she had started studying at home, it seemed inappropriate to switch."

"How do you feel about her achievements, sir?" Lee's voice.

"As proud as any parent can."

"Justifiably, if I may say so. Another question for Goldine," said Lee.

"Are you superstitious? Do you have a mascot, or some lucky charm?"

What a merchandising opportunity! Dryden thought: *Only my custom-made Adidas track shoes.*

"I don't think I am." She touched the medals so that they chinked against each other. "From now on, these are my charms."

She had already fed the empty seats enough quotes to fill a full-page spread. They came without apparent effort, as if they were scripted, but she delivered them with a verve that projected spontaneity. It seemed she was one of those rare individuals who could appear before the press and scintillate. Or was it the result of months of drilling in sessions like this? The only way to find out was to take Lee at his word and slip in a question she couldn't have had before from the machine.

Already it was feeding the next one to her. "Now

that you've had this success, do you plan to stay in track, or will you take advantage of the commercial opportunities open to you?"

"Are those things mutually exclusive?" said Goldine innocently. "I'd like to keep running, for sure. I can't say I know much about commerce. If it means reading the *Wall Street Journal,* I don't think it's my scene." She put her hand to her mouth. "Oh my God, which journal do you represent?"

Before the laughter died, Dryden pitched in. "There's a story that you trained in the Sierra Nevada. Did altitude training contribute to your success?"

There was a momentary hesitation which might have been a reaction to the different acoustic quality of Dryden's voice, but no doubt about the crispness of the response. "At six foot two, you could say all my running is at altitude. Yes, I did some running in the mountains. The air's a little sweeter there than it is in oily old Bakersfield, where I live."

"What do you think of Moscow?" Valenti asked, getting in on the act.

"At this moment, there's no place I'd rather be."

"How about the Russian people?"

"Everyone I've met has treated me kindly, and I'd like to tell them how much I appreciate that," she answered. "Unfortunately, I know just three words in Russian: *Na Mesta* and *Gotovo.*"

" 'On your marks' and 'Set,' " Melody translated for Dryden. "She's holding up pretty good, wouldn't you say?"

"She rates a gold medal for PR," Dryden answered.

"Have you ever raced against men, Goldine?" the machine resumed.

"Every day this week against you guys holding the cameras. I don't mean that unkindly, but when you're engaged in two semis and a final in one afternoon, you simply don't have time to stand and be photographed. No, sir, the answer to your question is that I haven't, to my knowledge."

"What do you feel about the sex tests for women athletes?"

She appeared to give it a moment's thought. "I recognize that a test is necessary. It's not embarrassing. They take a smear from inside your mouth and check your chromosomes. How do I *feel?* Just sad for the people who get rejected. A gene count might establish that the person concerned is not a one hundred per cent normal woman, but it doesn't make them a man either."

"Do you consider yourself completely feminine?"

That one. The machine wasn't sparing her. It was programed so that anything with controversial possibilities was taken up.

"From the amount I've talked since I got here, I wouldn't have thought anyone in this room could doubt it."

"Do you feel strongly about women's rights, Goldine?"

"Not so strongly as I feel about men's wrongs. You're asking me if I'm a feminist. Some years back, a famous woman sprinter was asked something like that. They wanted to know why she wore a bra under her trackshirt if she believed in women's lib. You know what she answered? Because I don't want two black eyes. I like that story. Do you have another question?"

"Yes." Dryden did. For some minutes he had speculated on the way Goldengirl dealt with questions. This was a long shot, but worth trying. "Do you think commercialism is destroying the spirit of the Olympic Games?"

"The spirit of the Olympic Games?" repeated Goldine. "You mean the ideas of that little French guy who set them up? Isn't that something like the important thing is taking part, not winning?"

Dryden pressed his question. "Is commerce a threat to those ideals?"

"I can't say I know much about commerce," answered Goldine. "If it means reading the *Wall Street*—" She stopped. The elation in her expression was supplanted first by a frown, then unmistakable fear. For a moment it looked as if she might flee the platform, but Serafin put his hand firmly over her wrist.

"She has given her answer. She knows nothing about these things, Mr. Dryden, but we thank you for your question. Do we have another now?"

"Do you have a special diet?" the machine faithfully chanted.

Serafin turned to Goldine with a paternal smile. She let her breath out slowly as if a crisis was past. The confidence seeped back. "Nothing most Americans would call special, though I guess what we eat is different from caviar and things. I like to have a balanced intake of food, and I take vitamins occasionally like everyone else, but I don't have fads, like living only on wheat germ."

"Another," ordered Serafin. This conference was going on till she had delivered enough good responses to erase the breakdown on Dryden's question.

"Do you have any message for the people back home in America?" Dr. Lee's finger was keeping strictly to the easy end of the controls.

"Gee, I'm not used to speaking to America at large. Just say I'm happy if my running pleased them. Does anyone else have a question?"

"Yeah. What are your plans for this evening, Goldengirl?"

"This evening?" For a second the repetition suggested she had been thrown again, but it wasn't so. She was fully in command, as she demonstrated by raising an eyebrow, smiling, getting to her feet and putting a hand up to shield her eyes as she peered into the limbo beyond the lights. "I've nothing arranged. Get yourself stilts, mister, and you might have a date."

It was a smart payoff, relished by all but one of the audience. Goldine could not have known the question came from the shortest man in the room: Gino Valenti.

[6]

IN the highly charged last minutes of the simulation session Dryden had been so absorbed watching Goldengirl that Melody had to tap him twice on the arm to get a response. The conference had been rounded off with the meticulous observance of detail that had characterized it from the start: Lee had formally thanked Serafin and Goldine for appearing, they had posed briefly in the flashlights, and their exit had cued in the press in full chorus.

"Show's over," Melody pointed out. "No second show."

Dryden offered her a cigarette. "Is this a regular thing?"

"She's done a few before. Wasn't that obvious? It's the first I've watched in weeks. Her technique's right on, I'd say, but she flubbed that second question of yours. They won't like that one bit."

"You mean I fouled it up?" Dryden innocently said.

"It's not important," Melody assured him. "They'll work on it with Goldengirl. Seems you located a fault. They should be grateful. *She* won't, but she doesn't know it came from you, so it shouldn't downgrade you. I see you liked her."

And Dryden saw that Melody wasn't pleased. He drew thoughtfully on his cigarette. "I admired her style, but I got the impression it was slightly out of character, almost as if she was high on something. Would that be an accurate reading?"

"Couldn't say, lover boy. They said Marilyn Mon-

90

roe was a dumb broad till she got in front of a camera. It could be that flashbulbs are Goldengirl's turn-on."

"They wouldn't do anything for me," commented Dryden. "I go for soft lights and music every time. What's next on the program?"

"Nothing for an hour," said Melody. "I was thinking maybe you and I—" She stopped.

Serafin had approached from behind and placed his hands on their shoulders. "I hate to break this up, but I thought you might welcome an opportunity to take a stroll in the fresh air, Mr. Dryden. I should be interested to have your impressions of what you have just observed—if you will forgive us, Melody."

She gave a forced smile. "Why not?"

Serafin walked him slowly into the open area away from the buildings. Purple mountain peaks surfaced above the tall fence to their right. Dryden stopped and stared about him.

"Is something wrong?" Serafin asked.

"In a way, yes. The wood fencing over there. I'm positive I saw it in your film yesterday. The shots of Goldengirl running."

"So you did."

Dryden laughed uncertainly. "Well, what have you done with the running track?"

"I see," said Serafin, with a rare smile. "We rolled it up, like a carpet. It's an all-weather strip, made to Tartan's specifications. They supply them to schools and colleges that use the same ground for a number of different sports. It's at the end, there." He pointed to a cylindrical object the size of a large roll of newsprint. It was mounted on a winch at one end of the enclosure. "We roll it up when it isn't in use, in case of aerial surveillance. But it's a genuine all-weather surface, I assure you. If that's all that puzzled you—"

"There is something else," said Dryden. "I don't see any gate in the fence. How do you"—he flapped his hand—"come and er . . . ?"

"As *you* did, Mr. Dryden. By helicopter. Does it make you feel immured? We are all in the same situation up here. You see, there isn't a road within six miles, so we have no use for a gate. If somebody *should* pass by, the absence of a formal entrance discourages them from calling. We can let a ladder down if anyone from here develops an urge to go mountaineering, but I haven't included anything like that in this weekend's itinerary."

"I didn't pack my climbing boots," said Dryden with a deadpan expression.

"That's all right, then. Tell me, how did the press-conference simulation strike you?" Serafin had come to the point at the first opportunity. He was almost childishly eager to learn how his party tricks had been received.

"Ingenious," answered Dryden. "Top marks to the effects department. That's a clever young man you've hired, that Mr.—"

Serafin brushed that aside. "What did you think of Goldengirl?"

"She's a most attractive—" Dryden began.

"Her handling of the questions," Serafin insisted. "Were you satisfied with the way she dealt with them?"

Dryden opened his hands in a gesture that conveyed nothing. His experience as a negotiator told him he had the edge on Serafin at this moment. Handled properly, the situation might yield something of interest.

"I have to give you credit," Serafin went on without waiting for a response. "You caught her off balance with one of your questions, and I believe it wasn't pure chance. It was perspicacious on your part to notice how she has been taught to respond. That was quite evident from the way you rehearsed your second question." He waited, his eyes boring into Dryden's, seeking confirmation before committing himself further.

It was necessary to give a little. "I thought it was

92

possible she was producing her best responses when certain trigger words came up. The way she reacted to being called the greatest woman athlete: a predictable question, but the answer was smooth, really smooth. On 'sacrifices' she was ready with her remark about things you can do after dark, and when Russia was mentioned, out she came with her three Russian words. I ask a question on altitude and she earns a laugh with her six foot two. I think, Let's try her with a trigger word she's already had, so I come in with 'commerce,' which has already produced a slick remark about the *Wall Street Journal*. She sidesteps me the first time, but I come again and . . ." He shrugged.

"You had the undoubted advantage of knowing it was a simulation exercise," Serafin reflected aloud. "If you had been in Moscow in the actual situation of an Olympic press conference, you would almost certainly not have detected the method. However, it's obviously something Lee must put right. I'm glad it came up."

"I wouldn't have guessed she had her answers ready from the way she put them over," Dryden said to soften the blow. "If she doesn't get her gold medals, you could always nominate her for an Oscar."

Serafin's expression froze. "If that is intended as a joke, it doesn't amuse me. You must understand that we think in positive terms here, Mr. Dryden. We should achieve nothing if we did not. The very fact that we hold a session like that is proof of our confidence. Believe me, we should not have gone to the trouble and risk of bringing you into our confidence if we were not counting on success. You are privileged this weekend to see the last coat of polish applied to an artifact master craftsmen have taken years to shape. *Years.* Your function—if you have one in regard to Goldengirl—will simply be to market her. I do not expect you to comprehend the work we have put into this, but I would have thought you might have sufficient respect to refrain from cheap humor of that sort."

Anyone in Dryden's line got into the way of talking of clients as commodities, but it jarred to hear a man discuss his daughter like furniture. And he objected to being put down as if he were some oaf in Queen Victoria's court. "I think there's something *you* should understand, Dr. Serafin. I'm aware that I'm your guest up here, but respect is something I don't believe I owe you. The girl performed well under questioning, and I commented on that. If each remark I make—"

"Then perhaps I spoke prematurely," Serafin cut in. "You will find I am not a man to trifle with. I have no sense of humor. If you took offense at anything I said, I withdraw it." He folded his arms and looked challengingly at Dryden. Deciding apparently that what he had said had been taken for an apology, he continued, "As to Goldengirl's facility in answering questions, I should make it clear that her answers are not rehearsed. She has a number of response phrases ready to introduce in her own way when certain key topics arise. The greater part of what you heard this afternoon was as fresh to my ears as it was to yours."

"If she's as good as that, why bother with trigger words at all?" asked Dryden acidly enough to show he was not ignoring the outburst.

"Ah!" Serafin nodded as if acknowledging a better-than-average question from a student. "They help her over difficult areas of questioning. The point you took up—the influence of commerce on the Olympics—is still a snare. Although it is common knowledge that people like Killy and Spitz made millions out of their Olympic victories, it wouldn't do for Goldengirl to admit she expects to make even more. So she is triggered —to use your expression—to say she doesn't read the *Wall Street Journal,* or something of the sort. It gets a laugh, which provides the bridge to another question."

"Neat. And you're confident she can do it in front of several hundred pressmen?"

"Certain. In fact, there is actually a delay between

question and response in an Olympic press conference while the question is translated into other languages. That is a feature we deliberately excluded from our simulation sessions to sharpen her reactions. TV studio interviews require immediate responses, so we cannot have her getting lazy habits. Did you notice anything about her manner?"

"She actually enjoyed the experience, if I'm any judge," answered Dryden. "I'd put it more strongly, in fact. She appeared to be exhilarated."

"It came over, then," said Serafin, looking pleased. "There are three obvious elements in the process of psychological reinforcement: the noticeable stimulus, the response, and the palpable consequence. The latter cannot be overestimated. In its most basic form it consists of reward or punishment. Lee has developed this quite brilliantly in terms of personality dynamics. As you observed, a correct response induces exhilaration in Goldengirl. She is motivated to derive pleasure from the press conference."

"It was apparent as soon as she appeared in the room," said Dryden.

"Splendid! You see, Lee's work with her has marshaled the motivating forces of her personality in the cause of our enterprise. For Goldengirl, the press conference is a situation in which she is involved—how shall I put it?—"

"Sensually?" suggested Dryden.

Serafin paused before answering. "You could say so."

"That was my impression. Is that good for her, Dr. Serafin?"

He frowned. "What do you mean?"

"I'm not a psychologist, but if Lee conditions her to be turned on by flashbulbs and tape recorders, what effect will it have on her personality?"

"I don't think you understand," said Serafin. "She is going to become a goddess overnight, worshiped by millions. What effect will *that* have on her personality

95

if she is not prepared? It will annihilate her. My duty is to prepare her, so far as I can, for life as a public figure, Dryden. If Lee can help her project facets of her private persona into her public appearances, he is giving her a lifeline."

"What you are saying, in effect, is that her private life is sacrificed on the altar of this goddess."

"I prefer the image of a butterfly emerging from a chrysalis," said Serafin without rancor. "An apparently dramatic transformation which has actually been in preparation unobserved for many weeks."

"Dr. Lee is an accredited psychologist, is he?" Dryden asked.

"But of course. He would be working for the government if they were not ultrasensitive about security. His early training was in Peking, and that has dogged his career ever since, even though he defected as long ago as 1966, the period of the Cultural Revolution. He has no affiliations or sympathy with Red China. Finding his Chinese qualifications were unacceptable here, he joined Columbia as a mature student, graduated and went on to take a doctorate. Then he moved West and obtained a lecturing post at Berkeley, which gives some indication of his caliber. Things went well for him for a time there, but you know what Berkeley is like. An imbecilic group of students calling themselves Maoists raked up his story from somewhere and proceeded to hound him as if they were Red Guards in Peking. They made it impossible for him to continue. He resigned his post and joined the psychiatric team at Los Angeles County General Hospital, which is where I met him four years ago on a public health committee. We found an instant rapport existed between us. As our acquaintance developed, we exchanged more confidences, and when he told me one evening of his experiences in China and at Berkeley, I realized what trust the man was reposing in me, for there are people in the medical world, just as there are in the academic, who delight in destroying reputations. When I needed the help of a psychologist here, it seemed quite natural to approach Lee. He listened to my account of Goldine and agreed to join us as soon as he had worked a month's notice at the hospital."

"Is he in the consortium?" Dryden asked.

"No. Lee is staff. He receives a good salary. I see to that. The only members of the consortium you have met so far are Armitage, Valenti and myself."

"Not Klugman?"

"Klugman, like Lee, is staff," said Serafin. "You assumed he was on the board? I asked him to meet you in the lounge out of courtesy, as one of the senior staff. Lee would have been there too, but he was working with Goldengirl. The schedule has priority over everything here."

"Could I see it?"

"The schedule?" Serafin took a half step backward and his face shaped into a refusal, but unexpectedly altered. "Why not? You are entitled to know how far we are committed to this project. Yes, you can see it. Come to the lounge."

If it was displayed in there, it was surprising he had not noticed it before.

"So Lee is in charge of the girl's psychological conditioning, and Klugman the physical?" Dryden said as they headed toward the built-up end of the camp.

"Broadly speaking yes. Klugman has two assistants: Brannon and Makepeace, both former athletes and coaches of some experience. And I am involved as well, of course, physiology being my specialty."

"How did you come to recruit Klugman?" Dryden ventured, making the most of this communicative mood. "He doesn't look to me like a Chinese defector."

Serafin drew in a sharp breath and stood still. "Mr. Dryden, I appeal to you for your own sake not to be facetious here. Klugman, since you ask, came here because I wanted a coach of Olympic class with the intelligence to bring Goldine to the necessary standard. He is one of the new generation of track clinicians. The day of the vulgarian trainer reeking of embrocation and incapable of using a knife and fork has passed. Klugman is eminent in his field, and commands the same respect from me as Lee. He came because I offered him double the salary his college was paying. Like Lee, he has no family ties, which was a factor I took into account in engaging him."

"Does he work in collaboration with Lee?"

"We are a team," said Serafin, making shapes with his hands and stepping forward again. "As you will see from the schedule, we have built in regular sessions for staff co-ordination. I am no autocrat. I believe participation in decision-making achieves the best results."

"You won't mind me asking, in that case, whether Goldine participates in the decisions?" said Dryden.

"Each phase of the program is fully discussed with her," Serafin evenly replied. "She does not attend staff co-ordination sessions, if that is what you mean, but her views, when she expresses them, are paramount in our discussions. In actual fact, she is not given to commenting much on the schedule."

"I'm surprised," Dryden said, matching Serafin's blandness. "I formed the impression this afternoon that she could put her point of view over pretty strongly."

"Has it not occurred to you that she might be perfectly satisfied with what is arranged?" said Serafin.

"Not having met the young lady, I couldn't say," answered Dryden.

Serafin nodded. "I take the point. You shall be given an opportunity of conversing with her this evening, after her workout in the gym."

"A private conversation?"

"Why not? That is to say, she has a personal companion, who must be present—a chaperon, so to speak. Yes, it sounds *démodé*, but in a community such as this, with a dozen men living in close proximity to her, I think you must agree that it is a necessary precaution. It is an inviolable rule that nobody except her companion is ever alone with Goldengirl in her quarters. Rest assured that you may speak with perfect frankness about any aspect of the project. The companion is not likely to betray confidences."

"Does Miss Fryer have a cháperon, too?" asked Dryden casually.

"No, Mr. Dryden, she does not. If Melody regarded herself as unprovided for in that respect, I should certainly engage one." Serafin peered over his glasses. "She has not raised the matter yet."

In the lounge, Valenti was practicing shots at the pool table, too engrossed to acknowledge the others' arrival. Serafin crossed the room to a framed Playmate dressed only in white suede boots, and touched a concealed switch in the gilt molding. A back projection displaced the girl for a blond without boots, varnishing her toes. Clicking his tongue in annoyance, Serafin pressed the switch again. This time a small, immaculately hand-drawn grid appeared in the frame.

"Examine it at your leisure," he told Dryden. "If you would like coffee or tea, there is a dispenser in the next room. In an hour, I should like you to come with Mr. Valenti to the gym. I'll pick you up at four."

Dryden traced his finger along the grid to 1600 on Friday. "Ergogenics," he read aloud. "That's new to me. I'll be there."

Before Dryden had finished inspecting the schedule, Serafin withdrew, or he would certainly have been asked questions. Some entries were self-explanatory and might have appeared on any athlete's training schedule. Others took a few moments' application to interpret. He soon realized that the letters below each activity represented the location and the staff required to be present. CR was the conference room; SKR stood for Serafin, Klugman and Robb. But what such

	0900-1100	1115-1230	1400-1545	1600-1730	1800-1900	2015-2130
SUN	PHYSICAL MR SK	TRACK T KBM	INTERVIEW IR LR	REACTION TG RC KBMR	WEIGHTS G KBM	FACIAL GQ FH
MON	TRACK T KBM	TACTICS CR KL	OLYM PROC CR SLR	ERGOGENICS G SLK	TRACK T KBM	SAUNA GQ H
TUE	PHYSICAL MR SK	CIRC TG G KBM	STRESS SIM IR LR	TRACK T KBM	TRACK T KBM	HAIR GQ FH
WED	TRACK T KBM	INSPIRL IR SLR	TRACK T KBM	REWARD GQ H	REWARD GQ H	REWARD GQ H
THU	PHYSICAL MR SK	TRACK T KBM	ACCL FILM CR LR	TRACK T KBM	ASSESSMENT IR SL	U/V RAY GQ H
FRI	TRACK T KBM	INSPIRL IR SL	CONFER SIM CR SLK	ERGOGENICS G SLK	MASSAGE GQ H	BRIEFING IR SLK
SAT	FLT 1 DEPARTS 0800 ETA 1100 SAN DIEGO MEET FLT 2 DEPARTS 1030 ETA 1330 SAN DIEGO MEET					
	STAFF CO-ORDINATION MEETINGS SUN 2015, TUE 2015, WED 1600, FRI 1800.					

jargon as REACTION TG and ERGOGENICS meant in human terms he was interested to discover.

Some things he now knew for certain. Project Goldengirl was a fact. Thousands of dollars were invested in plant and personnel. As a business proposition it was still bizarre in the extreme, but the possibility that it was a hoax could be dismissed.

Goldengirl herself had impressed him. He had no idea if she was capable of realizing Serafin's dream of three gold medals, but her exhilaration in the stimulation session had been riveting. It had definite commercial possibilities. If she wanted work on television he could fix it, never mind her six foot two.

But that was evading the real issue. He must soon decide what his objections were to the project. One that didn't trouble him was the English obsession with fair play. He would never have climbed the business ladder if he hadn't abandoned that at the outset. He wasn't wasting his sympathy on athletes disadvantaged by Serafin's planning. Nor was he troubled by the spirit of Baron Pierre de Coubertin, the founder of the modern Olympic movement. As anyone but the members of the IOC would admit if they studied the development of the Olympics, the ideals that launched the Games in 1896 had been sold out to commerce by 1900, when the second Olympics formed part of a trade fair. If the show had been handed over to businessmen then for perpetuity, it might not have been a bad thing. Unhappily, the politicians had jumped on board. Eighty years later, every team that would march its banner around the Lenin Stadium on August 10 had been nurtured for months on government funds, with the object of wresting national prestige from the Baron's brainchild. Why shouldn't private enterprise take them on?

If the real winners in the Olympic Games were governments and corporations, the losers were the athletes, persuaded or compelled by the prospect of gold and glory to sacrifice years of their lives to something they started out believing was sport. Slaves of the stopwatch, bloated by steroids, boosted with blood transfusions, vitaminized, immunized, screened and sponsored, they drove themselves to the point of agony training, lifting weights, endlessly lapping tracks and baring their lives to the scrutiny of the media. With what result? In most cases, to be beaten by millimeters or microseconds, robbed of victory because someone else's masters had developed a new refinement—an undetectable drug, an unimaginable technique, a more torturous form of training, a new argument to resolve the medical and legalistic objections attendant on any real improvement in performance.

Dryden was not so hypocritical as to question the manipulation of an individual athlete for profit. From what he had seen of the Goldengirl enterprise, it was simply an intensification of processes widely adopted in training for the Olympics. No doubt there were girls in Russia and East Germany being subjected to regimens just as demanding.

His objection wasn't on ethical or humanitarian grounds; it was business logic. Serafin couldn't guarantee gold medals, nor could oriental psychologists, Olympic coaches or ergogenics.

"What does it mean?" he asked Serafin, when he returned to show them the way to the gym. "Ergogenics?"

"You're still mystified?" said Serafin. "It is the science of increasing the capacity of physical and mental effort. How is it achieved? By eliminating fatigue symptoms. You will see."

By standards elsewhere in the "retreat," the gym was simple in construction, a functional timber building like a barn, furnished with enough gymnastic apparatus to stiffen an army's sinews. Lee, white-coated, and Klugman, in a black warm-up suit, were waiting beside a piece of equipment Dryden didn't recognize. There was a raised platform with a broad rubber strip along its center. At one end were an electric motor, hand controls and an instrument panel.

"Our treadmill," Serafin announced. He touched a button and the rubber moved smoothly over unseen rollers. "Don't look so scandalized, gentlemen. This isn't an instrument of torture. The treadmill is standard equipment in physiological labs. It is a reliable means of regulating experiments involving forward motion. It controls the leg cadence, you see. We use it here to analyze the movement of running, and additionally as a training device." He turned off the power. "This is the part of the schedule set aside for what we call ergogenics. This afternoon you will see how it is possible to raise the quality of a training session. Goldengirl will shortly give a demonstration of the principle in action. Dr. Lee and Mr. Klugman must take all the credit for discovering its application to our program, so I shall leave the explanation to them."

Klugman, his face set grimly for anyone about to communicate a principle, indicated that he was not the vocal side of the presentation by unzipping the top of his warm-ups to reveal a whistle on a cord nestling in the growth of black hair there. He jerked it to his lips and blew a short blast.

From a door at the end Goldengirl came running. She was wearing her gold leotard and white gym shoes; from the fluent movement of her breasts, nothing else. She stopped a yard from Klugman and stood erect, her eyes dipping a fraction to look into his. Her radiance during the press conference had given way to the expression of elegant insouciance Dryden remembered from the film.

Klugman issued instructions: "You are to demonstrate your ability to run at a speed of four hundred meters per minute. When I tell you, step on the treadmill and keep striding for as long as you can. I shall call out twenty-second intervals, so you will know how you are doing. Okay?"

Goldengirl fractionally inclined her head.

An Accusplit electronic stopwatch with a digital display was pressed into Dryden's hand by Serafin. Lee and Valenti were given them too.

Lee started the treadmill. Goldengirl had mounted the platform and was waiting for the order to step on the moving belt.

"There's a delay while we get up to the required speed," Klugman explained. "Don't start your watches before Dr. Lee gives the word." He put out a finger and tapped Goldengirl's calf. "Okay."

She stepped on, and began the unproductive exercise of running without forward movement, building speed in response to the motor's acceleration.

"Now," said Lee.

They touched off the timers.

She had whipped up her stride to a little below sprinting pace, compelled by the mechanism to drive her leading leg well forward to sustain the rate.

Lee turned his back on her and began speaking. "This is a simple demonstration of a phenomenon first noted sixty years ago by an American physiologist named Nicholson. He used a piece of apparatus called a Mosso ergograph which is obsolete now, but he obtained results which have been borne out by investigations since."

"Twenty seconds," said Klugman.

"In 1936, the Russian scientists Nemtsova and Shatenshteyn, working with weights and a bicycle ergometer, found clear metabolic evidence to support Nicholson's observations, by measuring oxygen consumption, pulse rates and chronaxia."

"Jesus! What's that?" asked Valenti.

"Chronaxia relates to the response of muscles to an electric current. The minimum amount of current that produces a measurable response in a given muscle is known as the threshold stimulus. Chronaxia is the time a current of twice this strength takes to produce a response."

"One minute," said Klugman.

"You give the dame electric shocks?" Valenti inquired.

Lee shook his head. "I didn't say that. I was describing the Russian experiment."

"Trust the goddamned Reds to think of something like that," said Valenti. "Hey, she's holding up good. Keep it going, chick. What's the record?"

"One minute twenty," called Klugman.

"Running on a treadmill isn't an activity for which records are kept," answered Lee. "She is moving at a speed equivalent to an eight-hundred-meter run in two minutes, which would have won each Olympic title up to 1972, but she has not trained for eight-hundred-meter running."

"One forty," called Klugman. "Keep going."

Signs of stress were starting to appear in Goldengirl. Her intake of breath was stertorous and her face was pink.

"The Russian girl Kazankina, who won the 1976 Olympic eight hundred meters, could probably manage something better than two minutes twenty at this

104

tempo," said Lee. "We shan't see anything of that caliber today."

"One fifty," interjected Klugman. "Can you hold on?"

Goldengirl's feet were drumming heavily on the rubber. Her head was going back. She closed her eyes. Suddenly the stride shortened, and she was carried back. She stumbled, tottered forward and finished on her knees beside the still-moving belt.

"One fifty-four point six," announced Klugman.

"Check," said Valenti.

"Check," said Dryden. Actually, he had omitted to press the stop button on the Accusplit.

"So what does it prove?" asked Valenti.

"Nothing yet," said Lee.

Klugman said to Goldengirl, "Take a ten-minute rest."

She moved obediently to a rubber mat and lay on her back. The sweat was breaking through her pores and her legs were trembling.

"She has to do something else?" said Valenti.

"The same exercise, but with ergogenic motivation," answered Lee.

"You sure it won't louse up her chances tomorrow?"

"Quite sure," said Lee. "If she wasn't on the treadmill, she would be doing this on the track."

It seemed a short ten minutes later when Klugman tersely ordered, "On your feet. Take up your position."

She sprang upright and ran toward them as she had the first time, the only indication of her effort a deeper coloration at points where the leotard was moistened by sweat.

Lee gave the instruction this time. "You are to try again now. First, let us be clear why we are doing this. You are going for gold. I want you to repeat that: 'I am going for gold.'"

She repeated the words with a conviction that would have paralyzed any rival who overheard.

"I am going to give you a tablet that will eliminate

fatigue," Lee went on. "I shall then count to five and it will begin to take effect. You will be able to stay on the treadmill until I tell you to step off. Instead of fatigue, you will have a sensation of weightlessness. You will feel your body grow lighter as the tablet is absorbed into your bloodstream. Are you ready?"

She nodded.

Lee handed her a white pill, which she swallowed. He counted to five and started the treadmill.

Dryden swiftly reset his timer to zero. Goldengirl was on the moving band of rubber again, steadily raising her stride rate.

"Now," said Lee, and they started their timers.

"This sort of thing won't get by in Moscow," said Valenti with a sniff. "They're going to be right down on anyone using dope."

"We have no intention of using this at the Olympics," Serafin assured him. "It is an aid to training, nothing more. If you eliminate fatigue, the quality of the athlete's workout is improved, and this will obviously assist her performances on the track."

They watched in silence except Klugman calling the intervals. With a minute gone, Goldengirl was showing no obvious strain.

Valenti put his timer on a bench and lit a cigar.

At one minute forty, she was moving smoothly.

Dryden listened to the metronomic beat on the treadmill and watched the illuminated digits replacing each other on the Accusplit display. One fifty-four, her previous performance, flickered by. When two minutes registered, he glanced up at Goldengirl. Her cheeks were flushed and the muscles were flexing round her neck, but she looked capable of enduring it longer.

"Two ten," called Klugman.

"That will do," said Lee. "Stop now."

Goldengirl clipped her stride, allowing the treadmill to take her back and off the belt like a skater leaving the rink. She leaned forward with her hands resting on her knees a few seconds, then walked to the mat and stretched out.

"What was she on—Dexie?" asked Valenti.

Lee shook his head. "As it happens—"

"Bennie, then?"

"The tablet was not an amphetamine," said Lee. "It had no stimulant properties at all." He took a wrapped tube of the tablets from his pocket. "They're called Sweetbreathers. I bought them from the coffee stand at Los Angeles Union Terminal. In other words, I gave her a placebo. Try one. It gave no chemical assistance to the metabolism."

Valenti cautiously touched the tablet Lee had given him with the tip of his tongue. "How d'you do it, then?"

"By motivational suggestion," said Lee. "Goldengirl is a good hypnotic subject."

"That was a trance?" said Valenti in disbelief.

"Correct."

"You could have fooled me. Don't you have to dangle a locket or something?"

"She is trained to respond to a phrase which induces a deep trance within seconds. You heard her repeat it."

"About going for gold?"

"Scientists have known for years—as I indicated just now—that physical performance can be improved under certain motivation," said Lee. "The existence of untapped energy that we use only *in extremis* is commonly acknowledged. A man pursued by a savage animal will clear an obstacle he would not attempt in less critical circumstances. A mother has been known to lift the side of a car to free her trapped child. There is a psychological barrier that tends to limit our aspirations. When that is removed, the physiological possibilities open up, as the demonstration indicated."

"Does she run her races under hypnosis?" asked Dryden.

"No," said Lee emphatically. "Nor will she. This

has a limited application. We use it to enhance the quality of her training in strength and endurance exercises. It is a way of tapping hidden sources of energy, but we apply the method with caution. She is limited to two sessions a week, and then we are careful to set tasks not much beyond her performances in the waking state. We cannot run the risk of overstrain."

Valenti started speculating. "But if she could run faster—"

"The point is that she almost certainly could not," Lee cut in. "All the best results have been achieved in tests involving strength and endurance. Research has shown that this won't improve her basic speed, but it will help her build strength for the twelve races she has in five days of competition in Moscow. I'm sure you appreciate, gentlemen, that it would be sheer madness to contest an Olympian final in trance."

"Shit stupid," Klugman confirmed.

"This is strictly a technique for use in training," Lee reiterated. "When Goldengirl goes to her mark at San Diego tomorrow, she won't be in trance. She'll need to be sharp."

"She will," promised Klugman.

Serafin brought his hands together with a small clap and rubbed them energetically. "Gentlemen, Mr. Klugman still has to put Goldengirl through the rest of her routine for this session, and I don't think we should delay them any longer. The demonstration is complete. I hope it has helped to enlighten you as to what we mean by ergogenics—a small but significant element in our program."

As Lee led the way to the door, Serafin drew Dryden aside. "I've told Goldine you would like to speak to her, and she's agreed. She'll meet you after the workout with Klugman. The door at the end of the gym— the one she came from—leads to her quarters. Go through now and wait in her changing room. She'll talk to you as she showers."

"As she showers?" repeated Dryden. "That's no

good to me. I asked for a conversation. I want to see her as we talk, not shout things over a shower wall."

"So you shall," Serafin said, putting a placating hand on Dryden's shoulder. "The shower in Goldengirl's quarters is open-fronted."

Dryden smiled, shaking his head. "Oh no, I've no intention of embarrassing the girl. Let's arrange it later."

"She has no inhibitions," Serafin said in a way that challenged Dryden to examine his own. "She suggested this herself. If it makes you feel better about it, Ingrid, her chaperon, will be in attendance."

"Chaperon?" said Dryden, with a determined effort not to seem facetious.

Serafin nodded as seriously as if showers and chaperons went naturally together. "I had better warn you about Ingrid. She is not communicative. A mute. Devoted to her duties, however, and powerful enough to carry them out efficiently. Keep on the right side of her, Mr. Dryden, and there should be no problems."

[7]

GOLDENGIRL was already back in action as Dryden walked the length of the gym to the door leading to her quarters. She was wearing a leather harness attached to the wall by two long steel springs. Urged on with quiet insistence by Klugman, she was repeatedly running forward, meeting their resistance and returning for another try.

He passed through a small corridor to her changing room, if that was the word, because it looked like a combination shower room and boudoir. The forepart was carpeted in white, and the walls were varnished pine. There was a dressing table no different in its jumble of pots and bottles from any other girl's, but the schedule of training was prominent on the wall above it. As well as the mirrors of the dressing table, there was another, full-length, attached to the adjacent wall. So, too, was a framed photo of a young woman in the uniform of an airline stewardess—by the length of skirt and style of hair, of sixties vintage. Keenly as Dryden examined it, he could trace nothing of Goldengirl in the face.

Opposite the dressing table was a tiled recess, half enclosed by a frosted-glass screen on runners, with a shower-bath sunk a few inches below floor level. To its left was a built-in wardrobe, the door open, displaying a collection of a dozen or more warm-up suits. He wondered whether Serafin's adopted daughter had ever worn a dress.

Studying the schedule again, he ran his finger down

110

the column on the right, the last session of the day, from 2015 to 2130, with the entries he remembered registering before as inconsistent with the rest: FACIAL on Monday, SAUNA Tuesday, HAIR Wednesday, REWARD Thursday and UV RAY Friday. Goldengirl was conceded a few of the vanities due to her sex. Somebody in the setup spared a thought for her feminine needs. Melody? Dryden doubted that: she was too obviously jealous. More likely Lee. He would be clever enough to see it as a support to the psychological indoctrination.

Each end-of-day session was listed GQ—Goldengirl's Quarters. Logically, somewhere nearby were a sauna room and a massage parlor. More to occupy himself than from inquisitiveness, he started toward one of the two doors opposite. He had not taken two steps when something soft caught on his shoe: a pair of nylon panties Goldine must have discarded when she changed into the leotard. Her tracksuit was lying across the stool in front of the dressing table. With a grunt of amusement, he lifted his leg and retrieved the panties from the toe of his shoe. It was reassuring to see they were white in color; Serafin's propagandizing hadn't penetrated to that layer of intimacy. But first appearances can deceive. On the front a small circular motif was imprinted in gold, with the Olympic rings surmounted by the letter M and two stars, and the words *Mockbá*, 1980.

He was shaking his head incredulously, dangling the panties from one finger, when the nearest door opened and Ingrid confronted him. She was black and very big. The outsize red warm-up suit she had on testified graphically to the strength of wool and polyester. Her bulk was mainly muscle. Her eyes widened and then narrowed as she took in the spectacle. She emittted a snort of fury, took a step toward Dryden, swung out an arm and snatched the panties away, stuffing them deep in her tracksuit pocket.

Dryden started speaking in a rush. "I'm the guy

who's meeting Goldengirl," he blurted out. "Dr. Serafin sent me. Told me to wait. Those got attached to my shoe. They were on the floor. You understand? I found them on my shoe." Ridiculously, he was lifting his foot and pointing.

Serafin had said she was a mute. Did he mean she was deaf as well?

He backed away as Ingrid lurched toward him, heaving stertorous, outraged breaths. There was no chance of cover if she turned violent. Dodging into the shower could only make his predicament absurd. The glass shower door was no defense against a woman built on this scale. His eyes caught the stool, but Ingrid, too, had seen it and veered sideways.

Instead of lifting it to poleaxe Dryden, she picked off Goldengirl's tracksuit, folded the trousers with concentration and carried them to the wardrobe, where she found a hanger and put them away. Then she motioned to him to sit on the stool.

The crisis was over.

"Thanks. I'm Jack Dryden. I don't believe I mentioned my name."

It made no impact on Ingrid. She took a last look round to check that no other personal items remained on the floor, and left as suddenly as she had arrived.

Goldengirl did not appear for another ten minutes. By that time, Dryden had ventured off the stool and as far as the schedule. The adjacent rooms could remain unexplored until he knew Ingrid better.

"Hi." Goldine was pink from the workout. A pleasant yeasty smell came with her. She tilted her head and took stock of him with wide blue eyes.

He introduced himself.

"I heard about you. Would you turn on my shower, please?"

"Cold," he inquired, going to the taps.

"You bet."

When he turned, she had one arm out of the leotard.

"Would you like me out of the way?"

"Why so?" She was genuinely surprised. "I asked you to be here. You'd like to see me shower?"

His English upbringing had taught him the basics of chivalry. "If that's an offer, I'm not turning it down."

"Anyone ever tell you about leotards? They're a lot of fun to wear, but hell to get out of. It's the arms." She gathered the thin fabric, persuaded it over her right shoulder and freed the other arm. With a wriggle of pleasure she peeled it to her waist. "Are they okay?"

"Superb," he said, so quickly that the force of the compliment was lost. Jesus Christ, she wasn't the first to flaunt a pair of breasts in front of him, but she was so casual with it for a first occasion that *he* was jumpy. Yes, they were charming, pink from the heat of her exercise, glistening damply, full enough to bob delightfully as she drew her shoulders back, but he had paid his tribute. If he added anything, she might take it for a pass. More crucially, Ingrid might, if she was listening through the door.

"I met your—er—companion just now."

"Ingrid?" She slipped her fingers inside the leotard and eased it over her hips. "She was civil, I hope. She can't speak, you know, but she's very protective. I told her to expect you."

"Thanks. I wouldn't care to be found here without an appointment. Isn't she supposed to be in attendance when we . . . ?"

"Sure." She let the garment fall in a small heap at her feet. "There's the rest of me—and Ingrid will come if I call her."

"Cozy." He hadn't decided whether she was simply exhibitionistic, or under orders to reduce him to a slavering wreck. Either way, he would treat this like a minefield. He knew enough about the way the training camp was run to put sex with Goldengirl right out of the question. This was strictly an information-gathering exercise. He needed to satisfy himself that she was just as committed to the project as everyone claimed. It was pure chance that the first steps in securing confidences and making a sexual conquest were identical: humor the subject.

"Possibly Ingrid wouldn't hear you with the shower going," he suggested.

"It's a hypothesis," she said, passing so close as she crossed to the shower that he felt her warmth on his face. She pulled the shower guard fully open and stepped under the jets.

Dryden returned to the stool and talked from there, watching as she scooped her hair forward to let the water penetrate the back of her scalp. "I was looking at the schedule on the wall—before you showed up, that is. It looks tough to me. How do you stand it?"

She tossed the hair back, with the spray cascading on her neck and breasts. "This is a soft week. Taking it easy for San Diego tomorrow. I had three rewards and a facial."

"What's a reward?"

She grinned, half stepping out of the shower, so that it played only on her back. With a strand of blond hair, she flicked water from her nipples, pinched into prominence by the cold. "Do you want a straight answer to that? For me, it's time off, an hour to do as I please."

"I get the picture," said Dryden. "But how do you earn the rewards?"

"Gee, you're a suspicious guy!" said Goldine, turning her back to him. "I earn them by working hard in training, reaching objectives."

"And if you don't work hard?"

She dipped forward and slapped herself sharply on the bottom. "No reward. But I'm smart. I don't cop out easy. There's generally something to work for at the end of a day—a facial, a sauna, ultra-vi. Motivation—it's a well-tried principle. There should be a towel hanging on the wardrobe rail. Would you be so kind?"

"Don't you ever rebel against it?" He found the towel and prepared to hand it to her, but she was already out of the shower and turning for him to put it around her shoulders.

"How do you mean?"

"Tell them you've had enough—you want to be taken down to L.A. to see a movie or look at department stores?"

"But I *don't*," answered Goldine. "I want to win the Olympics three times over. I can watch movies for the rest of my life."

And buy the stores, never mind what's in them, she might have added.

"You're dedicated to it, then. What do you expect to get out of it—setting aside the *Wall Street Journal* for once?"

"That's unfair!" she chided him, and tossed her hair, flicking water in his direction. "It's my right. I was born to do this. I'm a natural."

She said it in a categorical way that made him think of the Teutonic side of her parentage, but it didn't irritate him. She had been brought up to believe in a birthright.

"If you have a talent, why neglect it?" she went on, and added as a taunt, "What's yours?"

"Making money for talented people. That's why they sent for me."

"Name one."

"Have you heard of Jim Hansenburg?"

"The Grand Prix driver?" She picked a small towel off the rail and made a turban for her damp hair. "He's a dream! You've actually spoken to him?"

"I'm his agent," Dryden answered. "How did you hear of him up here?"

"I have a portable TV in my bedroom. I get too tired at night to watch much, but I've seen him on ABC news. And that gasoline commercial. Could I get to meet a guy like that, do you think?"

GOLDENGIRL

"After Moscow, who knows?" said Dryden. "You could be into commercials yourself."

She finished drying herself and wound the towel round her body. "I'd have to work on that. I get a little uptight about PR."

"You handled the press-simulation session this afternoon like a pro," said Dryden.

"I have to be tuned in first," she said. "Maybe Sammy will help me."

"Sammy?"

"Doc Lee. My shrink. Listen, I like talking to you. I'm due for a massage now. Sit in and talk some more." She opened the door Ingrid had come through. "This doubles for massage and facials." She led him into a narrower room with the same pinewood finish. Ingrid was standing beside a massage table in the center, pouring *Huile Clarins* from a large bottle into her cupped hand. "Mr. Dryden is going to talk to me as you do the rubbing, Ingrid," Goldine told her firmly. To Dryden, she added, "She's a fantastic masseuse. We have all kinds of tone-up gear in the cupboard, but Ingrid's hands beat them all." She unwrapped the towel and lay face down on the table, which was spread with a yellow blanket.

Dryden propped himself against the wall—there was no chair—and for the first time learned the practical difficulties of conversation with a naked girl under massage. On Goldine's side, everything was communicated in bursts of telegraphese between Ingrid's kneadings. When he understood enough to respond, he usually found that Goldine's head was turned the other way as he began to speak. Ingrid did it from malice, he was certain. The panties incident had done him no good at all.

But there was one moment to savor early on, when Ingrid was applying the oil. At Goldine's right buttock she slowed, staring at a pinker area of pigmentation —the imprint Goldine had made when she slapped herself. The outline of a hand was clearly defined.

116

Ingrid glared malevolently at Dryden, sniffed with indignation, and polished the flesh with the righteous vigor of a maid clearing up after a party.

Dryden tried a different tack. Up to now she had said nothing he could interpret as uncommitted. "You've got a strong backup—Lee, Klugman and your father."

"My father by adoption," she pointed out. "He's Doc to me."

"You wouldn't recollect much about your mother, being so young at the time of the accident."

"That's personal," she warned. "Keep off." As Ingrid paused in the rubbing, she added. "Doc provided all this. The least I can do is measure up to it."

"He told me the least he can do is provide facilities worthy of your ability. Sounds to me like a good arrangement." He let that sink in, confirming his tolerance of the project. "I just have the feeling it's a shade unnatural for a pretty girl like yourself up here in the mountains with a dozen men in attendance."

She laughed. "Unnatural! I'd say it was unnatural if they were girls. I'm not complaining."

She had used repartee like this to coast through the conference session. He didn't want the discussion back in that groove.

"You have Miss Fryer, of course. I saw the letter F on the schedule against Facial."

"Yeah. Estée Lauder wasn't available."

"Melody seems to do okay," he persisted. "She does your hair as well, doesn't she? It should be great for the newsmen to feature. I see it's natural."

"You do? Oh, I follow you." She rested her hand between her legs like a Botticelli Venus. "You're being personal again," she warned in a singsong tone that showed she hadn't taken offense.

"It was Melody who insisted I come," Dryden went on. "I was planning a quiet weekend on a tennis ranch. She's too persuasive."

"Too small," said Goldine. "We don't rate small

broads, do we, Ingrid?" She turned on her stomach with a force that set her flesh quivering. It was a rebuke for mentioning Melody. Between those two was a wall as high as the camp fence.

"How do you rate Klugman?" Dryden asked. "He looks to me like the masterful type."

"He has his job to do, same as the others," answered Goldine coolly. "He coached the Olympic squad a few years back."

It was difficult to tell whether this was the first hint of disaffection with one of the team. She could still be sulking over the reference to Melody. "They're in an odd situation, coaches," Dryden chanced. "Most of them seem to be former athletes who never quite made it. They transfer their ambitions to the next generation, as surrogates, you might say."

"And so?"

"They drive them even harder than they drove themselves, because if *they* don't succeed, it leaves the coach unfulfilled, impotent."

"You'd better try that theory on Sammy. You're talking like a shrink."

· He was determined to milk this one dry. "On a quick impression, Klugman strikes me as too intense for his own good."

"We employ him for *my* good," Goldine retorted. "If he has hang-ups of his own, so what? Turn me over, Ingrid. It's time you oiled my front."

Ingrid reversed her like turning the page of a book and lifted her lightly back to the center of the table. She lay relaxed, her eyes closed. Where she had pressed on her breasts and thighs, the white areas became pinker as the circulation of blood was normalized. Dryden confined his attention to the so far unfruitful progress of the interview. "Can I ask you about tomorrow—your plans for the meet at San Diego—or is that confidential?"

"No secret. I have to reach the Olympic qualifying standard in three events. There are five races in the afternoon—that's heat and final in the two short sprints, and just one run in the four hundred. In club meets you don't get many girls going for a full lap."

"The four hundred is the tough one. I recall you told us that in the press-conference session."

He shouldn't have mentioned it. He triggered another of her stock responses.

"It's a popular fallacy that most girls like to go the whole way."

He pulled a face. "Okay, I bought that. So you're not merely aiming to win tomorrow. You need good times."

"Uhuh. The plan is to make Olympic qualifying times and take off some of the pressure for the official trials next month in Eugene, Oregon. You're from England, aren't you? I don't know how much you know about track, but we have a beautiful selection procedure here in the States. The first three girls in each event in Eugene get nominated automatically for the U.S. team, no matter what. If the world-record holder gets edged to fourth on electronic timing, she's out, man, no argument. That suits me fine—I mean, where else could you make the Olympics after just two meets? But there's one catch, and that's to do with the Olympic rules. Each nation can send one competitor for each event, no matter how good she is, but if they want to send more, there's this Olympic qualifying time they have to reach. It's unlikely, but suppose there was a gale blowing in the trial at Eugene, and we all clocked slow times—or, if you like, wind-blown fast times, which don't count. I'd look pretty damned silly if I came in second in one of my events and didn't qualify timewise." She put up her thumb to Ingrid, who planted a palmful of *Huile Clarins* between her breasts and spread it assiduously over her neck and shoulders.

"So after tomorrow the secret's out," said Dryden. "You'll be tagged an Olympic hope. Will you know what to say to the press in San Diego?"

"There won't be many there," she commented. "Most of them will be in L.A. There's a big invitational at the Coliseum—for men. The press will make for that. One fast girl in San Diego isn't news."

It was another of her payoffs. From the smile and small shudder of pleasure as she delivered it, Dr. Lee's conditioning worked a treat.

"But your times will go into the ranking lists. Three qualifying times in one afternoon by an unknown girl: there'll be a stampede to get your story."

"I don't mind speaking to any pressmen I meet in San Diego tomorrow, but after that I go on ice again till Eugene," she told him.

"Do you like being a mystery girl?"

"You make girls sound like books—mystery, romance or Sci-Fi. I like to think I'm a blend of all three." She flushed as another programmed response slotted in.

Ingrid continued impassively anointing her stomach.

Dryden inwardly recoiled. He could see the prospect of any untutored statement disappearing as fast as the oil. "Won't the press keep tabs on you? Didn't you have to supply an address when you filled in your entry for the San Diego meet?"

"I'm P.O. Box Number 505918, Bakersfield."

"What about your club? Don't you have to belong to a track club?"

"Hadn't you noticed? I'm unattached." Again, the indulgent wriggle of pleasure.

"So after you've put up your times tomorrow, you'll just fly off, leaving the legend of a beautiful unknown blonde who burned up the track in San Diego?"

"You make it sound poetical. I like that." She gave him a dreamy smile.

"Goldine," he said as a last throw, "suppose you pulled a muscle in the heats tomorrow?" He had his hand on the door.

"How could I?" she answered. "I'm going to win the Olympics. Don't go. Try another question." She propped herself on an elbow and faced him. Her figure belied her. She was suddenly a child pleading for attention. "Ingrid can't feed me questions. Please think of something."

He shook his head in defeat. Lee had won this round. Out of compassion he asked her, "How does it feel to stand on the victory rostrum?"

She lay back with a whimper of gratitude. "Proud. Pleased for the American people." She squirmed on the blanket and brought one of her breasts against the massaging hands. "It really gets you here when you see your country's flag . . ." Her eyes closed tightly.

Dryden left.

That evening, a salad meal was served in one of the buildings. By monitoring the state of play on the pool table, he contrived to eat alone. The last thing he wanted just now was Valenti's company.

He brooded on his failure. In effect, the computer had beaten him by anticipating most of his questions. Once the programmed responses started coming, there was nothing he or Goldine could do to control her reflexes. No doubt about it: Lee had harnessed her sexual drive. Somehow he had linked it to the process of question and response. Each question she successfully answered was the equivalent of a caress. The afternoon press conference had suggested something like that was happening; the girl had projected herself in a way his own sexuality had recognized. In her quarters, he had involuntarily confirmed it by supplying her with enough questions to take her to the point of orgasm.

From the PR angle, he should have applauded Lee for a brilliant piece of psychological tinkering, certain to make electrifying occasions of Goldengirl's press interviews. But he could not put out of his mind her pathetic dependence on him as she had pleaded for another question. He had got it right earlier; her personal life had been sacrificed to Project Goldengirl.

Nobody cared about the mess it would be left in, least of all the man who had adopted her as his daughter.

As an attempt to discover how far Goldine was committed to the project, the interview had achieved nothing. Possibly if he had not allowed himself to be put down by her sharp "Keep off!" when he had mentioned her mother, if he had kept to matters that weren't likely to have been programed, he might have got somewhere, but he doubted it. If she was going to impart confidences, it wouldn't be in the camp, in front of Ingrid, and to a total stranger. Goldine, more than anyone, knew what was at stake.

What Dryden knew was still uncertain. That was the thing he found hardest to accept. He was used to making informed assessments, weighing probabilities and reaching decisions. He had spent the last twenty-four hours learning about Goldengirl. They had saturated him with information, shown him the film, told him about her background, declared their ambitions for her, answered his questions, let him see her undergoing physical and mental conditioning and allowed him to interview her himself. Yet paradoxically, the more he learned, the less certain he was that he understood. Earlier in the day he had felt near to achieving a total view of the project. At the end of it he was conscious only of uncharted areas on every side.

Worse, he had to admit that although he knew enough about Serafin and his associates to despise them, he was beginning to waver in his certainty that their scheme was impossible. Already he foresaw the dilemma he would face if he was persuaded that Goldine could win her three gold medals. His present objection—the risk to Dryden Merchandising—would not stand up. He would have the choice of going in with Serafin and condoning everything that was being done to guarantee success, or taking a moral stand and turning down a fortune.

Of course it was deplorable to tamper with a girl's psychology as they had done, forcing her under hypnosis beyond the physical limits her conscious mind imposed, and transferring her sex drive into a public-relations exercise. But suppose he took a high moral stand and refused to have any part in the project. For whose sake would he do it? Would it make any difference to Goldine? Even if there were some way of sabotaging the project, preventing her from qualifying for the Olympics, was that going to help her? She had been shaped and conditioned for one objective. Remove that objective, and where did it leave her? It could destroy her.

He spent an hour after the meal walking around the perimeter of the camp turning these thoughts over. Whichever way he looked at the problem, it came down to Goldine, and what could be salvaged of her personality. Goldine: he had slipped into the way of using her personal name when he thought of her in human terms. For all the layers of polish Serafin had applied to his "artifact," she had preserved some individuality. And Dryden liked her. She aroused him sexually—no point in denying it—but he also liked her directness, the way she had asked if her breasts were okay and the quick ripostes. *Estée Lauder wasn't available.*

He needed a chance to speak to her alone, outside the camp, without Ingrid in attendance or the possibility of bugging devices close by. That way he could judge for himself how far she was hooked on the Olympics. Then he could sort out his own priorities. The only chance of fixing it was by staging something at San Diego next day. Something they wouldn't have allowed for. They were certain to guard her like the President on a day trip to Dallas, but if there was one thing Jack Dryden had a name for, it was the knack of springing surprises.

He returned to the cabin they had allocated him. Earlier, he had just had time to put his bag inside. Now he unpacked. It was a single room with a view across the compound, simply but comfortably furnished, no worse than scores of hotel bedrooms he had stayed in for conferences. The only thing it lacked was a Gideon Bible. He had the feeling these people were not religious.

He lay on the bed trying to work something out for San Diego. Normally, he would prime himself with information. This time, all he had was what Goldine had told him. To compound his difficulties, he had not attended a track meet in years; he was an armchair fan.

How long he had juggled with the problem he did not know, when he heard a movement outside the door. It was well past sundown, but his eyes had adjusted to the fading light. He didn't need striplighting to think.

He left the bed and swiftly crossed the room to wait between the washstand and the door. The handle turned smoothly, with menacing slowness. There flashed into his mind the possibility that Serafin had decided to have him eliminated. He had asked questions, raised doubts. They couldn't see him fitting into the plan. Or risk letting him out alive.

Crazy. They wouldn't do a thing like that. Just the same, he picked up a glass toothmug, the nearest thing to a weapon within reach.

The door opened inward. The movement was stealthy, which was fortuitous, because it gave his keenly alerted senses a split second to pick up a trace of perfume. So, as he grabbed the intruder from behind, his brain telegraphed a reaction quick enough to prevent him crushing the toothmug into Melody Fryer's skull.

Instead of an automatic, it had been a bottle in her hand. It had hit the wall and smashed.

"Gee, lover boy!" she said as they toppled against the door. "I didn't know you cared. Whoops!" She sank to the floor.

"For Christ's sake!" he managed to say. "Don't move from where you are. I'll put on the light."

"Don't do that," she quickly said.

"Broken glass," he explained. "You'll cut yourself."

"Lift me up and put me on the bed. Then I won't get cut. I want to talk some. That was Campari. Pity. I'm partial to it. However, I have a flask of scotch in my pocket for you, and I think it's still intact. You won't mind sharing?"

"Why shouldn't I switch on the light?"

"Because I wouldn't care to be seen here," answered Melody. "No offense to you, Jack. It's just that I'm shit-scared of my boss. Fraternizing with you isn't on my job card today. Give me a hoist, lover boy. I'm only ninety-eight pounds."

He carried her to the bed. She was wearing a jumpsuit of some weatherproof fabric. From the feel, it was fleece-lined.

"Here's the scotch. I don't mind using that glass you nearly brained me with," she said. "Do you have a cigarette?"

He lit a Winston for her, poured her a drink and took a swig from the flask. "If you'd knock, I might have simply opened the door and let you in."

"*After* switching on the light," Melody pointed out. "Do I have to repeat that this visit is unofficial?" She curled her legs under her and arranged the pillow against the headboard. "Purely social. Aw, c'mon," she coaxed him. "What do you say to a civilized conversation? Sit down and tell me how you made out with Goldengirl."

"You heard about that?"

"Pete Klugman told me you had an audience with her ladyship after the workout this afternoon."

"That's correct," he cautiously answered. "I fixed it officially with your boss."

"And you now suspect I've been sent unofficially to get your reaction?" said Melody, holding out the glass for more scotch. "Don't fret, lover boy. I can tell you what happened. She stripped and did her floor show in the shower and then stretched out the body beautiful on the slab for you to look at from every angle. And when you took it as a come-on, you found how wrong you were, huh?"

"I went for conversation," said Dryden.

"She can handle a conversation," said Melody. "Oh, yes, Goldengirl's a smart talker. Trouble is, it never alters. When you give her a beauty treatment twice weekly, as I do, it jars a little. Like how she works hard in her training, and what standards she needs to get to Moscow. Like she's an achievement-oriented girl and she doesn't mind men looking at the goods so long as they keep their hands off. How do you like that?" She swallowed the rest of the scotch and used the glass to stub out her cigarette. "My, it's warmer in here than outside." She pulled down the zip of the jumpsuit to waist level. In the poor light, it looked like bare skin in the divide. "Did you find her stimulating, lover boy? You didn't stand a chance. Shall I tell you why?"

"If it pleases you," said Dryden.

"Come closer, then. I'm not radioactive."

Why refuse? He wanted a woman, and Melody couldn't signal more clearly that she was available. He kicked off his shoes and stretched out, gently pulling her down. Fumes of scotch, cigarette smoke and Clinique. "Tell me why I wouldn't succeed with Goldengirl."

"Kiss me first."

His hand moved inside the jumpsuit, between fleece and warm skin. She wasn't wearing underclothes.

She gripped his neck and pulled his face against hers until she was ready to take her lips away. This wasn't bluff. Melody wanted it badly.

His hand moved across her breast and slipped the suit off her shoulder. He heard her zip tugged down to its limit and he attended to his own. "What is it with Goldine, then?"

"Goldine?" She moved away from him to free her

legs from the jumpsuit. "Goldine doesn't exist. There's only Goldengirl."

"Goldengirl, then?"

She nestled against him once more, and her hand moved between his thighs. "Jeez, you should get a license for that . . . So you want me to tell you why you got nowhere with Goldengirl. She's a monster, that's why. I tell you, lover boy, Frankenstein had nothing on William Serafin. Maybe in time you'll get to understand, but if it's the real thing you want, you'll have to settle for me." She rolled on her back, tugging him with her. "Now you can fuck me, Jack Dryden, and I don't give a damn if it's Goldengirl you think about, so long as you fuck me good."

[8]

"NINE-EIGHT" VOWS MANLEY screamed the sports page of San Diego's daily, the *Union*.

SAN DIEGO, June 13——Milton Manley, San Diego Striders' latest sprint discovery, is set to dash 100 meters in a world-beating 9.8 in today's clash with San Jose State speedstar Pete Pagano at the Los Angeles Invitational. Manley, 20-year-old find of the outdoor season, states, "They tell me Pagano is the world's sharpest starter. Sure, he had the edge on me last time we met, over 60 meters in the AAU Indoor, but he'll find I blast that extra forty like I'm going for Mars. He'll need 9.8 and a ninety-degree dip to take me Saturday."

Crushed to the foot of the page by the promises of Manley and other stars appearing at the Coliseum, a paragraph coyly announced:

Today's track action in San Diego is confined to the Metro Track Club women's meet. With high-jump record-breaker Darrielle Newman a doubtful starter following a hamstring pull this week, interest switches to the hurdles duel between La Jolla's Jean Hampshire and UCLA hopeful, Marilyn Pinkton, with an Olympic qualifying standard of 13.2 as a possible prize.

The state of the newspaper, saturated by exposure to steady rain, said more than all the column-inches of predictions. There would be no world-beating performances in the speed events. The guarantees issued with a rubberized, plastic-coated, nonskid, all-weather track didn't yet include the sunshine essential to superlative sprinting. Even in San Diego in June it could rain on a Saturday.

Up in the Sierra Nevadas the visibility had been so poor by ten-thirty that the Jet Ranger was grounded for an hour, and even when they took off, the prospects of finding a safe route through the cloud screen looked slender.

As scheduled, Serafin, Lee and Klugman had left with Goldine in the Sikorsky, piloted by Lee's technical assistant, Robb, at eight o'clock, before the visibility had deteriorated. The second party was made up of Dryden, Valenti, Brannon (one of the coaching team, who seemed to have the idea he was in charge) and the pilot who had flown them up from Cambria.

"Ten flat in seventy-three. Compton Invitational," Brannon said, as if that established incontestably his status as flight commander. As he was six foot three in height and must have weighed two hundred pounds, the assumption went unchallenged. After that, he relaxed enough to tell them, "I'm called Elmer," and said no more for the rest of the flight.

Piloting a helicopter through low cloud in the Sierras is not to be rushed. They eventually touched down at the San Diego Heliport at two twenty-five. A taxi delivered them to the stadium at two thirty-eight.

With the rain had come a gusty wind and a sharp drop in temperature. Spectators, dressed in the lightweights the climate entitled them to wear with confidence, had clustered in the center of the covered stand along the home stretch on the principle that there was warmth in numbers. The numbers actually ran to about one hundred fifty. If each competitor was represented by a relative or friend, that didn't leave many there for the sport. This in no way discouraged the man in the public-address booth, who was working as hard as any World Series announcer.

"Fans, we have a great two hundred in prospect after those qualifying runs. Seems to me San Jose Cindergal, Debbie Jackson, who, remember, has twenty-three point five already this year, and just clocked twenty-four flat in Heat One, is going to be pushed by Marlene Da Costa, the Long Beach Comet, who won Heat Two in twenty-four point three, and there's Jilly Peterson, of West Coast Jets, one tenth behind in Heat Three. Also in contention we have Delia Calvert, of Lancerettes; Toni Burnett, San Clemente Superdames; and the tall blonde from Bakersfield, Goldine Serafin, who is listed as unattached. That's just one hour from now, but starting at this moment right in front of you is the long jump, featuring San Diego's lady of the leap, Cherry Harper, who, you'll remember, hung up her spikes two seasons back, and has them on again for this Olympic season. She's challenged by Glendale Gauchos' star, Mamie Van Dyck, and I'll pass up the temptation of saying she's an old master at the art of long jumping, but she won't mind me telling you she was over six meters fifty—that's twenty-one feet plus—back in seventy-six. Next on track we have what could be a sensational eight hundred . . ."

They found Serafin and Lee sitting apart from the main group of spectators, beyond the finish line. Two men Dryden had not seen before were on Serafin's left.

"Three hours in that goddamned flying goldfish bowl, and we miss the bloody race," Valenti complained.

"It was only a heat," Serafin airily assured him. "Gentlemen, I'm sorry if your flight was uncomfortable. Mr. Dryden, I'd like you to meet two other members of the consortium who have come to watch Goldengirl's debut: Michael Cobb and Oliver Sternberg. You know the Galsgear label? Michael owns it."

Cobb stood to shake Dryden's hand, a silver-haired, white-suited man with craggy, sensitive features redolent of bit players in prewar movies. Not a face you would associate with trendy clothes for the younger woman.

"And Olly is in wrestling," Serafin went on. "You could almost say he *is* wrestling."

Sternberg was younger. His skin was cherubically pink, and he had blue eyes. He was very fat. His features were confined to a last stand in the center of a threatening mass of bulbous flesh. It was impossible to say whether he looked friendly. He simply had two eyes, a nose and a mouth, with no room for anything so extravagant as an expression. His body was obviously too heavy to prize from the two seats it spanned, so he passed up the formality of shaking hands. Instead, he raised the flat of his hand like an Indian—an Indian in a white PVC raincoat, and with a red bow tie Dryden glimpsed when the chins shifted.

"It's not a question of comfort," said Valenti, determined that the problems of the helicopter flight should not be brushed aside. "It's my ulcer. We sat up there waiting for a mountain to come out of the mist and crush us. That's no help to a doozie, no help at all."

Sternberg looked up. "Do you also have piles?" he asked in a boyish voice. "If you do, stay on your feet. These seats are for Eskimos."

Before Valenti did more damage to his ulcer, Dryden asked whether he had heard the announcement correctly that Goldengirl had finished second.

"In twenty-four point six," Serafin confirmed. "She's through to the final, which is all we wanted. She has been told to save the real running for the finals. The one-hundred-meter heats take place in twenty minutes. Klugman is with her in the warmup area below us. He isn't permitted to coach her on the track."

"Twenty minutes?" said Valenti, still on his feet. "Do they have a bar in this icedrome?"

"I think I noticed a Coca-Cola stand downstairs,"

said Serafin. "Nothing alcoholic, if that's what you mean. We're among people who don't hold with things detrimental to the physique. The sponsors make most of their profits from toothpaste and soap. If you're desperate, Klugman is carrying a small flask of brandy for emergencies, and I daresay if you asked him—"

"Big deal!" said Valenti, lighting a cigar.

"Does anyone have a program?" Dryden asked, like Valenti, looking for an opportunity of using the twenty-minute interval, though not in the same way. If his plan to get time alone with Goldine was to succeed, he needed to know the stadium's layout. "I bought a paper, but it doesn't say a lot about the events."

"I know all the information of interest to us," answered Serafin, "but if you wish to go downstairs for any reason at all, please do, Mr. Dryden. I trust you won't take it personally if Mr. Brannon goes with you. Until we have come to an agreement about your participation in our project, we have to be a little security conscious. Here in San Diego we can't extend to you all the—er"—he gave a sly smile—"freedoms you enjoy in the retreat. By the way, Miss Fryer couldn't make the trip today on account of a headache."

"I don't mind having Elmer with me," said Dryden, ignoring the innuendo.

There was more action downstairs than on the track. The covered warmup area, with scores of girls working out in bright-colored tracksuits, had the purposeful confusion, speeded up, of an air terminal in high season. They had difficulty spotting Goldine. She was on the far side, bent low at her calisthenics and simultaneously listening to a lecture from Klugman. She was in a black warm-up suit, her hair tied in a gold scarf. This wasn't the moment to approach her, so Dryden applied himself instead to making sure where everything was located: dressing rooms, press room, director's headquarters, medical room, judges' and stewards' check-in. There was also a snack bar. He took Elmer inside for a hamburger and coffee.

When they heard the girls called for the hundred, they went upstairs, picking up a program on the way.

"Coming up to Heat One of the one-hundred-meter dash," called the announcer in his corn-belt twang, "and do we have a class field for this race! Debbie Jackson, fastest qualifier in the two hundred, goes again and meets Marlene Da Costa, winner of the two hundred Heat Two, and Goldine Serafin, the Bakersfield blonde, who also made the two hundred Final. Going with them is cute little Delphine Donovan, of the San Diego Mission Belles, at four-eleven a minisprinter, but watch out for her—she's no slouch. Then we have a clubmate of Marlene's in the Long Beach Comets, and never far behind her, Judy Winstanley. Lane six will be unoccupied, as Margaret Wales has withdrawn, but oh boy, these girls are going to have you screaming for them, never mind the rain. Do I hear those Long Beach Comets, down from L.A. in force? Two of your girls go in this one, and remember, it's just the first two in each heat who go through."

"Does this crap last the whole afternoon?" asked Valenti. "Can't we switch him off, or something?"

Serafin ignored him, totally occupied watching Goldengirl testing her blocks on the gleaming track. Klugman had rejoined them and was explaining the strategy. "She's going for second again. We figure Jackson will lead them in, so Goldengirl's job is to edge Da Costa."

"Wouldn't it be simpler to go for a win?" Dryden asked.

"With three finals to come, and Olympic qualifying times to set?" said Klugman, with a glare. "In these conditions? You have to be joking. She needs to conserve her strength. No sense burning it up in the heats."

"We defer to Mr. Klugman's judgment here," said Serafin. "He has worked things out with Goldengirl."

"You're bothered about the conditions?" said Cobb. "Is the surface slippery?"

133

"Maybe we should issue her skates," suggested Valenti.

"It gives a sufficient grip," Klugman answered, unamused.

Down in the rain, the whistle blew to bring the girls under starter's orders. They unzipped their warm-ups and dropped them in the baskets provided at the start. Debbie Jackson, the favorite, a slimly built black girl, was taking her time while the others waited in the rain.

"That's the kind of dodge you pick up when you've run a few," Klugman said pointedly to Serafin. "Look at Goldengirl. The first to strip, and she's that drenched you can see the bra through her shirt. Thank Christ she has the sense to keep on the move. Weather like this finds out muscle weakness sooner than anything."

"Coming up to countdown for this red-hot first heat of the one-hundred-meter dash," gushed the announcer. "We have five girls going, fans. From right, number seventeen, Debbie Jackson, San Jose Cindergals; fifteen, Marlene Da Costa, Long Beach Comets; twenty-four, Goldine Serafin, unattached; sixteen, Delphiné Donovan, San Diego Mission Belles; and thirty-two, Judy Winstanley, Comets. Over to you, starter."

Not till this moment had Goldine's height in relation to other girls made a strong impression on Dryden. The line-up might have been choreographed for some grotesque modern ballet: five girls—three black, two white—marshaled by two portly women in plastic raincoats. Goldine head and shoulders above everyone in the center. Next to her the smallest girl in the race, on a level with the number on her shirt. It was a definite relief when they got to their marks and sank their disparities in the uniformity of the crouch start.

The gun fired twice. A false start. "Not Goldengirl," Serafin emphasized.

For a second time they formed their unflattering row. Again, they moved forward to the starting line and got into their blocks. The rain drummed heavily on the roof of the stand.

"Set."

As the gun cracked, the first away was the announcer: "Good start this time. Jackson smoothly into her stride. Serafin picking up sharp, too. This girl can move! Looks like Jackson, from Serafin. Da Costa out of it. But here comes Winstanley! Watch this, fans."

Jackson was two yards clear and Goldine was cruising in behind her, glancing to her left to be sure there was no late challenge from Da Costa. What she had failed to see—it was stunningly clear from the stand—was the sudden surge of speed from the girl on the near side, who passed her two yards from the line.

"Jackson takes it from Winstanley," crowed the announcer. "Serafin third. Howdya like that for a sudden-death finish, fans?"

Klugman was making it very clear how he liked it. "She's blown it, the stupid bitch! My God, she wasn't even looking to her right. Left for dead by a second-choice club runner. It's unbelievable!"

Serafin was ashen. "Someone must do something. Not you," he told Klugman. "You'll be answering to me for that charade. Sammy, if you please. We must salvage what we can from this. There are two finals still to contest, and I want her in a positive frame of mind, not torn apart by abuse."

Lee nodded, and moved fast along the row to the exit.

"We can put it right," Klugman said defensively. "Dave Robb will have it on film. We'll analyze it, show her how she blew it. Okay, we'll put this one down to experience. Maybe we can get her entered for another meet. There's the South Pacific AAU at the Coliseum next week. I said before, she lacks experience."

"Save it," snarled Serafin without looking at him. "Of course she can't compete next week, you knucklehead. It would put the whole project at risk. After today—if this hasn't destroyed her confidence completely—the press will swoop on her wherever she appears. Oh no, we don't want stories circulating already about her training. We're keeping that for after the Olympic Trials."

"How do you like that?" said Klugman in an aside to Dryden. "I told him the girl needed experience, and now she flops, he shoots off his mouth at *me*."

On the field, four of the girls were trotting back through the downpour to collect their warm-ups. Goldine was leaning on the crowd barrier, shaking her head, unable to absorb what had just happened. An official with a golf umbrella approached her and spoke some words. She started slowly back toward the start.

"Maybe I'll take a stroll," Sternberg unexpectedly announced. He struggled to his feet and ambled in the direction of the exit.

"Better watch him," Valenti cautioned. "Wrestling's a rough sport. His idea of a stroll could include stepping on Miss Winstanley's foot."

"I have the times for that one," called the announcer. "Jackson eleven point thirty-eight, Winstanley eleven point fifty-four, Serafin eleven point sixty. The anenometer was reading one point three against. So Jackson and Winstanley make the final, scheduled for four-fifteen, fans, and I, for one, am mighty interested to see who's going to join them from Heat Two. Here's the line-up . . ."

Lee could be seen in the arena helping Goldine into her warm-up suit. The next set of girls were already trying their starting blocks.

When Sternberg returned, the heats were over and a 1,500-meter was in progress.

"How was the stroll?" Valenti asked.

"I can think of more fun-filled ways to pass my time," Sternberg evasively answered. "What's next on the track?"

"Hurdles."

"How will I stand the excitement?" He sank into his seat.

"What a race that was!" the announcer bawled into the public address, as the 1,500-meter girls doubled over to recover. "I'll give you the clockings just as soon as I get them, but first I have some news for you regarding the one-hundred-meter Final. Your Meet Director, Vince Sapperstein, has just looked in to tell me that at the special request of an AAU official, the number of girls in the Final is being increased from six to eight. Seems the quality of the heats impressed him so much he wants to see every lane in use at four-fifteen. So it's been decided that the six already due to appear will be joined by the two fastest losers. That's Edith Mercer, Millbrae Lions, who clocked eleven point fifty-two in Heat Three, and Goldine Serafin, unattached, with eleven point sixty in Heat One. Don't know about you, but I ain't complaining at the chance of another look at glamorous Goldine, the novice runner from Bakersfield."

"AAU official?" said Valenti. "They swallowed *that?*"

"Christ, no," said Sternberg. "Sapperstein's not dumb. That's just the cover. I told him what I wanted, making out I was rooting for Mercer, like I'm her sugar daddy, and asked him his terms. We have to underwrite the club's debts for the next two years."

"*We?*" said Valenti.

"It's a consortium, ain't it?" demanded Sternberg.

Serafin intervened: "We're profoundly grateful to you. Splendid work, Olly! Klugman, get down there and tell them what has happened, in case they missed the announcement. Yes, you can help Goldengirl with the warmup, but God help you if anything goes wrong in the Finals!"

The rain had eased to a vaporous drizzle when the finalists for the 200 meters appeared. Goldine had drawn the inside lane.

"That's good," Dryden remarked, airing his TV

expertise. "With the staggered start, she'll have them all in her sights."

"Not good," Brannon corrected him. "A dame with legs as long as Goldengirl's hates the pole position. The bend is tighter on the inside."

Jackson, who had drawn lane 4, again took her time coming to the start, but Goldine, too, had delayed, unfastening her headscarf to let her hair fall loose. She shook her head, not in the way she had after the defeat, but sharply, so that the hair whipped over her shoulders and had to be put back. From the way she went to the start, lifting her knees suddenly in a parody of the sprint movement, she was perfectly keyed up, free from the constraints of the heats.

Jackson pointedly shook hands with the winners of the two other heats before going to her lane. Second-placers didn't rate such recognition.

Words were pouring from the public address, but none of the group were listening, or had eyes for any of the runners but one.

"Set."

The shot echoed across the arena as Goldine powered off the blocks in a start so crisp that the first few strides were agonizing to watch in case a second shot signaled she had beaten the gun. Into the turn, she was yards up on everyone.

"Look at the blonde!" screamed the announcer. "See Serafin go!"

Eight seconds into the race she had nullified the stagger by overtaking everyone except Jackson, and she was poised to demoralize her. Arms pumping, spikes clawing the Tartan surface, she came into the home stretch emphatically clear, her hair streaming on the wind. She crossed the line more than ten yards clear, snapping the tape with her hands, like a distance runner.

"I don't believe it!" croaked the announcer. "Nobody in America can do that to Debbie Jackson."

"The time," Serafin asked. "What was the time?"

As if he had heard, the announcer called, "Twenty-two point eighty-five. Fans, this is straight out of Ripley! It's inside the Olympic qualifying time! You have just witnessed the fastest two hundred on American soil this year!"

Hearing this, Goldine threw up her arms. People were running to congratulate her as if they had known her all their lives—officials, other athletes, several spectators who had climbed the barrier. After a moment, she waved them away and jogged across the field to retrieve her tracksuit.

"That felt like a straight scotch," said Cobb.

Sandwiched between the two sprint finals was a walking race, dubbed by Valenti the 1,500-meter yawn. Before the last girls waddled across the line, the finalists for the 100-meter dash were making them look doubly ridiculous by trying starts at the end of the straight.

Having dipped deep into his store of superlatives through the afternoon, the announcer was hard-pressed to do justice to what was still to come. "Hope there's no one here with a heart condition, 'cause this is one that's guaranteed to give you palpitations. Debbie Jackson, the only girl in California to run eleven flat this year, meets the sensational winner of the two hundred, Goldine—I almost called her Golden—Serafin. Incredibly, Goldine only gets this chance because the line-up has been boosted from six to eight, and let's offer a small prayer of thanks right now to that AAU official who decreed it in his wisdom. This is shaping up as the race of the afternoon. What do you think: can Debbie hold off Goldine's challenge over one hundred meters, her favorite event? Hey, we've got the sunshine back to top it off. How do you like that? Let's not forget either that we'll be watching six other delectable dashers out to prove that what Goldine did in the furlong, they can do in the short sprint. I'll call them over now in lane order . . ."

"What's the Olympic standard?" Cobb asked.

"Eleven point twenty-five," answered Serafin. "It won't be easy. The wind's dead against them. Look at that flag."

As a spectacle, the line-up was improved by the addition of two extra runners. Again, Goldine had drawn a central lane, but the girls on either side were no midgets. Jackson, at far left, shook nobody's hand this time.

In the hunched ritual of the start, somebody was unsteady. The starter got them upright again.

They stepped forward to the blocks for the second time, got set, leaning across the line, tensed for the gun. As it fired, Goldine drove away as explosively as she had in the other final. The gun cracked again. A false start. The marshal spoke to Goldine.

"There was nothing wrong with that," Serafin protested. "She has faster reactions than the others. Is she to be penalized for that?"

"She'll be disqualified if it happens again," Brannon bluntly informed him.

But she was not. If anything, she got away a fraction late. That did not handicap her long. At twenty meters, still carried low by the thrust from the blocks, she was showing ahead, bringing with her the girls on either side in an echelon. The symmetry was short in duration. By midway, Goldine was alone, the others struggling to hold their form, a ragged line of no-hopers learning what it means to be utterly outclassed. Moving with a zest and rhythm rarely seen on any track, she parted the tape, ran on into the bend, turned and held out her hand to Debbie Jackson as she came level. Jackson's comment carried clearly into the stand: "Jesus, chick. What d'you use for fuel?"

Dryden touched Brannon's shoulder. "I'd like to go downstairs before the next race, Elmer. If you're my escort . . ."

In the excitement generated by the race they were able to leave the group without drawing comment.

Serafin registered Brannon's move with a nod and turned back to say something to Cobb.

"That run of Goldine's was electronically timed at eleven point zero eight," said the announcer in a voice that told you he was shaking his head, "and she was hitting a one-point-three-meter-per-second headwind. Fans, give or take a few hundredths, that's worth ten point nine in good conditions. This afternoon we've been privileged to witness a truly great double—Olympic qualifying times in each of the short sprints by this unknown blonde from Bakersfield, Goldine Serafin. I have the feeling this afternoon's doings in San Diego are going to cause quite some shake-up in the world of women's track. Incidentally, Goldine entered her name for the last event on our program, the four hundred, but I guess she'll settle for two finals in one afternoon, which ought to please those girls listed for the one-lap race, due off at four forty-five. Before that, the inter-club relay . . ."

On the stone steps leading to the warmup area, Dryden touched off the scheme he had worked out. He stumbled, tugged at Brannon's arm and landed heavily several steps down.

"Christ. Whassa matter?" demanded Brannon.

"I missed my footing. Wow, the ankle hurts!" He rubbed it energetically, still sitting on the stairs. "Can you help me up, Elmer?" On his feet, he groaned. "Feels bad. It may be a break. I have a weakness in my right leg. It went once before. Look, I need some-one to take a look at it. The medical room's below. Can you support me that far? You're a pal. God, it's like a knife thrust!"

Hanging from Elmer's shoulder, he hopped clumsily down the remaining stairs, past the sharp glances of the few girls still exercising in the warmup area and as far as the door marked with a red cross. Elmer pushed it open.

The meet physician in his white coat was attending to a pretty, dark-haired girl whose foot was bleeding.

141

She was lying on a rubbing table, wearing a tracksuit top and brief scarlet shorts.

"What's this, then? Someone else in trouble?" the physician asked, without putting down the swab he was using.

"Fell on the stairs. Hurt his ankle," Elmer explained. "Could you take a look at it, Doc?"

"Be my guest. Would you sit in the chair, sir, while I dress this young lady's foot. You're not in severe pain?"

"Not severe," Dryden confirmed.

"She was spiked in the walk," the physician told them. "Nothing too serious, but it needs cleaning up. You don't mind these gentlemen waiting here, miss—er—"

"Gee, no. It doesn't bother me," the girl said with a smile in Dryden's direction. "After all, it's only my foot."

Dryden was quick to see a chance to modify the strategy. "Well, there's really no need for both of us to stay. You could get a coffee, Elmer. It's clear I'll be here a few minutes yet."

"But I mustn't let you out of my—"

"Hey, you'll have these people thinking I'm a head case," Dryden quickly said. "No, I can't move with my foot like this, but it's too embarrassing for this young lady having treatment in this small room overlooked by two strange men."

"I really don't mind," she insisted.

"So beat it, Elmer, old friend," Dryden went on. "If you're concerned about me, you can wait right outside the door till I'm bandaged or whatever. Fair enough?"

Brannon scratched his head and looked around the room, possibly checking for a second exit, but there was none. Not even a window. To help him reach a decision, Dryden moved his right shoe and sock. The ankle was inflamed from the rubbing he had given it.

"Okay, I'll be right outside," said Elmer, defeated.

Dryden relaxed in his chair and enjoyed the leg

show a yard away. In different circumstances, he might have steered this situation toward a date, because she was quite a looker, with more than a hint of fun in her large, brown eyes, but there were other priorities. So far, his plan was working well. If the girl had not been there, he would have needed to persuade Elmer to report the accident to Serafin. This way was better. It detained him, providing more time to work on the physician.

When her foot had been lightly bandaged, the girl got off the table, swinging her legs Dryden's way. "I hope yours is as easy to treat as mine," she said with a smile.

"Thanks. Sorry we burst in like that."

"My pleasure."

It was cruel to pass up the invitation in those eyes. "There's one thing you could do for me," he ventured.

She smiled again. "Yes?"

But Dryden was a cruel man. "If my friend's still outside, would you tell him I'll be a few minutes yet? He agitates easily, and I don't want him coming in till I'm fixed up."

A little bleakly she said, "Okay. Leave it to me. Nice to have met you."

When the girl had left, the physician motioned to Dryden to climb on the table. Instead, he moved quickly to the door and flicked down the catch on the Yale lock.

"Hey, what the hell . . . ?" demanded the physician. He was a young man built like a football player, capable probably of thrusting Dryden straight through the hardwood door if he cared to.

"I'll be frank, Doc," Dryden said. "You're in a spot, and I can help you. Do you know what's been happening out there"—he jerked his head in the direction of the track—"while you've been bandaging that cute little foot?"

"What *is* this?" The physician took a step toward Dryden. "You told me you were injured."

143

"I needed to speak to you. You may not think it matters to the meet physician who wins the runs and jumps, but I think you should know that it does, and I'm here to tell you why. A completely unknown girl has just won the one hundred and two hundred meters in times inside the Olympic qualifying standard."

"So?"

"So you as physician in charge of this meet will have certain questions to answer unless you act fast. That girl has never run times like this in her life. She has to be on some kind of dope. Isn't it your job to test for that?"

The physician shook his head. "Not a chance. I can't carry out a dope analysis here. Listen, buddy, this is a club meet, not the Olympics. We don't do dope tests here."

"You could get her to a hospital and test her there," said Dryden.

"Who the hell are you to tell me my job?"

"A free-lance press reporter. If that girl isn't tested, I'll wait until her times have knocked the national rankings sideways, and then sell this story to the Los Angeles *Times*. I have your name right from the program, I hope—Julius Fishback, M.D.? And you're refusing to administer a test on Goldine Serafin on the grounds that this is a club meet, not the Olympics? I can quote that?"

"Now wait a minute," said Dr. Fishback, rubbing his hand through his hair. "Take it easy, friend. I want no trouble. If you're telling me you suspect this girl has taken an amphetamine—that's what you're saying, is it?—it's my responsibility to investigate that."

"I'm glad you see it that way," said Dryden. "It's of no consequence what *I* think. *You're* the expert here. If you exercise your professional judgment to arrange for the girl to go to San Diego General for a dope test, it might just save a lot of questions from the press when it's too late to do a thing about it."

"I follow you. What's in it for you, then?"

"If the test is positive, I have an exclusive. I'd like to travel with you to the hospital. Do you have a car, or should we ring for a cab?"

"My car will do," said Fishback, "but someone has to detain the girl. If she's finished her running, she may have changed and left by now."

"I think not," said Dryden. "She was running in the four hundred." He looked at his watch. "It's off about now."

"The four hundred—on top of two others? She *must* be doped," said Fishback. He picked up the telephone. "Is this the stewards' room? Fishback here—Meet Physician. I've decided to run a test on one of the athletes"—he cupped his hand over the mouthpiece—"her name: what did you say her name was?"

"Serafin," said Dryden. "Goldine Serafin."

"Goldine Serafin. I believe she's running in the four hundred meters. Would you have a marshal ask her to report to the medical room immediately after it finishes. Tell her it's routine, but make sure she gets here, won't you? Thanks." He put down the phone. "Why the big act about the ankle injury?"

Dryden smiled. "That was mainly for my friend's benefit. He works on the San Diego *Union*. In a way, I'm upstaging him. I didn't wish to hurt his feelings. Say, it would help a lot if you put your head round the door and told him you're taking me to hospital for a check. I'm not asking you to tell a lie. I think it might get rid of Elmer."

Dr. Fishback unlatched the door and spoke to Brannon, who presently came inside. Thoughtfully, Dryden was seated again.

"You're going to the hospital?" said Elmer, wide-eyed.

"You heard it from the doc," said Dryden. "Sorry, old pal, but there it is. You can't take chances with your health."

"What the hell do *I* do?"

"You'd better tell the others," said Dryden with a

vexed sigh. "I hope I don't spoil the arrangements. It's the San Diego General, is it, Dr. Fishback?"

"Er, yeah."

"Okay, Elmer? Maybe they can pick me up there in an hour or so. It's never very quick in hospitals."

Elmer backed out, agonizing over his dilemma. Fishback shut the door.

"I'm obliged to you," said Dryden.

The phone rang. Fishback picked it up, listened, said "yeah" a couple of times, and put it down. "That was the stewards' room. They're bringing over your junkie. She just won the four hundred meters in a time two tenths outside the U.S record."

[9]

A sound principle of merchandising practice is to exceed people's expectations. Events in San Diego so far had slotted neatly into Dryden's plan, but it was time to introduce another check against the predictable.

Dr. Fishback had not driven more than a few minutes along Park Boulevard in his Chrysler, with Goldine, white-faced, still in her tracksuit and clutching a bag containing her clothes, seated in the rear, when Dryden, at his side, said, "I don't suppose the hospital would look on this as an emergency. They get a lot of casualty work Saturday evenings, I expect."

"At the General, they keep busy most times," said Fishback. "No need for us to trouble them in emergency, however. This is a simple analysis."

"Do you work in the hospital, by any chance?"

Fishback shook his head. "I practice in a clinic in La Jolla," he said with pride.

"Nice," said Dryden. "The culture center."

"I guess you could say that. We have the University, of course, the Museum of Art—"

"Is there a hospital out that way—to save you driving to the General? Seems to me one lab is as good as another for a test like this."

Fishback thought about it. "We have the Salk Institute out there. They'd run a test for us. Hey, how about your friend? You told him to pick you up at the General."

"To be truthful, it's easier if he isn't around," said Dryden. "I wouldn't want to put my exclusive at risk, if you understand me. I'll catch up with Elmer all right. And I'll see Miss Serafin gets back to her people after the test."

"Suits me," said Fishback. At the next intersection, he followed the signs for Highway 5.

The springing of a drug test, as Dryden had anticipated, had caught the consortium unprepared. After the four hundred meters, a marshal, one of the dowagers in plastic raincoats, had rushed Goldine to the medical room with Klugman in tow, but she had very firmly closed the door on him before he could catch a glimpse of Dryden. And while Klugman had raced upstairs to report to Serafin, Fishback and Dryden had whisked Goldine to the car. The marshal had collected the clothes from the dressing room and delivered them to the car at the stadium gate.

The people at the Salk Institute for Biological Studies administered the test with the minimum of fuss. Before Goldine was taken by a female analyst to pass a specimen, Dryden put his hand on her arm and told her confidentially, "This is a safeguard for you. Don't be anxious. You've nothing to fear." Having said that, the thought crept into his mind after she had gone that if Klugman or someone had taken fright at the weather conditions, they *could* have slipped her a Dexedrine capsule. If the test proved positive, the consequences for Goldine's career, Serafin's ambitions, Dryden's future didn't need spelling out. He was in a sweat until the analyst appeared in half an hour and said, "She's clear."

"How about that?" said Fishback. "Could I have that in writing? Nobody's going to believe this." He turned Dryden's way. "Sorry about your exclusive, friend, but there it is. Happens Miss Serafin is just one fabulous running machine."

All this labeling. Artifact monster, machine . . .

"I just have to accept that I made a mistake," said Dryden. "Dr. Fishback, I'm sorry to have put you to all this trouble. There's not much I can do to com-

pensate you, but if anyone *should* suggest her performances this afternoon were upped, you may be sure I'll
publish a rebuttal giving you full credit for acting as
responsibly as you did."

"Doing my job, that's all," Fishback magnanimously
said.

As soon as Fishback had left, Goldine turned to Dryden. "We must call a cab, get back to San Diego."

"Easy," murmured Dryden. "Why the panic?"

Her eyes widened in surprise. "Doc. He won't know
what happened. If I don't check in quick, he'll go
crazy."

"He'll have heard about the test," Dryden pointed
out. "He knows these things can't be hurried. Look,
you've had a harrowing time. You need to unwind.
We'll walk a little. Twenty minutes more won't make
any difference."

"Will you clear it with Doc when we get back?" she
dubiously asked.

"Leave it with me. There won't be any problem," he
promised. "They're delighted you ran so well this afternoon. And when they hear you got a clearance on the
dope test, they'll be over the moon."

The stress lines in the center of Goldine's forehead
began to soften.

"I'm afraid I missed the last race," Dryden casually
continued. "How did it go?" He picked up her bag and
moved toward the door, and she came with him.

"The four hundred?" Her eyes were shining at the
recollection. "It was a lot of fun. The sun was out by
then. I just coasted through the first three hundred and
then kicked for home. I had a lot left at the end—
would you believe that? I never guessed it could feel
so easy."

"It's going to get tougher."

"Don't I know it! I had a peek at next week's schedule. Track, track, track. I guess it's necessary. I have
to be in condition for the Olympic Trials four weeks
from now."

"You looked fit enough today."

"I'll have to go faster than that, but it's coming."

They had come down the Institute steps and were strolling through the grounds toward the gate. Dryden nudged the conversation forward. "Goldine, I was hoping I would get a chance to speak with you like this, outside the retreat, away from Ingrid and all the others."

She smiled. "Ingrid's no snoop."

"I believe you, but the meeting we had in the massage room wasn't my idea of a relaxed conversation. I'll be truthful. I engineered that dope test to get some time alone with you. Don't feel threatened. I didn't do this to trap you. I just had the feeling yesterday that it wasn't fair to expect you to answer my questions frankly."

She stopped and regarded him pertly. "You mean I didn't reveal enough of myself?"

He put his hand behind her elbow and gently moved her on. "Goldine, you're a sensational bird, but I haven't brought you here just to chat. Can we be serious?"

"If that's what you want," she said flatly.

"Your father—your father by adoption—wants me to be your agent after the Olympics. When I met him first, I put him down as some kind of nut and told myself I wouldn't touch the project. It's a little wild to contemplate, you must admit. But underneath my cynical exterior, there's a streak of pure greed. I'm in business and I've had some success. I like to think I'm still moving up. When I stop thinking that way, I should retire. Now, that selfish streak of mine tells me you could be a winner, and I ought to take the Goldengirl commission. After this afternoon, if they asked me right now, I'd take a chance and say yes. But it's still a chance, not just because some other superdame might steal a medal you were counting on. You see, my vocation isn't nice. I trade in people. Successful people, celebrities, world champions. I invite combines and

150

corporations to bid for them. They make a pile of money and I take a cut. It sounds like a good arrangement, and for some of them it is."

"Jim Hansenburg?"

Dryden thought, and nodded. "He'll do for an example. Jim's a natural competitor. Give him any kind of test, from high school grades to Grand Prix racing, and he'll do his damnedest to finish on top. I had him playing with a toy the other day, a miniature racing circuit, and I asked him to make sure he didn't win—we were pitching for a contract, and I wanted our potential customer in a good frame of mind. Do you know, Jim raced that five-inch car as if he was on the Nurburgring, got ahead, and wouldn't give way for eighty laps? Then he drove it off the track, to my incredulous relief, but I'm sure he only did that because he'd proved to himself he was morally the winner. That's Jim Hansenburg, a nice guy, sexy—women adore him—but with this fixation to win. He knows exactly what he wants from life. Yes, he enjoys his money, girls, travel, but he only comes alive on the Grand Prix circuits. Give him five more years, when his reactions slow up a little, and that man will cease to live, Goldine. Literally, he may kill himself trying to keep up with younger, sharper drivers—plenty do— but if he does survive, it will be an empty old age, forever striving for success at pool, poker, ten-pin bowling. He knows. I've discussed it with him. It isn't in his nature to do anything different. My guess is that he'll be dead ten years from now, but it won't be on *my* conscience. Does that sound brutal?"

"I can understand," she said, lowering her eyelids. "Are you saying the same thing could happen to me?"

He shook his head. "I'm telling you I'm a money-grabbing bastard who'll push anyone who's a winner and take my cut."

"But you like to give them a rundown first on their prospects?"

"For my peace of mind, yes. There's a glimmer of conscience in there somewhere."

She stopped to perch herself on the concrete edging around a palm, one hand playing with her hair in a consciously feminine posture. "Go ahead, then. Tell me about the fate in store for me, Mr. Dryden."

"That's the catch. I can't."

"Come again."

"I understand Jim Hansenburg. Goldine Serafin, I don't."

"Why should that be?" she asked. "I'm a simple American girl who aims to win three gold medals."

"Why?"

"How do you mean?"

"To use a well-worn phrase, What motivates you, Goldine?"

She frowned, bewildered. "Is that important?"

"To me this evening, yes."

"I can only answer in another cliché: it's my life-style."

He watched her absently shredding a piece of palm bark. He was balked again. She looked ready to talk, but the defenses had been built too high, too strong. "How about a drink? The place over there looks okay."

"Thanks, but no. *Verboten*. I'd rather walk along the shore."

They followed the road down to the beach.

"You speak German, then?" Dryden knew how it was to be a laboratory rat; as one way through was barred, another opened.

"Very little. I had some from my tutor."

"Did your mother—"

"She brought me up to speak English," Goldine quickly said.

"May I ask about her?"

She frowned and thought a moment, studying his face as she made up her mind. Then she said, "I can't tell you much. I was very young. She was an air stewardess, born in Germany during the war. Her mother brought her to California after my grandfather was killed."

"Is that her picture in your quarters?"

"Uhuh. She was pretty."

"I thought so, too," said Dryden. "Strange, though. I couldn't recognize much of you in the face."

"That's not surprising. There isn't much of me left."

"I don't follow you, Goldine."

"Didn't they tell you about my rhinoplasty?"

"Your *what?*"

She touched her nose. "Cosmetic surgery. A nose job. Eighteen months back, I could have passed you in the street. Mousy hair, flat nose, pouchy eyes and saggy breasts. All I had was my six foot two. Doc sent me to a plastic surgeon. He remodeled my nose, removed the pouches from my eyes and gave some shape to my bustline. And they decided I should go blond. You thought I was natural?" She giggled a little. "I'll let you in on a secret. It's a masculine delusion that you can tell a peroxide blonde as soon as she strips. There's a great little product called Creme Bleach a girl can safely use anyplace from her eyebrows to her crotch."

"And that's how Goldengirl was created?"

"Most of her. Do you want to hear the rest? You've been honest with me, and I appreciate that. Nobody ever told me before that he was in this for the money. It's always like they recognize my talent or they want to see me fulfilled or we're doing it for America. You're smiling, but that's what Sammy Lee has started telling me."

"He's a smart psychologist," said Dryden. "Loyalty is a strong motivating force. You'll run harder for America than you would for yourself. It's one of the oldest principles in sports that you go better if you represent something: college, club or country. You've been prepared for Moscow as a loner, but by the time of the Olympics, he'll have you blubbing at the sight of the Stars and Stripes."

She looked impressed. "You know, I think you could help me, Mr. Dryden. What you just said is the kind of thing I need to understand."

The rainclouds were an unlikely memory as they strolled along the sand of La Jolla Beach, close to the waterline. She took off her shoes and linked her free arm in his as she talked. "You know, I'd like to answer that question of yours about why I want to win in Moscow. And let's be clear. I *do* want to win. That's *me* speaking, not Doc or Sammy or Pete Klugman."

"Or Goldengirl?" said Dryden.

"You got it. Not Goldengirl. Dean. I Dean Hofmann, mean to win those three gold medals. I'll try to tell you why, but you must understand some more about the way I was raised. They told you about that?"

"Not much. You had a private education."

"Tutors. I learned to read and write, and I made some progress, I guess. I wouldn't make UCLA, but I have the basics. From quite early on, the physical side of my development was paramount. By that, I mean I had my own little gym before I was out of diapers. It had a swing, ropes, parallel bars. I had to work out every day, morning and afternoon. I didn't mind that too much, but there was physiotherapy too, and that could be painful. Doc had a theory about oxygen intake which involved expanding my rib cage. So once a day I was put into something like an old-time corset, except it didn't compress you, it fastened under your ribs and pulled you out. I hated it. I hated the injections, too."

"Injections. What were they?"

"Iron, I guess. To supplement my strength. Once a week, right up to when I was sixteen. And my diet had to be regulated to my physique. No candy—I really do have my own beautiful teeth—and no jam or iced cakes."

"What *could* you eat?"

"Whole-wheat bread, skim milk or buttermilk,

grapes, oranges, honey, raisins, liver, beef and meat extract—by the spoonful."

"That's a lot of vitamins. Did Serafin measure your progress physically?"

"Each Monday morning. He still does. A full physical. Everything goes into the records."

"And Mrs. Serafin," ventured Dryden. "What part did she play in your life?"

Goldine smiled wanly and shook her head. "She slipped me a chocolate bar sometimes. She wasn't a dominant personality. If I was ill, she took over. That was nice. Don't get me wrong—I'm not bitching about my childhood. I couldn't be a champion if they hadn't taken care of my body. I have a very good cardiovascular system." She picked up a piece of driftwood and made as if to fling it far out to sea, then let it fall in the sand. "Did you know that Jean Serafin left him? That really surprised me. I never dreamed she had anything going with another man. She took off to the West Indies the fall before last."

"You didn't think of going with her?"

"Mr. Dryden—"

"Jack."

"Jack, you'll find this hard to credit, but I never really got to know Jean. She was younger than Doc, and maybe that made it hard for me to relate to her as a mother figure. I didn't make it easy for her. If you put together all the stereotypes you've ever seen of adopted kids rejecting their surrogate parents, I was it. Doc I could accept: I had no father, so he wasn't ousting anyone. But Jean I hated. In time, I tolerated her, but we never grew close. It's only since she left that I realize she had a part in my life."

"What was that?"

"I figure she was a moderating influence on Doc so far as my upbringing was concerned. I never heard them discuss it. I just see how things have gone through the past year and a half since Jean took off. Doc focused totally on me, and he's a determined man. He found some backers and had the training camp built. Since we've been up there, everything is stepped up. That's okay—I expect it, to be sure of winning the Olympics. Jack, I know I can win in Moscow. It would be a betrayal not to make sure I do, by training hard. A betrayal of myself, I mean. You see, winning is my way of making sense of my life so far. If I gave up, walked off right now to join a commune somewhere— I've thought about it—that's as good as saying all these years were wasted. I don't want that. I want to get my golds and give some meaning to my life so far. Then I can draw a line underneath"—she stopped and made a mark in the wet sand with her toe, and stepped over it—"and begin to find out who I really am."

"That makes sense, up to a point," said Dryden.

"I know what you're going to say. I've thought about that, too. I can't really draw that line, can I?" She turned. "Look, it's disappeared already. After Moscow, I shall really be Goldengirl. It's too late then to search for an identity."

"Do you want to be Goldengirl?"

She walked on in silence, looking at the waves.

"It's important," he gently insisted.

She stopped and looked earnestly at him, pulling a strand of gold hair between her teeth. "Jack, I have to admit that I do."

"You don't need to be ashamed. Almost any girl would answer yes to that."

"But almost any girl starts from a consciousness of her own identity. It's a reference point. I don't feel that I have that."

"Have you discussed this with Dr. Lee?"

"Sammy? His answer is that Goldengirl *is* me. When I accept it, all my anxieties will go. He's helping me to realize this through the simulation sessions. And it's true. When I attend stadium simulations and I see the crowd around me in their thousands, and hear the cheering and the announcements in Russian with my own name, I'm happy, Jack. In the press-conference sessions I come alive. It makes up for all the pain."

"Physical pain, you mean?"

"Sure. Pete Klugman is a great coach, and he's improved my track technique beyond belief. He doesn't do it with sugar cubes. I was raised to work hard at my sport, but nothing resembling the sessions with him. I don't like to talk too much about it. He can be very sweet at times, and he's doing all this for my benefit. For instance, my starting is immeasurably better with the practice I've had on the shock-start mechanism. It speeds your gun reaction. If you don't move your hands within fifteen hundredths of a second, you get volts up your arm. It hurts, but I go faster. You saw me today?"

"You went off so fast in the hundred that they called you back."

"That's the problem with quick starting. Starters *will* assume that if you leave the blocks before the others, you must have jumped. It isn't so. In Moscow, they plan to have automatic fault lights that can't operate after the gun has fired, so I should be safe from human error there." She dangled a piece of seaweed in the water like a child. "I can take the electric shocks. They're sharp, but they don't damage me. What I can't stand is being humiliated."

"How does that happen?"

"It seems to have crept into the training sessions lately. Pete used to be patient with me if I fell down on something. Say I run an interval in twenty-six instead of twenty-five. Not so long ago he would say something to encourage me, tell me where I could pick up a little more speed. These last few weeks if something goes wrong, he just lays into me, calls me a lazy cow and worse things, real ugly things, all in front of his assistants. Some days he gets them to bawl at me as I run by. "Get your ass moving!" they shout. "That was only twenty-six." It's supposed to get my spirit up —I've discussed it with Sammy—provoke some anger that raises the adrenalin. Sometimes it does, that's true. Other times it's plain dispiriting. He sets me goals we both know I can't reach, and then gives me a verbal larruping while the others look on."

"Have you complained to Dr. Serafin?"

"I've tried. He's sympathetic, but he won't alter anything. It's necessary to my preparation, he says. Light and shade. If I have it rough from Pete, that makes the sessions with Sammy nicer."

"And *are* they?"

The answer was in her eyes. "You bet. I'm Goldengirl already to him. He gives me stimulating things to do, like listening to tapes and watching films. Jack, I've seen so many films of Moscow, I know it like you must know L.A. And I've seen all the great sprinters in action from Jesse Owens on. Shall we sit down now? You've carried my bag a long way."

They had reached a wooden breakwater. They sat in the sand, protected from the slight breeze that had driven other people from the beach. From below the horizon, the sun colored the underside of a solitary cloud, but it would not be long before darkness set in.

"You say you enjoy the sessions with Dr. Lee," said Dryden, "but it isn't all films and conversations. You must have got through some hard work on the question sessions from the way you handled the press conference yesterday."

"Practice," said Goldine, smiling.

"But just as hard as running intervals, I should think," said Dryden.

She shook her head emphatically. "Sammy's methods are different. He never humiliates me. He's taught me how to treat the questions as a pleasurable experience."

"Most people regard that kind of experience as an ordeal," said Dryden. "What's your secret?"

She gave him a piercing look, and said, "Something anyone can buy for a few dollars. It wouldn't be much help to you, though." She turned away and shied a stone at the water. "You know about vibrators? Lonely women sometimes have a use for them. Sammy started me off with one. I wasn't embarrassed; I was raised to have no inhibitions about my body and its needs. We used it in the stimulus-response sessions—privately, not with all that jazz we had in the press-conference simulation yesterday. It was wired up so that each time I gave a good response I got good vibes—literally. I made a lot of progress that way. Now I don't need the vibrator. I get the same turn-on just from hearing the question and knowing I have the answer ready."

"We've come a long way since Pavlov."

"What do you mean?" asked Goldine.

"I was recollecting something your Sammy said about learning theory. He's no fool. He knows about people, how to win their confidence, make them more efficient."

"You don't like him?"

"I'm impressed by him," said Dryden. "I don't know whether it matters if I like him."

She turned to face him, her hair flame-colored in the freakish light. "How about me? Are you impressed by me?"

He wasn't used to such directness. "By your running—dazzled."

"And do you like me?"

"Too much," said Dryden.

She fingered her neck. "What does that mean, Jack?"

"I find it difficult to be objective about you, as a businessman should."

"You don't have to be objective."

"Sorry, but I do. If I'm to reach a decision about acting as your agent, I must make an informed estimate of your potential, both athletically and commercially. I'd be crazy to allow likes or dislikes to blur my judgment. I didn't build my agency by signing up all the nice people I know."

"Do you have any girls among your clients?"

"A few."

"And if one of them got to like you, I figure you'd just tell her to knock off the romance and sign the contracts."

"That's speculation," said Dryden. "It hasn't happened, I'm glad to report. Can you imagine telling a two-hundred-pound soprano from the Metropolitan Opera to knock off the romance?"

Goldine laughed, and flopped back on the sand. "We'd better not lose any time, then."

"What is that supposed to mean?"

"Tomorrow you make your decision, right? You sign me up, or walk right out of my life. From what you say, the upshot is the same so far as romance is concerned. If I want you, I must make it now. You said you like me."

This wasn't scheduled. Till now, everything had gone as per plan, with the characteristic smoothness of any Dryden operation. He had explanations to cover everything: his "accident," the dope test, the change of route, the delay at the Salk Institute. He was ready to admit to the consortium that he'd used the time to have a conversation with Goldengirl. Laying her on La Jolla Beach was another matter.

"When I said I like you, I meant it, but—"

"Kiss me, then." She parted her lips and confidently waited.

He leaned over her, keeping one hand on the breakwater, the other in the sand. "You must understand that this doesn't mean . . ."

She snatched at the kiss in a way that betrayed inexperience.

"Take it easy," he told her. "More like this." He showed her how to touch with the lips and gently increase pressure.

"I'm not much good," she said.

"That was better. Like everything else, it's practice. I'm useless at crouch starts."

She pressed her hip against his leg. "Hold me."

He shook his head. "Better not. I'm liable to take advantage."

With wide eyes she said, "But I want you to."

Time for the only ploy he could think of. "I'm—er—not equipped. Too risky for you."

"That's okay," she said with a sweet smile. "I'm on the pill."

"Not a chance," said Dryden. She had told him some weird things, but that beat everything. "In that case, what's Ingrid doing on the payroll?"

"Silly," she said, running the tip of her finger down the bridge of his nose. "Don't you know girl athletes have to regulate their periods? The pill is obligatory for Goldengirl. Hell, I'm not in high school, you know. Because Doc and the others treat me like a kid, it doesn't mean I'm untouchable."

"It's getting late." He was beginning to *talk* like a school kid. "Your father must be going crazy."

"We'll think of something to tell him," she said. "Jack, I want you. Christ, you're not refusing me, are you? Am I so grotesque?"

She was fumbling with the front of his trousers. This was becoming ridiculous: rape in reverse. He unlocked the arm that was around his neck and drew away from her, kneeling in the sand. "Goldine, this isn't the way."

She had pulled open the zip of her jeans. White cotton showed in the cleft. Practical and unalluring, it epitomized her situation in a way that touched his sympathy. Kept by the consortium, shaped to their specifications, trained to the breaking point, physically and psychologically abused, deprived of any feminine indulgence unless it suited their plans, here she lay on the sand in her plain cotton underwear, appealing for confirmation that she existed as a woman. He couldn't deny her that.

He moved close and whispered a lie. "Goldine, you're too persuasive."

As he expected, it wasn't ecstatic lovemaking. Melody Fryer's soft carnality was imprinted too clearly on his memory as he coaxed Goldine to relax her iron grip and let him perform the essential movements.

It was presently obvious that this was a pioneering effort so far as she was concerned, but she urged him on and accepted the discomfort like lifting weights. He closed his eyes and remembered her in the flashlights, parading the sexuality Dr. Lee had harnessed for her appearances before the press. At a cost now becoming apparent. He caressed her breasts and murmured endearments, but it was obvious he was not going to bring her to orgasm. After he had reached his climax he remained holding her and said, "Nice. You okay?"

She gave him a light kiss. "Thanks. I'm a beginner, as you must have noticed."

"After the first time, it gets better," he promised her. "I hope it did something for you."

More than she knew. It had brought him to a decision. He would agree to Serafin's terms and go in with the consortium.

[10]

BLONDE DASHER: METRO CLUB MYSTERY

By Grantland Davis

SAN DIEGO, June 15——Officials of the Metro Track Club were last night at a loss to account for the sensational running of a mystery blonde who mopped up three titles with Olympic qualifying performances in their San Diego meet yesterday. The tall, attractive girl, who gave her name as Goldine Serafin, is unknown to track specialists. Yet she posted times of 11.08 (100 meters), 22.85 (200 meters) and 50.52 (400 meters) to rank her among the world's top dashers in this Olympic season. Track nuts in Los Angeles on hearing of these clockings were inclined to put them down to faulty equipment, but Meet Director Vince Sapperstein stated, "We had the electronic timing mechanism checked by the Longines people Wednesday, and it's accurate to within a hundredth of a second. Besides, several observers clocked her independently. Believe me, those times were right."

Dope Test

The mystery of blond Goldine was complicated after her last event, the 400 meters, when an official escorted her from the arena, refusing press interviews. Later it was learned that Meet Physician Julius Fishback had called for a dope test. Said Dr. Fishback last night: "When I heard about those timings, I thought it proper to authorize a routine test on Miss Serafin. It was carried out at the Salk Institute and the result was negative. Her performances were definitely not assisted by drugs."

The girls who suffered crushing defeats in the wake of galloping Goldine included San Jose Cindergal Debbie Jackson, 21, who earlier this season ran 11 flat for 100 meters. "She took two meters off me in the first 30," said Debbie. "And that was into a wind. She'd have burned anyone off today. No, I didn't recognize her, but then I saw more of her back than her face. If this chick goes, the Olympic Tryouts next month should be a gas, a real gas."

No Trace

Late last night reporters were unable to trace Goldine Serafin. Her entry form listed her address as a Bakersfield P.O. Box number. A Dr. William Serafin and his wife Jean are known to have resided in Bakersfield until two years ago, but neighbors remember their only daughter as dark-haired and quite unlike the pictures taken yesterday of blond Goldine (above). The Serafins are believed to have separated in 1978. Their present addresses are not known.

Goldine was listed in the meet program as "unattached," meaning she has no track club affiliation.

Wild Theory

The possibility that the blond runner was a top-rank athlete from Europe over here to soak up some California sunshine, and using another name to disguise her from rivals in the forthcoming Olympic Games, was dismissed by an AAU official as "wild." But the mystery of blond Goldine remains, and may not be cleared up before next month, when the Olympic Trials take place in Eugene, Oregon. Stated the AAU official, "If the clockings in San Diego are authenticated, Miss Serafin should get an invite to the Trials. I mean no discredit to San Diego officials, but I'll be interested to see if this girl can repeat her performances under championship conditions."

Dryden tossed aside the Sunday edition of the *Union* he had picked up in the hotel lounge. It was a relief that nothing in it conflicted with the story he had told the night before. To give credit to Serafin, he hadn't gone berserk when Dryden and Goldine had finally appeared in the lobby of the Westgate Plaza Hotel at ten-fifteen. He had listened to the story, and it was watertight.

As Dryden had told it, Dr. Fishback of his own volition had ruled that Goldine must take a dope test. By good fortune, Dryden was in the medical room to have his twisted ankle examined, and overheard Fishback on the phone ordering the marshal to pick up Goldine after the 400 meters. Learning that the test would mean a car ride to the hospital, he had waited to see whether Klugman or anyone else was going along in support, learned that they weren't, and insisted that he be allowed to accompany her. Fishback had given his assent, provided Goldine was agreeable.

On the way to the hospital, Fishback had changed his mind and driven instead to the Salk Institute. They had arrived there at five-forty, the test had been administered at six-ten, but the physician in charge, who had to sign the medical certificate, was off duty till six forty-five. Satisfied by the analyst that the test was negative, Fishback had not waited any longer, but Dryden had thought it wise to collect the written evidence of Goldengirl's test. During the interval before the physician arrived, he had twice tried ringing the stadium, but nobody picked up the phone. Soon after seven o'clock, when he had collected the certificate, he got the idea of phoning the heliport. He had asked for a message to be delivered to the pilot of the Jet Ranger: that, as it was already too late to fly to Cambria Pines before sundown, he was taking Goldine, by then exhausted, for a meal in La Jolla. They had run into a little trouble afterward getting a cab, but finally stopped one at nine-ten. By nine-fifty they had found Brannon, deputed to meet them at the heliport, and got into another cab, which had delivered them to the hotel. Time: ten-fifteen. Supporting evidence: one certificate signed by Dr. Lyle-Gordon of the Salk Institute, one check from the Plaza Inn and—a nice touch—one crepe bandage around Dryden's right ankle. As he had mentioned to Goldine in the cab, it scored tactically to check in at ten, rather than seven. By then, the consortium was more anxious than angry.

How they felt after a night's reflection it was difficult to judge. When Dryden appeared in the hotel restaurant at nine-forty, he learned that several of the party had already breakfasted and checked out. A curt note left by Serafin informed him that a cab was ordered for ten-thirty. The second party would take off from the San Diego heliport at ten forty-five, destination Cambria Pines.

"You've read the report, then. She seems to have

created the right amount of interest at this stage, wouldn't you say?"

It was Lee. He must have arrived in the lounge when Dryden was deep in the newspaper.

"Looks like it," Dryden said tersely. The polite smile and couch-side voice were a little difficult to stomach this morning.

" 'The mystery blonde,' " Lee went on. "Isn't that a helpful start toward the image? I thought mysteries made good copy in the advertising business."

"It's a theory," said Dryden without enthusiasm.

"Perhaps I should stick to things I understand. The psychology of mass communications always overawed me. I am quite baffled by demographics and computer readouts. Did you sleep well?"

"You want me to tell you about my dreams?" said Dryden in a growl. "Yes, I passed a comfortable night. I believe some of the party made an early start this morning."

Lee's smile widened slightly. "As I understand it, yes. Dr. Serafin ordered seven-thirty calls for each of the consortium so that they should be in Cambria for a meeting at eleven. I can imagine certain of them were not too enthusiastic about that, but they have all checked out. Dr. Serafin usually gets his way."

"So who does that leave for flight two, apart from ourselves?"

"Just Klugman and Brannon, I believe," said Lee. "Goldengirl traveled with the consortium." He got up. "They are very likely still in bed. I'd better arrange for them to be called."

"Is that necessary? We could tell the cab driver to call back in an hour."

"That wouldn't do," said Lee. "Dr. Serafin has arranged for you to join the meeting at two o'clock."

Dryden got there at two-ten. There was no delay in the flight; the Jet Ranger managed the three-hundred-mile hop along the coast to Cambria in a little over two and a half hours. Time for a leisurely lunch before he ambled across to the casa Armitage had made available for the meeting. The ten minutes after two o'clock had been spent on a second cup of coffee. The consortium could wait awhile. He was playing this his own way.

They sat around a table in the big studio living room. Serafin grim-faced at the holdup in the agenda. Sternberg in the demanding act of removing his linen jacket with help from Armitage. Cobb politely stifling a yawn. And Valenti lighting his next Panatella from the butt of the last.

Dryden slid into the vacant chair opposite Serafin. "You *were* expecting me?" he mildly inquired.

"At two o'clock," snapped Serafin. "We don't have much time. I promised Mr. Sternberg to wind up by three, as his helicopter is coming to take him to an appointment in Las Vegas. Gentlemen, we come to the last major item on the agenda: the management of Goldengirl's commercial future. You will remember that Mr. Armitage suggested at our last meeting that we arrange for Mr. Dryden to be with us this weekend to acquaint him with our plans, with a view to inviting him to act for Goldengirl after her victories in Moscow. One way and another, Mr. Dryden"—he looked over his glasses—"you must have gained a pretty comprehensive insight into the project. I take it by now that you have come to a decision about your agency's participation."

"You coming in?" said Valenti.

"Can I get a few things clear first?" asked Dryden. This was his turn at bat and he was not going out with one swipe. "You're offering Dryden Merchandising the exclusive right to act as agent for Miss Goldine Serafin in negotiating contracts with commercial groups interested in using her name, picture, personal endorsement—"

"The lot," said Valenti. "How about it?"

"Radio, TV and movies," Dryden went on, "theater

and nightclub appearances, books, magazines and newspapers—all exclusive?"

"You're the top agent," said Sternberg, wheezing after the struggle with his jacket.

"And I have the reputation of my agency to protect," Dryden pointed out. "If Dryden Merchandising is better regarded by big business than most other agencies, it's because we have a name for taking one hundred per cent reliable people on our list. No junkies, jailbirds, political extremists—people who could destroy a brand image overnight. You understand that if anything adverse—I'm speaking hypothetically—became public knowledge, my agency couldn't have anything to do with Goldengirl."

Valenti looked suspicious. "What are you getting at?"

"It's a simple safeguard," answered Dryden. "Let's suppose, to take a wild example, one of you supported some controversial cause—the movement to ban dogs from urban areas, let's say—and you planned to use Goldengirl as a voice for your arguments. The moment she made these views known, she would be commercially finished."

"That figures," said Sternberg. "I like dogs, anyway."

"We understand that Goldengirl's character must be seen to be exemplary and uncontroversial," said Serafin, giving no hint that he took the comment as a personal imputation. "Is that agreed, gentlemen? Do we take it, in that case, Mr. Dryden—"

"Not yet. The timing of the promotional campaign," said Dryden. "You want everything to be ready to make an impact at the most favorable moment, the peak of public interest, as soon after the Olympics as possible?"

"That is the idea."

"In that case, quite detailed negotiations would need to take place *before* the Olympics. Contracts would still be conditional on her success, of course, but we should certainly have to talk with business executives at some level prior to the Games. To be realistic, the chance of keeping her ambitions secret after that is nil."

"We are resigned to that," said Serafin. "Candidly, there is no point in trying to conceal her intentions once the Olympic Trials have taken place from July fourteenth through the twenty-fourth. She will then be nominated for three events and must make it clear why she is not participating in the relays. There will be four weeks for your negotiations. Is that sufficient?"

"It will have to be," said Dryden.

"Do you accept the commission?"

"Hold it," broke in Valenti. "What's your percentage, Dryden?"

"For this assignment, fifteen."

"Jesus H. Christ. What does that leave for us?"

"Eighty-five," said Dryden. "If it makes the mathematics easier, you can pay me twenty."

"Don't push me," warned Valenti. "How much do you figure we can hoist?"

"Provided she gets the three, and is still breathing, something approaching twenty million dollars," said Dryden. "That's my estimate."

There was a pause for mental arithmetic.

"I'm agreeable," said Valenti.

"That goes for me, too," Armitage chipped in.

"We take out the expenses *after* Dryden's cut?" said Sternberg, "And split five ways? I make that a little over three million each."

Cobb had taken a calculator out of his pocket. "Check. In that case, it's okay with me."

"Just a minute," said Dryden. "What does Goldengirl stand to make out of this?"

"Five good friends!" squeaked Sternberg, convulsed with his wit.

Serafin was quick to intervene. "Of course, I am making provision for her. For administrative purposes, Mr. Dryden, we shall be forming a corporation to be known as Goldengirl Incorporated. It will undoubtedly simplify your agency's dealings with us. The board is, of course, constituted by the members of the consortium. My share of any profits that accrue will ensure that Goldengirl has everything she requires to finance her for the rest of her life."

"But she isn't on the board?" said Dryden.

Serafin shook his head. "Too young. Instead, I propose to set up a trust fund on her behalf. She will bet a generous proportion of my income from her activities. After tax, that is."

"May I ask what proportion?"

"It isn't settled yet," said Serafin, "but I had in mind at least a third. She will be a millionaire if your estimate is correct."

Dryden was thinking fast. He doubted if it would help Goldine materially to join the board. It was better to work through the trust. There wasn't much room for maneuver with hard-headed characters like Sternberg and Valenti, but he might try squeezing them a little. The best chance of a breakthrough was with Serafin. "I'm mainly interested in the backup the board could give to the merchandising campaign," he said. "I like the notion of a Goldengirl corporation. That's good business practice. What worries me a lot is the slice she gets of the revenue. It might create difficulties if the press got to know she had no direct interest in Goldengirl Incorporated. Okay, you have an answer to that in the trust, but anyone sharp enough to find out about the trust is going to ask what proportion of the Goldengirl millions goes into it. On a quick calculation, it's around five per cent. I appreciate the outlay of expenditure on this project, gentlemen, not to mention the risk you are taking and the long-term planning involved. Unhappily, the press and public won't, and it wouldn't be advisable to tell them. They'll see it simply as exploitation. I make no criticism—I'm thinking just from the PR angle."

"You're suggesting we should increase the girl's share?" said Cobb, eyebrows twitching.

"I'd like to see it raised to fifty per cent."

The silence this created was broken by Valenti. "What's in it for you if Goldengirl's cut is fifty per cent?"

"No more than if it's five," said Dryden. "I'm interested only in what the public is told. A hostile press could hurt the project a lot."

"That figures," conceded Valenti. "We don't want some wise guy shooting off his mouth in the Los Angeles *Times*."

Dryden nodded. "It's heaven-sent for some investigative reporter out to make a name for himself."

"How would you propose that we increase Goldengirl's share?" asked Serafin with caution.

"In two ways. First, by abandoning the percentage concept in favor of a guaranteed sum. Let's be candid —you weren't expecting me to come up with an estimate as high as twenty million. I could be wrong; this sort of thing is a crap shoot in many ways. But basing it on contracts we've negotiated lately on behalf of top-line stars, and allowing for the girl's exceptionally marketable personality, it's the closest I can come to any sort of estimate. It surprised you a little, I could see. None of you were counting on as much as three million a piece, or we would never have had such instant unanimity." He paused, preparing them for his terms. If they were led to expect a figure half as much, this ploy might be successful. "A guaranteed sum, I said, and I would be prepared to agree the same amount for my agency's services."

"How much?" asked Sternberg.

"Two million dollars each, to include all expenses." Before anyone commented, Dryden added, "And that brings me to Proposal Number Two. That is, to give the trust a controlling interest in Goldengirl Incorporated by having you, Dr. Serafin, on the board as its representative. You would receive a fee, of course, which we could agree upon with the trustees, but so far as press and public are concerned, you would not be a direct beneficiary. If we raised twenty million in revenue, Dryden Merchandising would then take its two million; Mr. Sternberg, Mr. Valenti, Mr. Cobb and Mr. Armitage would be guaranteed two million each; and there would be ten million for the trust fund. From the public's point of view, Goldine would be getting fifty per cent of the money. How much of that she was generous enough to give her father would become a private matter."

"You're a smart cookie!" said Sternberg.

"I like it," said Cobb, "but I have a query. Without prejudice to your reputation as an agent, Mr. Dryden, what would you propose if the revenue amounted to less than the twenty million you estimated?"

"I said the figure each of you would receive would be guaranteed," answered Dryden, "so I was implying that the trust fund would stand the loss, if we call it that. Equally, if the revenue topped twenty million, the excess would go to the trust."

"I'll buy that," said Valenti. "Two million guaranteed?"

"Subject to three golds," said Dryden. He was watching Serafin. The others, he had assumed, would agree; in their world, guaranteed sums in units of a million were more potent than percentages. With Serafin there was a question of status. Would he settle for anything less than his own share? The money was more, but he would have to rely on Goldine for his cut. Was it really the money he wanted from all this?

"I'm agreeable," said Dick Armitage, almost forgotten.

"Very well," said Serafin. "I think Dryden has a valid point about public interest. We shall not be making any of our financial arrangements public, but if questions were asked, it would obviously look better if the trust fund were seen to account for a sum large enough to satisfy any doubts. With your approval, gentlemen, I shall make arrangements for an agreement to be drafted on those lines. I appreciate your cooperation in this matter. It says much for our unity of purpose that we have reached a mutually acceptable arrangement in so civilized a way."

"It's important that this is formally agreed to without delay," pressed Dryden. "My participation must be conditional upon it."

"It will be done," promised Serafin.

"In that case, I'll get my lawyers to draft an agreement between Dryden Merchandising and Goldengirl Incorporated. It can be done without any breach of security. How do they get in touch with you?"

"Through my P.O. box in Bakersfield," said Serafin, handing him a card. "I'll mail copies to my fellow members of the board here. We can confirm everything when we meet next. I suggest an appropriate venue would be Eugene, Oregon, during the National Olympic Trials. Shall we say July tenth? I can arrange hotel accommodations. I assume you would all wish to be in Eugene for the period spanning Goldengirl's events. That takes us through to July sixteenth. The Trials follow the program of the Olympics."

"I'll give a progress report on the merchandising campaign," Dryden offered. "By then, most of it should be mapped out."

"But you won't involve anyone else until after Eugene," Serafin firmly ordered. "We can tolerate no breaches of security. This will be a solo exercise on your part until mid-July. Is that perfectly clear? Between us, we are a powerful group, and without going into detail I can tell you that any leakage of information about the project would do you and your group of companies no service, no service at all."

"I don't care for threats," said Dryden.

"Threats? We deal in facts, not threats," said Serafin. "And the outstanding fact is that the interest of everyone around this table is served by observing the rule of secrecy. During the weekend, you have heard a number of reasons why we think it advisable to avoid publicity. There is another which has not been mentioned, and that is Rule Twenty-six of the International Olympic Committee—the Eligibility Code. The essence of it is quite simple: to be eligible for participation in the Olympic Games a competitor must not have received any financial rewards or material benefit, except as permitted in certain bylaws."

"Hell, they'd need a commission to prove anything," said Sternberg.

"That is exactly what they have, Mr. Sternberg," Serafin acidly said. "Need I say that if Goldengirl were ordered to appear before such a commission, the consequence would be disastrous? We could hire a good lawyer to argue her case, quote precedents, and so on. There are hundreds, thousands of Olympic athletes receiving sponsorship of one sort or another. But the publicity, you see, the private training camp, the personal coaches, the psychologist, would destroy the image we are trying to create. Commercially, it would sink us. And, of course, names would be published—"

"Okay, okay, we follow you," squeaked Sternberg. "If we got a fink in this operation, we take care of the problem. I move next business."

When Dryden came to load his suitcase into the Excalibur at the end of the afternoon, Dick Armitage was standing there, the look of self-reproach restored on his features.

"Thanks, Jack. I guess I owe you an apology."

"What for?"

"Not telling you what I was letting you in for."

"A two-million-dollar ripoff?" said Dryden. "Skip it, Dick. Go and practice shots. We need a little prize money on the side."

"You haven't come in just on account of me?"

Dryden switched on the ignition. "Forget it. Mind you win Wimbledon."

[11]

"HI, Mr. Dryden. Good weekend?"

"Middling."

Zena on Reception pulled a face at the doorman.

Dryden stepped into the elevator. The morning routine—KNX/CBS News, coffee, Los Angeles *Times*, San Diego Freeway, parking lot, familiar faces on the sidewalk—had reinstated the world he had stepped out of on Thursday. The loose ends of last week waited on his desk. A stack of unanswered mail, the Colgate contract for Hansenburg, half-yearly figures from London. He applied himself to them, deliberately insulating himself from Project Goldengirl.

"My calendar, Jackie. What's it like for the next three weeks?"

"Busy, Mr. Dryden. There's the trip to New York Thursday, and Tokyo next week. Most other days I have lunch dates written in. Would you care to see it?"

"Later. I'll have to cancel New York and Tokyo. Something has come up. Would you have a look through and see which of those lunches I can put off? I shall need some afternoons clear."

She widened her eyes slightly. "I'll see what I can do, Mr. Dryden." She got up, a tall, bright-eyed girl in her twenties, never off work.

"Thanks. What's the secret, Jackie? How do you keep so fit? Sports, is it?"

She laughed. "My idea of sports is to have my guy Hal take me shopping in Beverly Hills. I keep in condition that way."

"Sensible."

When she had closed the door, he allowed the weekend to resurface. He wouldn't say he had it in perspective yet—it was too close for that—but he could begin to get a few things straight. By committing the agency to an agreement with the consortium, he had gone clean against his first intentions, performed an about-face he would hate to admit to any of the earnest young executives on the next floor.

What had influenced his change of mind? Two things: Goldine's running in San Diego, and the couple of hours he had spent with her at La Jolla.

He examined the reasons. Something in the way she had run in those two finals he had watched had convinced him she was a world-class athlete. The opposition had been mediocre; Debbie Jackson was the only runner there with any reputation, and she might simply have had a bad day. He was no authority on track. He couldn't tell you the world record for 100 meters, let alone the Olympic qualifying standard. All it came down to was a hunch that through that rain in San Diego he had seen the glint of gold.

And La Jolla? He was hard put to analyze *that* with any detachment. It had started so promisingly, as each development slotted into his plan. And ended in that grotesque coupling in the sand. Really, it was what she had said that influenced him: her statement of helplessness. That was all it had been—a statement. She hadn't asked for help or sympathy. She just believed her only chance of self-preservation was to win in Moscow. If that was her conviction, it was probably true. What Dryden knew was that when she won—*if* she won—she would need support of a kind he was uniquely placed to give. There was nothing he could do yet to preserve her from humiliation and perverted science, but when the time came he could save her from annihilation by the media.

The possibility that he was rationalizing, that his concern about the girl arose from the hunch that she was a winner, he put in the back of his mind. It was a practical decision. He could help Goldine survive as a personality. Nobody else would.

The dealing at Cambria Pines had been a first step. She now had the best share of the revenue she could reasonably hope for, and in the most secure form. There were details to watch—the terms of the trust fund were important—but the principle of her right to a major share had been established.

It still puzzled him that Serafin had agreed so readily to the changes. The specter of adverse publicity may have frightened him a little, and perhaps he assumed his influence over Goldine would guarantee him fat pickings, but the way he had capitulated without a syllable of protest was difficult to understand. It seemed he was not interested in haggling over terms. If that was so, it would be useful to know what *did* interest him in all this.

Now that he was back in circulation, Dryden could begin to check some of the details Serafin had mentioned in his account of Goldine. Her mother's accident: there should be something in the files of the Los Angeles *Times*. The Tamarisk Lodge children's home: did it exist? What were Serafin's professional qualifications? That kind of information was easy to verify in a library. It was the second stage of research, the business of visiting people and asking questions, that could raise problems. He would be in a spot if anything got back to Serafin.

Jackie came in again with the calendar. "I've put off all the lunch dates up to Friday, and I'm working on next week. By the way, Mr. Dryden, did you wear those shirts I bought?"

"Forgive me, Jackie. I should have mentioned that. They were fine."

"Your weekend was okay?"

"Fine. Just fine."

"I'll get back to the phone, then," said Jackie.

She had come to him a year ago with a rave reference from one of the top executives at Gulf Oil. So far, she had measured up to it. Quick, thoughtful and intelligent, she had not given him the least doubt of her integrity. He didn't like damaging the confidence between them, but he would rather say nothing than fabricate an account of his weekend.

The *Times* building on West First Street was nearer than the Huntington Library, so he used the Information Service there. He turned to the *Directory of Medical Specialists* and found:

SERAFIN, William Joseph. Physiologist. b. Salzburg Sept. 16, 1920. s. Anton and Olga (Merttens). M.D. Geneva, 1945; Ph.D. Yale, 1951; Research Fellow, Yale Sch. Medicine 1951–2; m. Jean Dixon, 1952; Calif. Inst. Hum. Sc., 1953–; Prof. of Anthropometry, 1969–; Weinraub Found. Med. Research Fellow, Vienna, 1962–3; Fellow, Amer. Ac. of Phys. Ed.; Member Amer. Assn. U. Profs.; publ. *Hereditary Factors in Human Physique,* 1964; *Anthropometric Data and Human Growth,* 1966; address: Calif. Inst. of Human Science, Bakersfield 3105, California.

On a quick inspection, nothing conflicted with the information Serafin had given out at the retreat. A second reference book, *Who's Who in U.S. Medicine,* carried the same details with the addition of Goldine's name among the family particulars.

He looked up another entry:

LEE, San Fen. Psychologist. b. Peiping, China Apr. 18, 1935; ss. Kwok Lo and Hui Tao (Tang); B.Sc. National Central U., Chung Kiang, China, 1956; M.Sc. Peking, 1959; B.Sc. Columbia, 1969; Ph.D. Columbia, 1972; Faculty, Berkeley, Calif., 1972–4; Consultant, Los Angeles County Gen. Hosp., 1974–; Member Amer. Inst. of Psych.; address: c/o L.A. County Medical Assn., 1925 Wilshire Boulevard, Los Angeles.

He wasn't learning anything of importance he didn't know already, so he went to the room where the *Times* files were kept, and asked for the April through June volume for 1964. According to Serafin, Trudi's death from drowning had happened in May. As he turned the pages, he reflected that Serafin himself had handled them in 1964, if his story was reliable.

He found the report in the issue for Saturday, May 25:

KILLER WAVE: FIVE DROWN IN BEACH TRAGEDY

LOS ANGELES, May 25——A 20-foot wave, described by oceanologists as a "one in a million hazard" caused five deaths on popular Huntington State Beach at 3:16 yesterday afternoon. From a sea so calm that surfers had mostly given up waiting for rides, the wave built into a vast wall of water within seconds. Eyewitnesses described it as "terrifying—like a street block coming at you." Parents along the crowded beach screamed to their children as it towered above them, but few got clear before it hit them, sweeping them as much as fifty feet up the beach.

The effect of the killer wave was clear seconds later, when scores of bathers were seen struggling in deep water, dragged out of their depth by its undertow. Many were temporarily blinded by the sand in the water. The six lifeguards on duty were assisted by volunteers in the rescue operation. It was thought for a time no fatalities had occurred, but a search of the water by helicopter revealed three bodies. Two more were recovered later. The dead were identified as John Paschal, 15, of Palm Springs;

Patrick Lamont, 24, Huntington; Darryl Horn, 20, San Diego; Miss Anne English, 30, Santa Barbara; and Miss T. Hofmann, 22, Inglewood.

The report went on for another column, but there were no other particulars on Trudi. He found those in the issue for May 27 on an inside page under her photograph: the one he had seen in Goldine's quarters.

BEACH VICTIM DIED RESCUING CHILD

LOS ANGELES, May 27——A victim of Friday's tragedy on Huntington State Beach, when a freak wave caused five drownings, actually died going to the rescue of her two-year-old daughter, who survived. She was Trudi Hofmann, 22, a TWA stewardess, of Lincoln Boulevard, Inglewood. The incident was described yesterday by Mrs. Diane Pershore, who was sitting near Miss Hofmann when the 20-foot killer wave reared up unexpectedly in a calm sea. Stated Mrs. Pershore, "I noticed the young woman playing with her daughter, and presently the child went down to the water's edge, leaving her mother sunbathing. As the screaming started along the beach at the sight of the advancing wave, she got up and raced toward her daughter. Next thing they both disappeared in the foam and must have been dragged way out of their depth, as other bathers were. The water was two feet deep where I was sitting, forty feet behind the tideline. In the confusion, I lost sight of those two, but later I saw the little girl carried from the water by a lifeguard. She was just a scrap of a kid."

Devoted to Child

Miss Hofmann's body was washed ashore on adjacent Newport Beach late Friday evening. The child, Dean, who will be 3 on June 6, is at present in the care of the Los Angeles County Welfare Service. No relatives have yet been traced.

Neighbors of Miss Hofmann in her Inglewood apartment on Lincoln Boulevard described her as a gentle person devoted to her child. German-born, she had come with her mother to California in 1953. She engaged a babysitter to be with Dean while she was on duty with TWA, but she frequently took the little girl to one of the local beaches. It is understood that Miss Hofmann was a nonswimmer.

Dryden leafed through the next half-dozen issues, but there was no more on the accident. Now that he had confirmed so many details of the story, he would not go looking for the back number of *Time* that Serafin claimed had first caught his attention. He was prepared to believe it existed. Instead, he turned to the more delicate assignment of digging out more information on Serafin himself.

He used a public phone booth to call the San Diego *Union,* and asked for the sports desk. "I'd like to speak to the guy who wrote the piece on the Metro Track Club Meet in Sunday's edition. My name is Frank Rademacher, Southern Pacific AAU."

In a moment a voice said, "Grantland Davis here."

He repeated the bogus name, disguising his accent. "I'd like to invite this mystery blonde of yours to our meet at the Coliseum, Saturday. The Metro Club people could only come up with a Bakersfield P.O. box number. I saw your piece on Sunday and figured you must have checked her out by now. It's getting late to start mailing box numbers. If I could phone Miss Serafin today, I might be able to get her name on the meet program. You don't mind me asking if you located her?"

"No luck, I'm afraid, Mr. Rademacher," said Davis. "After calling at the Salk Institute for the dope test, she vanished. I can't help you."

"That's tough," said Dryden. "It might have added a hundred or so to our gate. Too bad. That Dr. Serafin you mentioned in the piece. Is he the father?"

"Could be. We haven't traced him either. He was a professor of something I can't get my tongue around, at the CIHS in Bakersfield. Seems to have retired two years back."

"He must have left a forwarding address," said Dryden.

"Sorry to disappoint you. Seems Prof Serafin wasn't giving much away about his retirement plans. He called in a couple of times to collect mail, and that's all they know."

"He didn't have friends there?"

"Seems not," said Davis. "In the words of the Registrar—this is off the record—he thought he was God, but he had trouble convincing his colleagues. They were that glad when he offered to retire that nobody's kept up with him since. Of course, we can't even be sure he's the father of our blonde."

"You got nothing else on him?"

"We spoke to his neighbors in Bakersfield. He alienated them, too. Cut them stone dead in the street. His wife was a local doctor, nice woman, our man in Bakersfield was told, and there was this pathetic daughter who didn't resemble our whiz kid one bit. Frankly, the story's spiked till we turn up something new. If you get a lead, let me know, won't you?"

Dryden went back to the *Times* Information Bureau and looked for Tamarisk Lodge in the *Register of Social Agencies*. It didn't appear, yet he was sure he had the name right. He asked the girl if they kept old editions of the register. She said no, she thought they would have one at the County Welfare building on Wilshire.

There, he was shown a shelf of registers going back to the forties. In the volume for 1960 he found:

TAMARISK LODGE, Casitas Springs, Ventura. Acc. 25m/f under 11. Matron: Mrs. G. Van Horn.

He asked for a telephone directory and confirmed that someone of that name was listed and still lived in Ventura. He dialed the number. An elderly voice answered.

"Yes?"

"Mrs. Van Horn?"

"That's so."

"I wonder if I've got this right. Are you by any chance the lady who was formerly Matron at Tamarisk Lodge?"

"I am. Who is this speaking?"

"That's great. My name is Hofmann. I don't suppose by any chance you recollect a child named Dean Hofmann, a girl of about three years of age?"

"As a matter of fact, I do," the voice answered cautiously.

"Wonderful! Mrs. Van Horn, I'm one of the family visiting Los Angeles and I dearly want to find out what I can about Dean. We lost trace of her, you see. If she's the child I think she is, I'm her cousin. Could you spare me half an hour if I came out to see you at Ventura?"

"I suppose I might be able to, Mr. Hofmann, but I can't tell you a lot."

"Thanks, ma'am. What's the time now? I should be with you by five-thirty, if that's really okay."

He put down the phone before she could say no. He could make a sizable list of the mean things he had done in his life, but telling lies to sweet old ladies was new. He got into the Excalibur and drove west on the Hollywood Freeway.

Mrs. Van Horn had a small house one block past the Mission San Buenaventura on Main Street. A regiment of poinsettias, spaced and sized, lined the front. He saw the old lady watching him from behind her chintz curtains as he came up the path. He didn't blame her.

"Mrs. Van Horn? I'm Jack Hofmann."

"I supposed you were. Do come in."

The room was tidy, but stacked with ornaments, and smelled of lavender. A red-faced man in a dark suit was standing at the mock fireplace, fixing him with a penetrating stare.

"This is Mr. Hardaker, my lawyer," Mrs. Van Horn explained. "He—er—happens to have dropped by. You don't mind if he stays?"

"Lord, no," said Dryden. The old lady had got her reinforcement organized fast.

"And it's about Dean Hofmann, I understand?" she said. "Do sit down."

"That's right. I hope to trace her while I'm over here. I'm from London," he said, lowering himself into a leather armchair showing signs of wear.

"How interesting. Yes, I remember the child very clearly. There was an accident, you know."

"I just read it up in back issues of the Los Angeles *Times*. Terrible tragedy."

"Her mother was an air stewardess," said Mrs. Van Horn. "Now what exactly would your relationship be to her?"

Hardaker must have primed her. Dryden wondered why. He started on the story he had fabricated on the drive over. "It's a little complicated. My father was born in Germany, but he took a job making clockwork toys in London in the thirties and got married to an English girl. When war broke out in 1939 he found himself on the wrong side, you see. He decided to change his name to Harrison and stay in London. So I grew up as Jack Harrison. It wasn't till Dad's death last year that I learned our name was actually Hofmann. Going through his papers I found some newspaper clippings describing the 1936 Olympic Games. I'm not sure which paper they were from, but it was all in German. One name was underlined in each of them, a Fräulein G. Hofmann. My German isn't good, but I could understand enough to make out that she had been a member of the German National Gymnastics Team which had won the gold medal. I asked my mother about it, and she told me Miss Hofmann was Dad's sister. I found it incredible at first, he had always seemed so English to me, but the papers proved it. In the war he had bought a forged identity card—it cost him thirty pounds—and after that he'd had no trouble.

"Well, when I learned the truth and got over the shock, I was curious to know if I had relatives alive in Germany. After changing our name, Dad had never contacted his own people again. He was funny like that; it was as if he really had started a new life, and even the ending of the war made no difference. But Mother told me that Dad's sister had a child named Trudi, born, I believe, in 1940. The father was an army officer, who was killed not too long after. Last summer I visited Germany and tried to trace my aunt and my cousin Trudi. No luck. I discovered they had emigrated to the States soon after the war. Santa Barbara, I was told.

"But I'm not easily put off once I start something, and this summer here I am in your country. I tried Santa Barbara first, and managed to find out a little more. My aunt died when Trudi was eighteen or so, and Trudi moved into Los Angeles to work as an air stewardess, still using the name of Hofmann. The personnel section at TWA still have a record of her, and told me about the accident in 1964. Terrible. I heard there was a small daughter, and that she was taken to Tamarisk Lodge. How sad, I thought—that little girl of two years old with no family. I supposed she must have been adopted after a time, and maybe she's quite happy now. On the other hand, if she isn't, if there's any way I can help her, I'm not short of money now, and I'd like to. So I set about contacting you, Mrs. Van Horn. I found your name in the County

Welfare building on Wilshire Boulevard." Dryden held out his hands. "That's how I'm here."

"Can you prove all this?" asked Hardaker stiffly.

"Prove it?" repeated Dryden.

"Mr. Hofmann has said enough to satisfy *me*," said Mrs. Van Horn emphatically. She was small and fragile-looking, with a marked curvature of the spine, but she spoke to Hardaker as if he was a boy being difficult in Tamarisk Lodge. "Do you drink coffee or tea, Mr. Hofmann?"

"Tea would be most acceptable if you have some, but I didn't come to put you to any trouble."

She shook her head. "You won't do that, I'm sure. Mr. Hardaker can brew a pot of tea while you and I talk. You don't mind, Charles? I shall be quite all right with this young man. You know where the canisters are? You'll find the Earl Grey in the willow-pattern one." Practically before Hardaker had left on his errand, she leaned toward Dryden and said, "Don't mind Charles. He's what we used to call a dude when I was younger, but he has my interests at heart. Lawyers *will* ask for pieces of paper all the time. I know from what you just told me that you're not the FBI or anything. Darn it, they couldn't possibly know all the facts you've just given me."

"Would they want to?" said Dryden, mystified.

"I hope not." She looked toward the kitchen door and said in a whisper, "You see, the adoption was a little irregular, and we've had some scares since." In her normal voice, she continued, "What exactly do you want to know, Mr. Hofmann?"

"First, can you confirm that we're both talking about the same child?"

"No question of it," said Mrs. Van Horn.

"In that case, could you tell me how long she was with you, and what happened to her?"

"I don't have any records here, Mr. Hofmann, but I remember that it was the summer of 1964 when she came to us at Tamarisk. We gave her a birthday party a few days after she arrived, but I don't believe it made much impression. She was still in a state of shock. By Christmas, she had got over it enough to take a much livelier part in our celebrations."

"And after that?"

Mrs. Van Horn's brow puckered. "The adoption. A couple had visited the Lodge sometime in the fall and asked questions about Dean. They must have gotten her story from someplace. I don't know where, but they were clever people, both doctors. I liked the woman. She seemed genuinely warm toward Dean. You can tell."

"And the man?"

The old lady screwed her face into an expression of dislike. "He was more interested in the child's bones than her personality. I'll never forget it. I picked her up in my arms and he started touching her legs, not unpleasantly, I mean, but holding them in his hand like he was picking out a grapefruit in a supermarket. She didn't care for that one bit. Kids know, even at three years old. Damn. Charles is pouring. D'you hear? This will be the weakest cup of tea you've had in your life."

It looked as if it might be Dryden's last chance for information off the record. "Was there something odd about the adoption?"

Mrs. Van Horn hesitated. "I think it was all smoothed over with the lawyers, but the way it was arranged was unlike any other adoption in my experience. People can't go around homes picking out children as if they were unclaimed strays, can they? It wouldn't do, Mr. Hofmann. But these folk were doctors, as I mentioned, and somehow they squared it with the welfare authorities." Her eyes darted toward the kitchen again. "They sent us a garden swing two weeks after the papers were signed. If it had been money, I'd have sent it back, but what can you do about a darned swing? The kids saw it right away, and I was sunk."

Hardaker returned, tray in hand.

"Oh, Charles!", cried Mrs. Van Horn. "You've slopped it in the saucers. Mr. Hofmann is from England. They *know* about tea. Put it on the table here and make yourself inconspicuous. We're having such an interesting conversation. Sugar, Mr. Hofmann?" Before Dryden could say he didn't take it, she clicked her tongue and said, "Charles, you forgot the sugar. It's in the pantry. Second shelf, I'm almost certain." When Hardaker had gone through, she smiled and murmured, "Top shelf, but no matter. Where were we?"

"The adoption," said Dryden. "Did you hear any more about Dean after that?"

"Very little, I'm afraid," said Mrs. Van Horn with a sigh. "They were Bakersfield people, you see. That's eighty miles north of here."

"You don't recall what brought them to Ventura, then?"

"Oh, the man had some story. What was it now? I believe he claimed to have some interest in the family. A survey, would it be? Yes, he had been working on a survey into the way people grow, of all the darned silly things, and he'd managed to trace Dean from her grandparents. They would be your aunt and uncle, I guess."

Dryden nodded.

"That was what he claimed," said Mrs. Van Horn skeptically. "I'll say this for his story: he was looking the child over like she was a laboratory specimen. You know, I had nightmares about that adoption for years after. And I never liked that swing. We got rid of the thing the fall before last. Darn it, here comes Charles."

"I brought the biscuits, too—in case," said Hardaker, with an ungracious smile at Dryden.

"My, that was thoughtful," said Mrs. Van Horn. "Now, Mr. Hofmann, was there anything else you wanted to ask me?"

He didn't want to queer the old lady's pitch with

Hardaker, but this chance wouldn't come again. "You said a few minutes ago you'd had some scares since the adoption. What exactly did you mean, Mrs. Van Horn?"

Hardaker almost threw up his hands. "That isn't a question Mrs. Van Horn can answer."

"Why not?" queried Mrs. Van Horn.

"Lavinia, I urge you to take care. We don't know Mr. Hofmann. You might regret—"

"You won't gag me, Charles," Mrs. Van Horn said firmly. "Mr. Hofmann is a fine young man, can't you see that? He's the cousin of the child's mother. He wants to help Dean if he can. For Lord's sake, let's be candid with him."

"Against my advice, remember," Hardaker said, his face the color of the poinsettias at the window.

"Drink your tea, Charles, and don't fuss. Yes, Mr. Hofmann, I got a little distressed about two years back, when a man telephoned saying he was a newsman doing an article on children's homes. That didn't scare me at all, but when he got here, all he wanted to know about was Dean, and I could tell he was no reporter, because he didn't write a thing down. The questions frightened me. He was *very* abrupt. I could only suppose he was from the police, or something, and that they had turned up something awful on Dr. Serafin. Darn it, I wasn't going to say his name. Don't look at me with that death's head expression, Charles."

"What was this man like?" asked Dryden.

"A little older than you. Short. A small man, but forceful. What's the word they use? Machismo. Yes, he had machismo, all right. And he was a smart dresser. Do you have some idea who it was?"

"I don't know. Was he dark?"

"Swarthy, I'd say. He didn't have much hair, though. Oh, but he had two beautiful rings. Rubies, they were."

Gino Valenti. Two years back. The time the consortium was being formed. Trust Valenti to make his own check on Serafin's story.

"He was no cop, anyway," said Dryden. "They don't wear rings like that. And you told him what you've just told me?"

"If I recall it correctly, yes," said Mrs. Van Horn. "He was very insistent, you see, and I didn't have Charles here that time to speak for me." She gave Hardaker a warm glance. "It worried me for a long time after. That was when I had the swing moved out. I was getting this recurrent dream that Dr. Serafin had neglected the child until she died and then dissected her and kept her limbs in bottles of Formalin. It was very scary. If you find her, Mr. Hofmann, I'd like to know that she's all right. Would you let me know?"

[12]

TOWARD the end of Tuesday morning Dryden picked up a felt-tip pen and started listing potential merchandising outlets for Goldengirl. It took an effort to make a start; up to now he had brushed aside the detail, but it couldn't be shirked any longer. From July, *he* was giving the pitch, not Serafin. And without the backup of a film and a family saga dating back to prewar Germany. A campaign had to be prepared, if only in outline.

On paper, it was no trouble. The market possibilities were limitless. Earlier, he had looked up the press clippings on the merchandising Norman Brokaw had set up for Mark Spitz in 1973. His recollection had been right; by May of that year the potential value of Spitz's endorsements already under contract was reckoned at five million dollars. He had been featured in every major magazine from *Life* to *Stern,* and made TV specials with Bob Hope, Bill Cosby and Sonny and Cher. His poster had sold more than any since Betty Grable's, and he was pulling down $12,500 for every public appearance. It was good to read. Scale the whole thing up for inflation, the stepup in endorsement advertising and the built-in bonus for a gorgeous blonde, and there was no reason why Goldine should not top twenty million. The only figure she wouldn't be able to match was the $25,000 Schick had offered Spitz to shave off his mustache on TV. To compensate for that, she would have the edge in the lucrative cosmetics, fashion and domestic goods markets.

It was like surfing: you caught the wave at its high point and hoped it kept rolling all the way in. The timing was crucial. Like it or not, he had to sell the Goldengirl idea to big business in advance of the Olympics. That meant trading on his reputation, pulling every string he knew. The two-million fee he had settled for as payment wouldn't be easy money.

After lunch he drove out to Bakersfield. On the Golden State Freeway, he did some thinking about Serafin. The theory that he was conning Armitage and the others was out. You didn't equip an Olympic training camp in the mountains and employ a team of coaches, a psychologist and God knows how many ancillary staff to hoist the kind of money the consortium were putting up. Nothing Dryden had learned from Goldine, the newspapers or the reference books conflicted with the story Serafin had told that first evening at Cambria.

There remained the question: What actually motivated Serafin? Earlier, it was safe to assume it was the prospect of a fat profit. The meeting on Sunday had disposed of that idea. Having masterminded the operation from the start, Serafin should have had a large interest in the proposed carve-up of revenue. What had shaped up as a bloodletting had passed off with less dissent than a Quaker prayer meeting. He had relinquished his right to a direct cut of the profits without a murmur. Anything he made out of the project would now be at Goldine's discretion, and subject to the say-so of his fellow trustees. Yet he hadn't protested, hadn't seemed more than mildly interested. There *had* to be something else in it for him, more potent than dollars. A simple ambition to see his adopted daughter on the Olympic victory rostrum? Dryden doubted it. He was beginning to think along different lines.

According to the *Directory of Medical Specialists,*

Serafin had been born in Salzburg in September 1920. He had received his M.D. from the University of Geneva in 1945. In March 1938, Hitler's troops had annexed Austria for the Third Reich. Serafin would have been seventeen at the time, an automatic conscript to the Hitler Youth. Yet by the early forties, he was into his medical training in neutral Switzerland. How had he managed that when the Reich was committed to fighting on so many fronts? Either he had got out of Austria before the Nazis took over, or they had granted his exemption from military service to train as a doctor. To gain that concession, he would have had to convince them he was a committed Nazi.

The story of Gretchen in Hitler's Germany had been rich with detail of the *Napolas* and the operations of RuSHA, but that in itself didn't stamp Serafin as a former party member. Anyone who had lived through that era must have retained a vivid memory of the Nazi machine. And by implication at least, Serafin had more than once in his narrative expressed disapproval of the Third Reich. Its justification of racial elitism he had dismissed as a "crude philosophy."

Still, the impression that had emerged most strongly from that evening in Cambria was Serafin's fascination with Goldine's heredity. He had not been able to conceal his pride in pointing out that she was the recipient of Aryan genes. His preoccupation with the child's physique had been enough to give Mrs. Van Horn recurrent nightmares.

Then, there was the eccentric upbringing he had given the child, with the heavy emphasis on physical development: the home gymnasium, the exercises, the machine to expand her rib cage, the injections. And the cosmetic surgery, the bleaching of her hair. Was that to groom her for sporting and commercial stardom, or to create an Aryan ideal?

Thinking back to the Goldengirl film, its opening sequence had suggested Riefenstahl's influence before anyone had mentioned Nazi Germany. Allowing that

194

Serafin's formative years were almost certainly dominated by Hitler's propaganda, there was at least a
possibility he might be planning a triumph for Goldengirl at the Olympics as a vindication of the master-race
theory.

Fanciful? It fitted facts. Above everything with Serafin, there was a ruthless sense of purpose. If money
was not the motivating force, there had to be something of real power in its place. This afternoon was
dedicated to discovering what it was.

Bakersfield by California 99 presented an unprom-
ising location for a neo-Nazi plot. South Union Avenue
bristled with motels in landscaped grounds, with
billboards boasting steaks and seafood. The Serafin
address was in Alta Vista Drive, in the northeast
residential section, well away from the oil installations.
The house was brick, detached and large enough to
suit an owner with the status of professor. It had a
rose arbor and a lawn with a sprinkler working at full
pressure. He drove past slowly, parked one block up,
and walked back. The woman who answered his ring
was blond and in her thirties. Her hair was tied with
a blue chiffon scarf and she was holding a struggling
three-year-old.

She wasn't pleased at hearing it was another inquiry
about Dr. Serafin. She had answered questions for a
man on Sunday. Said he represented a San Diego
newspaper. Now, what was a San Diego reporter doing asking questions to decent people in Bakersfield,
she wanted to know, and how many more of these
calls was she likely to get? She had never met Dr.
Serafin, and knew nothing whatsoever about him. She
and her husband had the house on a two-year rental
due to expire in September, and they had fixed everything through Fox and Fox, the realty people on
Truxton Avenue.

The senior citizen clipping his hedge two doors
down was more forthcoming: "Would this be the CIA?
Say no more, mister. I can keep my mouth shut. What

do you want to know? Sure, I remember the Serafin people. Three of them, there was. A couple and their daughter. Used to drive a Buick. A professor, I heard. Not the college up the road, but the Human Science place, a couple of miles east, off Chester Avenue. I believe he threw up the job back in seventy-seven, or thereabouts. He was some years short of retirement then, I guess. Say, would that be significant? Yeah, he was five years my junior, I'm positive, and I got to sixty-five just eighteen months back. You thought I was younger? It's the outdoor life, mister. Keeps me in shape. What else interests you?"

"The daughter?" prompted Dryden.

"Didn't see much of her. She didn't hang about the street with the other kids, or I'd have talked to her for sure. I relate to kids. With me, the generation gap is nonexistent. But that kid never left the house except in the Buick. I never got what you'd call a face-to-face with her. Not sure I'd care to, candidly. She didn't rate as a looker. Had some height on her, though. She was inches up on both of them, and she couldn't have been much over fourteen. Is this helpful?"

"Sure," said Dryden. "Did you get to speak to the parents?"

"A few words now and then. Time of day, generally. Nothing to interest you guys. Hold on, now. I'm forgetting. Serafin had some kind of accent. Till now I never thought much about it. Funny how you just accept these things. Well, the Serafins liked to keep their distance, and people around here respect each other. When I heard the wife took off with some intern from the City Hospital, I kept it to myself, like it was no business of mine. You could see them each lunchtime holding hands on a bench in the Cunningham Memorial Garden." His eyes bulged. "Say, you don't suppose he was the *contact?*"

"Not a chance," said Dryden. "Thanks, anyway."

"My pleasure." His informant grinned conspiratorially. "I knew you was CIA when you parked on the next block. Saw you drive past the first time."

The campus of the California Institute of Human Science must have been symmetrically faultless when the main four-story block and tower were completed in 1915. A eucalyptus-lined drive exactly bisected five acres of lawn to end at the broad steps and fluted pillars of the portico, itself positioned at the very center of the red brick façade. At some point afterward, the symmetrical concept had been abandoned. A series of extensions in bricks an expert could probably date from their various shades of pink had extended the west wing toward the gate, while the economic strictures of the seventies had reduced further expansion to a colony of gray prefabs on the east lawn.

"I'd like to see the Professor of Anthropometry, if that's possible."

The porter looked Dryden up and down. "Professor Walsh, sir? You have an appointment?"

"I don't," admitted Dryden. "But I've driven up from Los Angeles."

The expression hardened under the peaked cap. "You some kind of rep?"

"I'm not selling anything, if that's what you mean. The name is Martindale, and I'm from England. Perhaps you'll be so kind as to convey that message to the Professor."

The porter gave him a doubtful look, and dialed a number on the intercom. "Patsy? Listen, some guy here from England wants to see the Prof. Name's Martingale."

"Dale," said Dryden. "Martindale." Having gone to the trouble of looking up the name of the English publisher of Professor Walsh's book on radiographic measurements, he wasn't going to have it mispronounced.

The porter repeated it correctly. "Yeah, I know, sweetheart, but see if it rings any chimes with the Prof, will you? This guy seems to think it should." He put his hand over the mouthpiece and told Dryden, "Professor Walsh just finished lecturing. There's this heap of letters to sign. I tell you straight, Mr. Martingale—What's that? Yeah. Patsy? Well, that beats everything!" He put the phone down. "Take the elevator to floor three, Mr. Martingale. Professor Walsh's secretary will meet you there."

Patsy got the name right. A small, efficient-looking blonde, she weaved a route confidently through a mass of students converging on the lift, and led Dryden along a corridor lined with bulletin boards. Through an office, presumably her own, to a room unlike any Dryden was prepared for. No filing cabinets, time-table, group photos on the wall. Not a skeleton in sight. It had a thick bottle-green carpet and biscuit-colored hessian wallpaper, three steel-framed chairs with white leather upholstery, and an occasional table with a tall Venetian glass containing white roses. A woman was adjusting the angle of the blinds at the window. Martindale's name seemed to have made an impact.

The Professor was obviously still in the lecture theater. There were sure to be questions afterward. He was welcome to stay there for the next few moments. The academic staff in all its robes wouldn't top the figure in this blue velvet pantsuit. She turned, a brunette with greenish-blue eyes, hair shaped to her head, with a thick fringe. She was near Dryden's age. The smile she gave him mingled mockery and invitation. "Mr. Martindale from England, I understand."

He blinked in surprise. "You wouldn't be—"

"Stephanie Walsh?" She put a cool hand into his. "I confess that I am. Won't you sit down?"

He sank into one of the steel chairs. "Excuse my confusion. They didn't tell me downstairs. I presumed Professor Walsh was—"

"A man?" She took a chair opposite him. "You're not the first. Perhaps we could both be excused some confusion, Mr. Martindale. You *are* Douglas Martindale of James and Martindale? The publisher of *Anthropometric Radiography and its Applications?*"

"Is there any problem about that?" he cautiously inquired.

"Just that I had it on very good authority—the London *Times,* I think—that you were dead." She held the smile impeccably. "Is it more disturbing, I wonder, to discover that a professor is a female, or that a publisher has risen from the dead? No, that's a presumption on my part. You haven't actually said you are Douglas Martindale."

It was a silk-glove job, but it was still a very firm put-down. Gulling Stephanie Walsh wasn't going to be easy. He studied her eyes as they waited evenly for his reaction. He decided he could trust them.

"Maybe your secretary didn't catch my name right. It's Dryden. Jack Dryden."

She gave a quick laugh. "I'm prepared to believe that's not the name she caught, Mr. Dryden. Do you smoke?"

She picked up a box of cocktail Sobranies from the table. He took a red one. A gold Ronson Varatronic followed.

"Thanks. Professor, I'm curious to know why you agreed to meet me when you knew Douglas Martindale was dead."

She held the lighter flame steady as she thought. "You're surprised you beat the security? Getting to see a professor shouldn't really be so difficult, but we do get bothered incessantly by sales reps. They have their job to do, I know, but you can get a little weary of seeing overhead projectors demonstrated, so we put aside a few days in July and invite them all to bring their books and hardware then. It ought to simplify matters, but there are still a few implacable gentlemen." She shrugged. "So they have to get past the porter first. When I heard the name you gave, I was amused, a little intrigued. It isn't customary for these men to resort to assumed identities. I decided to take my fate in my hands and have a look at you. You *don't* have a medical encyclopedia up your sleeve?"

"Not a single volume," said Dryden. "I won't deny that I am in merchandising, but I'm not here to sell you anything."

She smiled. "Try a little harder, Mr. Dryden. They all say that."

He nodded, grinning. "This is more in the nature of an inquiry. God, there's another cliché of the trade." He started again. "My job, Professor, involves managing the contractual arrangements for certain celebrities in sports and show business whose names are used in advertising. I have a client who, happily for both of us, has had a good run of success over the last two years. A fine sportsman, but a little innocent of the world. Easily taken in, I mean. Last week, he told me about a business venture he's investing prettily heavily in, even by his standards. It's all terribly sub rosa. In fact, at first I was worried my client was being conned, but now I'm satisfied it's on the level. There are others chipping in, some hard-bitten characters among them. Now they're asking me to join them in a promotional capacity. Before I do, I want to know some more about the scheme and the man who dreamed it up. His name is William Serafin."

"I see." She thought a moment, and felt in the box for a cigarette. Dryden supplied a light. "And you suppose I can fill you in on Bill Serafin? Mr. Dryden, before we go any further, how would you have broached this subject as Douglas Martindale?"

"I would have said we were considering a book Dr. Serafin had submitted for publication. As your English publisher visiting the States, I thought it opportune to visit you and at the same time get some background on your predecessor."

She weighed it. "Yes, I'll buy that. Did you have a title for this mythical work?"

"Would *The Influence of Heredity on Human Growth* get by?"

"His Vienna project. It figures." She was assessing him carefully before volunteering anything. Her eyes were worth watching. There was pale-green shadow on the lids, a brown liner above the lashes. "You seem to have the essential facts already. How do you suppose I can help?"

"You worked with him, I understand," said Dryden. "I find it difficult to credit that four years ago you were a deputy professor, but that's what *Who's Who in Science* states."

"I had three years as deputy to Bill," she said, ignoring the compliment. "I guess that was enough for him. He retired prematurely early in 1978. The chair was offered to me."

"Three years," Dryden mused. "You must have worked closely with him."

"That's debatable. Bill Serafin ran his department on a unilateral basis. He was one of the old school of academics. Anyone who questioned his interpretations could go look for a job elsewhere. Plenty did, before I ever arrived at the Institute. Frankly, Mr. Dryden, I wouldn't have tolerated him any longer myself, but it happened that he resigned before I got my letter in. There was nobody else at senior grade with the right experience, so that's how I got to be professor at thirty. If you're asking me whether Bill would be reliable with other people's money, I believe he would. I never had reason to doubt his integrity."

"That's reassuring," said Dryden. "The disagreements were mostly academic?"

She looked at her cigarette, thinking. Then she said, "If you want more information, Mr. Dryden, you must give some. You've told me Bill Serafin wants you and your client to join him in a business venture. I've given you my opinion that he would make a trustworthy partner. I don't see any reason yet to expand on what I've told you."

It was Dryden's turn to take a moment out to think. She was telling him, in effect, that there was more to

Serafin than she had said, but it had to be coaxed from her. "I understand your discretion, Professor. I really am honor-bound not to say anything about the project. I think what interests me is what motivates Dr. Serafin. I've reason to think this is more than a straight investment to him. That's slightly baffling, a little unnerving to a businessman. Would it be too much to ask whether you'd consider him an idealist?"

"I knew him professionally," answered Professor Walsh. "Ideals don't come into anthropometry, that I've noticed."

There was only one way he was going to achieve anything here, and that was by coming to the point. "He was a young man in Austria at the time of the German occupation. Things he has said make me suspect he has retained some of the Nazi ideology, in particular the theories about race."

She frowned and shook her head. "That doesn't sound like Bill Serafin. The work we do in this department draws certain physical distinctions between races, apart from the obvious one of skin pigmentation. I've never heard him make any kind of subjective comment about one ethnic group in relation to another. No, Mr. Dryden, I think you may have that a little wrong."

"He wouldn't have an interest in demonstrating the physical superiority of one race over all others?"

"My God, Mr. Dryden, where did you dredge these ideas from? Bill held certain theories about the human physique, but don't make him a racist. Anyone pushing that line wouldn't last ten minutes in this place, let alone get to be professor. It's an insult to the man's intelligence. Physical superiority—what does it mean? The average American is several centimeters taller than the average Chinese. So what? He's physically superior at reaching books off the top shelves of libraries, but he won't lick the Chinese at reaching the ones below."

Dryden nodded bleakly. The theory had seemed

quite plausible on California 99. "I'm not doing too well, am I?"

She returned a quick smile. "At least you're not trying to sell me encyclopedias."

He tried again. "You said he held certain theories about physique. Would it be unprofessional to ask what they were?"

"Not at all," she said. "He made no secret of them. He devoted the greater part of his career to investigating the characteristics of human growth. His comparative study on two generations of German women was quite a seminal piece of research. It confirmed a trend noted in a number of other studies this century: that average stature appears to be increasing at the rate of about one centimeter per decade. It was important because Bill's results were taken from subjects measured at maturity. Previous research relied heavily on military statistics, and since young men tend to be conscripted at eighteen, and growth is incomplete in many males of that age, some physiologists argued that the figures were more indicative of the earlier onset of puberty than a significant increase in stature. The tendency for puberty to begin earlier is not disputed; the average age now is below thirteen in America, whereas eighty years back it was around fifteen. The controversy arises when you consider the implications of the human race growing indefinitely larger."

"And ending like the dinosaurs?" said Dryden.

Professor Walsh smiled. "You've got it. If we extrapolate from Bill's figures, and mankind survives the next two hundred years, everyone should be twenty centimeters, or eight inches, taller. It's an open question whether the human skeleton is structured to cope with such an increase."

"Perhaps we'll level out before then."

She paused to consider the point. "Quite probably. I think Bill Serafin might admit that. But he's still convinced that average height will increase for several decades yet."

"Is there any reason why it shouldn't?" asked Dryden.

"A whole lot of people think it won't. They argue that the apparent increases this century are exceptional. They say the present average, that's one hundred and seventy-three centimeters, or five feet eight, is just about the optimum, and they have evidence to show that the size of the human frame hasn't changed much since the Stone Age. Measurements of skeletons show Old Stone Age man as averaging five feet nine, Neolithic five-six, Bronze Age five-eight, Iron Age five-six, Anglo-Saxon five-seven."

"When did the shrinking set in?"

"Almost certainly in the industrial revolution. Urbanization brought about a deterioration in living standards. People were literally stunted by the conditions. The theory is that it's taken over a century to recover from that, but now we're back to what the good Lord intended us to be."

"Sounds reasonable," said Dryden. "What does Serafin say about that?"

"He won't admit the validity of the measurements of primitive man. Only the strongest and tallest specimens would have survived to maturity, he says, so it's futile making comparisons with civilized times, when life is held precious even for the weakest. He contends that the average man today is the tallest in history. And he refuses to accept that we've reached the limit. The human frame has the structural capacity—I believe I'm quoting him accurately—to absorb the anticipated increase for at least the next six decades. By the year two thousand the average will be up another inch."

In the film at Cambria Pines, Serafin had presented Goldengirl as a prototype of the woman of the twenty-first century.

"Is it important?" Dryden asked.

"It is to Bill Serafin," Professor Walsh said emphatically. "His Vienna research is the main thing in his life. He sees it as the bed-rock of his theories—I'm calling them his, but many others share them. In his years here, he submitted numerous papers to the scientific press. Few, I'm afraid, ever got into print. He got the reputation of being obsessed with this theory of increasing growth, without ever adding anything of substance to his research in Vienna. And a lot of people, including close colleagues, I may say, began to wonder, like you, if it was important."

"It was, I expect, if you had to work with the man."

She nodded. "You must understand this, Mr. Dryden. Medical history rings with the names of men and women who devoted the greater part of their lives to investigating some hypothesis, often counter to the orthodoxy of current practice. As working associates, people like that can be extremely tiresome to get along with, but there's always the chance they will make a breakthrough that transforms our thinking. Yet I suppose for every one who makes it, there are scores who never do. Where fulfillment might have been, there is emptiness, a vacuum. Bill Serafin, I think, fits that category. He left this place an embittered man. The morale among the rest of us was pretty low when I took over. I had to make it clear from the beginning that I saw the role of professor differently. This room used to be his office. It didn't look like this. He would shut himself in here with his books and write papers no journal wanted to publish. Rightly or wrongly, the rest of the staff forgot about him. The department was managed by his secretary, a formidable character. I made it a condition of my appointment that she be transferred, and she was. Now she runs Bio-Engineering instead. I could see, too, that if I moved in here, where Bill used to shut himself away, I'd be sunk. Things wouldn't alter. So I took over a small office up the corridor nearer the rest of the staff, and had this place decorated and furnished as a general-purpose tutorial room. I use it as well for receiving VIP visitors, like publishers back from the dead."

Dryden grinned, but thought fast. She was rounding off the interview. There was something else to confirm. "Before I cap that by floating gently out of the window, may I ask a damn-fool question about Dr. Serafin's theory? He has to prove the human skeleton structurally capable of accepting an increase in size, is that right?"

"That has to be faced, if his ideas on growth are valid. Scientists from Galileo onward have argued that nature can't construct an animal beyond a certain size without altering the proportions and materials that give it its characteristic appearance."

"Well, what's to stop him pointing out that there are plenty of tall people around without apparent difficulties? Fellows of seven feet and upward are pretty common in basketball, and they're not on crutches, that I've noticed."

She shook her head. "That's missing the point. We're not talking about extremes. You're in merchandising, you said, so I guess you know all about graphs. If you plot the distribution of human stature, you get a normal curve, the bell shape, with the lip of the bell taking in your basketball players on one side, and midgets on the other. Unless some form of genetic selection is introduced, the graph will always look that way. Bill's theory says, in effect, that the entire bell is edging toward the right. Your seven-foot men won't look so tall in the year twenty-one hundred; they won't even make the basketball team. But giants don't prove anything. We're concerned with the norm; an increase of one centimeter per decade might not seem significant on present average height, but it could be too much for certain types of physique. The bell won't necessarily chip at the edge; it could crack in the center."

"So that's the point he has to answer if his hypothesis is correct?"

"He's been trying to answer it these last ten years," said Professor Walsh. "Sadly for him, it's in the area of speculation. Only time will tell us if he was right."

Dryden saluted this assessment with a philosophic nod. He wasn't making the mistake of leaping at the chink of light it revealed. "I suppose there's no way of inducing growth artificially?"

She gave him a long look, then shook her head. "You're thinking of anabolic steroids? They add muscular mass to the body, but there's no effect on height."

He nodded again. "You said only time would tell. There's no way around that?"

"You mean by augmenting growth?"

"Something like that."

"The process of growth is still a biological enigma, Mr. Dryden."

"I thought perhaps there might be a hormone . . ."

She hesitated. "That's in the area of biochemistry."

"But growth is governed by hormones, isn't it?"

She nodded. "From the pituitary gland. Somatotrophin—the human growth hormone. We generally call it HGH. But if you're suggesting Bill Serafin—"

"Without suggesting anything," cut in Dryden, "what would happen if you administered HGH artificially?"

"It's already used as a treatment to remedy a certain type of dwarfism. The pioneering work was carried out in the sixties at Tufts University, Boston. HGH was extracted from the pituitary glands of corpses at autopsy and administered to children with arrested growth. It proved successful with the Lorain type of dwarf, that is the well-proportioned small human being. We have a unit working here at the Institute."

"What happens if you administer it to normal children?"

Her eyes narrowed. "I have no idea. I can think of no reason why anyone should want to do that."

"Of course not." He reached for the ashtray and made a performance of stubbing out his cigarette. "It might make them taller at maturity."

She didn't comment.

"Of course, it's a grotesque idea, pumping growth hormones into normal children," he went on. "Nobody would do such a thing. If they've got a deficiency, okay, but not if they're normal. Maybe it's been tried with laboratory animals?"

She said in a voice that was thinking of other things, "In 1921, two American researchers administered a bovine pituitary extract to young rats, continuing through their normal period of growth to adulthood. The results were dramatic: giant rats, with a normal body configuration and without obesity, twice the weight of untreated controls. But before you draw any conclusions from that, Mr. Dryden, you should know that the rat has a built-in capacity for growth. Its epiphyseal discs, unlike ours, don't ossify. If that's blinding you with science, maybe I'm doing you a service. You're on very doubtful ground."

"Thanks for the warning. I was thinking aloud. Bad habit. Perhaps there are more natural ways of stimulating growth. Does exercise have any effect?"

"Very little, that we know," said Professor Walsh. "It possibly encourages some acceleration of growth. I believe there was some Swedish research carried out on girl swimmers in the twelve-to-sixteen age group which showed that their height as a group was accelerated above established norms, but that's not what you're interested in, is it? You want to know if there is any way of producing people taller than they would normally grow by natural means."

"That sums it up," admitted Dryden.

She stood up. "Mr. Dryden, I don't know what this project is of Bill Serafin's, and I don't wish to know. If you and your client are sponsoring research intended to substantiate theories about growth, there is one other thing I would care to say to you. There's a way of increasing people's stature that's been known for hundreds of years: the medieval torture rack. They justified its use as a means of discovering the truth. Think about that."

[13]

GOLDENGIRL came off the bend well clear, beginning the final phase of her run, hair fanned on the still air, limbs moving in parallel planes. Ninety meters to the finish. The muscles contracted on her neck as she gathered herself. The change from coast to maximum effort was smooth. Sixty meters out, she was still ahead, but not secure. The figure behind was cutting her down like a falcon. At thirty meters, there was space between them. At twenty, they were locked. From somewhere, she summoned the strength to raise her knees a fraction higher, stretch her stride by the margin necessary to meet the challenge. Then meters from the line she had powered herself centimeters ahead. As they crossed, she forced her torso forward, but she had got it wrong. The black runner beside her had dipped a microsecond earlier and stolen it.

"So where do we go from here?" Klugman demanded of Goldine's bowed, gasping form. "Back to forty-meter dashes, or what? We spend three weeks perfecting that dip. *Three weeks*. And for what? The first time we try it in a routine repetition session, you blow it. Okay, so we write that off to experience and try again. And again. And again. Harry takes you on the dip every goddamn time. If you got it right *once,* I wouldn't mind, but how many two hundreds is that now? Four? Five? Half of them you dip too late; the rest, it could be Groucho Marx running the last ten meters. We'll try it one more time."

Harry Makepeace straightened to his six foot three

209

and shook his head. "Not with me, you won't. That time I bust my hump catching her. Oh boy, I really must be getting old."

Klugman turned his contempt on Makepeace. "You mean you can't give fifteen meters in two hundred to a dame?"

"Four times, yes. I can lay back and leech off her, but that one hurt. It's the altitude, Pete. Right now I have spaghetti legs. What did she clock? Man, she was burning the last fifty."

Klugman glanced at the stopwatch in his hand. "Inside twenty-four again. The time's insignificant. We're working on technique."

"Five runs inside twenty-four—that's going some," said Makepeace. "I tell you, Pete, I'm screwed."

"Okay," conceded Klugman. "You take the gun. We'll give Brannon a workout. He'd better start level with her. I don't see him breaking twenty-four from fifteen meters back. Have him use lane one. We'll put her in three."

"Go easy on her," said Makepeace. "It's not easy judging it from up front. In a dip finish, the runner from behind has the edge."

"You're telling me nothing," said Klugman acidly.

He waited till Makepeace had started across the compound to give Brannon his orders, then told Goldine, "All right, Makepeace is no pushover. He learned his finishing on the boards, sixty-meter dashes with people like Williams and Borzov. We'll work on this some more and you'll take him. Elmer Brannon you can take right now. Treat it as a routine two hundred. Put him out of your mind till you're in the stretch. You can ease a little up to one-fifty meters, if you like, then turn on your burner. He'll come at you hard. Hold him level if you can. Make the dip just where you did this time, but make it like you mean it. Give it everything. Slam your boobs against your knees. Got it?"

Goldine stood upright, straightened her hair, looked evenly at Klugman, and gave a nod.

"You okay?" asked Klugman.

"Sure."

"Want to tell me something?"

She hesitated, unsure of him. "I'm putting plenty into this, Pete. It's not like it was six months back, when everything was a drag. I sometimes think you read me all wrong. I'm not a quitter. I'm going for gold, and nothing, but nothing, will stop me. I could just use a little encouragement now and then. There isn't much joy in training with guys and getting beat each time."

"You like to be a winner, you mean?"

The way her eyes shone answered that question.

"Like in San Diego?"

She was beginning to smile.

"That made you feel good, huh, queening it over a bunch of no-hopers? You'd like some more? Maybe I should tell Makepeace and Brannon to ease up a little, give Goldengirl another ego trip."

Her smile dissolved.

Klugman hadn't finished. "Get this straight in your head, chick. You blew it in Diego in that hundred heat, remember? Whipped by some lousy club runner because you looked the wrong way. By rights, you should have missed the final. When you think about Diego, remember that one. In this game, you learn more from one defeat than ten straight wins—if you've got sense. We're going to see you get it right in Eugene, understand? With the schedule you have, you could destroy yourself in the heats, no trouble. We have to play it cool, keep something back. That makes the last thirty meters crucial. You have to be sharp enough to read the race, inject a little speed if necessary, and dip for the line like there's a Samurai swiping at your head. That's what you could have learned in competition, what Makepeace picked up dashing sixties through six or seven indoor seasons. It doesn't just happen. The doc insists we keep you under wraps.

211

Great, but someway we have to teach you to take hold of a race. I don't know what San Diego did for you, but it scared me out of my shoes. So we'll try another finish, if it's all the same to you, and keep the ego trips for sometime after Moscow."

Her cheeks had reddened. She faced him, studying his eyes, as if seeking some clue to the bitterness simmering there. "And if Elmer edges me this time? What will you do about that—kick my butt?"

Quietly Klugman said, "Try me."

She turned and began walking to where the others were waiting. Klugman took a memo pad from his pocket, noted the time shown on his Accusplit and touched the button that returned the display to zero.

When the gun fired, her quick reaction stole a meter from Brannon, starting behind on the stagger, but he was soon into a strong rhythm, holding her pace.

They took the turn with five meters between them, Brannon clearly poised for the hairline finish this exercise was contrived to produce. As a sprinter, he was over the hill, but he could still get close to twenty-two seconds, fast enough to pass Goldine or any other girl. This was not a test of speed over the full distance, however. His instructions were to snatch the race by the narrowest margin, judging it on the run-in, as racing cyclists do.

As they came off the bend, he drew closer, playing it less adventurously than the younger man had. Makepeace was a lean, resilient sprinter, capable of controlling a duel of this kind from the rear, striking in the final second. That wouldn't work for Brannon, a one-gear man, used to holding on by sheer strength. Forty meters from the line, he drew level, his face a mask of resolution.

Goldine held her form, resisting Brannon's pressure, denying him any advantage in the run-in. When the moment came, and they dipped, her movement was so sharp that her hair stood momentarily on end. The judgment was exact. Brannon decisively beaten, in spite of ending face down on the track.

Nothing was spoken between Goldine and Klugman. It had all been said on the track.

After she had showered and changed, there was a session with Lee, listed "Assessment" on the schedule. It took place in a small room used by Lee as an office, and decorated to provide a relaxing setting for their conversations. The walls were ocher-colored, warm but unobtrusive. There was an olive-green carpet, suede-covered chairs, velvet curtains. The lighting was provided by an old-fashioned table lamp with a large red shade that gave both faces a pink glow.

Between them Lee's desk, the only thing on it a pack of Kleenex. Goldine was pressing one to her nose. Her eyes were moist at the lids.

"Should I turn the heater up?" Lee inquired. "We don't want you catching cold." His use of English was unerring; the only indication that he was an Oriental was his inability to convey secondary meanings through stress. In an analyst, that could be an advantage.

"I'm just fine, thanks." She raised a smile and toyed with the ends of her hair, fine against the coarse fabric of the sweatsuit. She wore the black suit exclusively for late sessions. It was pure wool. Even in July there was a chill in the air before sundown.

"You're not disheartened by anything?" asked Lee. There was a comforting ritual between them that always prefaced the sessions. He could be as piercing in his questions as anyone, when he wanted. Never at the start.

"Should I be?"

He raised his shoulders a fraction. His smallest gestures were eloquent, he used them so sparingly. His unusual height had not impaired the command of the physique that dignifies the Chinese.

"Perhaps I am," she conceded.

Lee waited.

213

"I'm not hitting the targets set for me in training sessions. Not most times."

Lee asked, "And do you interpret that as a shortcoming on your part?"

"Pete does."

"You haven't answered my question."

She creased her brow slightly. "If I'm not satisfying my coach, I figure I'm failing."

"So you measure your progress by the degree of satisfaction your performances produce in Peter Klugman." A flat statement. If there was irony intended, she had to extract it for herself. In all their sessions, Lee had never said a word in derogation of Klugman.

"He *is* an Olympic coach," she said in defense of her statement. "I'm bound to be influenced by his estimations of how I'm doing."

"Naturally," said Lee. "He is qualified to judge."

"And as he sets the targets," Goldine went on, "he must believe I'm capable of reaching them if I work at it."

"If that is the purpose of the targets, yes," said Lee. "Would you feel better if you achieved them?"

"I'd feel better if Pete treated me like I was a member of the human race. He used to, you know."

"I remember. You often spoke highly of him."

"He bought a lot of mileage with me then. He's a fabulous coach, and he's taught me everything I know about track, but lately he hasn't related to me at all. One day he slaps me down, the next he just clams up, and gives me a look like I'd be better off baton-twirling."

Lee listened, but made no comment.

She gave an illustration. "This afternoon, I ran six repetitions on the two-hundred strip. The idea was to go through my regular routine and sharpen up on finishing as well. We've put in a lot of work on my finish since San Diego. He had Harry Makepeace chase me and try beating me on the dip. He did—five times in a row."

"And the sixth?"

"He switched to Elmer Brannon. If Elmer nipped me, I'd give up. He's an old man."

Lee let that pass.

"Yesterday I was on hundreds," Goldine continued. "Eight altogether. The first six were around eleven-three, the others one tenth slower. That's slow running, Sammy, but I was bucking a headwind all the way. The other direction I could have made inside eleven each time. Pete knew it. We both knew it. Sometimes I run the other direction, but he wasn't having that. After four eleven-threes, the look on his face was unbelievable. I suggested we reverse for the other runs on account of the wind. You know what he said? Maybe I should ask the consortium to provide me with an astrodome, where the temperature is constant and the wind never blows and there's no rain. I thought that was mean. I sometimes think he wants to deprive me of any sense of achievement in my training. It makes me burn inside."

"And when you burn inside, do you perform better?" asked Lee.

She reflected on that. From the quick movements of her eyes, the question raised a conflict in her mind. "You could be right," she finally admitted.

"You said you beat Brannon in the final run this afternoon."

"Sure."

"Could injured pride have had some influence on that?"

"You mean I was sore at Harry beating me?"

"Or that you were denied the chance of beating him," said Lee. "Why didn't he make the sixth run?"

"He was used up," she answered matter-of-factly. "They're not so fit as me."

"So if Peter Klugman had insisted Makepeace make the sixth run, you might have beaten him. You weren't given the chance. It made you angry, and you

215

translated your frustration into action by defeating Brannon."

"Elmer's not much of a scalp," said Goldine with a grudging smile.

Lee developed his thesis. "It may not be a bad thing for you to feel things are being made difficult for you. If frustration produces a positive response, makes you angry, stimulates you to greater efforts, that is a valuable discovery to have made about yourself. It is quite inevitable, isn't it, that over the course of five days of competition in Oregon, and again in Moscow, you will encounter setbacks and frustrations? An official penalizes you for a faulty start, or fails to penalize another girl. You draw an unfavorable lane three times in succession. Someone makes a personal remark while you are warming up for a race. These things are unpredictable; the only thing you can bet on is that *something* will occur that could upset you. The way you respond is vital to your success."

Her eyes widened. "Is that why Pete is bugging me?"

Lee drew back from that. "I couldn't say. I'm simply making the point that it is not a bad thing for you to know what it is to battle against odds. Most of the great champions had to learn that. Babe Didrikson tore a cartilage in her first event in the 1932 Olympics and still beat world records in other events. Fanny Blankers-Koen had to wait till she was thirty and the Second World War was over before she became an Olympic champion. People had written her off. A calculated taunt from her husband that she was too old gave her the determination to dominate the London Olympics. Wilma Rudolph lost the use of her left leg when she was four, and couldn't walk till she was seven, but she got to be the golden girl of 1960."

"Okay," said Goldine, unimpressed. "We've been over this. It's all in the positive mental attitude. I have some fight in me, Sammy. I may seem like a spoiled kid up here with all these facilities, but I know what it is to have things tough. Pete doesn't need to knock me to teach me that. I don't expect training to be a pushover, but there could be a little joy in it, couldn't there?"

"The joy comes later," said Lee.

"I know, but—"

"Have you tried to understand the training sessions from Peter Klugman's angle?"

She sighed. "I wish I could. I don't know whether he hates me, or what."

"The relationship between a coach and an athlete has overtones neither may completely understand."

"Meaning he drives me hard because he wants me to succeed where he failed?" said Goldine, casually slotting Dryden's theory into the discussion.

Lee gave her a longer look before replying, "Certainly that could influence his attitude. A coach might sublimate disappointments in his own achievements by transferring his ambitions to athletes he helps, yes. But there can be a conflict, too. In passing on his knowledge and experience he can feel something being drained from him. Your acquisition of technique is his loss."

"That I *don't* understand."

"When you mount the victory rostrum in Moscow, the glory will be yours. Little, if any, will reflect on anyone else. The pride Peter Klugman, or any of us, will take in your success will be personal. We shall have the satisfaction of a job well done, a contract completed. But a coach may not see it so dispassionately. It is difficult to be dispassionate about an ambition that has dominated your hopes and efforts since high school, and become the mainspring of your life. On that day in Moscow, Peter could be forgiven for thinking some of your success might have been his, even for feeling some resentment toward you."

"I get your drift," said Goldine. "I can understand that. I have a strong sense of self, too. You need that to be a champion. But, Sammy, I'm still kind of perplexed why he must cut me up now, when it's all in front of me."

Lee's eyes focused on the ceiling. "Isn't it possibly an indication that your progress in training shows you are certain to win in Moscow?"

She put her hand to her face as a smile dawned there. "I never thought of it that way! Sammy, you're a genius!"

"We were speaking in hypothetical terms," Lee discreetly added. "But as I was starting to say just now, the human mind can actually be stimulated by frustration and discomfort. When things go well, without checks, there is a danger of overconfidence, of satisfaction with a less than sufficient level of performance. I remember a nice phrase I read once in a piece about the qualities needed in a champion: the ability to "function in disaster and finish in style." That's worth cultivating, Goldengirl. And it must come from within. It's right that Peter Klugman should treat you with detachment. Your motivation should be mainly intrinsic in these last weeks."

She nodded. "In the Lenin Stadium, I'll be on my own. Surrounded by a hundred thousand people, but really alone."

Lee took off his glasses and wiped them methodically. "Are you easier in your mind now?"

There was a slight hesitation before she replied, "I guess I am."

"There's still something?"

"Maybe."

" 'Maybe' usually means yes."

"Okay, there is," she admitted. "Last night, I lay awake trying to analyze what was wrong in my life. I decided it was Pete and the way he treats me now. I feel better about that, now you've explained it, but I'm still hung up, to a degree."

Lee replaced the glasses on his face.

"You know what I most miss up here?" she went on. "Affection. I don't mean dating. That can wait. I want

218

somebody to care for me. Don't take that unkindly, Sammy. You're a terrific help to me, and I couldn't function properly without you, but you know how it is —you're my shrink. You have to be detached, like you say Pete must be. Two or three months back, I didn't feel this way, and I guess that was because Pete was relating to me. He can be *so* considerate when he cares to." She sighed. "It seems you get cooled out by everyone if you're achievement-oriented."

Lee smiled and slowly shook his head. "Actually, the reverse is true. If it is affection you crave, you will find it the moment you win your first gold medal. You will be adored by everyone. Think of all the millions whose hopes you will have justified. You are running for America, for the free world, and your achievements will be watched by people sitting in their homes across the world, the largest TV audience ever. For those few days in Moscow, you will be the focus of more pride, more affection, than any individual on this earth. Even the Russians will take you to their hearts, because everyone admires a great athlete. To be Goldengirl is to know that wherever you go there is warmth, admiration, recognition. Let me show you." He went to a shelf and took down one of the video-cassettes stacked there. "I don't think you've seen this one before." He slotted it into the deck to the left of where he was sitting. "It's a tape Dave Robb put together from clips of various Olympic champions. Yes, you've seen a lot of them, I know, but this is different. You'll see why."

The TV screen on a lower level of the shelf unit flickered. The picture was black and white. An old film, scored with scratches. A blond girl in dark shorts and a white top crossed with a diagonal stripe was streaking to victory in a sprint event.

Goldine identified it at once. "Betty Cuthbert winning the hundred in Melbourne, 1956," she said, almost in a yawn. "I really have seen it before, Sammy."

"Watch," urged Lee.

Instead of cutting to the familiar slow-motion replay after the runners had crossed the line, the film stayed with Betty Cuthbert. People were running to congratulate her. There was no doubt about her victory; she had crossed two meters clear. They jostled around her, embracing her, kissing her.

"She was eighteen," said Lee. "A year younger than you. Now watch the two hundred meters."

Another sequence familiar from the training loops, the devastating bend-running that secured a three-meter victory in Olympic record time. And again the sequence ran on as the slim, smiling girl was mobbed by well-wishers and photographers. She was shown receiving her medal: a close-up of her face, happiness personified. The film cut to a Melbourne headline: BETTY YOU BEAUTY!

Then the relay. Overhauling the British girl in the final leg to break the world and Olympic records. A third gold medal. Her teammates lifting her on their shoulders. A lap of honor, waving to the cheering crowd. Another victory ceremony.

"This is her return to Sydney," said Lee as a motorcade sequence came up. "They even named a street after her."

Betty Cuthbert was standing in an open car. Crowds five and six deep lined the route, waving and cheering. Children were running beside the car.

Lee switched off.

"Isn't there more?" asked Goldine. "Doesn't she get to meet the mayor, or someone?"

"Tomorrow," said Lee, his purpose achieved. "There are others on the tape: Rudolph, Tyus, Szewinska, Stecher. The emphasis, as you saw, isn't on technique. It highlights the moment of victory. Did you like it?"

"It's set me up again," said Goldine warmly. "A little of that each day, and I'll get by, I guess."

"Running itself can be a satisfying experience," said Lee. "Winning is better. Being adored is best of all."

"Must be out of this world," said Goldine. Her expression became more serious. "But let's not kid ourselves, Sammy. The motorcades don't go on forever. Actually, I won't mind that. I don't need too much of that. I only need to feel I'm somebody." She laughed. "Not just one of Pete Klugman's hangups. I want people to like me, maybe even love me, for who I am."

"Naturally you do," said Lee. "And we know, don't we, that after next month you won't need Klugman. You'll have the independence you crave. A sense of identity. Because the world will recognize you as Goldengirl. You'll go before the press and handle their questions as you do in the simulation sessions, experiencing the excitement of all that interest. That's when you come alive, isn't it?"

Her eyes responded.

"This time it won't be simulated," Lee went on. "It will be real. And it will go on. The receptions and the motorcades come to an end, yes, but the identity you secure does not. You will always be Goldengirl, a celebrity, a focus of interest. The knowledge of what you have achieved will give you confidence in every situation. That's the way to resolve the conflicts you feel just now. Winning in Moscow is fulfillment." He smiled as he slipped in one of her phrases. "Does that figure?"

She grinned back. "It figures, Sammy. You put me straight again."

The meeting of staff in Serafin's room two hours later heard Lee's report of the conversation.

"She displays a certain amount of anxiety about the track sessions," he told Serafin and Klugman. "She expresses some resentment that the objectives are beyond her, that she is denied the satisfaction of achieving them."

"Didn't I tell you that would happen?" Klugman had turned impulsively to Serafin. "All this crap about stress! You can't keep chopping an athlete down. How much longer do I have to go on with this?"

"Is it achieving results?" Lee impassively asked. "How did she perform today?"

"Why ask me when you already know?" said Klugman.

"Isn't it a pertinent point?"

"I need to know anyway," said Serafin. "I know you're not entirely in sympathy with this, Peter, but let's at least consider the facts."

"She ran six repetitions under twenty-four seconds," said Klugman flatly. "That's great running."

"The best she has achieved?" asked Lee.

Klugman nodded. "She's a fighter."

"Doesn't that confirm the value of the exercise?" said Lee.

"Yeah, but *my* stock's dropped fifty points since we started this."

Lee disdained to comment.

"The question is, do we persist?" said Serafin. "There could be a danger of overstrain. It hasn't shown up so far in the physicals, but I can't risk letting this go on to the threshold of hypertension."

Lee said, "It is proved beyond doubt that there is a factor in the personality that can be stimulated by failure. Too much success leads to overconfidence. We have established that Goldengirl's performance has improved appreciably under stressful conditions. So far, there are no clinical symptoms of overstrain. I would be in favor of prolonging this, at least until Friday. If we switch her then to less demanding objectives, I believe it will give her the lift she needs for the Olympic Trials."

"Until Friday?" said Serafin. "That sounds reasonable to me. Would you settle for that, Peter?"

"Seems I'm in a minority of one again," said Klugman. "Okay, Friday." He took out his notebook and recorded the decision.

With that settled, Lee went on to say, "There are also some indications of a crisis of identity, as we anticipated. I think we can keep it under control by frequently reinforcing the Goldengirl idea. This after-noon, I showed her part of the tape Robb put together for me, featuring female gold medalists, with the em-phasis on their moment of triumph. All she has seen before has been technical film, which always cuts as the athlete crosses the finishing line. Seeing the girls she recognizes in this new role, being lionized by the press and crowd, made a definite impression on her. The scenes of Cuthbert in Melbourne were sufficient therapy for today. I watched the pupils of Golden-girl's eyes dilate as each victory was celebrated."

"This sounds an interesting innovation," said Sera-fin.

"Betty Cuthbert?" said Klugman, frowning. "You're using her for an example?"

"What is the matter with that?" asked Lee.

"You wouldn't find a more conspicuous example of a golden girl," said Serafin.

"Betty Cuthbert?" repeated Klugman.

"Three gold medals," said Lee.

"I know *that*," said Klugman.

"There are obvious parallels with our situation," Serafin went on. "She was blond, blue-eyed, young—"

"Eighteen," said Lee.

"And she first hit the headlines in Olympic year by winning the Australian championship for two hundred and twenty yards," said Serafin. "It would do Golden-girl no harm to identify with her."

"So long as nobody tells her what happened to Betty Cuthbert after the Olympics," said Klugman. "I can think of groovier ways to live with three gold medals than waking up in the night screaming with nightmares. When a kid of eighteen has to go on sleepers because her life has been taken over by the PR guys, that's sad. And that was twenty-four years back."

"Aren't you being a little overdramatic?" said Lee. "If you remember, the same athlete made a return to track, and won another gold in 1964."

"The four hundred meters," said Serafin, as if Klugman had not spoken. "That's another parallel, of course. Betty Cuthbert is the only athlete to have won the three events Goldengirl is going for. At an interval of eight years, so our achievement will be unique. It may be worth pointing out that Cuthbert demonstrated the possibility of the triple. Which brings us to you, Peter, and the prospects for the Trials in Eugene. We know how Goldengirl is shaping. What can you tell us of the opposition?"

Outmaneuvered again, Klugman glared at Lee, and gave his run-down on the U.S. sprint scene. "The black girls top the rankings for the dashes, as usual. There are two useful sprinters at Tennessee State University, names of Carroll and Devine. On the East Coast, Shelley Wilson is cleaning up around eleven flat. She could come big in Eugene. And there's Francie Harman of Texas Southern with a windy ten point nine and a legitimate twenty-three point five. And I guess Debbie Jackson will be back for more."

"She won't trouble us," said Serafin. "What's the picture in the four hundred?"

"Until San Diego, it was dominated by a Sacramento coed called Janie Canute, some kind of Jesus freak who's running in the name of the Lord. So far, she's done it no discredit. Below fifty-one three times this month. That's fast. The rest you can forget. Nothing under fifty-two."

"In the name of the Lord?" said Serafin. "That's something we didn't consider, Sammy."

Klugman laughed. "If Dryden's as good as you say, the Lord would have to pay a bundle for exclusive rights."

[14]

DRYDEN arrived in Eugene as scheduled on Thursday, July 10, making the 800-mile trip north along the Pacific Coast by air taxi. Mahlon Sweet Field seethed with pinch-fit people carrying trade-marked sports bags, Adidas nudging Puma as they converged on the taxi stand. Bystanders debated which of the bag carriers were hammer-throwers, which high-jumpers. Now that the University of Oregon track was established as a venue for national track and field, jock-spotting in July was a local pastime.

The Hotel Jacaranda, where Serafin had booked rooms for everyone, was a four-story modern building north of town on the Coburg Road, away from the University, where most competitors were accommodated. It stood in nine acres of landscaped grounds, with tennis courts, nine-hole golf and two heated pools. The room Dryden was shown into was in the forty-dollar class; he wasn't surprised there were no athletes staying there. "I've known big-name golfers come," the receptionist told him. "Track people, no."

He took a slow shower. No sense in hurrying downstairs and catching Valenti or Sternberg at the bar. He wanted a clear head for the afternoon. His plans for selling Goldengirl were scheduled for a thorough going over. He had dug a little into the business histories of the consortium. Valenti he had confirmed as a go-getting executive who had more than doubled his share of the pharmaceutical industry in the last ten years. Oliver Sternberg had wrapped up the wrestling game less overtly; the back-room deal with the meet director in San Diego typified his business style.

The real surprise was Michael Cobb. The Old World exterior masked a dynamo. The Galsgear label, currently selling every garment the factories could produce, was about to be superseded by a new Cobb line. Defying the dogma of brand loyalty, he had made a policy of limiting each promotion to a two-year run, launching the replacement at the sales peak. The results had transformed the trade. In the last five years he had moved into shoes, lingerie and men's casuals.

Add Serafin, and the line-up justified the groundwork Dryden had got through for this presentation. People like these weren't going to be sidetracked by the newspeak of marketing; they wanted firm proposals, and they would dissect them point by point.

When he did go down, he was pleased to see Dick Armitage in the elevator. In thinking of the consortium, he never included Dick. Nice to know there was one he could rely on for support.

When they reached the restaurant, the others were already seated at a table for four. After the necessary courtesies, it was easy to move to one of the small tables overlooking the patio.

"That's really too bad," Armitage said with a broad grin. "I guess we'll have to sit alone and talk tennis instead of track. Before you say one word about Wimbledon, Jack, I'm sorry. But I did take him to five sets this time, *and* I had a match point on my service. It's moving my way. I'll nail him in Forest Hills next month. See if I don't."

"Forest Hills? When is that?" asked Dryden vacantly.

"Last week in August."

"Of course. I seem to have a mental block about the middle of August. Will you be going to Moscow for the Games?"

"I'd like to," said Armitage. "Oh boy, just wouldn't

226

I? Goldengirl should be the sensation of all time. While I was in London they staged an international track meet with East Germany. I couldn't get there, of course, but I saw some on TV. The Germans have this girl Ursula Krüll, who is faster than Stecher ever was. She left everyone standing in the sprints. The way the sportscaster was talking, you'd think they might as well hand her the gold medals now. Cute-looking for a Red, but oh, so confident. You could see it all in the way her ass moved. Know what I mean? God, yes, I'd like to see how she moves after she's raced with Goldengirl, but I won't, Jack. There's no way I could take out the week before Forest Hills, even for this. You'll be there, of course?"

"Probably."

"You're not sure?"

"There's something to be said for staying in America, teeing up some merchandising," said Dryden. "Still, I suppose by that stage of the game I can bring someone else in at this end. I could be useful with the PR side of things in Moscow. That's what I tell myself, anyhow. If I'm honest, I want to be around in case of hitches. Your consortium is a volatile group, Dick. You didn't see the panic in San Diego when Goldengirl misjudged one of the heats."

"I heard about it," said Armitage. "Didn't Olly Sternberg fix things?"

"That's right. Very neatly."

"He's a useful guy to have around if you're down to the wire. That poundage is deceiving. He can move fast in a crisis."

"I can believe it," said Dryden, "but there are limits. Even Sternberg might be pushed to buy off the entire IOC Executive Board. I hope nothing goes wrong in Moscow. God knows, there's enough planning gone into the operation. I'll be happier if the next few days go as per schedule. Have you seen Goldine since you checked in? She isn't eating with them, I notice."

Armitage grinned. "Easy, Jack. She really is in Eugene. She's staying on the University campus like all the other competitors. It wouldn't do for her to put up here with the rest of us. The press boys would be wise to that in no time at all. It should do her a world of good, actually, mixing with other girls. The kid's had a sheltered life, when you think about it."

Dryden had thought about it. There were times when Armitage got under his skin. Remarks like that, tossed casually into a conversation, betrayed the shallowness of the man. He hadn't given a serious thought to Goldine's predicament. Yet there was no malice in him. He was one of the world's nice guys. He just assumed everyone else was nice, too. It was the formula for a trouble-free life. Tyrannies were founded on people like Dick.

It was still good to see his amiable face among the others assembled after lunch in the room reserved for the meeting. Serafin ushered Dryden to a chair at the head of a long oak table. In case of any doubt whether this was the place of honor—or the hot seat—there was a jug of water and a glass there. The only other object on the table was Cobb's electronic calculator.

For once, Serafin spent no time on introductions. "Mr. Dryden, this afternoon is yours. Do tell us what you have worked out for the merchandising of Goldengirl."

The five faces of the consortium turned his way.

"I hope it isn't exclusively *my* afternoon," he began, "because any ideas I throw up are intended for discussion. Around this table there's an abundance of marketing experience. Let's use it. Feel free to come in with your ideas at any point.

"I'd like to suggest that we agree first on the strategy. The details we can fill in after. I've done some thinking on this, and it seems to me we have two quite basic things to settle at the start. One is the phasing of the campaign. The other is the character we should like it to have. The image, if you like. My experience

228

is that you need to present a coherent image, whatever the range of your merchandising may be.

"Let's take the phasing first. From tomorrow on, and increasingly as the week progresses, Goldine—I tend to call her by her own name, if you don't object —will become a public figure, an Olympic hope. Provided she reaches the objectives you've set for her— I'm assuming she will—the media generally will take a lot of interest in her. I think we should capitalize on that. She projects herself well in interview situations, so let's use all the publicity she can get this week. It's not for me to make suggestions about the way she runs her races, but something special tomorrow or the next day would get the wagon rolling nicely. By Wednesday, she could be getting into feature status. It's important she isn't just a sports celebrity. She'll reach a wider public if she makes the other pages of the papers."

"Cleavage shots," said Valenti.

"Christ, they went out with Lyndon B. Johnson," said Sternberg. "Where you been all these years?"

Cobb looked slightly perturbed. "I don't know that I'd favor full exposure."

"Shall we leave it till we discuss the image?" suggested Dryden. "The main objective of this week's publicity, as I see it, is to provide the lift-off for the talks with big business. As I told you in Cambria, the selling of the project starts now, to have everything set up for the peak of public interest immediately after the Games. If I mention Goldine Serafin to an executive at Coca-Cola next week, I want him to know she was the blonde who went over big at the Olympic Trials without me telling him. Ideally, I'd go flat out on publicity from now on, right through the buildup period to the Games, but it's obvious that would play havoc with her preparation. The girl can do without being harassed nonstop by the media for the next four weeks. So I propose we give the press and TV boys all the interviews and pictures they can use this week, and then whisk her out of it to the Sierras where she can train without distractions. Two weeks later we pass the word along that she's visiting L.A. for a day, and lay on what will pass for a hastily arranged press conference at the airport.. If she can spare one day from her training, that should give the campaign the boost it needs. More photos, some exclusives, maybe a tour of the TV studios. Then we put up the shutters till Moscow."

"It makes sense to me," said Armitage.

Valenti wasn't convinced yet. "What kind of deal do you hope to fix with Coca-Cola or anyone else before she's got the golds?"

"Quite possibly a better one than if I started talking *after* Moscow," said Dryden. "I'll tell you why. This kind of deal is conditional. They agree to pay a fee for Goldine to endorse their product provided she achieves an Olympic triple. I make it clear we can't finalize anything until after Moscow, because it would contravene the Olympic rule on amateurism. But they see the advantage of having it all set up now, ready to sign on August sixteenth, the day she wins her third gold medal. On the morning she makes the headlines, they could run her picture in their ads, like the Grand Prix drivers touting gasoline the day after a big win. So we draw up terms in advance, and for them it's a speculative venture. Winning the Trials is still half a world away from the triple in Moscow. I can use that uncertainty as a negotiating point. They're more easily persuaded to agree to a figure of three hundred grand now, when it's speculative, than later, when it's fact."

"It's a gamble, in other words," said Sternberg.

"It is for us," said Cobb. "They risk nothing in this kind of deal except the possibility of Dryden pushing them to an inflated fee. The risk is mainly on our side. If Goldengirl succeeds, we collect. Otherwise, no deal. Correct, Mr. Dryden?"

"It's been my understanding from the start that this is all or nothing," answered Dryden.

"I confirm it," said Serafin at once. "The strength of our position is that we know those three gold medals are within her capability. We are not interested in silver or bronze. If you can use the fact to obtain more favorable terms, Mr. Dryden, you have our support. I must say that your suggestions so far sound eminently sensible. The more publicity Goldengirl can get this week, the better are your chances of being taken seriously by the companies you approach. There is one thing I was coming to, gentlemen, that I may as well tell you now, because it bears on something Mr. Dryden has suggested. After the Trials, Goldengirl is going to train in seclusion, but not in the Sierra Nevada retreat. I have made arrangements for her to complete her training elsewhere in America. She will continue to have the services of everyone who has helped her up to now, and the exclusive use of a track and gym vacated for the summer by a women's physical education college. In the interests of security, I would prefer not to divulge its location. It's not that I don't have confidence in your discretion, gentlemen; simply that I don't believe in burdening colleagues with confidential information they don't need to know."

Some glances were exchanged across the table at this, but nobody made an issue of it.

"What happens to the Sierra training camp?" asked Valenti.

"A good question." Serafin looked at his watch. "Two hours ago, work began on dismantling it. By the end of the week there will be nothing left there. The chance of that mythical wise-guy reporter from the Los Angeles *Times* pinpointing the site is almost nil, Mr. Valenti, and if he did, all he would find would be ashes. We are covering our traces, in other words. But the comment I wanted to make on Mr. Dryden's suggestions was that I can certainly arrange for Goldengirl—I tend to use that name, if nobody objects—

to spend a day in Los Angeles on a public-relations exercise. I like the idea, and so, I think, will she."

Dryden thanked him. So far, the proposals had met with better support than he could have hoped for, but the difficult part remained. "If you all agree on the timing of the campaign, let's talk about its character, the character we want Goldine herself to present to the world, because that's going to govern the way I pitch my campaign. There are some fixed points already: she's tall, blond, pretty, a natural athlete who comes from nowhere to make the U.S. Olympic team in three events. That's all good copy for the press, but she can't go on being a mystery blonde. We have to fill in the story. I wouldn't suggest we fabricate things; they'd soon be wise to that."

"We tell 'em what we want 'em to know," said Valenti.

"Right."

"How's this for starters, then? Her mother dies trying to save her from drowning off Huntington Beach. No father, so she's orphaned at three. Doc Serafin adopts her, spots her potential, and from there it's a straight rags-to-riches theme. Great copy!"

"Riches are out," said Sternberg, who seemed to relish pouring scorn on Valenti's suggestions. "The Olympics are for amateurs—remember?"

"Okay. For 'riches' read 'fame,'" said Valenti with a shrug.

"If you're suggesting the story is strong enough already, I think you're right," said Dryden. "It's more a question of what we leave out than what we add. Dr. Serafin has just told us the training camp is being demolished. That's obviously one thing we don't want anyone knowing about. Another is the backup."

"No one's going to argue with that," said Sternberg. "We all know the press would do a hatchet job on Goldengirl if they got on to the camp or the consortium."

"I think I see where this is leading," Cobb said to

Dryden. "After the San Diego meet, she was billed as the mystery blonde nobody had heard of who showed world-class form and then disappeared again. That was fine for San Diego. It's a good start for Eugene. Have you seen the papers, gentlemen? She isn't headline news, but more than one gives her a mention." He took a paper from his case. "This is the San Francisco *Examiner Chronicle*. I quote: 'Spice is added to the women's sprints by the entry of Goldine Serafin, who posted outstanding times in all three events in a single afternoon in San Diego last month. Track nuts, unable to trace previous performances in first-class track by this Bakersfield blonde, are keen to get a look at Miss Serafin.' She's still the mystery runner, you see. But the point about mysteries is that people want them solved. Once Goldengirl runs here and proves how good she is, everyone will want to know how she kept her form secret so long, and why. I agree we must cut the training camp from the story, but we need to put something in its place."

"What's wrong with saying she's just one hell of a runner who never took up the sport till now?" demanded Valenti. "Maybe you or I could win the Olympics, but we never tried. America is full of undiscovered runners. Track's a minority sport."

Cobb shook his head. "It's going to be obvious to anyone that Goldengirl is coached. She didn't learn the rocket start in Dr. Serafin's backyard. And she has to be superfit to get through—how many races is it she's running here?"

"Twelve," said Dryden. Cobb was emerging as an unexpected ally. It would be interesting to see how Serafin received this line of argument. He extended it a little himself. "I think what we're coming around to is admitting that Goldine has had expert coaching, and trained extremely hard for the trials. Is there any reason why we shouldn't tell the press about Klugman?"

There was a pause. Serafin took off his glasses and wiped them. He looked ten years older without them.

"It's not a point I had fully considered," he said. "I thought it advisable in the interests of security to keep Klugman's name out of it."

"But why?" asked Cobb. "We're not trying to prove she's Superwoman, are we? There's nothing to be ashamed of in having a coach."

"I must say I have reservations about this," said Serafin. "My idea has always been that we would attribute her success to natural ability."

"So we hired Klugman to bring out the ability," said Sternberg. "Every jock needs a coach. I don't see where the conflict is."

"You think Klugman is a risk?" asked Valenti, adding suspiciously, "What is it with Klugman? Does he have a police record?"

"No, no," said Serafin, obviously sensing the current of opinion against him. "I've nothing against Klugman. Perhaps you are right, Mr. Cobb. I was being unrealistic. We may as well admit that he has helped her."

"That seems to be agreed, then," said Dryden. "I think the spotlight will be centered steadily on Goldine. Once she has said Klugman is her coach, there won't be a lot of interest in him. He'll need to be briefed, of course, but that can be taken care of. The other question Mr. Cobb raised was possibly more important. How do we explain her meteoric rise to world class?"

Serafin quickly answered, "I'm sorry if I seem to be repeating myself, but the only explanation is that she is an outstanding natural athlete who first took to the sport seriously this year. It couldn't happen in any other event but the sprints, and you must take my word for that as a physiologist. Sprinting is an inborn ability. Some of America's most brilliant sprinters over the years spent more time on football than track technique. If the press want to know why Goldengirl avoided competition, it was because she didn't consider herself ready for it before June. Believe me, she will give satisfactory answers to questions of this kind."

"Those of us who saw her in the press-simulation session need no convincing of that," said Dryden. "To sum up so far, then, we're presenting Goldine as a girl whose childhood was scarred by tragedy, but who now emerges as a naturally gifted athlete who took to sprinting this year. Dr. Serafin recognized her potential and hired Klugman to coach her. She's totally surprised and elated by the success she's had, but determined to win for America in Moscow if she can. Is there anything anyone would wish to add?" He looked generally around the table, but the question was directed at Serafin. Nothing had been said about Nazi eugenics, nor trends in human growth. If he was right, and Serafin planned to use Goldine to justify his theories, this was a chance to build them into the sell. So long as the rest of the consortium collected their two million apiece, they wouldn't be bothered whether Goldengirl proved Aryan superiority, or anything else.

But the only contribution came from Sternberg. "Yeah. How do we get the sex thing in?"

"What precisely does that mean?" asked Cobb.

"We want to give Dryden something to generate commercial interest, right? She's a girl, so there has to be a sex angle. Maybe we can use some tit shots. Or she could start an affair with a French pole-vaulter. Nothing beats sex as a commercial sell. Why do you think I have dames wrestling in my promotions?"

"We could give it an artistic dimension with the nude sequence from the film," added Valenti, showing his ideas didn't stop at cleavage.

Cobb heaved a long sigh. "You're both missing the purpose of what we're doing. At this stage, Mr. Dryden is peddling an idea. It's quite simply that an unknown American girl can become the star of the Olympics. He's selling success, and just now there's a big demand for it. Americans have had enough of scandals and exposures, statesmen with feet of clay, corruption in public life. They're looking for a simple, supremely successful hero figure, and that's what Goldengirl can be. She's pretty, and that's a bonus, but turning her into a sex symbol would just confuse things. The people Dryden has to deal with aren't fools. They know how to market a girl, but that's up to them, not us. All they want to know from us is that she really can do what we claim. The way she runs in Eugene this week should help them decide. They'll be more impressed by a set of track results than close-ups of her bust."

There was nothing Sternberg could say. Dryden's respect for Cobb was growing by the minute. To salve damaged egos a little, he added, "I think we'll find Goldine makes a physical impact this week without any help from us. Let's not underrate the spectacle of a tall blonde in a tracksuit."

"You said it!" Valenti perked up. "The start of a women's dash is one of the finest sights in sport—if you get it from the right angle."

"We appear to have reached agreement that you present Goldengirl as a simple success story," said Serafin.

"So who do we approach?" said Sternberg. "Coca-Cola, you mentioned."

"Why not?" said Dryden. "But let's look at it systematically. There are different spheres of potential commercial interest. Most obviously, the sports industry. The war between Adidas and Puma is waged more strenuously in track than any other sport. It's an old game to play one off against the other, but I'm for trying it again. It usually succeeds. Equally, I hope to get something going among the manufacturers of track surfaces—3M, Reslite, Grasstex and the rest. The electronics industry now has a sizable market in stopwatches. 'Goldine's World Record was timed with a Cronus.' For 'Cronus,' read 'Accusplit,' 'Tempo' or 'Olympia' if they care to top the Cronus bid.

"The next group who will have a lot of interest in Goldine are the food manufacturers, particularly those whose selling point is health. An endorsement from a sports star can move a lot of wheat germ, liquid food, breakfast cereal, milk, oranges. I have a very extensive list, which you can examine at leisure after this.

"Next, bearing in mind that she'll be America's best-known woman, there are the luxury markets: cosmetics—how about a Goldengirl line? Fashion—I'm hoping to get something going with Galsgear, or at least one of your groups, Mr. Cobb."

"Why not?" said Cobb.

"Pharmaceuticals, too," put in Valenti. "You can come to an arrangement with me."

Sternberg shook with laughter. "How the hell do you expect a track star to sell Valenti cough cure?"

"No trouble," said Valenti, turning petulantly away from the vibrating fat man. "It's nothing new. You might not think a basketball star could push nasal spray, but Wilt Chamberlain did. They found the right slogan, you see. *Afrin Nasal Spray Has Long Duration of Action with Virtually No Rebound Problems*. Count me in, Dryden. Valenti Products will do business with Goldengirl."

"That's good to know," said Dryden. "I was about to say, anyway, that the multimillion-dollar concerns aren't too bothered about having any obvious tie-in with sports. If the celebrity is big enough, they'll buy. I'm thinking of the automobile industry, domestic goods, detergents and so on."

"Cigarettes?" said Armitage. "The tobacco industry has strong links with my sport."

"I'm not sure that is such a good idea," said Serafin, frowning. "I think we should be selective about this."

"That's why it's important to have a clear idea of the image we're presenting," said Dryden. "I think Dr. Serafin is right here. Product identification counts. It may mean turning down some big offers, but you have to weigh that against contracts you might lose. For the present, Dick, I think we'll hold back on that suggestion."

"Just as you say," said Armitage.

"Before we leave the endorsement possibilities," Dryden went on, "there's one other angle that might get us some business. I've been looking at the range of products that utilize the concept of gold as a selling point. You have the jewelry industry itself, naturally —I should be able to work out some merchandising there—but then, there are all those products packaged in gold. You know them; let's not take up time by listing them. Dick, I know cigarettes are still on your mind, but this takes in confectionery too. Food products. Manufactured goods. Every sales campaign that uses the old gimmick of a gold seal or a gold star to confer distinction on the product."

"If I sense the feeling of the meeting accurately, you've satisfied us that the opportunities are there, Mr. Dryden," said Serafin, finding it impossible not to take the chairman's role. "I'm confident, too, that you will preserve Goldengirl's image. I think people now have come to accept that athletes are entitled to cash in on their success, and need expert help like yours. Things have moved on a lot since the Los Angeles *Times* suggested that the merchandising of Mark Spitz presented him like a 'chunk of plastic livestock.' You don't expect any unfavorable comment on your activities?"

"It's a free country," said Dryden ambivalently. "Actually, I'm working on something that could dignify Goldine a lot in the eyes of the public. Quite by chance, the Olympics are held in the same four-year cycle as U.S. presidential elections. By August, the campaigns should really be heating up. I'm no authority on politics, but I have the feeling that an approach to the President himself after Goldine's victories might secure something mutually advantageous. I'm thinking along the lines of a TV linkup by satellite with Moscow, or the President to congratulate her and invite

238

her to a White House reception on her return to America."

"That I *really* dig," said Valenti.

"At the proper time, I'll sound out the campaign managers," said Dryden. "Like all these things, it's a question of timing it right. I think we can count on the White House reception and a ticker-tape return."

"This is starting to shape up," said Sternberg. "You have any other ideas?"

"Initially after Moscow, we'll let the media take over," said Dryden. "She'll spend two weeks doing civic receptions, TV talk shows, phone-ins, magazine interviews, and somehow making commercials in between. After that, it's up to me to keep her fame flowing. There's a well-tried formula: posters, some fashion modeling, a little fund-raising for charity, but otherwise strict cash on the nail for guest appearances, some sportscasting, possibly a pop record and definitely a movie. She'll write a book, of course, and a syndicated column for the newspapers. The market should hold up for eighteen months to two years with some infusion of interest here and there. You know, rumors of marriage with some big-name celebrity. That's the way I see it, gentlemen. If you have other ideas, I'll be glad to have them."

"The center spread in *Playboy*," said Valenti. "They pay fantastic money."

"I figured he'd move into the twentieth century if we gave him time," Sternberg commented in a loud aside to Armitage.

"That's something we might consider later," said Dryden evenly, as La Jolla Beach flickered across his memory. He wanted to get through this session without disclosing a personal interest in Goldine.

Serafin nodded to Dryden. "Gentlemen, I think we have heard enough to give Mr. Dryden's plans our backing. I take it you are all in favor of the scheme as outlined?"

"There is one point I should like to have clarified," said Cobb, lifting his eyebrows deferentially.

"But of course," said Serafin. "What's the problem?"

"No problem," answered Cobb. "It's just that the businessman in me likes to have everything cut and dried. When I joined the consortium two years back, it was simply as an investment, a profit-making venture. A bit of a gamble, perhaps, but that's what business is about. If you examine my career, you'll find I made my way up through a number of biggish gambles—perhaps 'calculated risks' is a better way to put it. I take a long look at what's involved, who is involved and what the return might be. Project Goldengirl appealed to me from the start as a smart idea. You want to give the girl her chance, so you approach people who might invest in her and we all share in her success. As a cautious cuss, I took a careful look at the other members of the consortium. We're an oddly assorted bunch—and I'm not getting at anyone—but we've all come into this with the simple aim of turning a profit. I like that. I like your team: Lee knows his psychology, Klugman has obviously got the girl into shape, and Dryden has just convinced me he can raise that twenty million he predicted. Just one person worries me in all this."

"The girl herself?" said Valenti.

"Fortunately, no. I think she's as committed as the rest of us. The cause of my concern is you, Dr. Serafin."

"Do you suppose I'm not committed to this?" said Serafin in amazement.

"On the contrary, I'm sure you are. What concerns me is *why*. When we met on the tennis ranch last month, Dryden came up with a new proposal for dividing the profits. We agreed to it without any hassle at all."

"The agreements are ready for you to sign," said Serafin.

"Fine," said Cobb with a smile. "I'm not asking for

changes. The terms suited me, as I'm sure they suited everyone else. Except *you*. In effect, you forfeited your right to a direct share of the profits. Okay, you represent the trust, and Goldengirl isn't going to let you starve, but I still find it baffling that you surrendered your right to a guaranteed two million. Either you're a fool, which I don't believe, or there's something in this for you worth more than two million bucks. If there is, your fellow members of the consortium are entitled to know what it is."

Serafin eased a finger around his collar and blinked as if pained. It was an understandable reaction. If Valenti or Sternberg had put in the knife, he might have turned the thrust aside. From Cobb, it wasn't a wild stab; it was an incision, carefully measured, precisely completed. And now the wound gaped.

He made an attempt at evasion, almost as a reflex. "I'm not clear on the relevance of this to our meeting. We are here to discuss Dryden's proposals, aren't we?"

His appeal was to the others around the table, but Cobb replied, speaking in the mild, urbane manner he had used throughout. "You'd like *me* to explain the relevance? I thought possibly you'd prefer to speak for yourself."

Serafin shrugged. "You started this. You'd better go on. I'm still not sure what it is about."

"Very well," said Cobb. "Gentlemen, I've reason to believe Dr. Serafin intends to use Goldengirl's forthcoming fame to give publicity to certain theories he holds. As I made clear a minute or two ago, when I joined the consortium I took steps to learn what I could about everyone involved. I've no doubt that the rest of you did likewise. My inquiries into Dr. Serafin's career revealed that he has devoted much of his working life to propounding certain physiological theories. I believe he masterminded Project Goldengirl as a genuine attempt to justify these theories. We've been backing a scientific experiment. That's okay. It still happens to be an attractive commercial proposition. Once I was satisfied that the object of the experiment was three gold medals, I was in. So long as I collect, I don't mind *what* this venture proves. The thing that needs discussing now is what effect it will have on the merchandising campaign if Dr. Serafin gets up after the Games and claims Goldengirl is the triumph of his experiment. That's the relevance to our present discussion. What will it do for the image if Goldengirl is admitted to be a golden guinea pig?"

Serafin was ashen. "It wouldn't be like that," he said in a voice tremulous with shock. "A scientific paper, that's all I have in mind. Something in the *American Journal of Physiology*. It needn't affect the merchandising. The public at large isn't interested in my theories. I want to demonstrate the truth to my colleagues in the world of biological science. It's far too technical to be of wider interest."

"I feel like Dow Jones just dropped fifty points," said Valenti.

"Would somebody fill me in?" said Sternberg.

Dryden obliged. Why should Cobb do all the running? "Dr. Serafin supports a theory that the human race is growing taller from one generation to the next. He contributed some important research to the argument in the sixties. Physiologists who contest the theory say that the human frame isn't capable of adapting to indefinite increases. They believe the trend Dr. Serafin and others have reported is just a process of restoration to normalcy after bad conditions in the last century produced stunted people. Goldengirl is an exceptional individual, a prodigy, as tall as Dr. Serafin expects people to become in the next century, but with a physique to match her height. A six-foot-two-inch mesomorph, perhaps unique among women. If she wins in Moscow, he can claim her performances prove the body capable of functioning efficiently—no, superlatively—with the larger frame he projects people will have in the future."

"I see someone else has been digging," said Cobb.

"That's all we're sweating over?" said Sternberg. "Do you think anyone gives six bits whether we're all growing taller?"

"No," said Cobb. "But think about what will happen when people read in the papers that Goldengirl was running in Moscow to prove a scientific hypothesis. That she has an exceptional physiology. They're going to translate that into something simpler. The girl they saw winning all those medals on TV wasn't the kid next door, after all. She was some kind of weirdo. A freak. It wasn't Uncle Sam she was running for, bringing a lump to their throats; it was a group of scientists. What do you think that's going to do for her image? Do you suppose the orange growers of California will want her in their ads after that?"

Serafin was shaking his head. "How can I make you understand? I don't intend it to be like that. This will be a scientific paper. It need not mention her name."

"Do you suppose that's going to fool the press—Miss S, who won three gold medals?" asked Cobb relentlessly. "After Moscow, the girl will be a world celebrity. Everything about her is of interest. You know as well as the rest of us that nothing sells papers faster than dirt on some big name."

"Dirt?" Serafin was almost speechless. "This isn't *dirt*."

"It doesn't have to be," said Cobb. "All it wants is a headline 'Goldengirl Was Guinea Pig' and that's our revenue cut—by how much would you say, Dryden?"

"It's true. We'd be sunk."

"Spooked," said Sternberg.

"So how do we handle this?" said Valenti, mashing his half-finished cigar into an ashtray.

"We keep cool," said Cobb. "Let's be reasonable. Dr. Serafin was the architect of Project Goldengirl, and he's still essential to its success. If he hasn't been entirely frank with us about his intentions, that wasn't from any wish to do us in. I'm satisfied he didn't realize the damage he could do the project by publishing his paper. I think there's room for compromise here. Dryden has said the merchandising campaign needs eighteen months to two years. I'd like to suggest that Dr. Serafin delay publication until August 1982, or earlier if we hit our twenty-million-dollar target before then." He looked around the table. "Would that be generally acceptable?"

"Sounds like you have the answer," said Valenti. "Do you see any problem, Dryden?"

"Not if Dr. Serafin agrees. Publicity of this kind would be damaging early in the campaign. Actually, at the end, it might give it a lift. We won't be pitching for contracts at that stage."

"How about it, then?" Cobb asked Serafin. He put the question as genially as offering a drink, but there was no doubt in anyone's mind that it was an ultimatum.

Serafin's eyes had the glazed look of a man on trial who knows it's all over, the sentencing is done. The consortium he had created had taken over. "I'll delay publication," he promised. "When you have waited as long as I have to prove yourself right, you can hold on for longer."

"That's all right, then," said Cobb, picking up his calculator from the table. "I just wanted to clarify the point."

[15]

"ANYONE want a pair of track shoes, as once used in the U.S. Olympic Trials?" The girl in the Kansas University tracksuit was close to tears. She stood at the dressing-room door, hot from running, black hair moist with sweat, warm-ups dangling from her arm, the spikes in her hand. Nobody was listening to her. "Size 6a, urethane-coated kangaroo uppers with wraparound heel," she read from the label in a voice that demanded attention. "No takers, huh?" She held them at arm's length over the wastebasket to the right of the door. "Positively your last chance, girls, to bid for the shoes that took fourth place in Heat Three of the one-hundred-meters Qualifying Round. Do I hear an offer? Too late." She let them drop into the basket. "That's *my* contribution to the U.S. Olympic Appeal." Buoyed up a little by what she said, she crossed the tiled floor to the open cubicle where her things were. Around her, other girls obliviously continued changing for their turn in the arena. She got no response from anyone before a second loser came dejectedly through the door. "What did you do?"

This girl was in the Crown Cities Track Club colors. She held up her right hand with all fingers extended.

"Fifth? Too bad. Join the club. I'm through with track. I just threw my spikes away. What time did they give you?"

"Eleven-five."

The Kansas girl shook her head. "That's slow. I made eleven-three-six. My best ever, but I'm still quitting. Did you see Heat Three? It was my luck to draw the Serafin dame. What does the G stand for—Giant? It was like lining up with the Statue of Liberty. She wasn't even trying. Eleven-one. I'll never go that fast. What's the pleasure in going on, if you know you can never be the best? I tell you, from now on, it's non-stop dissipation for me: cigarettes, champagne and S-E-X. I shall burn my letter sweater the moment I get back to Kansas. I want to know the bliss of walking around college without guys giving me the elbow and saying 'Hey, stud.' " She tugged off her damp trackshirt, unfastened the bra underneath, and took the weight of her breasts in her hands. "As of now, buddies, you're going to live a little. You can thank Miss G. Serafin, unattached, for that."

Midway up the terraced stand along the home stretch of the University of Oregon's Hayward Field, Dryden was sitting between Serafin and Melody. There was no obligation to sit with the consortium, as there had been in San Diego; Sternberg and Valenti had stayed beside one of the pools at the Jacaranda, claiming they had such confidence in Goldengirl that watching qualifying rounds would bore them. Dick Armitage had a previous arrangement to use the University tennis court for practice. Cobb was standing with Lee and Klugman beside the track barrier, in conversation with Goldine on the inner side. She looked relaxed after her stylish success in the 100-meter heats. The second round was starting in twenty-five minutes, after the finish of the race in progress, the men's 10,000 meters.

Dryden might have been down there with them, but for a late-night drink he had taken with Cobb. After the disclosures at the meeting, it had been logical to compare notes on Serafin. Cobb's information had been commissioned from an inquiry agent. There was nothing in the report Dryden hadn't learned for himself in Bakersfield. But they did agree it was vital to provide Serafin with reassurance. They didn't want him deciding the meeting had been a takeover. Dryden had volunteered to take first turn.

Melody's job for the afternoon was listing the detailed results of every heat in the two rounds of the 100 meters, including anemometer readings. As well as the information coming from the public address and the bulletin board, Serafin dictated his own observations on the way each race was run, pinpointing likely rivals in the rounds to come. From the care he took in distinguishing between winners who were fully extended and others with something in reserve, his commitment to the project hadn't evaporated yet.

The draw for the second round had just been announced.

"Number one twenty-six. Who was that?" Serafin asked.

Melody consulted her clipboard. "M. Devine, Tennessee State University. The little black girl with Afro hair who won the heat after Goldengirl's. I'll tell you her time. Eleven point sixteen. Wind reading point zero eight against."

"Mary-Lou Devine," said Serafin. "That's strong opposition for the Quarter-Final. How about one hundred three?"

"J. Pharoah, Valley of the Sun Track Club."

"We can forget her," said Serafin. "She was a poor third in Carroll's heat. The others I remember. Shadick should be among the qualifiers, but the rest were stretched to survive the first round. This might, after all, be an easier day than any of us planned for. She has a hard one coming up tomorrow."

Dryden had checked his program. "Not the hardest."

"Quite a severe test for the second day," said Serafin. "The Semi-Final and the Final of the hundred, with the qualifying round of the four hundred sandwiched between. Did I show you her schedule for

247

the week?" He took a card from his pocket and passed it to Dryden.

FRI., JULY 11	11:00	100m Qualifying Round
	15:00	100m Quarter-Final
SAT., JULY 12	15:00	100m Semi-Final
	15:30	400m Qualifying Round
	17:30	100m Final
SUN., JULY 13	15:00	400m Quarter-Final
MON., JULY 14	10:50	200m Qualifying Round
	16:20	200m Quarter-Final
	17:15	400m Semi-Final
WED., JULY 16	15:15	200m Semi-Final
	17:30	200m Final
	18:00	400m Final

"It's not the most imaginative example of program planning I've seen," Dryden commented. "Two finals, with just a half hour between, on Wednesday—that's really brutal."

"Don't blame the people here," said Serafin. "This closely follows the program for the Olympics. If you examine it, you'll see that the four hundred provides the problems. They don't envisage anyone combining that with the short sprints. There's no difficulty for runners doubling in the dash events, because there's a day's rest between the hundred Final and the first round of the two-hundred. However, we've known about this for months, and planned for it. It's one of the challenges you take on board when you attempt something nobody has achieved before."

"She has to beat the program planners as well as the world's best athletes," said Dryden.

"Exactly." Serafin smiled. He seemed to like the notion. "You're a perceptive thinker, Dryden. We could have used your help in the early stages of our planning. If there had been a little more active help from the consortium in those important discussions, I might have been encouraged to confide in them more readily. Yes, I wish you had been with us for the whole of the last two years."

Melody seconded that, with a gentle pressure of her left thigh against Dryden's right.

At four forty-five, when they returned to the Jacaranda, Sternberg was asleep in a peacock chair under a large pink canopy. Valenti was sipping something from a tall cocktail glass. Two empty ones stood on the metal table beside his sun-lounger.

"She made out okay, then," he said. "You think I'm clairvoyant? I only have to look at your faces. She do a good time?"

"Eleven flat in the Quarter-Final," said Melody. "That was the second fastest of the day."

"She judged it beautifully," said Dryden. "I think she'll go faster."

"She'll have to," said Valenti. "Second fastest won't do tomorrow. Christ, no, she'll have to step on the gas then."

"Second fastest would be sufficient, in fact," said Serafin. "That would get her a place on the team."

"Yeah, but let's not kid ourselves. This isn't just about making the team, is it? It's about shooting for contracts. Dryden has to put her over as America's number-one Olympic hope. I tell you, I'll be looking for something faster in the Final tomorrow."

"With your support, I'm sure she'll produce it," Cobb told Valenti, adding solicitously, "Did you pass a relaxing afternoon?"

Valenti looked up from his lounger. "Now, don't you guys get the idea Gino Valenti ain't committed. Matter of fact, I went into the TV lounge to watch, but all they showed was some lousy long-distance run. I wasn't passing a beautiful afternoon like this sitting indoors watching twenty or thirty stumblebums going endlessly in small circles. I got another vodka and vermouth and came out here. And that gave me a great idea. The vodka, not the vermouth. Seems to me there's a market you haven't considered, Dryden. Goldengirl wins her medals in Moscow, right? So there's a Russian connection. Under the U.S.–Soviet Trade Agreement there's a whole lot of Russian merchandise coming on the market. Vodka, furs, watches. There has to be some percentage in that for us. Why shouldn't Goldengirl endorse the goods? We could work something out with the Soviets while we're over there, tell them Goldengirl could move a lot of vodka for them in America. You like it?"

"If they paid us in rubles, it could help the U.S. balance of payments," said Dryden to humor him.

"Just an idea of mine," Valenti murmured in modesty.

"I got my dips in today," said Goldine.

"You were good," said Klugman. "You hear that? I mean it. You took them like a champion. Tomorrow will be tougher, because you'll need to run from the front. Your start looks okay. Keep low, even if the others are upright. Remember Borzov. With luck, you won't see any others. When you hit the front, don't turn it on too hard. Hold your speed, don't force it. Gather for the finish and dip, even if you're home by a mile. Did you see who you drew in the Semi?"

"Debbie Jackson, for one. She was looking sharper than she did in San Diego."

"Eleven-fourteen," said Klugman, "but she was spent doing that. Shelley Wilson is the girl in form: eleven point zero five, eleven point zero three. She's the main opposition. And in the Final, Francie Harman, of course. She'll be sleeping on that ten point ninety-eight tonight. Something good from you in Semi-Final One could throw her, but I think she'll follow you home in the Final. Any problems?"

Goldine smiled. "Not any more. It's a long time since you said I was good, Pete. Francie can sleep on her ten point ninety-eight. I'm happy."

U.S. TRACK AND FIELD TRIALS

GOLDINE'S RUSH

By Ches Nottingham

EUGENE, Ore., July 12——She's 19, blond and the fastest girl in America. You don't have her phone number. You don't know her name. No need to write it down, fellows, because after today in Eugene, Oregon, you'll hear a whole lot more about Goldine Serafin.

Tall, attractive Goldine from Bakersfield was the sensation of Day Two of the U.S. Olympic Track and Field Trials at the University of Oregon's Hayward Field. Bursting from the blocks with a sharpness that had the 12,000 crowd cooing like wood pigeons, she zipped to U.S. records in Semi-Final and Final of the 100 meters. In the Final she clocked 10.81, just three hundredths slower than the still unratified world record posted recently in Warsaw by East Germany's speed queen, Ursula Krüll. And between appearances in the 100 meters, Goldine fitted in a qualifying run in Round One of the 400 meters.

Goldine's action-packed afternoon started with coffee and Danish at 12:15 in the University restaurant. From then, her schedule went as follows:

1:30 Change for a warmup for the afternoon's racing.

2:45 Report for Semi-Final One of 100 meters. Rivals include Debbie Jackson (San Jose Cindergals), who has twice recorded 11 flat, and Mary-Lou Devine (Tennessee State), one of the favorites for the event, with 11.04 in the Quarter-Final yesterday.

3:02 Goldine produces a perfect start, steals a me-

251

ter from Jackson and Devine, holds it up to halfway, and then surges another meter clear to record a new U.S. record of 10.90. Second, Devine 11.08; third, Jackson 11.13.

3:35 400 meters Heat Two, First Qualifying Round: Making it seem like strolling, Goldine glides to an easy win in 53.42, second fastest time of the round.

4:00 Time out from jogging for a Coke and sandwich at the refreshment car.

5:15 Report for 100 meters Final. The line-up, with Semi-Final times, Mary-Lou Devine 11.08, Jean Shadick (Will's Spikettes) 11.02, Goldine Serafin 10.90, Francie Harman (Philadelphia) 11.13, Shelley Wilson (Atlantic City Astro-Belles) 10.97, Debbie Jackson 11.13, Therese Newhart (Tennessee State U.) 11.14, Janice King (Valley of the Sun Track Club) 11.20.

5:31 100 meters Final. After one break, Goldine leaves the cream of U.S. sprint talent meters back as she stakes her claim for a place on the plane to Moscow. Knees going like a majorette's, golden hair slipstreaming, she rips through the wire in 10.81, the third fastest ever—and that into a light breeze that slowed runners-up, Shelley Wilson and Mary-Lou Devine, to 11.04 and 11.07.

No Serious Running

After the Final, Goldine treated reporters to an impromptu press conference in the center of Hayward Field, casually throwing out the incredible fact that she did no serious running before this season. Her father, Dr. William Serafin, 59, a former professor at the California Institute of Human Science, persuaded her to try track as a recreation, recognized that she had extraordinary spint potential, and arranged for her to be privately coached by Pete Klugman, former track coach to the Cornell and U.S. Olympic teams. "Pete advised me to concentrate on technique through the first few months," said Goldine, "so I didn't get my feet wet competitively before June, when I reached the qualifying standards in a San Diego club meet. This is only my second meet, and now I guess Moscow will be my third." Asked if she had expected this afternoon's victory, she commented, "In some ways it's a dream, it's all happened so soon, but I came to win, yes. It's no use mentally settling for a minor placing, or you get nowhere."

Triple Aim

Goldine's 10.81 clocking makes her a clear challenger to East Berliner Ursula Krüll for the Olympic title, but before that she has more business to attend to in Eugene. "I enjoyed my run over 400 meters, and I'm definitely going for that as well as the 200," she told me. "If I could make the U.S. team in all three events, that would be nice. It means a lot of running, but I don't give up easy." Goldine, 6'2" and 163 lbs., looks to have the strength to get through the seven races remaining on her schedule here. If so, she could emerge as the first U.S. girl to represent the nation over 100, 200 and 400 meters at one Olympic Games. Whether it would be wise to attempt this ambitious triple on so little experience is an open question. Commented Jake McMurty, an AAU official: "After her running in San Diego we guessed this girl was saving something special for Eugene. She's proved us right today. Maybe she would be wise to settle for two events, but it's not for us to interfere."

Meanwhile, Goldine is quickly learning what is involved in becoming an instant Olympic hope. "Next time I come out, I'll make sure I have my comb in my sweatsuit pocket," she quipped as photographers closed in.

"Campari?"

"Uh?" Melody groped for the fastener on her bikini top and snapped it shut. "Say, that's a nice surprise." She rolled over on the tiled surface of the patio and squeaked at the contact. "Jeez, it's hotter than I thought out here!" Sitting up, she massaged the backs of her thighs before accepting the glass. "How did you know?"

"About Campari?" said Dryden. "A whisper I heard somewhere. You don't mind me interrupting the cooking? I allowed twenty minutes each side."

"You've been here that long?"

"At the table there, across the pool. I was reading the paper besides admiring the view."

Her free hand slid behind her back to the waistband of her white bikini pants. The upward tug she gave the elastic didn't quite obscure the peach effect.

"You have Sunday morning free, then?" said Dryden. "You seem to have been kept busy since you got here."

"I finished collating my notes at ten last evening," said Melody. "They have to be ready for Dr. Serafin to look over before the action in the stadium this afternoon. It was a lot of work. What a way to spend a Saturday night!"

"I could say the same," said Dryden. "I was in a poker game. Lost twenty-three bucks. Oliver Sternberg knows how to call a hand."

"You don't look too dejected."

"How could I be after yesterday? Moscow's still a long way off, but that U.S. record was good for my anxiety neurosis. So was that four-hundred heat. She made it look so easy, like tumbleweed blown by the wind."

Melody chipped some varnish from a toenail. "You make it sound positively lyrical. To me it was fifty-three point forty-two. Track's a drag."

"What brought you into the job, then?"

She shrugged. "I had some complications in my personal life. Needed to get out of Bakersfield for a while."

Dryden had the tact to leave it there. "It can't all be work. You've managed to get a gorgeous tan up in the mountains."

"Ultraviolet," said Melody. "Why should she have it all to herself?"

"Fair point."

"It wasn't so bad in the mountains," Melody admitted.

"I second that."

They exchanged smiles.

"But now you're moving camp," said Dryden as casually as he could.

"Uhuh."

"Change of air?"

"I guess so."

"An undisclosed location?"

"That's the ticket."

"Wild horses wouldn't drag it from you?"

"One Campari wouldn't."

"You'd like another?"

"Jack Dryden, I'm suspicious of your motives."

"Melody Fryer, you have reason to be. The entertainment page of the *Oregonian* lists all of three nightclubs. I don't know what passes for an All-Star Revue in swinging Eugene, but I'm fumbling toward a proposition. Think about it while I fetch that drink."

"Hi. I'm Janie Canute."

Goldine looked up from the bench where she was untying the laces of her spikes after her 400-meter Quarter-Final. The girl who had spoken looked frail for a runner. Her fine black hair was parted at the center like a squaw and clasped at the back with a leather thong. She had a thin row of beads around her neck.

"If I may say so, you have a beautiful style," said Janie. "You don't mind me speaking?"

"That's kind of you," said Goldine. "I believe I should know your name. You won the second heat, is that right?"

Janie nodded. "Not so fast as yours. You were really motoring over the first half. Someone over there took a split at just on twenty-four. Do you always start fast?"

"It's inexperience, I guess," said Goldine. "I was too anxious to make up the stagger. By the end, I was short of breath."

Janie handed her a training shoe that was out of reach. "I read about you in the paper. You must have a lot of talent, Goldine, going for three events."

Goldine smiled. "Or a lot of cheek."

"Don't say that. If you have talent, don't bury it. Unto every one that hath shall be given." She stopped and smiled. "You guessed it. I'm the one they call the Jesus freak. I run because I believe it's God's divine plan for me. You have to have something to run for, don't you, or it's meaningless? I'm always asking people why they run. I mean, a girl has to have a good reason to stand the guys teasing her about being a jock. You don't mind me talking? I don't embarrass you?"

"I like to talk," said Goldine. "I don't know many people in track."

"I'll introduce you to a few. They all think I'm a nut, but they're okay really. Mind if I ask you my question?"

"About why I run?" said Goldine. "I'm not religious, Janie, but it's a kind of compulsion, like yours, I guess."

"Mine's more of a conviction. Does it come from within?"

"I couldn't exactly say. I find it difficult to analyze

like that. It's not a thing I have much control over, but the more I go on, the more committed I become."

Janie nodded earnestly. "I understand exactly. Goldine, wouldn't it be great if we both got to Moscow?"

"The topless dancer!" giggled Melody as Dryden unlocked his hotel room door and hustled her inside. " 'Get a load of Ann-Marie, the topless dancer!' I never saw so many disappointed men in one place together. You should take out an action for deception."

"It wouldn't stick," said Dryden. "Topless they promised, and topless she was. As topless as I am. They're covered."

Melody fell onto the bed laughing. "They should be!"

"I've seen some poor entertainment in my time," went on Dryden, "but for an All-Star Revue, that beat everything. One topless dancer, with nothing to exhibit."

"No beefing, Jack," said Melody, still simpering at the memory. "It was all star. All star and no boob! 'Get a load of Ann-Marie!' Do you think I might have drunk too much champagne?"

"If that was champagne, it was as flat as Ann-Marie," said Dryden. "Thank God I had the foresight to take the cognac in with us. Melody, I'm sorry it turned out like that."

She sat up. "Sorry? Don't be sorry. I haven't laughed so much in years. I nearly wet my pants laughing. Say one word more about Ann-Marie and I won't answer for your bedspread. No, that's mean. I like to be humored. Which door is the john?"

Dryden used the interval to open the bottle of Campari he had picked up from the bar.

"Get a load of this, then!"

Melody was standing in the doorway of the bathroom wearing a pale-green silk-satin underslip, her arms burlesquing the action of a go-go dancer. "It's

257

cabaret time for disappointed guys. How about some backing?"

He tuned the radio beside the bed to something Latin-American. Still giggling, but moving rhythmically with the beat, she glided and bobbed toward him, stopping a couple of steps short, and by degrees easing the lacework straps simultaneously from both shoulders with her fingertips.

He watched the fine grain of the material slip over her breasts until they emerged, undulating gently with the music, the nipples pink and promising as the first buds of apple blossom. With a wriggle she persuaded the slip over her hips, turning suddenly to cheat him of more than a glimpse of her coppery pubic wedge, mockingly rotating her bottom where it had been. As an erotic display, it more than compensated for the nightclub fiasco, and the entertainment didn't stop at visual arousal. Dryden slipped his hands around her ribs and got a load of Melody Fryer.

"You're pretty good at it," she announced, an indefinite interval later, as he lit her cigarette. She lay facing the ceiling, on the bedspread, coyness forgotten. "Now spoil it by adding 'for an English guy.' "

"No, I'm being sincere, Jack. Too bad I should meet you now, after two years of sexual deprivation."

"Really?" said Dryden. "You mean not one of those guys in the training camp . . . ?"

"You have some sauce, Jack Dryden, asking a girl things like that! Deprivation doesn't mean total neglect, but if it panders to your male ego, I can tell you I haven't met anyone who tops you in a long time."

"And just when you've found me, you're taking off again," said Dryden. "Sad."

She blew cigarette smoke at him. "You don't give up, do you?"

"Would you prefer it if I did?"

"I guess not."

"If I thought it would end like this evening, I

wouldn't mind taking a chance on some other night-spot in an undisclosed location."

"You'd have to be determined. It's a long way from L.A., buster."

"I get around in my line of business," said Dryden. "Like the shore of Lake Erie?"

"That is a little remote." Dryden took stock. "I shall be in New York toward the end of next week. If I knew which part of Lake Erie . . ."

"You have an office in New York?"

"That's where I shall work from," said Dryden, encouraged. "It wouldn't take long from there by helicopter."

"Okay, if I feel like sampling the Erie nightlife, I can call you up, can't I? That's as much as I'm telling, Jack, and I think you know why. Now, how about finishing that Campari?"

U.S. TRACK AND FIELD TRIALS

GOLDINE HAS GOLDEN LOOK

By Ches Nottingham

EUGENE, Ore., July 14——Goldine Serafin, 19, sensational winner of the 100 meters here at the U.S. Olympic Trials on Saturday, today filed her claim for representation in two more events with brilliant runs in the qualifying rounds of the 200 meters and the Semi-Final of the 400 meters. This morning, she coasted through the first round of the 200 with a 23.02 win, the morning's fastest. In this afternoon's Quarter-Final, she stunned her rivals with 22.72, clipping one tenth from the U.S. record, and leaving the 1979 AAU champion, Mary-Lou Devine, five meters down. Less than an hour later, go-getting Goldine was on the track again to buzz to a 51.30 victory in the Semi-Final of the 400 meters. Until today in these Trials, nobody has looked like heading blond Goldine, but there is a fine race in prospect in Wednesday's 400-meter Final, when she will clash with Janie Canute, whose 50.45 in the second Semi-Final was a personal best, just fifteen hundredths short of the U.S. record.

"Pete, that four hundred didn't feel right."

"What do you mean?" said Klugman. "You qualified. That was all you had to do."

"My legs felt heavy, like I was unfit."

"That's not surprising after two hard races. You can't expect to beat records in qualifying rounds and feel no effects at all."

"They *still* feel heavy."

"Then you must ask Ingrid for a massage. That's why we brought her to Eugene."

"You don't think I should tell Doc, in case there's anything wrong?"

"I'll tell him. You're a little jumpy, that's all. One day's competition to go—you're sure to feel like this."

"Janie Canute didn't tie up. She's going to be hard to beat on Wednesday."

"You don't really have to beat her. We just want you to make the team."

"There are two other girls in her Semi-Final faster than me."

"I know that. Don't get yourself disturbed. You'll take them in the Final like Grant took Richmond."

"Would you tell Doc about the stiffness in my legs?"

"I'll tell him. I'm going up to the Jacaranda right after this. Now don't forget. Fix that massage with Ingrid, and you'll be fine tomorrow."

Klugman was less sanguine when he reported to Serafin. Possibly the way he related the conversation was influenced by the circumstances. He had found the consortium in one of the Jacaranda's three cocktail bars. Melody's perfume waged battle with Valenti's cigar smoke over a table cluttered with empty glasses.

Sternberg was telling jokes. Everyone was there, even Lee, sipping tomato juice and eating an olive.

This was the first time Klugman had visited the Jacaranda since arriving in Eugene. He and Ingrid had rooms in a four-story walkup, chosen for its proximity to the residence hall where Goldine was staying.

"What's yours?" Armitage convivially asked.

"I won't bother, thanks," said Klugman. "I only wanted a few minutes with Dr. Serafin."

"No trouble, I hope?" said Sternberg. "Now, where was I with this broken-hearted camel?" He picked up the threads of his story.

Klugman moved behind the chairs to Serafin, and squatted to give him the news. "I don't want to cause alarm," he said in an undertone, "but I'm a little concerned about Goldengirl." He reported the symptoms.

"Heaviness?" repeated Serafin.

"I'm wondering if this could be a reaction to the change in altitude," said Klugman. "Years ago I did some training at the U.S. altitude camp at South Lake Tahoe, and they warned us to expect a reaction when we came back to sea level."

"You think we don't know about altitude effects?" Serafin said in a hiss. "Of course the body has to make an adjustment. It wouldn't be the reason for this. She's already gone past the time when that would make any difference. This must be psychological. I'll get Lee to come outside."

"You sure there's nothing wrong?" asked Sternberg, as Serafin stood up.

"Nothing, I assure you. Just updating on the tactics for tomorrow," Serafin announced. It didn't carry a lot of conviction.

When Lee had heard Klugman's account, he was emphatic in his diagnosis: "A common anxiety symptom. She's had no competition today. It's given her time to dwell too much on what she still has to face. All athletes exhibit symptoms of anxiety and helplessness prior to major competitive events. The desire to find a let-out can become quite obsessional. Simulated illnesses or injuries are usual in these circumstances. I suggest you prescribe a mild sedative, William. By tomorrow morning, the physical manifestations will have miraculously vanished."

"Of course. Just as I thought," said Serafin. "If you come upstairs," he told Klugman, "I'll give you something to take back to her now. You're going past the hostel?"

"She'll be with Ingrid just now," said Klugman. "I told her to get a massage. That should help relax her."

"Sensible," conceded Serafin. "You'll see them both, then. Tell Goldengirl I shall look in right after breakfast tomorrow. And tell Ingrid I shall want a word with her as well. There's a small service I want her to perform."

Klugman had to admit next day that Lee had been right. When Goldengirl arrived at Hayward Field for the afternoon's events she was bubbling with confidence. "Sure, I slept well, Pete. I really am primed to go." She hooked a thumb in the waistband of her tracksuit. "See, I'm wearing my gold shorts today. The first time this meet. That's how great I feel."

"You took the tablet last night?"

She grinned, and blushed. "Between you and me, Pete, I didn't. I knew I could sleep okay without it, and I did. I was that tired. No sense taking sleepers if you can manage without. Maybe *you* should have taken it. You look *terrible*."

"I'm okay. It stirs up memories, watching the finals. Makes me realize I'm getting no younger. Come on, it's time you started limbering. The Semi goes at three-fifteen."

"Don't I know it! The Final at five-thirty, followed by the four hundred Final at six."

"Press conference six-fifteen."

"That's positive thinking," said Goldine.

Most of Eugene had turned out for the afternoon's events, which included Finals in the men's 400 meters and 110-meter Hurdles, as well as Day One of the Decathlon, but there was no question that the real draw was the girl the papers—still casting around for an epithet that would stick—described as the Bakersfield Express, the Runaway Blonde and Galloping Goldine. The moment she appeared in her white tracksuit, there was a rush of autograph hunters. Officials, obviously alerted, diligently headed them off.

When the moment came for her first run of the afternoon, the concentration of interest was exceptional for a Semi-Final. Ice cream vendors squatted in the stands, their trays on their knees. As the starter raised the gun above his shoulder, all conversation stopped. A motor mower was audibly at work on one of the fields outside the stadium.

In the beer tent behind the main stand, Valenti heard the buzz of excitement that followed the shot. There wasn't time to get to a point where he could see the finish. These things lasted twenty seconds or so, no longer. He would definitely catch the Final.

"I figure that was the Semi," he told Sternberg as he deposited the glasses on the table outside.

"Yeah?"

"We missed it."

"Does that grieve you?"

"Well, I aim to watch the Finals."

"Will it make one scrap of difference if you watch?"

"I guess not, but I *have* invested some."

"You're the kind of guy who sits beside a ticker-tape machine looking at stock prices," said Sternberg.

Over the public address came an announcement: "The result of Semi-Final Number One of the two hundred meters: first, Goldine Serafin, unattached, twenty-three point twelve seconds . . ."

In the stand, Serafin asked, "That's odd. It looked faster. What was her time on Monday, Melody?"

"In the Quarter-Final? Twenty-two point seventy-two."

"She won," said Cobb. "The time is insignificant. Better she saves herself for the finals to come."

"You're right, of course."

By the Competitors' Entrance, Klugman turned on three small boys brandishing ballpoints and programs. "Piss off, you kids. She's signing no more autographs. That's definite." He put an arm around Goldine and steered her toward the training field.

"Pete, something is wrong," she said. "I don't have the lift in my limbs any more."

"You won," he pointed out. "You're in the Final. Okay, maybe you're a little tired, but you were still good enough to beat Devine."

"Shelley Wilson ran twenty-two point nine in the other Semi."

"Don't start fretting about the other girls. Run your own race. Just two to go."

Ingrid was sitting alone in a TV lounge adjoining the student common room on the University campus. Dr. Serafin had told her to keep well away from the stadium after she had carried out his instructions. Her steps had taken her through the deserted campus. She had passed the common room, noticed that it was open, and looked inside. It was all right to go in there: Goldine had taken her there for a coffee after the massage. So she had walked through to this empty room, with comfortable chairs and a TV. "Be inconspicuous," Serafin had said.

On NBC, they were showing the Trials.

". . . took the bar off with her heels," the commentator was saying as the screen showed a high-jumper in slow motion upended inelegantly on the air cushion. "Dani won't be pleased with that. You really can't afford to leave your legs trailing in this style. That's reduced it to three, then: the two Crown Cities girls and Janis Nelson."

A switch of cameras brought a close-up of shapely buttocks encased in gold stretch-nylon.

Ingrid frowned.

"The girls are testing their blocks prior to the two-hundred-meters Final, which gives us a chance to take another look at this tall, attractive blonde they're already calling the greatest find in years, Goldine Serafin, winner of the one hundred meters, now seeking to add to her tally with the first of two appearances in finals this afternoon. In Monday's Quarter-Final, Goldine destroyed a brilliant field and set a new U.S. record for this event with twenty-two point seventy-two seconds, and although her Semi-Final earlier this afternoon was a little slower at just outside twenty-three, I can't see anyone threatening her, can you, Herb?"

"No, Dave. She's the girl in form. She looks unbeatable. I just hope she can hold this form till one month from now in Moscow, because she's going to give Ursula Krüll one hell of a shock if she runs anything like she has this week in Eugene."

"Thanks, Herb. Let's take a look at the rest of the line-up as they go to their positions. That's Jean Shadick, one of the two white girls in this Final, and the youngest in the race, at seventeen. Fifth in the one-hundred-meter dash. A good run here might clinch a place for Jean in the relay squad. Debbie Jackson, the girl in green, disappointed a little in the hundred, but came through with a second place in the Semi-Final this afternoon. Number two ten is Shelley Wilson, the fastest qualifier, with a twenty-two point ninety-three, and candidly, the one girl in this event who looks remotely capable of matching Goldine Serafin. Second in the hundred, she regards the two hundred as her strong event. In your picture now, Jo Carroll, a sophomore at Tennessee State, unlucky not to make the Final in the shorter of the two dash events, eager to join that relay squad if she can. One seventy-eight, the familiar figure of Mary-Lou Devine, undefeated last season, finding it tougher this Olympic year, but already assured of her place in the one hundred line-up for Moscow. But no question who the favorite for this event must be: the Runaway Blonde, Goldine Serafin. She has the outside lane this time, so I don't think she'll be seeing too much of the opposition. How do you dig those gold pants?"

She was shown in close-up, lifting her feet to check that her spikes were clear of mud, then tossing back her hair, almost white in the low-angled sunlight.

"The sort of girl you only see in commercials," said the commentator's sidekick. "Each time she comes in focus, I expect to hear violins playing."

"On your marks," said the starter's voice.

"In lane order, then," came in the commentator. "Number one ninety-one, Shadick; one eighty-two, Jackson; two ten, Wilson; one seventy-six, Carroll; one seventy-eight, Devine; one eighty-eight, Serafin. The two-hundred-meter Final."

"Set."

A long shot of the six girls in the hunkered regimentation of the start.

The shot.

"Away first time, and Serafin gets another bullet start. Wilson looks good in lane three, but it's the Bakersfield blonde who's running clean away again. Coming off the bend, the rest are making no impression on the stagger. Into the stretch, it's Serafin out alone. But Shelley Wilson's moving up with a late run. She's cutting back the lead. It's going to be close. Here she comes! On the line, Serafin! Snatching it on the dip. Wow, that was closer than she expected, I'll bet. Devine third, Jackson fourth. The time, Herb?"

"Just outside twenty-three seconds."

"Confirming what we saw for ourselves, that Shelley Wilson was running close to her best, but Goldine Serafin isn't quite the runner we saw earlier in the week. She was tying up in that last fifty meters, understandably showing the strain of a very active week. This must raise doubts of her ability to hold off Janie

Canute in the four hundred, but now let's take a look at that finish in slow motion."

Ingrid switched to Tom and Jerry.

"You okay, chick?" asked Debbie Jackson. "You don't look so good."

Goldine didn't look up from the bench where she was sitting, slumped forward with her hair draped over her knees. "I'll be okay. Would you please ask the photographers to let me alone?"

"You should put your sweatsuit on. It's getting cool out here."

"You want your coach?" asked Shelley Wilson. "They won't let him into the park, but we could walk you over there, keep the press off."

"I just want to sit here for a while. I don't need anybody."

"Please yourself, honey." Debbie Jackson draped the sweatsuit top around Goldine's shoulders, then turned to the cameramen. "Okay, fellows, you got your pictures. Now let the chick alone, will you? She has another final in twenty minutes, and she needs to psych up."

Serafin jammed his Zeiss binoculars against his eyes again and brought the group of girls into focus. "Why doesn't she get up?" he said. "She ought to be loosening up for the four hundred. Where's Klugman? He should be with her."

"Coaches aren't allowed in the center," said Lee. "That's one of the meet regulations. It's printed in the program."

"To hell with the program. We hired the man to do a job. She needs him at this time."

"Not necessarily," said Lee. "She knows what she has to do. There's no way Klugman or any of us can help her at this stage. It's a question of whether she has the inner resources to produce another all-out effort. We always knew this afternoon would be the crunch."

"I don't understand why she made such heavy weather of winning the two hundred."

"We must teach her to phase her effort more economically over several days," said Lee. "It's no use breaking records in the heats if you have nothing left for the finals. Look, she's on her feet now."

"Hi, Goldine." Janie Canute's greeting was as friendly as before; the note of strain in the voice had to be nerves. She pulled off her tracksuit top, revealing the incredibly narrow span of her shoulders. Where she got the strength from was anyone's guess. "You all set?"

"I wouldn't say so." Goldine mustered a smile. "How about you, Janie?"

"I always get the shakes. Watch the two girls in lanes five and six. Speedburners. They move off fast. Nearly threw me in my Semi."

"Thanks."

Janie had shut her eyes. When she opened them, she crossed herself. Then she went to her mark in lane 1. She was wearing knee-length striped black-and-white socks.

"Good luck, Janie."

"God bless, Goldine."

Dryden had left his seat and walked around the track perimeter, away from the finish where the crowds were, to watch the race from a point on the last bend. When the girls reached there, the discrepancies of the staggered start would be neutralized. They would know what real position they held, what remained to be done in the seventy meters or so to the finish. A shout of encouragement there might be timely.

They were down in their blocks at the opposite end. Goldine was in lane 2, the girl Canute on her inside. The shot that started them cracked across the stadium with an echo Dryden took for a recall shot. But all the girls were striding out. So far as he could judge, Goldine was maintaining the gap between Canute and herself, but the two girls in 5 and 6 were pouring it on, stretching away from the rest.

In the back straight the eight finalists chased their elongated shadows on the ocher-colored track. The crowd was muted, reserving its support for the home stretch. Now he could hear spikes pounding the surface.

Going into the last bend, against all expectation, the two on the outside had held their lead. It looked awesome. Canute was moving up on Goldine, who seemed unable to find much more.

The leaders hurtled by, ten or twelve meters clear. Dryden heard their breath, they passed so close. Canute in her striped socks was level with Goldine, but it was obvious neither could catch the leaders. This was a battle for third, for the only place left.

There was an instant when the curve of the track brought Goldine's eyes square with his. He didn't expect her to spot him, nor did she. Instead, he glimpsed a look compounded of agony and near-despair. He had seen it once before. La Jolla Beach. *Am I so grotesque?*

He leaned over the barrier like a kid at a football game, and yelled, "You can do it, Dean!" And then he was watching the two girls' backs as they forced themselves up the long stretch to the finish. The crowd, spotting the real issue of the race, had come to life.

From where he was, it was impossible to tell the outcome. He drew back from the barrier and looked at his hands. They were shaking. He wanted a cigarette, but he knew he would either crush it or drop it.

"Martinez wins," called the announcer. "Jones, second. We'll have to wait for the photo for third."

People were kneeling at Goldine's side where she had flopped on the turf. Someone was warding off a TV camera. A physician asked if she was okay.

She sat up. "Tell me who got third."

"We don't know yet. Won't be long."

A short way away there was another group around a lolling figure.

"Is she all right?" Goldine asked. "Help me up, would you?"

Rubber-legged, she took the few steps to where they were assisting Janie.

"I guess we underestimated the opposition, Janie. Still, thanks for a great race. It's up to the judges now."

Janie smiled. "One judge, Goldine. I'll abide by His decision."

Someone peeled down her socks to assist the circulation.

"Don't do that," she said quickly.

But it was done. Her exposed right calf was discolored by a large bruise, the skin badly grazed.

"Janie, what happened?"

"There was no reason for anyone to know. I had a small accident on my way out of the hostel this afternoon. One of those things."

"What exactly happened?"

"Someone bumped me on the steps by the entrance. A black lady. Poor soul, she seemed unable to speak. It was a shock, but I had a couple of hours to get over it. It didn't affect my running just now, really it didn't."

There was a movement behind Goldine. A hand touched her arm. "Would you please come over here and talk to NBC-TV, Miss Serafin? The judges have just confirmed the result. You made third, so you've qualified for three sprints in the Olympics. That has to be some kind of record."

Janie looked up. "That's marvelous! The Lord willed it, Goldine."

[16]

"SATISFIED?"

Dryden was well into the Los Angeles *Times* story on Goldine. Scattered round him in the coffee lounge of the Jacaranda were copies of all the morning papers the hotel supplied. He looked up. The question came from Klugman. The resentment in it wasn't well concealed.

"With the press coverage, you mean?"

Klugman nodded.

"It's a start," said Dryden. Nothing he had read so far had struck him as objectionable. Aside from straight reporting of the Finals, the emphasis was mainly on Goldine's reaction to becoming an instant Olympic hope. The tabloids featured her on inside pages, captioning pictures with quotes from her press conference. Some of the more serious papers raised the question whether it would be wise to contest as many as three events in Moscow, but that was predictable. It couldn't take away her right to compete. "Anything wrong?"

"Just tell me one thing. How much longer is it going on?"

"What, exactly?"

Klugman flapped his hand over the papers. "All this. When do we get the lousy newsmen off our backs?"

Dryden put down his paper. "You're being harassed?"

"Not me," said Klugman, glaring. "Well, I gave

271

some interviews yesterday. I agreed to talk to them, so no sweat. I'm talking about Goldengirl. You were at the press conference last evening. You know how long it lasted. Was there one question they didn't ask her, do you reckon?"

"It was a pretty thorough going-over," Dryden agreed. "She didn't expect any different. Actually, I thought she held up well."

"Me too. But would you believe they're back for more this morning, asking the same damn-fool questions? I just came up from the hostel. She must have a dozen of them in her room."

"That would include some photographers?" said Dryden.

"Yeah. Taking pictures of her sitting up in bed reading telegrams." Klugman almost spat out the words.

"So?" said Dryden. "It's been done a thousand times before, but can you think of a better excuse for photographing a pretty girl in bed?"

Klugman's lip curled. "She's a runner."

"A brilliant one. She's also a good-looker. If you want an answer to your question, I reckon she'll be getting a lot more attention from the press. When the sportswriters are through, the gossip columnists and the features editors move in. Sports provide the press with new faces every day, but how often are they pretty and can talk? Words and pictures sell newspapers. Look, without publicity, this project won't get off the ground. I thought you understood this."

"The further we get into this thing, the less I understand," said Klugman, shaking his head in a slow, victimized manner.

"Such as?"

"The way she ran yesterday. Those Finals should have been sensational. They were crap. You saw her earlier this week. Monday, she looked invincible. A U.S. record easing up in her two hundred Quarter-Final. Yesterday, it's like one cylinder is jammed.

Twenty-three dead and fifty-two. Christ, she was faster in San Diego when it was pissing with rain."

"Maybe the record-breaking earlier in the week was a mistake," said Dryden. "The papers seem to think she hit her peak too early."

"You telling me my job?" Klugman's face reddened menacingly.

"I'm telling you what the papers say."

"Screw the papers. What do *you* think went wrong?"

"Hard to tell," Dryden warily answered. "I didn't get the chance to talk to her about it. Could it have been nerves? There was a lot on those two Finals."

"Every athlete suffers nerves," said Klugman, unimpressed. "You run on your nerves. I've heard Olympic champions say the reason they won was they were so shit scared of losing. No, I don't rate nerves at all."

"Let's hear *your* theory, then."

After a quick look around the lounge, Klugman said, "Something physical."

"Her time of the month, you mean?"

"Not that. That's two weeks away. No, I figure she picked up a virus. Tuesday she complained to me that the four hundred had felt wrong. Her limbs went heavy on her. I tried to tell her it was understandable after two hard races, but she insisted I report it to Serafin."

"Did you?"

"The same evening. Remember when I came up here that evening Sternberg was telling stories?"

Dryden nodded. "Serafin and Lee left the room with you."

"They diagnosed an anxiety condition. Said she'd be okay next morning. She was—until she ran again. After the two hundred Semi, the heavy sensation returned. When she told me that, I saw trouble ahead. I mean, it's wild enough planning to beat America's best in two different events in the space of a half hour, without going to the mark less than one hundred per cent fit. Man, I suffered through those races."

"I'm sure. We all sweated," said Dryden. "But she qualified even though it was touch and go in the last. If you're right about the virus, it's unlikely we'll have the same scare in Moscow."

"Yeah, but we don't know for sure," said Klugman. "I'm no physician. This is just a hunch I have."

"It sounds reasonable," said Dryden. "Serafin should be able to confirm it. If we asked him to check her over—"

"I already did," said Klugman. "That's why I'm here this morning."

"What did he say?"

"He'll get around to it sometime tomorrow evening, after we get to the new training camp." Klugman's tone left no doubt how he regarded that.

"Tomorrow? That's too late," said Dryden. "If it's a bug, she could have shaken it off by then. He needs to check her today."

"Try telling *him* that," said Klugman.

"What's his objection?"

"He figures there are too many pressmen around. He doesn't want people getting the idea Goldengirl is sick. That would tarnish the image, he says. We have to wait till the spotlight is off her. When he came out with that, I lost my cool. I told him I don't give a fuck for the image. Screw the media—I've given two years of my life to this project. I'm entitled to know if she's liable to fold up in Moscow."

"You're not the only one," said Dryden. "I'm damned sure the consortium would feel they have the same entitlement. Do you really suppose this could happen at the Olympics?"

"Look, I'm not clairvoyant. All I know is something was wrong yesterday. Don't tell me it was too much racing, like the papers say, because I know that's a lie. She trained for three hard runs. Any day she can reel off five or six two hundreds—fast ones—and then a four hundred inside fifty-two. She should have beaten records in the Finals, not dragged her ass into third place."

"She won two," Dryden pointed out. "Let's keep it in perspective. That four hundred was the only race she lost, out of twelve in the Trials."

"She damned near lost the two hundred," said Klugman. "You want it in perspective. Okay. Goldengirl ran that in twenty-three flat. On Sunday in the Karl Marx Stadium, Berlin, Ursula Krüll took the East German title in just outside twenty-two. One second may not sound much to you, but it's an awful lot of space between two sprinters. All right, mister, you're the PR guy in this operation, so I don't see you telling Goldengirl to quit acting the showgirl and get up here for a physical, but someone should."

The press interest in Goldine had really got Klugman's hackles up.

"I think it might be arranged without interfering with the publicity," said Dryden. "After all, Dr. Serafin is her father. He's entitled to some privacy if he visits her at the hostel. He could check her there. The main problem is convincing him it can't be put off till tomorrow. If I canvassed support in the consortium, it might be managed. Will you leave it to me?"

"I have no choice," Klugman said without much gratitude. "He wouldn't take it from me."

Dryden didn't lightly volunteer for another confrontation with Serafin. Goldine's slightly jaded running on the final day of the Trials hadn't bothered him once it was confirmed she had qualified for Moscow in her three events. With two U.S. records from earlier in the week, the Goldengirl idea had enough going for it now to justify trying it out on big business. That was all that had concerned him, until Klugman told him about this heaviness in the limbs. Klugman was too obsessive for his own good, or Goldine's, but he knew about track. He had taken this seriously enough to report it to Serafin the evening it cropped up. Despite the way

Serafin and Lee had dismissed it, events had come very near to justifying Klugman. He was right; it had to be investigated, and it was obvious there should be no delay. This had to be discussed with Serafin.

The chance came at lunch, the last occasion the consortium would come together in Eugene. Dick Armitage was leaving for a tournament in San Francisco immediately after, and Sternberg, Valenti and Cobb had taxis coming from three o'clock on. Serafin and his team were obliged to stay another night, as Goldine had exclusives lined up well into the evening.

"When are you leaving, Mr. Dryden?" Lee asked. Two tables had been pushed together to accommodate everyone. Lee was diagonally opposite, so the question was heard all round.

"Probably tomorrow," Dryden answered. "I'll be calling Mahlon Sweet Airport this afternoon to make a reservation."

"Don't trouble yourself," Serafin airily said. "Melody can fix it. Now that she's through transcribing notes on the Trials she's looking for something to occupy her again, aren't you, my dear?"

A look of laser intensity passed between Melody and her employer.

"If you'd mentioned it to me, I would have stopped over," said Valenti, winking archly.

Melody selected a breadroll of the long variety from the basket and wrung it savagely in half.

Sternberg laughed. "What do you say to that, Gino, apart from 'ouch'?"

"I have no trouble making it with girls," said Valenti, unamused.

Armitage cued in Dryden. They had conferred over a pre-lunch drink. "Look, I'm leaving right after this. Is there anything else to settle?"

"I think not," Serafin started to say.

"Really?" said Dryden. "You cleared up the mystery over Goldine's physical condition?"

"What's that?" said Cobb at once.

"You heard about that?" said Serafin, eyeing Dryden nervously.

"Observed it," Dryden smoothly answered. "I mean, it was obvious she wasn't totally fit yesterday. I take it you've established the cause. A muscle strain, perhaps?"

Serafin hesitated, as if deciding whether a quick affirmation might get by, but the pause itself defeated him. "We're not entirely sure. She complained of some sluggishness in the limbs after the Semi-Final of the four hundred meters, and it seems to have affected her performance yesterday. Fortunately, she did enough to qualify, but you are right—she was not at her best. I have no explanation to offer yet. I simply assure you, gentlemen, I shall investigate this at the first opportunity."

"When will that be?" asked Dryden.

"Tomorrow, when we arrive at the new training camp."

"Why not before?" asked Cobb, quick to pick up the point. "If there's anything the matter, it should be looked at now."

"Let's not get this out of proportion," said Serafin, taking off his glasses to polish them. "She ran slightly below our expectation, but she still did all that was necessary. All athletes occasionally run below form. The human body is not an automobile; it has a complex metabolism. There could be scores of possible explanations. Something in the diet, perhaps. The onset of a cold. Some mild infection. Things that wouldn't disturb you or me in the least can take the edge off the running of a top-class athlete."

Lee at once took up the thread: "The physical sensations could be psychosomatic. Goldengirl is unaccustomed to the strain of competition. In six days there's quite a buildup of tension."

"Okay," said Cobb in his easygoing way. "Maybe it's physical, maybe not. You're the people who can tell. I'm not making an issue out of this, but it seems to me if there was something wrong with the girl yesterday, there's no sense waiting forty-eight hours before you check it out. Why the holdup?"

"I should have thought that was obvious," Serafin peevishly replied. "Goldengirl is getting a lot of attention from the press just now. We don't want stories circulating that she is having medical attention. That wouldn't help Mr. Dryden's campaign one bit."

"You're right there," admitted Dryden. "But does this have to be done in a way that alerts the press? You're her father. You have the right to visit her and spend some time alone with her. The press are constantly juggling schedules. I'm sure we can slot the physical in without creating undue interest."

"If you really think so," said Serafin dubiously.

"I'm with Mr. Cobb on this," Dryden went on. "I think the important thing is to establish the reason why Goldine ran below her best yesterday. If it was something in her food, or a virus, surely your chance of locating it is better today than tomorrow? I'd like to think she's going to Moscow without the possibility of a sudden loss of form. What happens there matters more than all the publicity here."

"Very well," said Serafin, replacing his glasses. "I'll visit her after this."

The conversation shifted to the arrangements for the day Goldine was to spend in Los Angeles meeting the press and touring TV studios. Valenti had ideas to secure maximum attention: a presidential-style welcome, with a band and majorettes. He wasn't pleased when it was pointed out that a publicity backup on that scale didn't square with the amateur image. "So what does an amateur athlete rate?" He demanded hotly, "—the Mormon Tabernacle Choir?"

Sternberg, too, favored something spectacular. "To go over big, you need an angle," he said. "Like, for instance, she meets that dame you told us about, won all the medals in Los Angeles. That Babe. They meet by chance on the plane and come down the steps together. Two golden girls. How about that?"

"Babe Didrikson died in 1956," said Serafin flatly.

"Who cares? It's still a great idea," said Sternberg. "We can find someone else. No trouble."

"It's too obvious," said Dryden. "We don't want this to look like a publicity stunt, even if it is. These ideas might work *after* the Games, but not before."

Sternberg wasn't finished yet. "Maybe we could use her speed someway," he said thoughtfully. "Yeah, she spots some kid stepping off the sidewalk and runs across and grabs him just before a three-ton truck squashes him flat. That ought to make the front page."

"Just tell me how you stage an incident like that," said Dryden, growing impatient. "How do you synchronize a small child with a three-ton truck in a street in Los Angeles as Goldine walks by? And even if you managed it, do you think the press would be taken in by that kind of stunt? They're not so dumb."

"Okay, wise guy. Tell us *your* idea."

"I'm against stunts," said Dryden. "Look, the interest in Goldine is there already. You must have seen the papers today. Already she's been interviewed by two TV networks and God knows how many radio stations. The magazine feature writers are with her most of today. Two weeks from now, she'll be getting known to a wide public. It takes a little time for the thing to gather momentum. About then, the stories will be ready for some reinforcement, but nothing phony. What the media will want are new pictures, extra information—how she's training for Moscow, what she feels about the opposition, how her life has changed since she got to be an Olympic hope, and so on. I'm for playing it straight."

"Dryden is right," said Cobb. "She'll be giving them the sensational stuff in Moscow. Our business now is to lay foundations. We have to get her established as a marketable personality. We want people to see her on their screens next month and recognize her. We want them to know a few heartwarming details from the magazines: that she was the kid whose mother drowned saving her from the sea, that she's a novice taking on athletes with years of experience in track and that she does it for fun, and for America—isn't that wonderful?"

By degrees, and grudgingly, Sternberg and Valenti backed down. The pre-Moscow period would be used for image-building, not shooting for headlines. The Dryden-Cobb alliance was proving effective.

Toward the end of the afternoon, sometime after the consortium had dispersed, Serafin entered the Jacaranda lobby. Dryden was waiting for him.

"You examined her?"

"I did," said Serafin, "—as well as I could in the conditions. It wasn't so thorough as the physicals I give her at the camp."

"Did you form an opinion?"

"She seems to have picked up a mild virus infection of some kind. There's definite inflammation of the throat. Nothing serious, but enough to account for the quicker onset of fatigue yesterday. I've put her on an antibiotic. There's no reason why she shouldn't get through the rest of her interviews."

"That's a relief," said Dryden. "Things still look good for Moscow, then?"

"But of course."

"And you managed to get in without the press jumping to conclusions?"

Serafin gave a smile. "Yes, as it happens there were no questions. There was just one photographer outside, with a young woman from *Cosmopolitan,* I think. They seemed to recognize me, and made no objection when I went in or came out."

"Cosmopolitan," said Dryden, making a mental calculation. "And you went in soon after three. At that rate, she has three more interviews scheduled. She could be through by six. I'd like a session with her my-

self this evening, if that can be slotted in. There are some details I must check before I start the rounds of the advertising executives. Funny the small things they want to know that can clinch a contract—the pitch of a voice, the shape of the hands. I've known a twenty-thousand-dollar deal to hinge on the hairiness of a tennis player's arms." He laughed. "No problem with Goldine, but I need to have the answers ready."

Serafin twisted his mouth into something like a smile. "So you want more time with her?"

"More?" repeated Dryden.

"Come, come," said Serafin. "Do you reckon I have forgotten the five hours you spent with her in San Diego? Are you actually asking me to believe you need to be reminded of the shape of her hands? Let's be candid, Mr. Dryden. You're a resourceful man, or I wouldn't have hired you. You submitted her to a very thorough interrogation in San Diego. By the end of it, there wasn't much you didn't know about me or Goldengirl. And now there are two more points you need to check with her: one is that I actually carried out that physical this afternoon, and the other—unless you have it already from another source—is the location of the new training camp. To save you the trouble, I'll tell you now that it's Thomas Jefferson College on the shores of Lake Erie, a mile or so west of Cleveland. The director happens to be an old friend from my postgraduate days at Yale."

"I thought you weren't telling anyone that."

"You'd have found out," said Serafin simply. "You would need to know, anyway. There are sure to be things we must discuss in the next four weeks. You and I are the principals in this enterprise now. Without disrespect to the others, they don't need the information. They could be a nuisance, pestering me for progress reports. I don't mean to be unsocial, but there's a lot to do. If you still want a meeting with Goldine, I suggest you don't make it too late. My guess is that she'll be pretty exhausted by this evening."

"Don't kid yourself this is leading up to anything," Goldine said as she flopped on the bed. "It's just so much sitting. Bliss to stretch my legs."

"Your training is all wrong," commented Dryden, smiling. "I get a lot of practice sitting. I could win medals at that. Would you say I have an elegant style?" He posed stiff-backed, with arms folded.

"Championship class," she said in an effort to sound amused.

The room overlooked a shadowy square of lawn. One corner of the quadrangle glowed vivid orange in the sun.

"How did it go?"

"The interviews? Great," she said with more animation. "Maybe I shouldn't say that till I see what they write, but I had a ball."

He raised an eyebrow.

"I *have* been trained to talk about myself," she went on. "This was for real, with people I never met before in my life, people who want to know about *me*. Jack, I wallowed in it. I gave some cute answers, too."

He nodded, but with slight unease. "I'm sure you did. No problems, then?"

"My throat's a little sore. Doc figures I have a virus infection."

"He told me."

"Myself, I think it's the talking," said Goldine. "The press conference last night, and then all the interviews today."

"You don't feel unwell, then?"

"Thirsty, that's all," said Goldine. "I must have drunk a gallon of water." She giggled. "I kept stopping to visit the john. I hope they don't put *that* in the magazines. But I still feel thirsty, so I guess Doc is right. He gave me something to help my throat. Say, I had a visit from one of the U.S. team managers. A real nice woman."

"What was that about?"

"They wanted me to get some altitude training at

Colorado Springs." She gave another quick laugh. "I had to confess I've done a little already. I told her Doc has arranged for me to have the use of a track where I can train in seclusion, and she seemed to think that was okay. So long as I report for the U.S. team briefing and medical on July thirtieth, they'll let me alone. Doc already sent them a letter saying I wasn't available for the relay teams. Some committee is considering that. I don't see how they can object. I mean, I know it's traditional for the girls in individual events to make up the relay teams, but nobody has ever tried three events before. If I ran the relays, that would make seventeen races in eight days. Somebody must see that's ridiculous."

"They might suggest you drop out of one of the individual events instead."

"The four hundred, I suppose. They could suggest it, but I wouldn't back down for anything. I mean, I had to fight for that place, all the way up that home stretch. Okay, maybe I only got third because I have a better chest measurement than Janie Canute, maybe Janie was shook up from her fall, but the fact is that the photo showed me ahead of her."

Some of this was news to Dryden. "She had a fall, you say?"

"I heard some talk of it," said Goldine vaguely. "She stumbled on the hostel steps, I understand."

"Tough," said Dryden. "So that was why she couldn't go faster in the Final." Before he got the words out, he was cursing himself for being so tactless. His voice trailed away in embarrassment.

Goldine propped herself on her elbows, eyes burning. "Tough for *her?* How do you think *I* felt, getting beat by two girls I could have run off their feet if I hadn't caught this bug? I know people are saying I tried too many events, I should stand down and give Canute a run in Moscow, but, hell, she can run in the relay team. I'm not giving up my place to anyone."

The bedsprings rattled as she thrust her head back on the pillow.

"Why should you, indeed?" said Dryden quickly. "After all the training you put in. It sounds to me as if Canute was looking for an alibi."

He expected her to latch on to this, but she spurned it.

"What the hell—it's all history. The fact is that I took third place. I'm thinking of Moscow now, what I have to do there. You have to be single-minded if you aim to excel in sports."

"Or anything else," said Dryden.

"This has been good for me," she continued. "Out on that track, I was coming to terms with myself. There was a moment in that four hundred when I realized the first two girls had got away, and I was fighting for the last place on the team. I was in desperate trouble, but I had a fantastic sensation of power. Not in my legs; they were dragging. In my head. For the first time in my life, I controlled my own destiny. And other people's. There was nothing Doc, Pete, Sammy or anyone but me with my two stupid tired legs could do to get that place. If I chose, I could ease up a little and settle for fourth and they would have to watch helpless while all their plans, all that cash, fizzled in front of their eyes. There's no money at all to speak of in an Olympic double. It's been done so many times. The triple is the only one that counts. So there I was with this marvelous feeling of self-determination. It was as good as adrenalin. And when I got it, I knew I wanted more, so I had to get that third place."

"Just for yourself," said Dryden.

"You bet. It's something I'd never experienced, never even thought about before, carrying people's hopes. Jack, I like it. I like the feeling that I could get to the Finals in Moscow with the whole of America watching me and if I chose, I could win, but just as easily I could"—she paused, considering, then laughed

—"I could stop running and pee on the track to show how much I care about gold medals."

"What an idea!" said Dryden, trying to treat it casually. "Look, you're undermining my confidence."

"That's why I'm saying it. Nobody can take Goldengirl for granted any more. She's not an automaton. She's an independent human spirit. You think I'm feverish? I'll tell you another thing. Coming up the home stretch I knew I could beat Janie Canute. I can take anyone on a dip finish. All I had to do was stay close up. She's a Jesus Freak—I suppose you know. Real charitable. I talked to her earlier in the week. You wouldn't meet a more generous-hearted girl. Really, there's nothing to dislike in her unless you have a hangup about religious people. But in that final hundred meters of the race I felt quite savage toward her. A cat-and-mouse thing, letting her steal a few inches ahead, knowing all the time I was dominant. When you run shoulder to shoulder with someone there's a special kind of intimacy between you. And if you're the one with the whip hand, hmm, that's fabulous. Ugly, maybe, but an experience I savored. Relished, even. Now you know the kind of person I am. I'm discovering myself as I go on with this."

"You're sure it *is* yourself?"

"What do you mean?"

He chose his words judiciously. "You seem to be suggesting that this experience revealed your true nature. I'm not sure that this is so. It could be the first chance you've had to release some inner tensions."

Scornfully, she snapped back, "Don't talk like Sammy. It doesn't carry conviction. Are you telling me I'm basically a sweet little girl, not mean at all?"

He answered with a generalization. "In top-class sports it's unusual to be friendly with your rivals. You can make a show of it, shake hands with them before the race, but inside you're hoping they drop dead on the track."

"I know. The killer instinct," she said in a bored

voice. "Now tell me that's just something you put on, like track shoes."

Dryden shook his head. "I know plenty of sports stars, remember. As personalities, they differ a lot. They have one thing in common: when they're down to the wire, they are ruthless, Goldine, ruthless. It takes an experience like the one you had yesterday to discover that."

She laughed. "You're a smart talker, Jack. What am I supposed to do—shout Eureka, I have the essential quality of a champion? You don't have to preach to me. I've had a bellyful of therapy. I'm on another trip now. Self-discovery. I'll let you know how it works out."

[17]

PAN Am Flight 164 was three hours into its five-and-a-half-hour schedule between Los Angeles and New York. From his pile of papers in the First Class bay of the Boeing 747, Dryden picked up a copy of *Sportscene* that had caught his eye on the bookstand at L.A. International Airport. It was dated August 1. Instead of the usual baseball player, the cover photo featured the shapelier back view of a girl athlete, her face turned to glance over her shoulder, a bright-eyed, confident look, framed in soft brown hair. She was in the blue-and-white strip-costume of East Germany. The picture was artfully cut off at the thighs to focus attention on the tightly stretched white shorts. The creases on view were not in the fabric. The caption read: URSULA KRÜLL: "MOSCOW IS MINE." He turned to the cover story.

In a classroom in a Luckenwalde junior school, thirty miles south of Berlin, sit 34 eleven-year-olds, straight-backed, arms folded, girls with hair ribbons, boys in white shirts. One place is empty: the center column, second from front. "Nobody sits there until after the Spartakiad," explains head teacher Heinz Krämer. "That place is reserved for the outstanding athlete of the class. It is the place Ursula Krüll once occupied. I taught her myself," he proudly adds, his thoughts darting back to 1969.

Ursula is currently the fastest girl runner in the world. When she was no bigger than Herr Krämer's

287

pupils, she competed in the Spartakiad, a festival of sports at regional and national level involving over four million children. She was a slimly built child with two red hair ribbons. Those ribbons got to be a familiar sight as she raced to easy victories over all other girls of her age group.

East Germany spends five per cent of its national income on sports development. The State Secretariat for Physical Culture and Sport draws together athletic activities in schools, factories, co-operatives and recreation zones into a cohesive program, ensuring that talents like Ursula's are fostered from childhood through maturity. She was sent to one of the twenty sports schools for children of precocious physical ability. At twelve, she was already listed as a potential competitor for the Olympic Games. At seventeen, she won her first national title, over 100 meters, and at eighteen, in 1976, she competed in the Montreal Olympics. She qualified for the Final, but was not among the medal-winners. "It was the experience I went for," she explains. "Montreal was never intended as my Games. I've been working to a ten-year program since I was twelve. Montreal was for other girls. Moscow . . . Moscow is mine."

At twenty-two, Ursula is ready for Moscow. Her teasing gray-blue eyes, cutely bobbed brown hair and svelte figure may not accord with stereotypes of Eastern-bloc athletes, but her progress places her emphatically in the tradition of East Germany's former sprint queen, the powerful Renate Stecher. Over the last three years, Ursula has headed the world rankings for the 100- and 200-meter dash events. In 1978, she zipped to a convincing double in the European Cup Final. Since then she has not lost a race. And she has got faster each year. Going into 1980, she looked the undisputed claimant for Olympic gold.

Now, just weeks from the Games, has emerged a threat to Ursula's ten-year plan. It happened in the most unlikely way. Last winter, while Ursula was grinding out her four-hour schedule of sprint training and weightlifting in one of Berlin's newest indoor sportsdromes, a retired California professor was urging his daughter to take up some physical activity. "It's not good for an eighteen-year-old to spend all her time around the house," Bill Serafin told blond Goldine. "You should try getting some exercise. Like jogging."

To please her pa, Goldine put on some sneakers and took a turn around the Bakersfield block where they live. She didn't easily identify as one of the Jogging Generation, so her progress was brisker than gurus of the jog would recommend for a maiden run. She stretched her legs and went. And she enjoyed it. "This could be fun," she told her father when she got home. "But I'd like to run on a track, not around the block."

Next afternoon, Goldine made a circuit of the Bakersfield College Stadium. And another. At the end of the week she tried a 100-meter dash. Someone nearby was holding a stopwatch. "Get a coach for that kid, and she could run the Olympics," he told Prof Serafin.

So they did. They hired Pete Klugman, former coach to the U.S. Olympic squad. "Soon as I saw Goldine, I knew she was a natural," says Klugman. "She had everything: stride length, style and basic speed. All I had to teach her was technique."

He had seven months for that. In East Germany, Goldine's gift for running would have been spotted in junior school, shaped and honed to perfection over years. Track in America is a more haphazard affair. Prompted by Klugman, Goldine decided to go for broke on the Olympics, training in secret, with the U.S. Trials in July as a deadline. She had just one competitive outing before that, at a San Diego club meet. She won the 100, 200 and 400 meters in top-class times. Experts who had never heard of Goldine Serafin queried the timekeeping.

At the Trials in Eugene last month, the Bakersfield blonde posted her challenge to Ursula Krüll, setting new U.S. records in Ursula's pet events, the 100 and 200 meters. For the hell of it, she also entered and qualified for the Olympic team in the 400 meters, finishing third. No U.S. girl has ever run all three sprint events at one Games.

Tall, elegant-featured Goldine, with sparkling blue eyes, pink cheeks and a sharp turn of conversation, is dismissive of her Eugene performances. "It's Moscow that counts," she says, sighing. "I'm very inexperienced. I'll run the best I can for America, but don't overdo the buildup, will you? I'd rather surprise people than disappoint them." But she is losing no sleep over the clash with Ursula Krüll. "I haven't had time to study other girls' form. Krüll is just a name to me. It might as well be Schmidt, or anything else. Somebody has to be top girl in East Germany. It's a system I'm running against more than any one girl."

The system is geared to producing champions. Unlike the Russians, whose performances in track have shown a marked decline since the Soviet republics gained more autonomy in sports development, the East Germans bring their superstars together for intensive training and competition. At the Leipzig College of Physical Education, where Ursula Krüll graduated from school, the pick of German athletes train under the guidance of professional coaches to a program based on extensive scientific research into physiological development. There are strong incentives to excel: for students, larger cash grants for better performances, and for coaches, extensions of their contracts if their charges win championships. "I have kept the same coaches for a long time," says Ursula.

If Goldine Serafin has a system, it is based strictly

on free enterprise. Women's track is a backwater in the U.S.A. Few girls persist with any kind of sport after leaving high school. Diver Micki King, who took the gold medal for springboard in the Munich Olympics, put it like this: "We're mystery people. We have our place in the sun once every four years, and then we disappear."

For her place in the sun, Goldine is presently training up to four hours a day to coach Klugman's schedule. What is her incentive? "It's the joy of running," she explains. "If I'd been made to do it since I was a kid in kindergarten, I think the fun might have gone out of it by now. Put me down as a souped-up jogger. That's all I am."

Sportswriters in Olympic year can be forgiven for seeing it differently. U.S. women's sprinting has been dominated by black girls—Wilma Rudolph and Wyomia Tyus the most brilliant—since the Olympics recommenced after World War II. The last white American of top class was 1936 Olympic champion Helen Stephens. A fast blonde may be a cliché, but she's rare enough in reality to rate star treatment in 1980. Since her breakthrough in Eugene, Goldine's story has made the pages of almost every publication except the *Harvard Business Review*. And her tall, shapely figure (36–24–36) is becoming as familiar as the smiles of the presidential candidates.

While Goldine adapts to the pressures of the media, Ursula in Berlin bears the ballyhoo of Olympic year with the cool of a seasoned campaigner. Since her European Cup triumphs a year ago, she has taken over as East Germany's most glamorous sportsgirl. Previous incumbents include the beautiful (and since twice-married) blond diver Ingrid Krämer, a triple gold medalist, and attractive gymnast Karen Janz, who robbed Olga Korbut and comrades of two gold medals in the Munich Olympics. Any idea that glamor has no place in a Communist society is given the lie by pinup posters of

Ursula, in tracksuit, that share many a German bedroom wall with Marx and Lenin. Her running shorts are cut with a dash that beats all records. "If you have good legs, it does no harm to show them," she explains in a highly serious tone. "Running is kind to my legs. It keeps them in shape. Skiing and cycle racing aren't so good. If I was a cyclist, maybe I would wear less revealing shorts." She still admitted slight irritation at the maneuvers of our cameraman. "Always the back view. What is it about my butt? People say I turn my back on the camera deliberately, but I don't. I'm conscious of my body, but only important things, like knee lift and leg cadence."

If such dedication argues total indifference to the effect she creates, it is reassuring to learn that Ursula spends up to an hour each day answering fan mail, much of it requests for a certain photo in which she is bent forward as if to receive the baton in a relay race, but winking at the camera. She has no steady boyfriend, despite persistent offers of dates. "There will be time after Moscow," she says. "I don't think I should want to go out with an athlete. I like to talk about other things than track."

Goldine, too, has had to curtail her social life since joining the gold rush. "I'm a normal girl, and I like going out with guys as much as anyone," she confides, "but you have to make sacrifices. I'll make up later." Nineteen, with cornflower-blue eyes that light up in surprise each time anyone suggests she is America's Olympic hope, she reveals an innocence of her commercial potential that would gladden the hearts of the International Olympic Committee. "Endorsement contracts? What are they? Look, I'm only just beginning to think of myself as a runner. Don't confuse me any more by turning me into some kind of merchandise."

Goldine might deny it to herself, but the middlemen who made a killing each Olympic year are already jostling on the sidelines over the right to manage the girl who could become the hottest property in U.S. sport. "There have been inquiries from agents, it's true," says Professor Serafin. "Of course, Goldine isn't considering anything like this. If she won a gold medal, I wouldn't know what to advise. It's really up to her. We're just ordinary people with no experience of sports. She's doing this for America, not with any profit motive."

How do track experts rate Goldine's chances? "She's unquestionably a brilliant talent," says Dale Dennigan of *Track and Field News*. "She made a lot of mistakes in Eugene through inexperience, and still did more than any girl in U.S. track history. If you analyze her best clockings of 10.8, 22.7 and 50.52, they indicate that she has a great chance of Olympic medals in all three events, but let's remember that her best running in the 200 was achieved in the Quarter-Final, and her personal best in the 400 was made a month back in San Diego. She must learn to spread her effort more judiciously. She's short on experience, of course, but that could mean she's capable of improvement. It's not unknown for a sprinter to take the Olympic title on a slender competitive record. Helen Stephens is an outstanding example, coming from a farm in Missouri in 1935 to set world records and then win two gold medals the next year, but it's right to point out that she had a lot of intensive coaching before the Olympics. By any criterion, Ursula Krüll remains clear favorite for the 100 and 200 meters with her personal bests of 10.78 and 22.0 in the German trials. Remember, she hasn't lost a race in two years. Taking the events in isolation, I'd put Goldine's chances highest in the 400, but I'm afraid the short sprints will take a lot of her steam, as they did in Eugene. I'm picking her for silver in the 100 and 200 and hoping she can surprise me."

Goldine accepts this estimate as a reasonable

summation of the evidence available. "I'd rather not go to Moscow as favorite for anything. I'll take it as it comes. Of course, I have my ideas of what I can do, but they won't be helped by speculation in the papers."

Ursula, too, is reluctant to make predictions on the outcome of her clash with Goldine. "I don't know much about this girl, but her times I must respect. Do you have a picture of her? I send her my good wishes and I look forward to meeting her in Moscow."

Ursula now possesses a photo of her U.S. challenger in action. "I'd like to send Goldine one of my pictures, so we'll know each other in Moscow," she says, "but the only ones I have just now are taken from the back. Well, I'll send her one," she adds with a mischievous smile. "Maybe she ought to get used to seeing me from that position."

Smiling, though not at the wit of Fraulein Krüll, Dryden treated himself to another look at the cover picture. He was pleased because the *Sportscene* article chimed in well with the chorus of publicity Goldine was getting from the media. The rivalry with Krüll could become a highlight of the Games—the souped-up jogger versus the peerless product of the German machine. He liked that.

He opened his briefcase. Before landing at Kennedy Airport, there was work to do. The past ten days had seemed like 1969 again, when he had started the agency in London with the help of one part-time temp, and lived on sandwiches and four hours' sleep, spending the other twenty generating business. These days, he was used to farming out the work to those sub-executives on the next floor, not seeing it through himself, every stage from the pitch to the signing. Still, he had kept control of the thing; if there were leaks, they wouldn't be traced to Dryden Merchandising.

All told, he had done pretty well on the West Coast.

The old sales patter hadn't deserted him. On a quick count, he had logged upward of two million in endorsements, all provisional, of course, and peppered with escape clauses, but it wasn't bad at all. If he could do as well in New York this week, the project would be right on target.

Already, the agreements had chiseled some shape into the Goldengirl image. She was hooked on California oranges, eggs and soft drinks. She drove a four-seater sports coupé with a V-12 engine, wore cashmere sweaters and white pantyhose and welcomed visitors to the U.S.A. Her hair was shampooed nightly with Goldtress, she showered under a Softspray de luxe and always took a malt drink last thing. Her preference in tracksuits was still under discussion, but shaping promisingly; enough gear had arrived gratis from the major sports manufacturers to outfit the entire agency staff if they ever fielded a track team.

The pleasing thing about the negotiations was that top management had heard of Goldine. That extra day in Eugene had repaid handsomely in publicity. Executives might not believe she was capable of three gold medals, but they knew enough to talk about her, and that was a foot in the door. The take-up had been better than 60 per cent, with less than 15 per cent outright refusals. Moreover, nobody had wanted to know who was behind the project. To a man, they swallowed the line that Goldine was Superjogger, the girl who found by accident she was America's fastest sprinter.

The ingénue image had gone over strongly, as the *Sportscene* story testified. It fulfilled all requirements at this stage, providing good copy for the press and prime material for the admen to work on. No question of it: Goldine had done everything right in the interviews after Eugene. There was no hint anywhere of the self-indulgent stirrings she had admitted to him afterward. Just as well: the media would have a field day if they heard she was developing a power thing.

He took out a cigarette. No future in worrying what

she might say. She had the intelligence to preserve the image, whatever her private statements revealed. In a way, that conversation in the hostel had been a demonstration of the point she was making. She had shown she had power over him. She could destroy his work with a few words in a press conference. He had to believe she wouldn't, that it was enough to know she had the power. For, like her more explicit threats, it was self-defeating. To execute it, she would have to destroy Goldengirl, and if she did that, she removed herself from her position of influence.

He started sifting through his papers.

It wasn't pure chance that he bought an evening paper before he left the Pan Am terminal at Kennedy Airport. He wanted to see how his golfers were doing in the Philadelphia Classic. It was a long time before he found out. His eyes were riveted by something else:

TRACKSTAR VANISHES: KIDNAP THEORY.

NEW YORK, Aug. 1.———Goldine Serafin, 19, blond star of the recent U.S. Olympic Track and Field Trials, was today reported missing by her father, Dr. William Serafin. Early Wednesday morning she left Cleveland Hopkins Airport, Ohio, to travel by air taxi to New York, where the U.S. Olympic team had been asked to report for a pre-Games medical check. She did not arrive. This came to light yesterday afternoon, when Dr. Serafin contacted Murray Randal, of the U.S. Olympic Committee. Police are now investigating Goldine's disappearance. A spokesman confirmed they were working on the theory she was kidnaped.

Goldine made headlines last month, when she raced to U.S. records for 100 and 200 meters in qualifying for the U.S. Olympic team. She also qualified in a third event, the 400 meters, which makes her the first U.S. girl to attempt this triple in the Olympics. Prior to the Trials, she was almost unknown as a runner.

Dr. Serafin today described how he escorted Goldine to the airport from the house in Cleveland where they have been staying with friends. "I saw her into the plane, a light aircraft, red and white in color," he said. "I actually lifted her baggage aboard."

When Goldine failed to return to Cleveland Wednesday night, Dr. Serafin assumed she had been delayed in New York and made arrangements to stop overnight in a hotel. It was late Thursday afternoon, when she had still not contacted him, that he thought of phoning the U.S. Olympic Committee, and heard from Murray Randal that she had not reported for the medical. Dr. Serafin then informed Cleveland Police of her disappearance.

Heading the inquiry in Cleveland is Police Captain Sam Mortenson. "It's too early to be definite, but we're working on the possibility that she has been kidnaped," he said this morning. "This girl is big news, with the Olympics coming up in ten days. Her abductors could believe they have a strong bargaining position. People with a big interest in the Olympics might be persuaded to put up a ransom so that Goldine can compete."

Dryden didn't read any more. He crossed the hall to the telephones, found the Cleveland book, looked up the Thomas Jefferson College, and stabbed out the number. In seconds he was speaking to Serafin: "Look, I just saw a paper. Is this true? She really is missing?"

"Unhappily, yes," said Serafin. His voice was strained. "There's no news of her. The police are waiting for a ransom demand. When I picked up the phone we thought perhaps . . ."

It was a clear warning to watch what he said. The police had a tap on the phone.

"I've just arrived at Kennedy Airport," said Dryden. "If there's anything I can do to help . . ."

"Not at this stage," said Serafin. "It's in the hands of the police."

"I understand. Do they think she got to New York?"

"Probably not. They're proceeding on the supposition that the pilot of the air taxi was implicated. I gave them a detailed description, but there doesn't seem to be anyone like that known to the other pilots."

"You walked into a trap?"

"It seems so. Listen, if I should get any news, can I contact you?"

"Through my New York office," said Dryden. He gave him the number. "It looks as though I'll be here till August sixteenth, or thereabouts. When does the team fly out?"

"August ninth."

"Christ, I hope you hear something soon. This can't be helping her preparation for the Games."

"Leave *me* to worry about that," said Serafin tersely. "There's nothing you or any of my friends can do. It's a police matter. Don't let it interfere with your visit to New York. I'm confident we shall hear something soon. I must ring off now. I don't want to miss the call if it comes."

As his taxi headed up the Van Wyck Expressway, Dryden sorted through the theories his reeling brain supplied. A kidnaping might appeal to the police, but it seemed likelier Goldine had arranged her own disappearance. At the first opportunity, she had slipped Serafin's leash and hidden herself in New York like any teenager on the run. She had talked about doing it that evening in La Jolla, hooking off to join a commune somewhere. At that time she had rejected the idea, but the pressures had mounted since. The urge to escape, go into hiding until the Olympics were over, could have overwhelmed her.

A more devious, but possibly more credible explanation was that this was a try-on. The next round in her power game. She was getting back at Serafin and the consortium, making them suffer a little. She would lie low for a few days to make them aware how much they depended on her. When she reappeared, she would have the gratification of seeing how relieved they were, knowing they dared not antagonize her. It was perverse, but so were some of the things she had said in her room in Eugene.

Then he remembered Sternberg and Valenti. They had wanted to pull stunts, stir up press interest in Goldine. When it had come up, he thought he had squashed the suggestion with Cobb's help, but they could have decided later to stage something of their own. He could imagine Valenti crowing over the idea of a kidnaping.

There remained the theory the police were working on. If they were right, and it *was* a kidnaping, a genuine one, disturbing possibilities were raised. Professional crooks didn't kidnap amateur athletes on the off chance that some sports-loving millionaire would put up. The chances were high that somebody had got wind of the money involved in Project Goldengirl. They knew the consortium would pay heavily—perhaps up to a million—to get Goldine back. Some ugly questions had to be faced. Not only did the kidnapers know about the stake in Goldine; they must have learned she had transferred from California to Cleveland. In the consortium, only Serafin and Dryden knew about Cleveland. The only others who could have leaked the information were Klugman, Lee or Melody.

By the time the taxi dropped him at the Roosevelt on Madison Avenue he had dismissed the kidnap theory. This had to be Goldine playing games of her own. A porter carried his cases inside. The desk clerk recognized him from previous visits.

"Mr. Dryden, sir. How nice to see you. We have a message for you to call your office. Urgent, they said."

"My office here?"

"That's right, sir. The booth over there is free, if you'd care to use it."

This signified some kind of emergency. The New York office knew his time of arrival, of course, but they weren't expecting to see him before tomorrow. After the flight from L.A. he always spent the evening relaxing.

The switchboard operator stammered her apologies. "I wasn't sure what to do when I took the call, Mr. Dryden, so I asked Mr. Helpern, and he said as it was personal, I should leave a message for you at the hotel."

"Fair enough. Who was the caller?"

"That's why I was doubtful, sir. The lady wouldn't give her name. Just said she wanted to contact you urgently, and it was personal. She asked if you were in New York, and I said you were expected late this afternoon. I hope I didn't do anything wrong, but she was very insistent."

"A young lady? I suppose you couldn't tell."

The pause at the other end of the line was palpable with embarrassment. "She sounded like she was my generation, sir. I'm twenty-two."

"Lucky for you. Did you tell her where I'm staying?"

"Most certainly not, sir! I wouldn't do that. Not to a caller that wouldn't give her name."

"So what did she do—ring off?"

"She gave me a number you can call." Another diffident pause. "Would you care to take it down, sir?"

He noted it, and assured the girl she still had a job. In return he got an unsolicited promise that nobody else in the agency would hear about it.

In his personal appointment book were the phone numbers of two girls he occasionally met on his visits to New York. The numbers he had just written down were different from either.

Goldine? If it was, he had a few things to say to her.

He dialed the number and waited.

"Who is this?"

"Jack Dryden."

"Hi, lover boy," said Melody. "So sweet of you to call."

[18]

HE met Melody in the main cocktail lounge of the Century Paramount. She was on a stool at the bar in a jade-green cheongsam. Dryden ignored the leg show. He wasn't there for a sexual encounter. She had told him she had news of Goldine. If that was just a come-on, he wasn't staying.

She was drinking tomato juice, and asked for another. He ordered a straight scotch for himself.

"Surprised to find me in New York?" she asked. "I guess you must feel flattered, being paged to call me the moment you check in."

"Surprised, I'll give you," said Dryden, measuring his response. "What brings you here—orders from Dr. Serafin?"

She wrinkled her nose. "I don't follow you."

"I thought you might be assisting the search for Goldine."

"You thought what?" She broke into a ripple of laughter. "Hey, that's priceless! Casing the clip joints to see if her ladyship is sold into white slavery! Honey, I'm here because I walked out. Quit. I'm finished with Serafin."

"What happened exactly?"

"Got a spare smoke?"

He opened a pack for her.

"It was obvious he was going to boot me out in a couple of weeks," she went on. "There's no job for me once the Olympics are over. Klugman, Lee, everyone on the payroll has to look for a new job."

302

"I see what you mean, but what makes you give up now? This way you miss a trip to Moscow."

Melody grinned. "I'm not so dumb as that. It was my job to fix the travel arrangements. You don't think I'd walk out and leave my ticket behind?"

"He won't like that."

"He's in no position to argue," said Melody. "I know enough to blow the project sky-high. The price of an airline ticket and a Russian hotel bill is peanuts to what I could collect in overtime pay. I'm thinking about that. No use trying to negotiate anything yet."

"You mean he's too distracted over Goldine's disappearance?"

She studied him amusedly with her green eyes and said nothing.

"You, er, mentioned on the phone that you had news of Goldine," he prompted her.

"That's right, lover boy. I can tell you where she is right now."

"You know that?"

She was savoring this, pouting with her lower lip and fingering her hair as Dryden assimilated what she was saying. Two statements of fact had emerged: she had walked out on Serafin, and she knew where Goldine was. The facts didn't trouble him so much as the implications.

"Sure I know," she said.

"Did you ask me here to let me into the secret?"

"Depends."

"On what?"

"What I get in return," said Melody.

"Like Campari, for instance?"

She laughed, shaking her head. "Fancy your chances, lover boy? Later, maybe, but I was thinking of a different kind of arrangement, as a matter of fact. Something less romantic, more . . ." She held up her right hand, passing the thumb lightly across the fingertips.

"Let's have it straight," said Dryden. "Who do you represent?"

She frowned. "I miss your drift, sweetheart."

He didn't disguise his irritation. "Less than two hours ago I got off a plane and bought a paper. It carried the news that Goldine has disappeared and is probably kidnaped. I get to my hotel and there's a message from you. Urgent. So I meet you, and what do you tell me? You walked out on Serafin, and you know where Goldine is. Am I supposed to believe you have no part in her disappearance, you have nothing to do with the people who abducted her? You're in this up to here, Melody."

She clasped her hands over her knee and rocked back on the stool laughing. "Jack Dryden, you fracture me! You really believe I arranged for some hoods to kidnap Goldengirl and I'm here to fix the ransom? Melody ripping off the consortium, huh? Oh boy, that's really wild! I just wish I had the nerve to do it." Her face became more serious. "Listen, I'm here strictly on my own account. I'm out of a job, as I told you. I figured you might use some extra help in the agency after Moscow, someone with experience as a confidential secretary and inside knowledge of the Goldengirl project. I'd like to stay with the assignment, if you think I could be useful. Jesus, I'm no kidnaper! Just one of America's unemployed angling for a job."

"But do you know what's happened to Goldine?" Dryden said, without indicating whether he believed her.

She nodded, studying his reaction. "You can't blame a girl who has information for wanting a return on it."

"I suppose not." The prospect of Melody on the agency staff didn't enrapture him, but it might be tolerated. There could even be an advantage in having someone in the New York office with knowledge of the project. She wasn't the type to stay long. It was a small price for the information she had. "How's your typing?"

She leaned forward and kissed him lightly on the cheek. "I shall adore working for you."

"So what happened to Goldine?" he asked.

"She never left Cleveland. You'll find her in Caradock Lodge. That's a private sanitarium on Euclid Avenue, the road out to Cleveland Heights, east of the city center."

"Someone has locked her up in a sanitarium?"

"That's putting it a little strongly," said Melody. "I'd say she was under observation."

"Say what you like, we must get her out of there," said Dryden. "Do you know who is responsible for this?"

"Sure I do." She took a sip at her drink. "Not the Mob, honey. Bill Serafin arranged it himself. Okay, you don't believe that, because you read in the papers he informed the police she was missing, right? But listen to this. You remember how she complained she didn't feel so good at the Trials—her legs were going heavy on her, or something?"

"It was a virus infection," said Dryden. "She had a dry throat as well. You mean it didn't clear up?"

"You're getting there," said Melody. "On the flight from Eugene, she was all the time asking for water. If I'd been the stewardess, I'd have chucked the jugful over her. By the time we landed, it was obvious Goldengirl was pretty unwell. She was sweating plenty, and said she felt real weak. Soon as we got to Jefferson College, we put her to bed. Next morning, Bill Serafin checked her, and then told Pete Klugman there could be no training for at least a week. You can imagine Pete's response. I've never seen him so mad. He was laying into Serafin like it was his fault Goldengirl was sick. He said he had three weeks to get her in shape for the Olympics and now it was cut to two, just like that. Serafin had an answer. He said he had ten days to get her ready for the U.S. team medical. If she didn't pass that, the whole project was ditched."

"I don't see why," said Dryden. "If she was sick,

there would still be time to get over it. It's not as if she has the plague."

"Nobody knows what she has," said Melody. "Except possibly Bill Serafin. One thing he was adamant about: she wasn't going to that medical before she was fit again. You know what I think? He's afraid she strained her heart. They pushed her too hard in the training sessions. He's terrified it will show on one of those cardiograms."

"I am still trying to get the picture of what happened," said Dryden. "He arranged for her to move into the sanitarium. Was that because her condition deteriorated?"

Melody shook her head. "The break in training definitely helped her. After a week at Jefferson College, she was feeling stronger. She'd lost a little weight, but otherwise she was eating well and getting back to normal. Last Monday he gave her another physical and we all thought she would resume training and go to New York Wednesday for the team medical. Instead, he said she needed further tests, and he was moving her into Caradock Lodge. There was a meeting with Sammy Lee and Pete Klugman. I don't know what was said, but afterward Doc Serafin called me in and told me he was putting out this story that Goldengirl had disappeared. He said it was a way of buying time. When her health was restored, she would reappear and report for a special check by the team doctors."

"Crazy," said Dryden, shaking his head.

"You think so? Actually, it's smart. It gets Goldengirl's name in the news, and that can't be bad."

"Telling the cops isn't smart. What happens if they find her? What sort of publicity is that, playing the cops for suckers?"

"Aw, come on," said Melody. "Think about it. She's just one missing nineteen-year-old. She's been in the news, so they give out press releases, but what can they do in a case like this? They have to take Doc Serafin's statement on trust, or why would he report her missing? They file her as a missing person and wait to hear something. If it's a kidnaping, they can expect a ransom note to arrive. It won't, of course."

"They must be making some kind of inquiry."

"Naturally, but that's routine. When they've finished checking the leads Doc Serafin gave them, all they can do is sit and wait. One missing girl—even an Olympic hope—isn't a case for the FBI."

"All right," said Dryden. "It buys a little time. Now tell me how Serafin proposes to explain her reappearance."

"He's got it all worked out, lover boy. He'll put it out that she was kidnaped and the ransom has been paid by a group of his business friends, who remain anonymous. The kidnapers contacted him direct and threatened to kill Goldengirl if the police got to hear about the deal before it was finalized. It's neat, because this way she has a good reason for signing commercial contracts after the Games: she wants to repay the people who put up the ransom. Then, if anything should ever break about the consortium, there's a heartwarming cover story. Like it?"

"I think I need to get a few things straight with Serafin," said Dryden, unimpressed. "I've teed up two million dollars' worth of endorsement contracts already. If Goldine isn't training at all, I'm in deep trouble, whatever stories he cooks up. I need to know just what *is* going on in Cleveland." He upended his glass. "Right, Miss Fryer. You've joined the agency staff. Here's your first assignment. Make two flight reservations for Cleveland, for tomorrow afternoon."

"Two?" said Melody. "You want *me* to come?"

"I want to look inside this sanitarium before I tackle Serafin. It could be helpful to have you with me."

"Okay, boss," said Melody. "But count me out of the face-to-face. I've made my exit once. That's enough. You did say tomorrow afternoon?"

Dryden nodded. "I have a busy morning coming up, which is why I'm going back to my hotel now to get

307

some rest." He noticed Melody's eyebrows tilt in surprise. "You can leave a message with the desk clerk. Oh, and have a taxi pick us up from our hotels in good time, would you?"

Melody snapped her features into an intelligent response. "Certainly, Mr. Dryden." When he had said goodnight and turned away, she added wryly to herself, "That will definitely be all, Miss Fryer."

In the New York Institute of Sports Medicine next morning, Dryden put this question to the Director, Dr. Fassendean: "What are the symptoms of overstrain in an athlete?"

Dr. Fassendean, a small man in his thirties with a startling crop of red hair, smiled indulgently. "You might as well ask me how you cook eggs. You'll have to be more specific than that, my friend."

"I'm thinking of an athlete who might have trained too hard. A runner."

"Long distance?"

"Sprints, actually."

"Not common at all," said Dr. Fassendean. "You don't mean muscular injuries? The hamstring is the classic sprinting injury."

"This isn't a muscular thing," said Dryden. "I'm wondering if it has to do with the cardiovascular system."

"Athlete's heart?" Dr. Fassendean chuckled. "Good old athlete's heart. That's been running longer than any athlete I know. It's a rare condition, actually. I've seen electrocardiograms showing overstrain of the heart's left ventricle, which I guess is what is generally known as athlete's heart, but modern knowledge of training methods is rapidly eliminating the syndrome among serious athletes. The dabbler in track is more at risk."

"But what are the symptoms?"

"Acute overstrain manifests itself quite dramatically," said Dr. Fassendean. "Asthenia develops rapidly, as well as a syncope at times, vertigo, vomiting, lowering of the arterial blood pressure, dilatation of the heart. Look, maybe it would save us both some time if you described the symptoms your athlete has. I guess they're a little different, huh?"

Dryden nodded. "Well, it started with a sensation of heaviness in the limbs after a fairly intensive series of competitions."

"Nothing too alarming in that."

"Dry throat," Dryden went on. "Tiredness, excessive thirst, some loss of weight."

"This athlete eating normally?"

"I understand so."

"But drinking plenty?"

"Yes."

"Urinating frequently?"

"Now you mention it, yes."

"That's no heart condition. Get a physician to run a blood-sugar test. Sounds like diabetes to me."

"Diabetes?" Dryden mouthed the word without giving it credence. "Could that be caused by overtraining?"

Dr. Fassendean shook his head. "Caused, no. Not directly. If an athlete has the disease, it's more likely to reveal itself under stress conditions, like training. Physical malfunctions of any kind tend to become more readily detectable in the trained athlete. That doesn't mean athletics causes them. Plenty of people have mild forms of diabetes without realizing it. Around two-and-a-half-million Americans are registered diabetics, and surveys suggest almost as many again are undiagnosed. If those people took part in sports, there's a good chance their condition would be detected."

Figures were spinning in Dryden's brain. Two-and-a-half-million diabetics. Twenty million dollars. "Diabetes," he repeated mechanically. "That's when the body can't absorb sugar, isn't it?"

"Starches, sugar, yes," Dr. Fassendean confirmed.

"The pancreas—the gland at the back of the abdomen below the lower part of the stomach—fails to produce enough of the hormone insulin, and as a consequence excessive amounts of sugar accumulate in the blood and urine. Left untreated, the poisons in the blood attack the brain, inducing a state of coma and ultimately death. With the help of diet and drugs, insulin especially, it can be effectively controlled."

"There's no cure?"

"None," said Dr. Fassendean. "Before insulin treatment was discovered in the twenties, it was a death sentence."

"Do we know what causes the pancreas to stop functioning?"

"Not really. Just that certain stress conditions seem to make it more likely. If there's a potential weakness there, obesity appears to aggravate it. Pregnancy is another stress factor, and so is growth."

"Growth?" Dryden seized on the word.

"Sure. Diabetes is often diagnosed during the adolescent growth spurt. There's research evidence showing that young people who develop the disease are characteristically at least twelve months ahead of the average in the onset of growth. But look, it wouldn't be wise to make presumptions in advance of a proper diagnosis. My interpretation of the symptoms you describe may be wrong. A blood-sugar test would settle the matter."

"Thanks, Doctor. I'll see that one is carried out. I'm grateful for your advice."

In the entrance hall of the Institute, he looked at his watch: 12:15 P.M. In the Pacific Time Zone, it would be 9:15 A.M. He went to a phone booth and called a Bakersfield number.

"The California Institute? I'd like to speak to Professor Walsh, please. Yes, it's very important."

Her voice came over crisp and efficient. "Stephanie Walsh. Who is this?"

He pictured the half-smile under the fringe. "Dry-

310

den. Jack Dryden. I called at the College—sorry, Institute—a few weeks back. There was some, er, confusion over my identity."

"I remember—my dead publisher. So they have phones up there, do they?"

Of course she couldn't know he was in no mood to trade humor. "Actually, I'm in New York. Something has come up—"

"New York? Isn't that where the Serafin girl is thought to be? I saw the item on NBC News last evening. Bill must be out of his mind with worry. Is there any development yet?"

"Nothing," said Dryden. "Everyone's waiting for a ransom demand. Professor, when we talked, you were good enough to tell me a little about the growth hormone, HGH, and the work that's being done in your Institute with children suffering from arrested growth. If you recollect, I put a question to you about the possible effect of HGH on normal children, and you were pretty short with me—warned me I was on very doubtful ground."

"I remember saying that, yes." The note of coolness carried over on her voice.

"I'm back on the same ground," he admitted. "Believe me, I wouldn't trouble you if it wasn't important. I have just one question pertaining to what you said before. The answer could profoundly influence things here."

"Go ahead," said Professor Walsh. "I'm listening."

"Would the reason for your reservation about the use of HGH be that it has a connection with diabetes?"

"You've got it in one," said Professor Walsh. "If you administer HGH in large amounts over a considerable period of time, you produce a condition of hyperglycemia that stimulates the beta cells of the pancreatic islands. It causes them to hypertrophy and degenerate, resulting ultimately in chronic diabetes.

HGH is diabetogenic, Mr. Dryden. Anyone who uses it knows that."

Melody had arranged a 1350 flight from Kennedy Airport. They landed in Cleveland in a little over an hour and a half. The conversation between them was minimal. From Cleveland Hopkins Airport they took a taxi into the center and east along Euclid Avenue.

Caradock Lodge was not visible from the road. Dryden asked the driver to let them out a hundred yards past the gate. They settled the fare and walked back. There was a drive lined with tall, green-barked trees. A short way around the curve was the Lodge, mock-gothic to the pointed roofs of its ivy-covered towers. Inside, a dog barked. Melody slipped her hand inside Dryden's arm.

The bell, at least, was modern. It was answered by a uniformed nurse, sallow-skinned and tight-lipped.

"Yes?"

"Visitors," Dryden announced, "for Miss Goldine Serafin."

"There must be a mistake," she said without blinking. "There is nobody of that name here."

"Definitely no mistake," said Dryden. "This is Miss Fryer, Dr. Serafin's secretary. My name is Dryden, and I look after Miss Serafin's business interests. You probably have orders to admit nobody. We understand your difficulty, but"—he took a step forward—"this is an emergency. It is necessary for us to see the young lady, whatever name she is using here. Would you kindly take us to her? We flew in from New York specially."

The door slammed in their faces.

"I guess the answer is no," said Melody.

"I shouldn't have mentioned New York," said Dryden. "Serafin will have warned her about newsmen."

"So what do we do now?"

"You keep ringing the bell at regular intervals while

GOLDENGIRL

I scout around the outside, hoping that dog is tied up.
Give me three minutes, and then walk back up the
drive and wait at the gate."

He stepped over an ornamental chain and started
across a lawn, taking stock of the leaded windows on
ground level. Every one was fastened. The interior
was too much in shadow for anyone to be visible from
where he was. He heard Melody ring the bell.

He moved around the projecting turret at the left
of the house and found a paved area surrounded by a
low hedge. There was a garden table there with a
bentwood chair beside it. The breeze lifted the corner
of a magazine on the table. A jug of water had ice
cubes floating in it. Someone had moved fast.

On this side of the house was a french window. It
appeared to be closed, but as he approached, he noticed it move slightly with the wind. He eased it open
and stepped inside.

The room was wood-paneled and thickly carpeted,
but had an institutional look to it, the armchairs,
shabby from much use, facing each other in two arc
shapes across a low table supplied with glass ashtrays.
A potted palm beyond them was a geriatric case itself.

Dryden jerked at the sound of the doorbell, remembered Melody, and crossed the room into a corridor
redolent of lavender polish. He could hear the voice of
the nurse speaking on the phone in an adjacent room.
No mystery who she was calling: "Yes . . . Yes . . .
I sent her upstairs, to her room . . . Certainly, I will
. . . Yes, in fact, they are still ringing . . . Very well . . ."

He glided past, turned a corner, saw the front door
ahead and opened it before Melody touched the doorbell again. He held his hand up in a silencing gesture.
Her face twitched in surprise. He tugged her inside,
closed the door and hustled her to the staircase across
the hall. They were upstairs before they heard the
phone receiver being replaced.

Melody started trying doors. The first two bedrooms

313

were unoccupied, the beds stripped. Before there was time for a third, steps sounded on the stairs. Dryden nudged Melody into the second room, gently closing the door behind them. There was nothing they could do but stand together in the only place unseen from the door, the angle formed by one end of the wardrobe and the wall.

"Dryden Merchandising certainly looks after its staff," Melody murmured, wriggling pleasurably against him.

They heard a door opened, and voices nearby. Scraps of the conversation carried to them. The nurse was passing on orders. ". . . stay in your room at least until we're sure . . . I know, my dear, but he insisted . . . can't take risks . . . I have to check the doors and windows."

Her steps receded. Melody gave a small sigh as Dryden eased away from her and moved to the door.

In the passage he pointed to the door opposite, turning with eyebrows raised inquiringly to Melody. She nodded. He turned the handle and pushed it open.

"Jack!" Goldine ran to him and wrapped her arms around his neck before she saw Melody was there. She was wearing a white bathrobe and slippers. Her face was drawn, definitely thinner than it had been when he had last seen her in Eugene. "Melody!" she said in surprise. "I didn't expect—"

"Skip it," said Melody. "It's good to see you have the strength."

"I'm a whole lot better," said Goldine, disentangling herself. "The treatment is just marvelous. You knew I was ill, Jack? Doc has been giving me injections. I should be back in training by the weekend." She motioned to them to sit on the bed. "Say, how did you get in? Nurse Piper said there were people about, but I never thought—"

"No matter," said Dryden. "This illness—has it been diagnosed?"

She nodded. "It's not an illness. It's a diet problem.

You know how people are allergic to things? There was something in my food—"

"Sugar, perhaps?"

"Maybe. They're giving me Sweet'n Low with my coffee. Doc says I shall have to be careful what I eat in the future. He wants to get me right before I have my medical for the Games. I was a little anxious at missing the team briefing, but Doc has explained everything to them and I'll catch up next week."

Dryden exchanged a glance with Melody. "You haven't seen the papers?" he asked Goldine.

"All they have here is very old *Reader's Digests*," she answered. "Is there something I should see? Nurse Piper hasn't mentioned a thing. The Olympic Committee does understand I was ill, don't they? There isn't any complication about that?"

"Nothing that can't be retrieved," said Dryden. "You still expect to run in Moscow?"

A look of annoyance crossed her face. "Why shouldn't I? I earned the right, didn't I? You think I'm a quitter?"

"Easy," murmured Dryden. "I was only suggesting, if your health—"

"My health's okay," Goldine cut in vehemently. "I had a diet problem. Have you got that straight in your head? I'm going to Moscow and I'm going for gold. God help anyone who tries to stop me now." She kept her voice level; the intensity of her eyes was emphasis enough. She held the look until it was clear that the assertion stood unchallenged, then relaxed it and inquired, "How's the merchandising shaping? Have you made a start yet?"

"It's well under way."

"Tell me about it."

She seemed genuinely interested, so he outlined the results of his negotiations to date, explaining how an image was emerging already. Once or twice she stopped him to ask if a contract was firm. Far from being overawed by commercial commitments, she listened to Dryden in mounting excitement. She was entirely taken up with the publicity possibilities, building her own picture of what Goldengirl would be. She took little interest in the financial terms. "It amounts to over two million pledged already," Dryden told her with excusable pride. "That's only the West Coast. New York should be good for at least as much again."

"New York?" she responded dreamily. "Are the Helena Rubenstein people based there? I'd like to have something going in the beauty business."

"You will," promised Dryden. "It's high on my priorities here. I have plenty of contacts in New York."

As he was speaking, the door opened. "In that case, what are you doing in Cleveland?" asked Dr. Serafin.

[19]

DRYDEN had been waiting for this.

When Dr. Fassendean in New York had mentioned diabetes, it had registered nothing. It had made no sense. An alien suggestion. Only when Fassendean had described the types of stress associated with its onset had Dryden begun to see a possible pattern of cause and effect. His call to Professor Walsh had hardened possibility into suspicion. For three hours he had contained his anger as, detail by detail, the certainty had grown that Serafin had cynically destroyed his daughter's health.

Now the man stood in the doorway in the posture of an outraged parent.

The essential thing was to take control, keep it rational, prize out the truth.

Serafin addressed him again: "I think you and I should have a talk."

"I agree."

"In private," said Serafin.

Here was the first issue. An important one. As soon as Dryden had heard the phone call going through to Serafin, he had realized this would come up. Serafin would come to the sanitarium and find them with Goldine. He would not want to talk in her presence.

Dryden shook his head. "This affects Goldine. She has a right to hear it."

Serafin tersely said, "She knows nothing."

"Exactly," said Dryden. "You're about to rectify that, Dr. Serafin."

Goldine frowned in bewilderment, looking from one to the other.

"I have to consider her health," said Serafin. "This is no time to subject her to shocks. As her physician—"

"Save it," warned Dryden. "It carries no conviction. She's nineteen years old and she is entitled to know what's wrong. And why."

The force of that last word showed in Serafin's face. Creases rutted the pallid cheeks as if he had taken a punch. It stung him into a fresh offensive. "I don't propose discussing anything in front of Miss Fryer. She has left my employment."

"I know. She joined mine," said Dryden. "Melody stays. I want corroboration. Would you shut the door and come in—unless you want Nurse Piper in as well."

Serafin listened to this with his hands working convulsively at his jacket buttons. His knuckles were white.

"You wonder how much I know?" said Dryden. "Is that your problem? You think perhaps I'm bluffing? No, Doctor, I've dredged deep. Shall we start by talking about the growth hormone? What do you call it— HGH or somatotrophin?"

Serafin's face twitched. "For God's sake, man, not in front of Goldine!"

It was Goldine who answered him. "Doc, if this has to do with me, I intend to hear it." She went to him and gripped his arm, more in duress than endearment. "Don't you think you owe me that?"

She was strong. Serafin took an involuntary step forward. The door closed behind him. He rested his hands defensively on the back of the only chair in the small room. Goldine stepped away and sat on the edge of the bed, facing him. Dryden stayed leaning against the wall opposite. Melody had propped herself on the windowsill overlooking the garden.

Dryden was in control. "Okay. Let's take you back.

Vienna, 1963. The focal point of your career. Your research showed that a group of German women grew significantly taller than their mothers at maturity. It created interest among scientists, brought you recognition. Some had reservations about your theories, but nobody could dispute the results. And if one generation was taller than its predecessor, why shouldn't future generations grow indefinitely taller? Your critics said the human skeleton was structually incapable of further increase. Do I have it right?"

Serafin's mouth was set in a tight line. He gave a shrug that could have meant anything.

Dryden took it as an affirmation. "For years after that you immersed yourself in the controversy, writing letters to the scientific press, lecturing up and down the country, producing papers on every aspect of the subject your research had touched on. But the problem was that you had no new evidence to support you. You had milked the Vienna project dry."

Serafin didn't like that. His mouth shaped to protest.

Dryden gave him no chance. "Toward the end of 1964, you traced Goldine to the Tamarisk Lodge children's home. You had been trying to locate her mother, but she was dead. As it turned out, the child was a more exciting discovery, a member of the generation *after* the one you had studied. You visited the home, examined the little girl. Goldine won't remember this—"

"But I do!" Goldine said emphatically. "The matron held me while he handled my arms and legs. I cried."

Serafin admitted this with a nod, averting his eyes from Goldine's.

"When you saw the child you realized that here was a possibility of extending your Vienna research," Dryden went on. "If you were right, Goldine was destined to be taller than her mother and her grandmother. What an opportunity for you! There she was, an orphaned child. You could adopt her, take her into your home and monitor her growth, measuring her week by week, recording everything until she reached maturity. You would have a unique record of her development from the age of three. You would publish the results as a case history supporting your Vienna thesis. Correct?"

"Completely," said Goldine without turning to look at Dryden. "I was a guinea pig."

"That's untrue!" Serafin angrily protested. "After the adoption we genuinely tried to make your life as normal as any child's."

"Then, why didn't you send me to school like other kids?" Goldine simply asked.

The question hung in the air unanswered.

Dryden pressed on. "The tests you gave Goldine increasingly revealed that she was unusually strong for her age—'physically precocious,' I think you said yourself. And that was how the Olympic idea took root. What a boost it would give your research paper if Goldine won a gold medal! It wouldn't be the proof of your theories, because you don't convince scientists with isolated cases, but it would bring much-needed publicity to your ideas. By this time, editors were rejecting the papers you wrote. You had nothing new to say, so they weren't interested. I can see it must have depressed you profoundly."

"Who told you these things?" demanded Serafin.

"Does it matter?" said Dryden. "What obsessed you wasn't whether you were right: you were convinced you were. You had a compulsion to *prove* you were right, put the theory beyond dispute. But how? You had gone as far as you could in your thesis, and that was gathering dust. To answer your critics required something out of science fiction: a subject of average stature from the twenty-first century."

Goldine swung around to face Dryden. There was surprise in her expression. And fear. She was afraid of what he would say next. She looked pathetically vulnerable in the white bathrobe, fingering her neck, eyes opened very wide, brow fretted with anxiety.

He was moved.

He would have liked to take her aside, tell her gently, but she wouldn't have believed him. This had to be said in Serafin's presence.

He glanced briefly back, trying to give her courage. Then he returned to Serafin. "In the early sixties, there was an important development. You heard about HGH and the experiments to promote human growth. Using hormones extracted in autopsies, doctors treated children suffering from pituitary deficiencies, with spectacular results. The treatment was taken up at a number of centers. A unit was opened at your own Institute in Bakersfield. You suddenly saw that this could have an application to your research. With HGH, you could create what you had thought was a science-fiction fantasy. You were measuring Goldine's growth from week to week. You knew how tall she was likely to be as an adult. But with HGH it was possible to augment that. You could increase her height to the level you believed it would take three generations of evolution to attain. And you could prove beyond dispute that her frame could adjust to that level of increase."

Goldine stared white-faced at Serafin. "*Those* were the injections you gave me? All those were hormone injections?"

Melody said in a low voice, "Christ, I don't believe this!"

Serafin pushed aside the chair and went toward Goldine, putting out a hand to touch her shoulder. "My dear, put this way it sounds indefensible, but, believe me, I didn't go into this lightly. I learned everything I could about the treatment in the growth unit. I made the most intensive study of HGH and its effects."

"*That's* how I got to be as tall as I am?" said Gol-

321

dine, horror written on her features. "You planned for me to be six foot two?"

Serafin nodded. "I planned for you to be tall, yes, as tall as women will be a century from now."

A phrase came back to Dryden. Something Goldine had said on La Jolla Beach when she had told him about the cosmetic surgery she had undergone. *All I had was my six foot two.* Even that was denied her now.

"To prove your theory, huh? Like someone had to have the first smallpox vaccination, the first heart transplant? What do I get—a one-line credit in a medical encyclopedia?" Goldine continued speaking in a rush, coming to terms with what she had learned. "So you made me exercise, gave me physiotherapy as a kid to make me a perfect physical specimen—some kind of superwoman?"

"But you are!" said Serafin passionately. "You are Goldengirl. I'll tell you what you get. Glory, fame, more money than you can spend!"

"Who gets all that?" she demanded. "The kid you took out of Tamarisk Lodge? Is that who I am? Does the glory go to Dean Hofmann, or a bunch of hormones taken from corpses?"

"You were born a natural athlete," said Serafin as if he had not heard. "Your grandmother won a gold medal. Your father was on the U.S. Olympic team. The ability is inherited. The injections weren't given to make you a champion runner—they wouldn't do that. They made you taller, bigger, that's all. Through your running you are proving that your frame has adapted to the extra growth. It has no weakness. You are six foot two and a mesomorph and you can power your body faster than any woman alive. That's the triumph of my life's work, Goldine."

Dryden was no scientist, but he could see huge gaps in Serafin's rationale. The man had become so obsessed with his theory that he had abandoned scientific method for a kind of biological alchemy. It was so crackbrained that to take up points would lead no-where. He had to leave all that, try at least to get to the truth of what it had produced.

"It's a hollow triumph, Dr. Serafin, because you daren't publish now. Isn't it time you told Goldine why you put her in this place?"

She turned quickly, looking at Dryden with fright-ened eyes. "What does that mean?"

"It's for him to tell you," answered Dryden.

Serafin was shaking his head, but it was a gesture of submission, not defiance. "My dear, I would like to spare you this, but he leaves me no choice. If you are to hear it, then it is best I tell you myself. When I started giving you the hormone all those years ago, I was aware that there was a certain risk attached, a chance of damaging your health. I didn't know how high a risk it was. Later, I learned that it was proba-ble, if I persisted with the injections, that they would permanently damage the gland known as the pancreas. That, I must tell you, has happened. The reason why you have been unwell since the U.S. Trials is that you have diabetes. The stress of competing in the Trials brought it on, but the injections were really responsi-ble."

"No, Doc," said Goldine in a voice steady, but thick with emotion. "The injections weren't responsible. *You* were. I have this thing wrong with me and you knew it would happen. Now would you tell me if it's permanent?"

Serafin put a conciliatory hand toward Goldine, then let it fall limply as he met the contempt in her eyes. He turned his face away and nodded. "I gam-bled that it wouldn't happen so soon. I wanted you to get your gold medals first. Then, when it was diag-nosed, I would tell you why I did this. You would be compensated by your success in the Olympics. You would have the fame, the material benefits, as a con-solation, knowing I had provided you with the training, the conditioning, the backing that transformed you into Goldengirl."

"While the injections were transforming me into an incurable," said Goldine bitterly. "What did *you* stand to get out of it?"

"Not money," insisted Serafin. "Dryden can confirm that. The consortium was necessary to provide the facilities you needed, but for me the money wasn't important. I didn't trade your health for profit, Goldine. For a principle. To demonstrate a scientific truth."

Goldine suddenly started to laugh, a shrill peak of laughter verging on hysteria. She tossed back her head, showing her white teeth, and then rocked forward till her long hair cascaded over her shoulders. The others in the small bedroom watched with petrifying unease. "Oh, Christ," she said when she had recovered herself enough, "it's just incredible! Fifteen years creating your six-foot-two-inch scientific truth, and what happens? Four weeks before the big demonstration it goes down with diabetes. The bones are great, the bodywork is okay, but the inside's seized up. You pathetic little man! You proved your theory, but nobody will know. There isn't a medical institute in the world that would publish it, knowing how it left me. You just have the bills to pick up, and the job of telling the consortium what happened to their multimillion-dollar ripoff."

She was close to tears, but her words were shaped in the white heat of her new knowledge. They were razor-edged.

Serafin stood in silence, spastically stretching and clenching his fingers, suffering, Dryden suspected, more from the destruction of his dream than shame at what he had inflicted on Goldine.

Of those present, Dryden had least reason to feel emotionally involved. He had engineered this confrontation, anticipated what Serafin would say.

But he had not anticipated Goldine's reaction.

He had watched her and listened in genuine surprise turning to admiration. For it took courage to
speak like that to Serafin, her virtual slavemaster for
fifteen years. Maybe it was an isolated outburst of
defiance, but it showed she was no automaton. Her
own personality had survived and was struggling to
be free.

And Dryden cared.

There would be no Goldengirl. No triumph at the
Olympics. Nothing in it for Dryden Merchandising. But
stumbling toward him out of this wreckage was the girl
who had been Dean Hofmann.

Yes, he cared passionately.

Jack Dryden in love? Crazy. It couldn't happen.

He approached and put a hand gently on her arm.
This was not the time to analyze his feelings. She
needed to know he was going to help. "We must
get you out of here," he told her. "Out of Cleveland.
I'll find you a good doctor, a specialist, in New York."

She stared at him in surprise and frowned. "I figured now that I'm out of the Olympics . . ."

". . . you need help more than ever," said Dryden.
"I take it, after what you said, that you want to get as
far away from this skunk as you can. Okay, I have
an office in New York. I can get you into a clinic with
the best medical treatment."

"You'll do that for *me?*" She caught her breath in
disbelief. "I don't understand."

"But you'll come?" said Dryden. "You trust me?"

Her eyes moistened. She was shaping to reply when
Serafin interrupted.

"You think you can take her away from me, Dryden?
You think she'll go with you?" His voice was pitched
manically high. "It's a delusion. Goldengirl is mine.
I made her what she is. You can't alter that."

"He's off his rocker," said Melody. "Ignore him."

Goldine wasn't letting it pass. "What do you mean
by that? You figure you have a claim on me, like I'm
some possession?" She stood up and advanced on Ser-

afin with such menace that he put up an arm to shield his face. "Understand this, Doc. I despise you. I've hated you for years. The only reason I never walked out of your life before is that I wanted to collect those medals. Hell, I earned them. They were going to make some sense out of the mess my life has been up to now. Yes, you're right—you made me what I am. And by God I mean to change it."

"You won't," said Serafin with a quick uncanny laugh. "You're Goldengirl."

"Let's get out of here," Melody appealed to Dryden.

"There's no Goldengirl any more," Goldine told Serafin, stressing each word with categorical force. "You created her and you destroyed her. All that's left is bitterness and this wreck of a body I have to drag around. I guess I'll make out, but I don't ever want to see you or hear from you again." She turned away from him and told Dryden, "I'll need to get dressed."

"We'll wait downstairs."

"Before you go, there's something you may wish to know. All of you." Serafin spoke more slowly, with an effort to regenerate authority. "You make the mistake of assuming Goldine's diabetes is incapacitating. There are degrees of this condition, and hers is actually quite mild—so mild, in fact, that I doubt if it would have been diagnosed if she had not made heavy demands on her body as an athlete."

"Look, this doesn't help," Dryden said. "Salve your conscience any way you want. We don't wish to hear it."

"But you will," said Serafin more urgently. "Despise me if you like, but respect my knowledge of medicine. I brought Goldine here to check the extent of the diabetes and bring it under control with insulin."

"What are you trying to say?" asked Goldine.

"The injections I've been giving you supply the insulin your body requires, but no longer produces in sufficient quantity. Already you have regained most of the weight you lost. With regular insulin and dieting you can lead a normal life." Serafin took a step toward her. "Do you see what this means? There is nothing to stop you competing in the Olympics. I've stabilized the insulin requirement. We'll have to make adjustments to allow for the blood sugar you burn up in exercise, but it can be done."

"You're saying I have diabetes, but I can still run in the Olympics?" said Goldine, floundering through the medical jargon.

"Why not? It's nothing unusual for diabetics to reach the top in sports. There are international tennis players, swimmers—"

"Just what are you up to?" Dryden angrily broke in. "Goldine has accepted it's all over. God knows she has problems enough without you poisoning her mind with false hopes."

"Wait, Jack," said Goldine in a calm voice. "I must hear this out. He can't hurt me any more."

Dryden looked into her eyes and understood. He had thought she was free, but she was not. The idea of being Goldengirl still possessed her. That was what Serafin had meant.

"You must go to Moscow," Serafin was saying. "You won your place on the team. It's your right."

"What about her health?" demanded Dryden, refusing to let go. "You say the diabetes is mild. If competing in Eugene set this thing off, couldn't the Olympics make it worse?"

"That doesn't follow at all," Serafin answered. "I have it under control now. I will monitor her blood-sugar level from race to race."

Dryden shook his head. "The Russians will scream drugs the first time you take a blood sample."

"Nobody would ban a diabetic athlete from the Olympics," Serafin stated emphatically. "Insulin isn't on the list of prohibited drugs. It simply allows a diabetic to function normally. It gives them no unfair advantage. When Goldine competed in the finals at Eugene she was suffering from an insulin deficiency.

With an injection she might have beaten world records."

"That was why the four hundred was so tough?" said Goldine, the excitement rising in her voice. "It was the diabetes that beat me?" She wheeled round toward Dryden, eyes shining. "You see—I could have won that race."

"Of course you could!" crowed Serafin. "You exhibited your symptoms early in the Trials. Klugman reported them. But undue tiredness and a dry throat can result from a dozen different causes. Even if I had recognized the condition at once, it is doubtful if I could have helped you through the remaining races. It takes time to check the insulin requirement. It's a very fine balance that varies from one individual to another. Yours is stabilized now, but it's taken nearly two weeks."

"You mean I could get back to training at once?" asked Goldine.

Dryden put his hand on her arm. "I know how much this means to you, but it isn't wise. Even if you limit yourself to one event in Moscow, what use will it be if you go out in Round One? Isn't it better to be remembered as a winner than someone who failed in the Olympics?"

"Why should she fail?" Serafin hotly demanded. "She is the finest woman athlete in the world."

"How much training has she missed?" said Dryden. "Twelve, fourteen days? No Olympic athlete can afford to lay up like that before the Games."

"Never mind!" Goldine cut in. "You can bet he'll think of someone who did and won a gold medal. He has a story for every situation you could name. Before we go into that, has it occurred to any of you that I might decide to make up my own mind about running?" She paused challengingly. "Obviously not. You're not accustomed to Goldengirl having ideas of her own. She isn't programed to think. You'd better understand, all of you, that as of now, that's changing.

These last two weeks have taught me a lot, about my-self, and the people around me. What you just told me underscores my principal conclusion—that it's crazy letting any of you take charge of my life. Thanks, I'll pick up the bits and see what I can do with them myself."

Dryden had lost. What Goldine was talking about wasn't freedom. That had beckoned briefly and gone. Goldengirl had taken possession again.

"But you will run," said Serafin, sensing what Dryden had. "You can't pass up the chance now you know it's possible. You will do it, you know. You're going for gold."

If Serafin was expecting a good response, he didn't get it. Goldine ran her eyes over him and said with contempt, "Would you get out of my sight? Don't you understand it's all over for you, whatever I do? I don't need you any more. Like Jack said, there are other doctors."

"But you'll run," Serafin persisted with fanatical certitude, "and you'll prove that you can beat the world. I'll publish your case history. Oh no, Golden-girl, it's not all over for me! It's the summit of my professional career. The public will never hear about the diabetes. Shall I tell you why? Because it would tarnish your commercial image. Ask Dryden." He held up his hand. "All right, I'll go, I'll even keep out of your sight if that's what you want. But you won't totally shut me out. You're still my adopted daughter, and the police and press believe you were kidnaped on the way to your U.S. team medical. I don't think you realize how much media interest there is in this story." He smiled and lowered his voice, "What would you like me to tell them?"

She breathed the one word, "Bastard!" and looked for help from Dryden.

He knew he must give it. Her bid for self-determination had not lasted long.

Next morning, Sunday, August 3, the press were called to a mid-day conference at the Metropolitan Hotel, Cleveland Heights, where Serafin read the following statement:

"I am pleased to announce that my daughter Goldine, who has been missing since Wednesday, was this morning reunited with me. She is physically unharmed but suffering from shock and nervous exhaustion. She is at present under sedation, and will not be making any formal statement to the press. Remembering that the U.S. Olympic team leaves for Moscow three days from now, I ask for your forbearance in giving Goldine the chance to recover from her ordeal. I am not able to state at this stage whether she will be fit enough to travel with the team or, indeed, to compete at all.

"The circumstances of her release from captivity were as follows. Yesterday morning, a business associate of mine in Los Angeles received a telephone call from a spokesman for Goldine's abductors, demanding a ransom in dollar bills. A condition was stipulated that the news of the ransom demand should not be communicated to me or the police until the transaction was made. So, unknown to me, my associate raised the money with the help of a consortium of business colleagues interested in America's representation in the Olympic Games. I have no knowledge of the amount of the ransom, but I should like publicly to express my appreciation of their generosity.

"Goldine was released at six o'clock this morning on Shore Boulevard, East Cleveland, and phoned me at once. When I picked her up, she was extremely tired and in a state of shock. She was unable to say much about her kidnapers, as she had been kept blindfolded or under sedation throughout the four days and nights of her abduction. Otherwise, she appears to have been treated well. I informed the police of Goldine's safe return, and she has made a statement to them. She is now resting at an address I shall not disclose, for reasons already stated. As soon as a decision is reached about her participation in the Olympic Games, I shall be in touch with the U.S. Olympic Committee, and a further statement will be issued to the press."

"Could we have the name of the guy in Los Angeles?" asked a reporter.

"And the others?" added a second.

"What were the arrangements for the pickup?"

"Gentlemen, I have made my statement," said Serafin. "There is nothing I can usefully add. These last few days have been something of a strain for me, so I must ask you to bear with me when I insist on leaving it at that."

Whatever Serafin insisted, the press had a job to do. In the next three hours, Cleveland's transient accommodations—from plush hotels on Euclid Avenue to seedy bed-sitting-rooms downtown—were thoroughly checked for a new arrival. Hospitals, sanitariums and nursing homes were visited. Caradock Lodge, which some bystander had seen Serafin leaving the day before, came in for special attention, but Nurse Piper insisted nobody was staying there, and finally got rid of reporters by allowing them to make their own examination of the rooms. Jefferson College, too, was combed. It was known Goldine had stayed there prior to the kidnaping—a local paper had established that on Thursday—and that Serafin, Klugman, a redheaded secretary, and an unidentified Chinese had been in the party, but none of them could now be traced. By late afternoon, newsmen were talking of a professional coverup. It was thought the police might have taken a hand, but they denied it, seeming put out about the whole affair.

In fact, Goldine and Klugman had left Cleveland in a privately chartered helicopter an hour before the press conference began. In a little over two hours they landed in New York City, where they were met by a senior executive of the Dryden organization and driven to his home. That afternoon, while Cleveland was being scoured, Goldine was walking an Afghan hound in Central Park.

Dryden, with Melody in tow, took the scheduled flight from Cleveland Hopkins Airport at 2:10 P.M. He had masterminded the entire operation. This kind of exercise he performed automatically, laying on a press conference, fixing flight schedules, arranging accommodations. The others had seen the sense of co-operating when he had outlined the plan last evening in Jefferson College. Goldine, convinced she had achieved independence of action, and determined to preserve it, coolly consented to the arrangements so long as they committed her to nothing more than a flight to New York. Serafin, no less convinced that she would run in Moscow, had agreed to go through with the press conference as the best way of resolving the complications of the "kidnap" story. Dryden had written the statement and waited to hear that Serafin read it and didn't get drawn into questions. Nothing had gone wrong: Serafin was still fanatically interested in the success of Project Goldengirl.

Secure in the plane, Dryden might have been excused for congratulating himself on a smooth operation. In reality, he felt distinctly uneasy. Till yesterday, he had been scrupulous in keeping his participation in the project on a professional basis, avoiding any involvement in what happened to Goldine prior to the Olympics. There were huge risks even in that, but if things got hot before the Games, he had reckoned on pulling out without irreparable damage to the agency's reputation.

Not now. He was caught up in it with the rest of them. He had conspired to issue a false statement to the police and—potentially more damaging—he had hoodwinked the press. The alternative had been the inevitable collapse of the project. Nothing would have saved it if newsmen had talked to Goldine or Serafin on Saturday.

Then, why hadn't he washed his hands of it as he

had always intended if things went wrong? He could have walked out of Caradock Lodge, taken the first plane to New York and started calling his business contacts in Los Angeles to tell them the deal was off. Instead, he had organized this salvage operation. Why?

It was because he cared deeply now what happened to Goldine. He couldn't abandon her.

There had been a moment in that grim showdown with Serafin in Caradock Lodge when Goldine had believed the diabetes had put an end to her brief career as a track star. Ended everything her upbringing had prepared her for. As her world collapsed, he had offered to take her to New York and asked her to trust him and she had answered with her eyes. Nothing of significance had been said. There had just been this spark of understanding that passed between them, but it meant more than anything they had said to each other before, in the Sierras, on La Jolla Beach or in Eugene.

Then Serafin had let slip the shattering possibility that Goldine might, after all, compete, and the moment had gone. She was going for gold. The impulse was too powerful to resist. She had found the strength to reject Serafin, but she couldn't reject the idea he had nurtured in her. She had convinced herself she was free to decide her own future, but she had no choice at all. It was settled.

"Thinking about her, huh?" said Melody.

He nodded.

"I guessed it," said Melody. "Do you figure she'll win in Moscow?"

"She has to get there first."

Melody smiled. "Listen, I know Goldengirl, lover boy, and I know what three gold gongs mean to her. She'll be on that plane for Moscow, take it from me."

"Even if she decides to go, she'll have to get medical backing," said Dryden. "Can you see the Olympic Committee letting her compete so soon after the onset of diabetes?"

"They don't have to know," said Melody casually. "She could tell them she's had it for years."

He looked out the window.

Next morning in the office he listened to phone messages the machine had logged over the weekend. Before running out of tape, it had taken calls from Adidas, Puma, Pepsi-Cola, Chrysler, TWA and a dozen others anxious to know if the kidnaping meant the end of Goldine's Olympic ambitions. He put Melody on to answering them with a standard message that Mr. Dryden was unable to add anything yet to the statement issued by Dr. Serafin on the weekend, but was energetically pursuing the matter.

There had also been calls from Valenti and Sternberg. He rang them personally. Valenti was convinced the whole thing was a publicity stunt—"Got to hand it to you—great idea—wish I'd thought of it myself." Sternberg wanted to know who had put up the ransom, because if they expected a cut of the profits, they could go stuff themselves.

Around midmorning, a call came in from Serafin. He had been contacted by the secretary of the U.S. Olympic Committee, demanding to know whether Goldine still planned to compete. They had reserves standing by, but the girls were entitled to more than a day's notice to get through the formalities for the flight on Wednesday.

"What did you tell him?" asked Dryden.

Serafin answered in the same flat tone he had used to make the press statement. "I admitted I was not certain where Goldine was, but I would see that the message reached her. He told me they are fixing a medical for nine o'clock Tuesday morning. If Goldine doesn't report, she is off the team."

"I'll tell her. It's her decision alone."

"She'll be there," said Serafin positively. "By the way, I'm flying back to Los Angeles with Lee this afternoon. Goldine left me in no doubt that my presence is no longer congenial, and I think the same would go for Lee. She appears to find you a more sympathetic mentor."

"That's not my function, Dr. Serafin."

"Is it unwelcome?" said Serafin. "Mr. Dryden, I believe in facing facts. Goldine has no further use for me. For all practical purposes, you are now in charge of the project. Does that alarm you? Really, it is nothing. A sinecure. The important decisions have been taken. She will compete, and she will win. I doubt whether I shall go to Moscow at all. I can see it all on television in my own home. I have so much work to do, updating my case study."

When Dryden put down the phone he was bothered. It was unlike Serafin to bow out now, when everything was building to a climax. True, he had taken a tongue-lashing from Goldine, but he wasn't the type to let that influence him. He had been at the center of this scheme from the start, dominating it with an obsessiveness bordering on monomania. Just to retire from the scene at this stage didn't make sense. Either he knew something, or he was up to no good.

That was not all Dryden had to worry about. A few minutes after he had put down the phone, a young man walked into his office. They had phoned from downstairs to say he was from NBC-TV. People in Dryden's business didn't turn away callers from the media.

His name was Esselstyn. He was probably not thirty, short, tanned, with the cool of a croupier behind a wide smile. A sharp dresser, with fawn trousers, brown velvet jacket, pale-yellow shirt and green silk scarf fixed with a gold ring.

"Great to meet you," he told Dryden. "I'm in sports, on the production side. You remember *The Superstars?* Met several of your clients. Jim Hansenburg. Dick Armitage—or could that have been in *The American Sportsman?* Anyway, they told me you're a fabulous guy. When I heard our research people had turned up your name I homed in. Volunteered to come up here myself and meet you."

"Research people?" repeated Dryden. "What exactly is this about, Mr. Esselstyn?"

"Right to the point, huh? I heard you were a tough cookie, Jack. I'm Wayne, incidentally. Well, I'll come clean. We're putting together a TV special on this kid who made the headlines yesterday. The Cleveland kidnap girl. Goldine Serafin. You with me?"

Dryden gave him a nod that committed him to nothing.

"One hell of a newsmaker, that chick," Esselstyn went on. "Unknown blonde beats top-class track stars in San Diego, goes to the U.S. Olympic Tryout and rewrites the record book. Then this kidnaping. If I was a PR guy, I couldn't script it better. Next thing, Moscow—yeah, I know it's shaping up as a cliffhanger, but she'll get there. And whatever she does out there, it's news. It can't miss. So NBC Sports aims to put out a major feature on the kid when she makes it big in Moscow. It's come my way."

"Nice for you," said Dryden, "but I don't see—"

Esselstyn cut him short with a wagging finger. "Oh no, don't let's prevaricate, Jack. We were going to come clean, remember? I happen to know that you can put us wise to plenty in the Goldine Serafin story. Don't panic, I'm not asking you to go on film. We'll keep it off the record. I want you to know that this is planned as a tribute to Goldine. We want to touch the emotions. It's a great story. I just want to get it right, you follow me? Now, my people have been digging, as I told you. We happen to know half the stuff the press have printed on Goldine is hogwash. Crap. Take the superjogger bit. You know, the story that she first discovered she could run when her pop sent her jogging around the block. Palpably untrue. We've spoken to a guy in Bakersfield who saw her working out on the college track two years ago. No mistake. He identified her old man. Goldine Serafin may be an overnight sensation, but she's no novice to track."

"Does that matter?" said Dryden indifferently.

The finger wagged again. "Ah, but hear this. That same guy in Bakersfield has a good memory for faces. Someone else was at the track watching Goldine's workout, someone this guy had seen on *Wide World of Sports*. A mutual acquaintance, Jack. U.S. tennis champ Dick Armitage. Now, there's a turnup. I never knew Dick was a track fan. Candidly, I would have thought he'd never seen a track in his life from the way he bucked those hurdles on *Superstars*. Still, he seemed to take an interest in young Goldine. We thought he had eyes for the chick at first. That would be some scoop—revealing that Dick is the man in her life. Too bad he knocks around with that broad in the Martini ads. There had to be some other tie-in. So we dug deeper. Learned Dick was in Eugene for the Trials last month. Keeping up his interest apparently. Suite at the Jacaranda. We took a look at the guest list and found your name. Dick's agent. Now, what is a merchandising agent doing at an amateur track meet?"

"Watching the sport," said Dryden flatly. He was torn between ending this interview and learning how much Esselstyn knew.

"Yeah." Esselstyn paraded his neat line of teeth. "But let's not kid ourselves. You guys don't wait for sport stars to hit the jackpot before you move in. Okay, the Olympics are for amateurs and I'm not aiming to get Goldine banned. That would be counterproductive. So how about leveling with me? You have a stake in this girl—am I right?"

"Just because I watched the Trials—"

"You're saying there's nothing on paper? I'm prepared to believe that," said Esselstyn.

"I'm saying you're wasting your time and mine," said Dryden. "If you think you can link Dryden Merchandising with this girl on the basis of a track meet I attended with one of my own clients, you're in the wrong business, Mr. Esselstyn. You should be in Disneyland, not NBC-TV."

"You have no professional interest in Goldine Serafin?"

"Mine is a large and successful organization," said Dryden. "I don't spend agency time chasing after amateur girl athletes."

Esselstyn's eyebrows pricked up. *"Personal* time, then?"

Dryden stood up. "This is leading nowhere."

"You think so? You have no interest in Goldine? Maybe I should unscramble your memory, Jack. You were in Cleveland at Serafin's press conference after the kidnap. Saw you there myself. Going to tell me the whole thing wasn't a PR stunt? Pull the other one, Jack. I'll believe anything."

When he had finally prized Esselstyn out of the office, Dryden called NBC-TV. As he suspected, the man wasn't employed by them. He was a free-lance, specializing in hatchet jobs on people in sports. It was lucrative work; he had an extensive organization and the TV networks used a lot of his material. Dryden had told him nothing, but he wasn't the sort to give up.

Within minutes, a call was put through from Goldine.

"I need help."

It must have cost her something in pride to admit that.

"What's the problem?"

"The press. They found me. I went training with Pete on the New York Athletic Club track early this morning. Someone must have spotted me and tipped off the papers. First thing I knew, I was mobbed. Cameramen, questions, everything. I don't know what to say to them. It's out of control. Pete's no use. He just bawls at them, and they won't go away."

"Where are you now?"

"In the club building on Central Park South. We're under virtual siege here."

"You expect me to handle this?"

"Who else can I ask? What can I say to them?"

His pulse quickened. This was the crunch. His professional judgment told him it was crazy to get involved. Serafin and Lee had dropped out. Sharks like Esselstyn were moving in.

"I thought you were taking charge of your own life now," he stalled.

"Jack, give me a break, for Christ's sake. I'm scared. Do I have to plead with you?"

She had said something like that on La Jolla Beach, and he had responded. This time his entire career was on the line.

"Think about it," he flatly told her. "If I show up, they'll want to know who I am. They might recognize me, put two and two together. Agents aren't generally tied in with amateur athletes."

The followup was swift and savage. In the abrasive voice she had used with Serafin, she said, "Okay. If you don't come, I'll give them a story. All those fat contracts you have ready for signature. The complete rundown, every lousy company. I'll get Dryden Merchandising blacklisted all over America. Watch me." The phone clicked.

He held the purring receiver, staring at it, stunned by the change in Goldine, hating what this was doing to her, to him. He tried to figure a way out. There wasn't one. He couldn't ignore the threat. Goldine's story would destroy the agency overnight. It would be blown up into a major scandal: secret deals with big business, a pretty girl exploited for profit, the Olympic rules violated.

Melody was in the office, on the other phone. His eyes met hers. "Call the New York Athletic Club. Tell Goldine I'm on the way over. And don't look so bloody smug."

On the short drive through Manhattan, he let the full implications sink in. Goldine would realize soon—if she hadn't already—that she needed someone to take over from Serafin. The talk of running her own life had hit its first snag, and he was the remedy. It was no comedown for her: she was firmly in control. He was bound to co-operate, knowing she could set a match to his career anytime she liked.

So how would he handle this? Was it worth one more try to persuade her to drop the whole idea of Moscow? If he told her how he felt about her, made it personal—Christ, it *was*—would that achieve a break-through? He knew it wouldn't. She was groomed, conditioned, programed for one thing only. She was going for gold and needed his help. They both knew that.

He wouldn't be blackmailed into helping her. Damn it, she was only doing this in desperation. He must show her their interests were identical. It would hurt, but he had to be professional about this, think of her as Goldengirl, not Goldine. When she started picking up medals, her interest would be vested in the agency. No more blackmailing.

Goldine, a threat: Goldengirl, a client.

He relaxed. He knew what he had to do.

Pressmen thronged the entrance of the stately NYAC building at the corner of Seventh Avenue on Central Park South. Klugman barred the door like a Kremlin guard. "Upstairs, first left," he muttered to Dryden as he let him through, ignoring the protests and the flashing cameras.

Goldine stood putting on lipstick in a small committee room, using a sepia photo of a baseball team as a mirror. She was in the black tracksuit, her hair tied with a white velvet ribbon. When she turned to face him, he noticed she was also wearing eyeshadow.

"You came then," she said sarcastically, "the genuine English gentleman. Did you tell the newsmen to get the hell out of here?"

"You know very well they won't go without talking to you."

She turned away and pursed her lips at the picture. "So what can I say?"

"You can answer their questions. They'll want to know about the kidnaping. Tell them what you told the police, that you must have been doped, so you don't remember much. Say it didn't seem like four days. You're grateful to the people who paid the ransom, but you don't know who they are. Okay so far?"

She nodded.

"Then, naturally, they'll want to know if you're fit to go to Moscow."

Turning back to face him, she asked, "What do you suggest I say?"

He frowned in frank disbelief. "Haven't you made up your mind?"

"Not yet," she answered off-handedly, inspecting her fingernails. They were lacquered.

"It's time you did. The U.S. Olympic Committee have set a deadline. If you're going, you have to report for a medical at nine tomorrow."

"So?"

He gave an exasperated sigh. "Christ, Goldine, do you want to run, or not? You got through some training this morning. Is the speed still there?"

"It appears so."

He breathed more evenly. "Well?"

"This medical," said Goldine. "It's pretty comprehensive, I guess. I'd have to tell them about the diabetes."

Dryden nodded. "It's confidential between you and the doctors. No reason why the press should hear about it."

"You're missing the point," said Goldine. "What will those doctors make of it when I tell them I came down with this thing during the Trials? I'll be sidelined."

"That's putting it at its worst," said Dryden. "Frankly, I don't think that's likely. You can tell them you're stabilized on insulin and training normally. You

341

might need extra support standing by in Moscow, but if they want you to bring home the medals, that's not too much to fix. Have you seen the New York *Times*? You're America's answer to Ursula Krüll. This is shaping up as an East-West contest. There's political prestige in it. People in high places have an interest in giving you your chance. You say the running is still there. Even if they decide three events is too much, they should agree to let you try the one hundred meters. If that goes well, why not the two hundred? Under medical supervision—"

"Don't give me that crap!" she broke in angrily. "I'm not going to Moscow to try one event and see how I feel. If I settled for two sprint titles, where would that leave me? At the end of a list so long it's boring to recite. No, I'm Goldengirl, or I'm nobody." She started toward the door, her face flame-red.

He gripped her arm. "Hold on. Where are you going?"

She glanced down at his hand. "To tell the press I've decided to pull out, if you'll let go my arm." She flicked away a tear with her free hand.

He continued to hold her, his emotions churned up again. Why was she doing this? In effect, she was asking him to make the decision. She wanted it to come from him.

He let his hand slip down her arm till their fingers met. For a moment she gripped him tightly like a threatened child, then let go.

He suddenly knew she wasn't bluffing. She really meant to quit unless he stopped her. It was up to him.

He could stop the nightmare Serafin had started. Simply let her go and she was free. The papers would splash the story, write the valediction, and it was over. She could begin to pick up the threads of the life she had been plucked from fifteen years before. Dean Hofmann. The girl he loved.

But was it possible to extricate the girl from the nightmare? Faced with it, he knew it was not. You couldn't wipe away fifteen years of dedication to one idea. There would always be a sense of deprivation. Dean Hofmann had ceased to exist. There was Goldine, and for her sake there had to be Goldengirl.

She was already at the door when he said, "Ursula Krüll can sleep easy, then."

Over her shoulder, she asked, "What's that supposed to mean?"

"She'll be the golden girl of Moscow now. You were the only threat. Your clash with her was tipped as the centerpiece of the Games."

"Too bad," said Goldine without interest.

But she didn't open the door. She was waiting to hear more.

"What about you?" he asked without challenging the assumption that the decision was made. "Ursula is Goldengirl, so where does that leave you?"

"Didn't I just tell you?" she said, stung into a response. "If I'm not Goldengirl, I'm nothing. Nobody. Take a look at me. What you see is all phony—face, hair, figure, stature, even my name. I have no family, home, friends, job, no high school grades even."

"Two U.S. records," put in Dryden.

"Big deal. What use are those to an employer?" She was crying now, mainly in anger. "No, I don't know where I go from here. They got it right when they called me the mystery blonde. I'm a mystery to myself." She dabbed at the tears with a tissue. "What am I doing, leading off like this? I guess my eyes are a mess now."

"Not that I can see," said Dryden. He smiled. "I like them made up. New, isn't it? Is that for the photographers?"

She snuffled through a half-smile. "First thing I bought in New York. My own contribution to Goldengirl's image. I read a magazine feature on Ursula Krüll. She never wears make-up. Say, could that be why photographers make so much of her rear view?"

They exchanged smiles, conspiring to break the tension.

"I understand she has a highly provocative walk," said Dryden. "If she'd walk into the West, she could make a fortune modeling Levi's."

"What will *she* get out of winning?"

"Not so much as you could, but then it's commonplace for East German women to do well in sports. Who was that swimmer in Montreal? Kornelia Ender. She won a stack of medals. I believe it set her up nicely. The state looks after its champions. Still, it damned well should. Ursula Krüll has been earmarked for gold medals since she was twelve. Believe me, she'll deserve her success."

Goldine took the bait. "Deserves it? When she's second-best?"

"No," said Dryden matter-of-factly. "Best. The Olympic champion is the best. That's indisputable."

She reddened. "I could have run Krüll off her goddamned legs!"

"I'm sure," said Dryden, "but forget it. There's nothing so boring as an athlete's hard-luck story. Think of Klugman—that Achilles tendon."

"It isn't like that," protested Goldine passionately. "I know I could beat Krüll. Those medals are mine by rights."

"It's time to let go, Goldine," he insisted, confident now that she wouldn't.

"If there was some way to convince the doctors . . ." she said.

He made it sound as if the idea dawned that second, instead of an hour before, when Melody had casually put it to him. "How about telling them you were diabetic before the Trials began? You qualified for three events, so they can't stop you running the same three in Moscow."

She caught her breath, attracted, but hesitant. "It wouldn't be true, but—"

"There's nothing to it," said Dryden. "They *want* you

to pass the medical, remember that. If those doctors kicked up, the whole of America would be down on them. It isn't as if you're cheating anyone out of a place on the team. You won the right to represent your country. How could they object if you tell them you're a long-term diabetic? That would be blatant discrimination. The media would crucify them."

"Jack, you're right!" She closed her eyes and pressed her hands to her face, resurrecting her dream.

Each of the New York papers carried the same front-page picture next morning: Goldine in close-up, radiantly smiling. One headline consisted simply of the single word "SET."

[20]

DRYDEN was not in the Lenin Stadium, Moscow, on Saturday, August 9, 1980, when the Twenty-second Olympiad of the modern era was ushered in, watched by 103,000 people. Nor was he one of the two billion TV audience. This was not from contempt of the marching athletes, flags, pigeons, flame and oath that comprise the opening ceremony; who was he to knock this supreme sales vehicle as it was rolled out? Pressure of work was his reason, pressure that would keep him in New York till the eve of the one hundred meters Final on August 16. Ever since the kidnap story had broken, phenomenal interest had been generated in Goldine. The news that she was definitely going for three golds, despite almost a week's loss of training, was seized on by editors as front-page material. Rumors of records broken in training runs watched only by Pete Klugman (who was to join the U.S. team as a supernumerary coach) and bodyguards kept things bubbling right up to the team's departure on August 6. By then, with the name Goldine intelligible as a headline across America, and her picture splashed with each report, New York was no place for her to be. Dryden downed a double scotch as he watched the Boeing 747 Olympic Special take off from Kennedy Airport.

The next week was the busiest in his experience, but the potential revenue in endorsements soared beyond the target he had privately set. The take-up was so promising he steadily raised the asking price, and still they couldn't wait to shake on it. The sportswear deal alone was finalized at a million-dollar guarantee, with a built-in percentage bonus. The West German managing director, who had flown to New York to clinch it, afterward admitted it was the biggest endorsement contract he had ever negotiated, but the personal satisfaction he would get if Ursula Krüll took a beating was worth every Deutschmark. Cosmetics, electronic stopwatches and gold jewelry joined the list: the only problem was dissuading manufacturers from sending Goldine presentation boxes of their products, care of the Olympic Village. The most unaccountable thing to Dryden was that people now assumed the triple was not merely achievable, but in prospect. The kidnap publicity and rumors of a million-dollar ransom had created a legend that could only end as fairy tales do.

The first five days of the Olympic program were taken up with basketball, cycling, gymnastics, swimming and weightlifting, but it is fair to say they were generally regarded as appetizers for the main course of track and field, starting August 14. There was more interest in the gossip percolating from the Olympic Village than the activity in the Luzhniki Sports Palace. The *Herald Tribune* ran a story that after watching an impressive workout by Goldine, East German officials were considering adding the 400 meters to Ursula Krüll's program, because the girls already nominated were unlikely to match the U.S. *Wundermädchen*. Krüll, the article reported, had rarely run 400 meters, but earlier in the year had dipped under fifty seconds in a relay event, and was eager to challenge Goldine over any distance. Her form suggested it would take world records to beat her over the shorter sprint distances. "I shall do what is necessary in my principal events," Krüll was reported as saying, "and if the team manager decides I would strengthen the four hundred-meter squad, that's fine. The main thing is that East German girls should take the medals. I'm not seeking personal acclaim." Dryden pictured the hip swivel as she walked away.

The good news from Moscow that week was that a U.S. doctor had been appointed specially to monitor Goldine's physical state during her five days of competition. The reason officially given was that no girl had attempted the "triple" before, and Goldine was blazing a trail. Pulse-readings, heartbeat, blood count taken regularly through the program would provide a physiological profile certain to assist physicians in advising girls whether to emulate this formidable schedule. Not a hint of the diabetes was leaked. From the pictures appearing daily in the press, Goldine had put back the weight she had lost, and recovered her zest for running.

Dryden, by contrast, showed the strain of a week he wouldn't care to repeat when he and Melody checked in at Kennedy for Pan Am's 0810 Moscow flight on August 15. Moscow time is eight hours ahead of New York, so the final edition of the New York *Times* they bought before embarking carried the first news of the 100-meters heats. "GOLDINE QUALIFIES" ran the headline to the AP Report:

MOSCOW, Aug. 15——(AP) Goldine Serafin, victim of the recent kidnap drama in Cleveland, Ohio, reached the Quarter-Final of the Olympic 100 meters by finishing second in her First Round heat in Moscow this morning. The winner, Carol Estrada (Cuba), clocked 11.26 secs, to the U.S. girl's 11.34. Goldine was not extended in qualifying, but her East German rival, Ursula Krüll, showed outstanding form by taking Heat Three in 10.95 secs, a new Olympic Record. The other U.S. girls, Shelley Wilson and Mary-Lou Devine, came through safely, winning their heats in 11.21 and 11.36 secs respectively.

Higher up the page was an article comparing Moscow's staging of the Games with Nazi Germany's propaganda exercise in 1936. If the intention was similar, the techniques of persuasion had altered in forty-four years. Mass demonstrations, salutes and military uniforms were out; the propagandizing was more subtle. These had been billed in the West as the "Security Olympics"; in fact, there were fewer restrictions on movement than there had been in Montreal four years before. The emphasis in Moscow was heavily on cost efficiency. Eight billion dollars had been spent by the eleven-man Presidium, but buildings were designed for adaptation: the five twelve-story blocks of the Olympic Village, accommodating twelve thousand athletes and officials, would become a housing estate; the Press Center was to be taken over as headquarters of the Novosti Press Agency; and the Olympic Committee Offices would become the new base of the Soviet Journalists' Union. These would be the last grand-scale Games—the IOC were determined drastically to reduce the number of sports by 1984—and the Russians had provided an organization equal to the logistics of staging the greatest sports occasion ever. The opening ceremony had set new standards in precision; as the *Times* man commented, "it was the May Day Parade without the missiles—unless I nodded off when they went past."

Dryden himself dozed through most of the nine-hour trip, and Melody, who had surprised him with her diligence and efficiency all week, seemed content to catnap between Camparis. She had fixed the flight and obtained a hotel reservation from Intourist, no slight achievement. It meant she would be pretty constantly in his company—he hadn't inquired too closely into the details of the booking—but as she was one of the select group who knew the truth about Goldine's condition, it would be perilous to neglect her.

They touched down at Cheremetyevo Airport soon after midnight, Moscow time. As soon as they were through the formalities in the new Olympic terminal, Dryden picked up a copy of *Izvestia,* hopeful of deciphering some news of the Quarter-Finals, and learned that you just can't skim through a Russian newspaper.

They saw little of Moscow but pinpoints of light as the taxi skirted the western edge of the city on the Circular Motorway, but when they joined Mozhaiskoye Highway, Melody told Dryden they would soon see the River Moskva on their left. "Now we're in Kutozovsky Prospect," she confidently announced. "There's the river, and this is our hotel coming up. Not that; the skyscraper. The Hotel Ukraina." It was immense, twenty-nine stories high, and built in the gingerbread style known locally as Stalin Gothic. Floodlights played on the massive main tower. It wasn't Dryden's idea of a lovenest.

Everything was very proper when they checked in at the Service Bureau. They were greeted in English and politely asked to produce their passports. The clerk herself transcribed their names into the register, they signed and learned they would occupy Rooms 811 and 812. Melody's lips parted in a slight smile, which the girl returned. Two stone-faced porters approached and carried their suitcases to an elevator. The ascent to the eighth floor took all of three minutes, but the smile was still on Melody's face when they stepped out. Even the scrutiny of the large woman behind the desk didn't shift it. Only when the porters collected the keys, picked up the luggage and carried Melody's in one direction, Dryden's in another, did Melody blink and make a small sound of incomprehension. 811 and 812 were situated on either side of the forty yards or so of open area fronting the elevators and stairway. The duenna with the keys squatted between.

"Seems we'll meet at breakfast," Dryden said, stepping after his luggage. He was grinning when he stood looking at his room. It was large, a little ornate for his taste, with dark furniture, but comforts too, notably a large tiled bathroom with a tub long enough for a basketball player. He decided to sample it at once.

Sitting in bed afterward, he tried again to extract news of the Olympics from *Izvestia*. When he had scanned the back pages twice, it occurred to him that the Russians would give pride of place to gymnastics, which had reached the final stages, rather than track and field heats. Working down a column topped by a picture of a small girl poised on a beam, he got to a tabulated section with figures interpolated in the Russian alphabet that looked about right for 100-meter clockings. It didn't take long after that to divine that Goldine had come through the Quarter-Final in second place in 11.05 seconds. The fastest qualifier was Krüll. She had set a new Olympic Record in the fourth heat in 10.94. Dryden put out the light and slept.

He didn't meet Melody at breakfast, after all. Possibly, he decided, as well as having boned up on Kutozovsky Prospect, she knew something about coffee and Danish, Soviet-style, but later he learned she had taken breakfast in her room.

It was not a solitary meal for Dryden, however. He had just picked up his table napkin when he heard heavy breathing and sensed the imminent presence of someone of great size.

"You don't mind if I join you? One doesn't eat alone in a Soviet restaurant. We're all comrades, see?"

Oliver Sternberg. The inquiry was academic. He was already in the act of depositing his weight on the chair. "How long you been here? I never noticed you before this."

Dryden explained that he had arrived late for the Games, and why. "I didn't know anyone else was staying here."

Sternberg stopped to order, speaking apparently fluent Russian, then resumed the conversation. "You didn't? Besides you and me, there are one thousand, nine hundred and ninety-eight others, including Valenti. He won't be down to breakfast. We hoisted a few last night. Getting jumpy, I guess. It don't look so good from here as it did back home in California."

"Ursula Krüll beating the Olympic Record twice?" said Dryden. "That is a little awesome, I admit. Did Goldine appear to have anything in reserve?"

"Sure, she can go faster," said Sternberg. "The heats don't count a damn. It's a poker game till the Final. What bugs me is the digging."

"Digging?"

"Sure." Sternberg's eyes darted to left and right. "The media."

Dryden frowned. "They're bothering *you?*"

"Before I flew out, there was this creep sniffing around the gym asking my boys what my interest is in track. Seems he knew I was in Eugene for the Trials."

"Did you talk to him?"

"Did I hell! Boys gave him the bum's rush. I took a look at him first. Smooth character. Flashy dresser. Wasn't operating on a low budget."

Dryden gulped his coffee. "You didn't get his name?"

"Not then. But I know it now. What would you say if I told you I wound up sitting next to the guy in the flight out here?"

"I'd say his name is Esselstyn," said Dryden. "A free-lance digging up dirt on Goldine to sell to NBC if they'll buy."

Sternberg gave a low whistle. "You've met the jerk?"

"What did you tell him?" asked Dryden.

"What do you think? I clammed up. For ten hours. But Esselstyn don't give up easy. Yesterday he was trying to put the screws on Valenti. You see why we got jumpy, Dryden? He knows things. He could spook this one just when we're due to collect."

"I doubt it," said Dryden. "He has the guest list from the Jacaranda, but not much else. If we keep stonewalling, we're okay. He's seen you, me, Valenti.

Dick Armitage and Cobb aren't in Moscow. Nor are Lee and Serafin."

Sternberg pulled a wry smile. "I have news for you. Serafin has a suite in the Hotel Rossiya. NBC flew him out here Sunday. He'll be doing proud-father interviews after each Final. Just thinking about it brings a lump to my throat."

While Sternberg systematically disposed of a vast fried breakfast, Dryden weighed the developments. Serafin's presence in Moscow troubled him no less than Esselstyn's. He had thought it was too neat, Serafin going back to watch TV in California, where he couldn't upset Goldine. If NBC planned to get father and daughter into a studio together, they were due for a shock. After what she had learned in Cleveland, Goldine was going to throw a blue fit if she set eyes on Serafin again. So what did he plan to get out of this? Reflected glory? Dryden had an ugly idea it went further than that.

"Proud-father interviews?" he said, thinking aloud. "Would NBC bring Serafin all the way here just for that?"

Sternberg was chewing. He nodded as he wiped grease off his lips. "You figure they have something else in mind? Like Esselstyn has told them he can lift the lid on Goldine's backup, and some wise-guy producer plans to spring it on Serafin in front of the cameras?"

This exceeded anything Dryden had imagined. "Let's not leap to conclusions," he said. "Unless Esselstyn has learned a lot more than he knew when he spoke to me, he doesn't know enough to fuel a demolition job like that. NBC wouldn't touch it without cast-iron proof. You say Esselstyn is still digging. There's no one else to see except Klugman. He won't get much from him." He stopped, as another shuddering possibility hit him. "Esselstyn couldn't have spoken to Goldine, could he?"

Sternberg swallowed the last of his breakfast. "Relax. No pressman has got near the chick yet. You haven't seen the security. Fort Knox ain't in the same league."

"My paper said that was overstated, all that talk of the Security Olympics," said Dryden. "I got the impression the Russians were more relaxed than anyone expected."

"Who's talking about the Russkis?" squeaked Sternberg. "It's U.S. heavies you have to get by if you want to meet Goldengirl. She has a two-man bodyguard day and night, orders of the team manager. No statements, except in scheduled press conferences. It's obvious our people have realized Goldengirl is a national asset. They wouldn't let a fink like Esselstyn louse up her chances bugging her with stupid questions."

"Well, that's a help," said Dryden. "You're sure of this?"

"I was drinking with newsmen last evening," answered Sternberg. "There's a story going around that one guy wasted eight hours yesterday trying to lay on an exclusive with Goldengirl. He ended up joining the queue for Lenin's Tomb—said he was making sure he got a goddamned face-to-face with *somebody*."

Dryden and Melody started before midday for the afternoon's events in the Stadium, but still found the buildup of traffic in the approach road so heavy that they paid the taxi driver almost a mile from the Stadium, and made their way with the crowd along Pirogovskaya Street. In the dazzling sunshine, progress up the wide pavement was slow, but anticipation ricocheted from group to group regardless of language. Occasionally it broke into chanting and cheers as the walkers spotted flags and emblems in the crawling line of cars. Then someone glimpsed the flame, just visible on the Lenin Stadium, beyond the volleyball arena. *"La voilà!"* Coos of recognition and a frenzy of photography.

Dryden had decided he must get to Goldine and

warn her about Esselstyn. A man smart enough to fix a flight reservation next to one of the consortium wasn't going to be held off for long by U.S. team security. Goldine would need to know what to expect and how to freeze him off. She was sure to be preoccupied with the running. Dryden's problem—if he got close enough to speak to her before Esselstyn—was convincing her it was important. Her moods were so volatile. But it couldn't be shirked.

Instead of moving with the mass of the crowd toward the Stadium approach, they turned right at the street's end and headed toward one of the three training tracks where athletes warmed up for their events. There was a better chance of seeing Goldine here than trying to penetrate the security at the Olympic Village, which was organized with the 1972 shootout in Munich still much in mind.

The track was a full 400-meter circuit surrounded by a double wire fence patrolled by officials. The public enclosure extended along one side of the stretch. There must have been two hundred or more spectators seated on the tiered benches simply watching athletes in warm-ups jogging around the perimeter and exercising on the grass. Almost as many again were clustered around the competitors' entrance: autograph collecting is a popular activity in the Soviet Union, engaged in by adults as well as children.

And as Dryden and Melody arrived, something was happening there. A team bus had drawn up and officials had swung metal barriers into place to provide a passage through the converging crowd. The athletes debouched at speed, ignoring the papers and pens hopefully thrust toward them.

Dryden was looking through his field glasses at some girl athletes limbering up on the far side.

"No chance?" Melody asked.

"None at all. They aren't even Americans."

"Who are these people arriving?"

"Not Yanks, for sure. We obviously picked the wrong training track."

A small Latin-looking man at his elbow seemed agitated when Dryden started to replace the glasses in their case. He tugged at Dryden's sleeve, jabbering unintelligibly, stabbing his finger in the direction of the crowd at the gate. It seemed ungracious to push him away; he was evidently doing this from the best motives. He didn't want Dryden to miss the excitement at the gate.

One word came through the spate of sounds and by repetition made itself understood: "Krüll." The little man wanted them to know he had spotted Ursula Krüll.

"Krüll. Oh, yes. Ursula Krüll," said Dryden, nodding energetically. He turned the glasses on the slim brunette who had just run the gauntlet of autograph hunters.

She was talking with two other girls dressed similarly in the blue tracksuit with the letters DDR displayed. Cameramen were crowding around them, but she continued the conversation with the cultivated indifference of someone who has lived in the public eye for a long time. It was a pretty face, whatever preconceptions you had about Eastern Bloc athletes, the cheekbones shaped high, the curving top lip lifted interestingly even in repose. Her blue eyes continued to look steadily at her companions, undistracted by the cameras.

"Cool," said Melody.

"Krüll, *si*," said the little man.

"Let's go," said Dryden. "If the East Germans are here, you may be sure the Americans aren't coming."

As they were moving off, they saw Krüll slip her thumbs in the waistband of the tracksuit and ease it over her hips, still talking as she lifted her lightly tanned legs from the garment. She checked the level of the famous shorts with a quick movement of her hand, turned abruptly and wagged a playful finger at a cameraman, then trotted leisurely away around the track. If she felt any tension at the prospect of the afternoon's events, it didn't show.

They fared no better at the next training track, except having it confirmed by some U.S. 800-meter men that Goldine wasn't likely to appear on the public training tracks at all. "The only place you'll see that chick is in the Stadium racing," one told him. "She works out on the Village track, then they rush her to the Stadium in a hired Zim, along with two musclemen and her physician. Man, you have to be somebody to rate that class of service."

At three o'clock that afternoon, eight girls bucked from the blocks in the first Semi-Final of the 100 meters. In the tiered seating beyond the finish, Melody tightened her grip on Dryden's hand. From their foreshortened view, it was difficult to tell who had started well. The line of runners moved without the impression of speed you got from seeing them side-on; but the energy of sprinting, the rhythm and power, were dramatized in the hammer motion of legs—knees raised, it seemed, extravagantly high, shoes pounding the track.

They had covered more than half the distance, and the symmetry was threatened by two girls in lanes 4 and 5 edging ahead—a Russian and a British girl. Goldine, in lane 2, was in the pack with the rest. The first four would qualify for the Final.

"It looks bad," said Melody gratuitously.

"It's the angle," responded Dryden, hoping it was.

The roar that greeted the Russian victory was worthy of the Final. The Soviet girl was overcome, covering her eyes as officials crowded around her.

Goldine had crossed at least two meters behind, third or fourth. Mary-Lou Devine was out.

The time was flashed on the scoreboard: a new Soviet Record:

1	MURATOVA	URS	10.98
2	HAWKINS.	GBR	11.06
3	SERAFIN	USA	11.15
4	SCHMIDT	GER	11.18

"How do you read *that?*" asked Melody.

He didn't answer. He was training the glasses on Goldine. She was walking back to the start with the British girl. Muratova was besieged by pressmen. The others couldn't get near to make the token touch of congratulation.

"Playing possum?" suggested Melody.

"She does have a four hundred-meter heat to run before the Final. The object was to qualify, and she did."

On the track, the next set of girls were already testing their blocks.

"This could be instructive," said Dryden. "Krüll is taking on the Cuban girl who beat Goldine in the heats yesterday."

A small section of the crowd was chanting "Ur-su-la." Their idol ignored them, ignored the girls lining up beside her, the photographers positioned to capture the start.

The chanting stopped as the eight got into the crouch position. The gun cracked.

A fraction over ten seconds later, Krüll crossed the line emphatically clear of the rest, eased to a trot, corrected the coverage of her shorts, waved away photographers and jogged smartly back to the start. Before she reached there, the scoreboard flashed the news that for the third time she had improved the Olympic Record. The latest—10.83—made the Russian girl's time look ordinary, Goldine's pedestrian.

"Wishing you could change your meal ticket?" Melody asked.

It was not long till the 400-meter First Round heats. They noticed two late substitutions: Canute, J. (U.S.A.) replaced Jones (U.S.A.) in Heat One; Krüll,

U. (G.D.R.) replaced Muller (G.D.R.) in Heat Six.

"So Janie Canute gets her chance, after all," said Melody. "How did she manage that? The power of prayer?"

"Didn't you hear? Jones came down with glandular fever a week ago. She didn't make the trip. What interests me is that Krüll has come in. I heard the Germans were considering this, but it's a hell of a gamble when she hasn't trained for three events."

"How do you know she hasn't?" asked Melody. "Wouldn't it be typical of the Commies to train her in secret and then spring this at the last moment? They could figure it's a way of psyching Goldengirl."

"Equally, Goldine could have psyched *them* by holding herself back in the heats of the one hundred. The Germans could believe Krüll has the sprints so buttoned up it won't hurt to take in the four hundred as well."

Melody shook her head. "That's not the way Germans think. They're methodical. They don't gamble."

"The coaches might not," said Dryden, "but politicians would. If those people saw a chance of proving their system produced a super-woman, do you think they'd pass it up? Krüll is the prestige vehicle of an ideology. She's running in the name of Marx and Lenin. Since she's running well, those ideologues can put enormous pressure on the coaches to try her for the triple. What do they care if she's a spent husk at the end of it?"

"You wouldn't, by any chance, be justifying anything to yourself?" said Melody without looking at him.

The heats of the 400 meters resolved none of the speculation. Goldine qualified in second place in Heat Three, cruising through easily in slow time. Ursula Krüll, too, ran well within herself in her race, third in a marginally faster time. The fastest qualifier of the round was Janie Canute, with 51.02 secs.

In the next hour, Dryden twice approached the

covered warmup area below the stand in hope of contacting Goldine, but security guards intercepted him. The only consolation was that if he couldn't get through, neither could Esselstyn.

In the arena the Finals of the men's 800 meters and 400-meter-hurdles came and went, and a protracted struggle developed between the Swedish and West German pole-vaulters. Many of the crowd seemed disengaged from what was happening, waiting only for the last event of the day, the women's 100-meter Final. Two girls, Muratova and Krüll, had beaten eleven seconds in the preliminaries, so it seemed set as a Soviet-German clash, with the rest scrapping for bronze.

While officials cleared the track of hurdles, Dryden was scanning a section of the crowd through his field glasses. "Come on," he abruptly said to Melody. "We're moving. I want a better view this time. Some people up there are leaving." He hustled her along the row, down a gangway and past two officials in conversation. The seats were situated high up, almost level with the finish. The people sitting alongside gave them suspicious looks, and then someone said, *"Amerikanka,"* which seemed to explain everything.

The eight finalists had appeared in the arena. For the first time in the afternoon the atmosphere was charged with that tension that can bind a hundred thousand people into a unit, totally absorbed in a human activity as simple as a ten-second run. Across the world millions more watched and waited. And the eight who had earned the right to a few seconds' attention from the biggest audience in history jogged about the small grass enclosure, preoccupied, heads down, steeling themselves. The vast majority of those watching regarded this as a mild diversion to be looked at, enjoyed, forgotten, but those eight pent-up athletes had lived with this moment for years and would relive it till their lives' end. A faulty start, a lapse of concentration, a cramp, and how much was lost? A race? A professional contract? An Order of Lenin? A way of life?

One conclusion was certain: when that 100 meters had been run, not one of those eight girls would be quite the same person.

The starter touched a button that sounded an electronic signal to the finalists. Warm-ups were peeled off, spikes checked, secret prayers uttered.

Dryden had Goldine in focus. She appeared to be smiling, saying something to Ursula Krüll. The German looked away. In the stands, people were chanting her name. The Russians were responding with "Mu-ra-to-va."

The starter spoke into his microphone, and the chanting stopped.

"*Na Mesta.*"

The girls moved forward. Each starting block was fitted with its own loudspeaker, so that there should be no split-second's acoustic advantage.

"*Gotovo.*"

Goldine was in lane 3, Krüll 5, Muratova 6.

One hundred and three thousand spectators, and you could hear a flag flapping on the lip of the Stadium.

Suddenly it was happening. The gun had fired and they were off their blocks, building speed, oblivious to the deluge of sound from every side. Goldine was angled low, impelled by the power of her start. There was a purpose to her running that had not been evident in earlier rounds. She was declaring herself now, when it counted, running with an action that made the others look mechanical. Meter by meter she imposed herself on the race. Her will reached up the strip to the finish, as clear as the lane markings.

A meter down, Krüll was summoning the power acquired in those years of weightlifting. Although it was taking her clear of the other runners, it hauled back nothing from Goldine. The muscular effort for a 100-meter sprint theoretically requires about seven liters of oxygen, but the lungs cannot supply more than half a liter in the ten seconds. So when the muscles have used the oxygen available, they incur a debt. They gather lactic acid and other alien substances that the body can tolerate only for a short time. Krüll's capacity to surmount the oxygen debt had been calculated by East German physiologists to be worth a full meter in the last thirty. But where was it?

Goldine held her head to the line, dipped as Klugman had drilled her, ran on, turned, bowed to draw breath, and was engulfed by cameramen.

SERAFIN USA 10.81 flashed the scoreboard. NEW OLYMPIC RECORD.

"How was that for openers?" said Melody.

Dryden didn't answer. A pulse was beating in his head and his whole body was shaking.

"Snap out of it," said Melody. "You look like death. She won—okay?"

He still sat in silence, feeling the tension subside, startling him with his physical involvement in what had happened.

Around them, as if they had needed time to make a mental adjustment, people were beginning to clap, many standing for a better view. It had percolated that Ursula Krüll had been decisively defeated, not by Muratova, but the blond American, who had concealed her devastating form through all the previous rounds.

Dryden, who knew Goldine's ability, who had touted it around the board rooms of Los Angeles and New York, should not have reacted this way. Now he secretly admitted to himself that after the Semi-Finals he had written off her chance of gold.

He stood with the others to see Goldine approach Krüll, now being consoled by teammates. They touched hands. The German girl nodded, looking Goldine up and down as if she were from another planet, then turned to retrace the 100-meter stretch she had believed was hers.

On NBC-TV William Weston said, "Watching that instant replay with me was Dr. William Serafin, the proudest man in this Lenin Stadium. How about that, Doc? Wasn't she just incredible?"

"Oh, quite credible to me," said Serafin. "Without presuming to boast, I knew ·she would win. She is unique, you see."

"No one here is going to disagree with that, Doc."

"Yes, but I wasn't using the term superficially. She is physiologically unique. Her skeletal development—"

"Her *what?* I didn't catch that."

"Her skeletal development. The configuration of her bones. If I may explain—"

"First tell us how you *feel,* Doc."

"Feel?"

"Yeah, you must be over the moon right now."

"There's an element of satisfaction, yes."

"Well, how about that for Quote of the Week? 'An element of satisfaction.' Just now I said you were the proudest man in the Lenin Stadium. Maybe 'coolest' would be more apt. And there we must leave it. With the first U.S. gold medal in track going to Goldine Serafin, of Bakersfield, California, I return you to Dave Yardley in New York."

In the Stadium, two large men in U.S. blazers were steering Goldine off the track to the competitors' tunnel in a throng of pressmen and cameras.

"What happens now?" asked Melody. "Does she get her medal?"

"Tomorrow. The action's over for the day, so the crowd are going home," said Dryden. "There should be a press conference shortly, and I want to get a word with her, if I can, before it starts. Would you wait?"

He made his way below. One of the architectural achievements of the Lenin Stadium is that a capacity crowd can be dispersed within six minutes. This assumes that everyone is making for the nearest exit. Dryden wanted the press center under the west stand.

GOLDENGIRL

He got there by degrees and brute stubbornness. It was a good thing he had left Melody upstairs; anyone as small as she would have found themselves outside and halfway to the metro station by now.

He confirmed with a photographer by the entrance that Goldine hadn't yet arrived for the conference. Uncertain which direction she would approach from, he waited there till he spotted a face he knew among those streaming inside: Klugman, actually smiling.

In time, he remembered Klugman's personal stake in this, and held out his hand to him. "Congratulations! Beautifully managed!"

"Thanks." Klugman was pink with pride. "I'll enjoy it myself when I see it on TV. She did everything right. But for the crosswind, she'd have taken the world record."

"The important thing was taking Ursula Krüll. Where is Goldine now?"

"The doctor's looking at her," said Klugman. He held up his hand. "No sweat, it's routine. You'd like to see her? I can get you in."

He led Dryden back along the covered area under the stand to where each team management had its individual office. There was a cluster of cameramen outside the U.S. office. Klugman spoke to the two men on the door and Dryden was allowed past.

He pushed open a second door. It looked unlike any office in his experience. There was a bed in the center and Goldine was lying on it, still in her tracksuit, except the shoes. At a table to the right a girl in a blue nylon coat was testing urine in a chemical flask. Two men in white jackets were by the bed, one making notes, the other holding a syringe containing blood. He turned as Dryden entered and asked, "Who the hell are you?"

"It's okay," said Goldine, glancing expressionlessly at Dryden. "Personal friend."

The doctor wasn't satisfied. "Look, this isn't—"

"Save it," snapped Goldine. "I said he was my friend.

364

Well," she asked Dryden, "are you here to congratulate me, or not?"

Something in her tone stopped him. "It'll keep," he said. "You'll get plenty of that. There's this press conference coming up. I want to speak to you about it. There's a man called Esselstyn." Dryden described him briefly. "You haven't met him already? Good. If he's there, he could be difficult. Likes to put the knife in. He, er, has a theory that you trained a long time for this. He doesn't believe the jogging story. If I were you, I wouldn't mention it unless you have to. You follow me?"

"You came here to tell me that?" she said without showing if it had registered.

"There's something else," Dryden quickly added. "Did you know the TV people have brought your father to Moscow?"

"Doc? He's not my father. You know that."

"That's a technicality so far as the media are concerned," said Dryden. "They may want to lay on some kind of meeting between the two of you."

"They can go jump," said Goldine. "I won't go near him."

He moved closer, trying to exclude the medical team from the conversation. This had got off to a bad start. She was edgy, and so was he. Damn it, it was like prison visiting. "I'm not suggesting you agree to meet him," he said in an undertone. "Just keep it on a low key. Tell them you need to rest, or train, or something. Remember what they've written about the adoption, your happy childhood . . . I know how you feel about this, but it's important to be consistent, to come up to the Goldengirl image. If anyone mentions your father—"

She cut him short with an obscenity. "I just won a gold medal and all you can talk about is that megalomaniac." She turned to face the doctors. "This is a private conversation, okay? If anyone present—that

365

includes you"—she called to the girl—"repeats things I said in confidence I'd—"

"You see what I'm driving at?" said Dryden.

She ignored him and spoke to the doctor with the syringe. "Had you finished examining me?"

He nodded and made an effort to respond with clinical detachment. "You will have the glucose tablets with you in your tracksuit pocket, but you shouldn't need one."

"Uhuh." She brushed that aside. "What time is it?"

"Six-five."

"They can wait some. I'll be worth it. Are you sweating, Jack?"

He didn't answer. He could have said things all right: said this was no time to act the prima donna; after all he had done in lining up a fortune in endorsements, he had a right to expect she would co-operate. But who was he to take a moral line when he was asking her to lie to the press? What was at stake was the image, the revenue, his livelihood. She knew that.

"Do you think you can depend on me?" she asked. "Or are you just a little scared of what I'll say? Tell you what. If you want to be sure, you must give some. I'll do the devoted-daughter bit as a favor to you in return for something. You can kiss me, Jack."

Idiot! He had been so taken up with the threat of Esselstyn that he had missed the importance of this moment. Goldine had won. The whole of America had its arms outstretched to her, but she was turning to him. She had wanted him to kiss her, and he had talked about Serafin! "But of course."

He smiled warmly and moved close.

She pushed her hand in front of his face. "Not my lips, Jack. My feet. You can kiss each of my feet. You owe one hell of a lot to them."

He was wrong. It wasn't affection she wanted, but abasement. Goldengirl was demanding her tribute. It was absurd. Adolescent. It warranted turning her over and slapping her bottom, but he didn't. He did as she commanded, bent and put his lips to her feet in the un-comprehending presence of the medical team.

The only thing he was thankful for was that Melody wasn't there to watch.

[21]

THE victory ceremony for the 100 meters opened the program in the Stadium next day. As Goldine took her place at the top of the rostrum there was generous applause. Her press conference had been seen in full on Soviet TV the evening before. The candor of her answers had made a good impression. She had said complimentary things about Moscow, the Russian people, Muratova, Ursula Krüll, but she was proud of her victory and admitted she had worked hard for it. There had been no questions about Dr. Serafin or the consortium. If Esselstyn was present, he had kept quiet.

She shed no sentimental tears as the Star-Spangled Banner was played and the Stars and Stripes edged up the center flagpole behind the Olympic flame. *"She stood serenely in her white tracksuit as if she had always expected to be there,"* reported the New York Times. *"And when the ceremony ended, she shook the hands of the other girls and left the arena. It was as if she didn't need to maximize the moment, because she knew there would be more."*

This was to be the easiest of Goldine's five days of competition, with just the 400-meter Quarter-Final to contest. She ran in Heat Two, allowing a Jamaican girl to scud away in the stretch for an easy win. Goldine's time was 53.23 secs, making her one of the slowest to go through to the Semi-Final, which after her tactics in the 100 meters fooled nobody.

The sensation of the round happened in Heat Four, when Janie Canute clashed with Ursula Krüll. It had clearly been decided in the German camp that Krüll needed her confidence restored as soon as possible after the previous day's defeat, and a respectable time in the 400 meters was prescribed. The talk in the Olympic Village that morning had been that she was ready to demonstrate that her strength would turn the tables on Goldine in the longer events. She had come to Moscow to collect two gold medals, and she would settle for the 200 and 400 meters.

Janie Canute had been told that a fast time was on. She said it suited her. She wanted to get the measure of Krüll, the one girl whose ability over the distance had not seriously been tested. When they went to their marks, Krüll was in lane 2, Janie in lane 4. There was a good Finn in one of the outside lanes, but the rest had never got inside fifty-two seconds. Janie crossed herself and asked for fifty flat.

People were edgy. There were three recalls. A French girl was disqualified and left the track weeping. You could hear her sobs between the starter's instructions.

When they got away at the fourth try, Janie put in a lot of hard running around the bend, completely negating the stagger between herself and the little Australian in 5. She was moving well. By the end of the back stretch she was up with the Finn. Then on her inside, Krüll hurtled through as if it were a 200. Approaching the bend, Janie passed the Finn and gave herself to the pursuit of the East German. Each stride was obviously hurting, but she was cutting the gap between them. There were seventy meters to cover. The danger was that in pursuing Krüll she would fold, letting the others pass her in the run-in. She glanced behind to see where the Finn was, a sure indication that she was relinquishing the race. She was safe, but second. She concentrated on stride length, and came home five meters behind Krüll.

When Janie had got her breath under control, she straightened, jogged a little to ease the stiffness, and looked for Krüll. The German girl was surrounded but leaping for joy above the cameramen, arms raised high. Janie looked toward the scoreboard, 49.22. Krüll had set a new world record, the first of the Moscow Olympic Games. In an event she had not intended to run. That was style.

In *Izvestia* that evening, there were two pictures of Ursula Krüll: one solemn-faced on the rostrum with her silver medal around her neck; the other, head flung back, arms outstretched, at the moment she had the world record confirmed. At the hastily arranged press conference, she had said she believed she could improve the record in the Final. "I am just a novice in this event," she was reported as saying. "Who knows what is possible if I get some real competition?" Which must have tested Janie's Christian charity when she read it, for in finishing second in 49.89, she had set a new U.S. record.

At 10:30 P.M. a phone call was put through to Dryden at the Hotel Ukraina from Barney Helpern, the senior executive in his New York office.

"Jack? I hope I didn't catch you in bed. Is the line okay at your end?"

"Fine. Matter of fact, I was in the bar, acquiring a taste for Armenian brandy. How's business?"

"It's humming, Jack. Your Miss Serafin's press conference was on the tube in prime time last evening. Went over big. I mean that. The TV manner of that kid—breathtaking. This morning we've been stampeded with inquiries from people you spoke with last week, the guys who wouldn't jump then but are falling over themselves to get in now."

"They'll have to pay, Barney."

"Sure. I can handle that. The reason I called is that I heard from Simon. I can't spell things out, for obvious reasons."

"I'm with you, Barney." Simon was Dryden's contact in the presidential office.

"Those soundings you made a week or two back. They could come to something. There's definite interest in the idea. If she pulls off the triple, it's on. All we have to agree on is the timing. This bloody eight-hour difference complicates things. The people here are talking in terms of a TV linkup around ten Wednesday night. That's six on Thursday morning, Moscow time."

"We can lay it on at this end," promised Dryden. "This is one arrangement that isn't negotiable. Mind, the advantage isn't all on our side. Setting aside a certain event in November, when you add it up, we're going to give a useful nudge to the gross national product."

"I'll say we are. You should see the papers here. She made every front page this morning, and that's after one gold. I must tell you one cute headline I picked up. 'GOLDINE RAN SOME.' Get it?"

"I like it, Barney."

"Say, this East German broad—what's her name?—Kill?"

"Krüll."

"Yeah, Krüll. I heard she made some kind of record today. Don't get me wrong, but could that foul things up at all?"

"It was a world record," said Dryden. "People were pretty impressed here, which is what the Germans planned, I'm sure."

"But you're not worried?"

"I'd have to be a total idiot not to be worried," said Dryden. "We're hoping she'll burn herself out. It's the Final that counts. I still have my money on Goldine."

"Great. Just one thing more, Jack. The TV transmissions. You know NBC has brought in Goldine's father a couple of times to comment?"

"I heard about it."

"We get it over here. Cranky old guy. You know him, Jack? He doesn't come over too good. Bloodless character. Carries on about her bone formation until they cut him off."

"He is a professor of physiology, Barney."

"I can believe that, Jack. I'm just a little apprehensive of this program they're slotting into Tuesday evening."

Dryden's grip tightened on the phone. "Which program is that?"

"You haven't heard? You know there's a rest day Tuesday. No track. NBC has just announced they are running a half-hour prime-time special on Goldine. *GOLD TOMORROW*. Something like that—there could be a query in the title. I guess it's a curtain-raiser for the Finals Wednesday, mainly clips of the action so far, but they have an interview lined up with Serafin. What worries me, Jack, is how that old man will come across. You follow me?"

"I do." Dryden had followed, overtaken and raced ahead. It looked worse from there. "Thanks for the tip, Barney. I'll try and find out what's happening."

He replaced the phone, his head reeling. *GOLD TOMORROW?* He needed to find out what was happening all right. The program could be the curtain-raiser Barney imagined, but with a title like that it could just as easily be Esselstyn's hatchet job.

Monday's program included the First Round and Quarter-Finals of the 200 meters, and the Semi-Finals of the 400 meters. At ten-fifty in the morning, when the 200 meters got under way, the Stadium was less than half full. As expected, the top-flight girls treated it as a workout, burning the first 150 meters and coasting the rest. There was no Olympic Record from Krüll, as there had been in Round One of the 100. She hit the stretch in line with the Russian third string and ran alongside her, twice turning to urge her on, and deliberately easing five meters from the line to let her cross first. As she returned to collect her warm-ups, with photographers in tow recording every step, she left no doubt in anyone's mind that her confidence was buoyantly back.

Goldine's heat followed. She qualified in a faster race, declining to dispute first place with two African girls. After it, she dodged the press by removing her spikes and making barefoot for the competitors' exit. A U.S. official collected her clothes.

Earlier, Dryden had visited the Hotel Rossiya. Locating Serafin was not easy with a guest list six thousand strong. He visited each of the three blocks before tracking him to one of the restaurants.

Serafin looked tired. He attempted no explanation of his presence in Moscow. "I didn't expect to see you here," he told Dryden. "You should be careful. People recognize me since I've been on television."

"That's what I want to see you about. This program scheduled for tomorrow night."

"*GOLD TOMORROW?* I'm taking part," said Serafin. "It's going out live to America. I have to be at the TV Center at five o'clock Wednesday morning. Ungodly hour."

"Have they told you what to expect?"

"Yes. I insisted on a proper interview, not the insulting treatment I've had all week in the commentary box, where they push a microphone against your face and snatch it away before you have a chance to finish a sentence."

"They haven't discussed the subject of the interview?"

"Goldengirl. What else? As she won't condescend to appear on the program herself, I'm the star guest."

"What will you tell them?"

Serafin gave a thin smile over his coffee cup. "Afraid of what I'll say?"

"Afraid of what a hostile interviewer might get you to say," said Dryden. "A TV interview can be a grueling experience."

"I'm not new to it," Serafin pointed out. "I've been on *Science Forum*."

"This may not be so cozy," said Dryden. He told Serafin everything he knew about Esselstyn.

At the end, Serafin was unmoved. "I can't see the producer having any truck with a man like that," he said. "Just let them try taking up my time with impertinent questions. I've been pushed aside all week. It won't happen this time."

When he got to the Stadium, Dryden went looking for Klugman. He spotted him in the section reserved for team officials. Klugman came out looking worried.

"Anything wrong?"

"I hope not," said Dryden. "Has a character named Esselstyn been bothering you? Short, curly hair, dark, around thirty. Fancy dresser."

"What did you say his name was? Could be the creep that tried to buy me a drink Sunday," said Klugman. "Something about going on TV. I told him what to do with his TV show."

"You didn't discuss Goldine's training with him?"

"What kind of goof do you take me for?" said Klugman, flushing.

"Sorry. I needed to know. Esselstyn is dangerous," Dryden explained. He brought Klugman up to date. "I believe they tried to get Goldine for this program."

"People are trying all the time. TV, radio, papers. You name it," said Klugman. "She's giving no more interviews till Wednesday night when it's all over. Team management decision. Would you believe they had to move her into the U.S. Embassy last night? You can ban the press from the Olympic Village, but you can't stop competitors setting up as free-lance journalists. They try to interview big-name athletes with the idea of selling exclusives to the papers. Goddamned racket. Soon as anyone brings a gold medal back, they go for them like jackals. Plays hell with the chance of anyone trying to psych up for the other events. I hear the East Germans have moved Krüll out for the same reason. Since that world record yesterday, she's back in business."

"It was smart psychology," said Dryden.

"Smart running. She tied up at the finish, but if she can learn to coast the back stretch, she'll go faster. That's what the German coaches will have told her. We can expect something under forty-nine seconds in the Final. Goldengirl's best ever is fifty point five."

Dryden had heard Pete Klugman on his lugubrious tack before, but still felt his stomach lurch. "First they have to run the two hundred Final," he pointed out. "If she tops Krüll in that . . ." The "if" betrayed him. He started again. "She was invincible in the one hundred. After the illness, the layoff, we had no right to expect her to run so brilliantly."

"Looks like the time out helped her," said Klugman. "I've known it to happen before. The diabetes is mild, it's under control now, and the break in training was mentally beneficial. The whole experience sharpened her motivation. She's hooked on success. Totally." He sighed, shaking his head. "It makes her pretty insufferable. Another reason they moved her out of the Village is she refuses to share a room with other girls." He shrugged. "Wouldn't surprise me if she had breakfast with the Ambassador. Caviar on toast."

The Quarter-Finals of the 200 meters, in midafternoon, provided more confirmation that Ursula Krüll was under instructions to take a rest from record-breaking. She tagged the U.S. girl Shelley Wilson, keeping a conspicuous two meters adrift all the way up the stretch, finishing in 22.83 secs. In her heat, Goldine, too, refused to be drawn by Muratova, who delighted the crowd by equaling Eckert's gold-medal performance of 1976, with 22.37 secs. To underline the achievement, a small girl was waiting near the finish to scamper across the track and present the Russian with a posy of flowers.

Dryden was alone in the stands that afternoon,

Melody having declared herself more interested in shopping at GUM. Since that first evening when they had met the vigilante between their rooms at the Ukraina, Melody had been disenchanted with Moscow. There was no room service, the waiters in the restaurants ignored you, and Soviet vermouth was no substitute for Campari. He wasn't expecting a rave report on GUM.

One of the consortium, at least, was more sanguine about the city. The previous evening, Valenti had arrived in the bar with Sternberg. After remarking that the kidnaping had obviously done Goldengirl no harm, he went on to describe his experience the previous evening, when the phone in his room had rung and he had taken a call from an English-speaking girl offering to play Olympic games for five rubles. "The best five rubles I ever spent!" he assured them. "If you guys had some sense, you'd be up in your rooms now, sitting by the phone. Me? I'm sated. Besides, I must keep back some rubles for a fur hat."

There was a surprise when the line-up for the second Semi-Final of the 400 meters was announced, for it included both Ursula Krüll and Goldine. The crowd needed no prompting at the significance of this; the news reverberated around the Stadium in scores of languages.

The clash raised the possibility that the two would be drawn into a struggle to gain the psychological prize of finishing ahead. It did not materialize. As if by tacit agreement, they ran side by side to the line, aligning so closely that they shared the same time of 50.43 secs. The photo finish gave Krüll the edge because technology will not admit that ties are possible in the modern Olympics, but nobody seemed to mind. The girls posed for pictures with their arms around each other's shoulders, giving caption writers the world over the opportunity to comment that sport is about friendship, not international rivalry.

Tuesday, August 19, was the rest day from track and field. Dryden planned to use the morning to confer with the NBC-TV team about the linkup with the White House. He would also find out what he could about *GOLD TOMORROW?* He hoped to wangle an invitation, if only to watch it live on a monitor.

Before leaving the Ukraina he was handed a message asking him to meet a Mr. Ford in the lobby. He was suspicious. Every traveler to Russia hears stories about tourists who inadvertently offend the authorities by photographing military personnel or violating travel regulations, but Dryden hadn't stepped out of line. He hadn't even checked his room for listening devices. Yet a message to meet someone with one of the best-known names in America was odd, particularly as he didn't know a Mr. Ford.

The man was U.S.-raised, whatever he was called. Tall, gray-haired, in a brown lightweight, he greeted Dryden in an elegant Boston accent. "Hope I didn't interrupt breakfast, Mr. Dryden. James Ford." He gripped Dryden's hand firmly. "U.S. Embassy staff. Don't let that alarm you. This isn't official. It just happens that you might be able to help someone over a small problem. Not concerning you directly at all. It's, er, kind of confidential, not for discussion in a Soviet hotel lobby. I have an Embassy car outside, if, er . . ."

"Do you have any form of identity, Mr. Ford?" Dryden asked. "One hears stories . . ."

"But of course."

Dryden wasn't used to examining diplomatic identity cards, but the photo matched and the bald eagle was prominent.

"I also have an American Express Card," said Ford with a half-smile.

"That won't be necessary. You don't wish to see my papers?"

"We just want your advice," said Ford, leading the way across the lobby.

The car was chauffeur-driven and bore the U.S. insignia. If this turned out to be a KGB trick, at least he would arrive at the collective labor camp in style. But they headed in the right direction, across the Moskva by Novo-Arbatsky Bridge, up Kalinin Prospect and into Tchaikovsky Street. There was a moment of unease when they pulled up at a gray stone building with Soviet soldiers on guard at the gates, but the eagle was over the door and the Stars and Stripes fluttered overhead. James Ford was on the level.

Dryden followed him up the Embassy steps, across the small entrance hall and into an elevator. They got out on the second floor. Ford stopped at a door and said, "This is where I leave you, Mr. Dryden. This isn't official business at all, you understand. You've met two of the people inside, so introductions aren't necessary." He held open the door.

Dryden walked in, still mystified. And though two of the faces that looked his way *were* familiar, he couldn't immediately place them. It was a fairly ordinary office, not the Ambassador's suite for sure.

The man he hadn't seen before stood up to welcome him.

"So good of you to come, Mr. Dryden. I'm Don Mc-Corquodale of the U.S. Olympic Committee. I believe you already met Doctors Dalton and Nagel."

Doctors. Of course. They were the two he had seen with Goldine in the Lenin Stadium. He nodded at them, finding no clue in their faces to explain what this was about.

McCorquodale had an easy style of speech and made it plain from the beginning that he was seeking co-operation. In his mid-fifties, he carried enough weight to suggest that relaxation was intrinsic to his way of life, not staged for the occasion. "You'll have guessed that we want to talk about young Goldine Serafin," he said. "Quite some runner. Surprised a lot of people Saturday, me included. It's raised her into the superstar class, that gold medal." He smiled. "Given us a few problems, keeping the media out of her hair, but that's one of our functions as I see it, ensuring that an athlete has the chance of getting through the Games without undue harassment. I believe you heard we had to move her out of the Village."

"Pete Klugman told me," Dryden confirmed.

"Klugman, yeah," repeated McCorquodale without showing interest. "Do you smoke? I'm getting quite a taste for these Soviet cigarettes with the cardboard filters, *Papirosi*. Care to try one? Don't suppose you medics would."

The doctors looked on while McCorquodale and Dryden lit up.

"The press aren't the only problem," McCorquodale resumed. "You know about the medical complication? That's another thing we have to take care of, which is why we have a team of first-class physicians with us—for *all* the athletes on the squad, I mean. When you take close to three hundred sportsmen and women abroad, you're going to have a few problems. You need an expert on hand to cope with emergencies. Goldine's condition isn't new in our experience, Mr. Dryden. We've had diabetics on the team before, not in track that I recall, but other sports. We can handle it. That is, Ben Dalton can. When we knew about Goldine, we assigned him to monitor her condition throughout the Games. It may look to an outsider like she's being singled out for special treatment, but, hell, she *is* special. Between ourselves, there's a lot more on tomorrow's Finals than Goldine herself realizes. If she comes up with more gold medals, she could find herself on the hot line to Washington. It's as big as that." He drew on his *Papirosa*, letting the information sink in. "Could do us all a lot of good—Goldine, the team, the Committee and good old Uncle Sam himself."

Dryden noticed McCorquodale didn't include him in the list. He was surprised. This had to be leading up to something, and a charge of jeopardizing the amateur status of an Olympic athlete seemed likely. But if this was in McCorquodale's mind, he wasn't pouncing yet.

"So we all want her to go out there tomorrow and leave scorch marks on the track for those Russians to remember," McCorquodale went on. "And you guessed it—there's a complication, which is why we brought you here. You're a personal friend of Goldine's. She told us that herself. Mr. Dryden, we know damn all about the girl. She's new on the track scene, and one thing and another prevented us from getting to know her before we flew out here. We figure you may be able to help us understand what's going wrong."

"Something's wrong?"

"Ben, would you explain?"

Dr. Dalton took over. His manner was direct. "Two problems, Mr. Dryden. One concerns the diabetes. You understand that we control it by balancing the carbohydrate intake with insulin injections? Before we left New York, Goldine told us her normal requirement. It should simply be a matter of adjusting that to the lowering of the blood sugar due to sever exercise. You follow me?"

"I think so. If you exercise, you need less insulin."

"Right. The difficulty is that since we got here, Goldine's blood-sugar readings have been extremely erratic. If she hadn't told me she was a long-term diabetic, I'd think she had recently contracted the disease. If she did, she shouldn't be running at all. In treating diabetes, you have to get the patient stabilized. If she isn't, it's goddamned dangerous to take any excessive exercise. There's a high risk of inducing a coma, and that could mean brain damage. At worst, death. I understood the condition was mild, and my readings confirmed that earlier in the week. This morning I had to administer an injection fifteen units up on the figure she's supposed to be stabilized on. Question one: are you able to confirm Goldine's own statement that she has been a diabetic more than two years?"

"If you are, no trouble. We'll instruct the doctors to cope," emphasized McCorquodale. "I regard this as a management decision."

"You've explained the problem to her?" said Dryden. "Does she understand the danger?"

Dr. Dalton turned to McCorquodale. "This is bringing us to question two. Could we first establish his answer to my first question?"

Dryden had to stall. "It's somewhat irregular, isn't it, questioning Miss Serafin's statements like this?"

McCorquodale said, "He's right, Ben. Make your second point." Turning to Dryden, he added, *"This* is why we're asking you."

Dr. Dalton shrugged and said, "Okay, then. The fact is, Mr. Dryden, that we are concerned about Goldine's behavior. I was commissioned to monitor her diabetes, and I'm quite well up on the disease. I can tell you patients often react emotionally when their balance of insulin isn't right. Nervousness is common. Irritability, emotional upset, this kind of thing. But this young woman is displaying behavior that has me baffled. It's new in my experience. To be candid, I don't think it is related to the diabetes."

"What kind of behavior?"

The other doctor spoke: "We had an example the other afternoon when you visited her after her victory in the one hundred meters. The way she acted—didn't *you* think it was odd?"

"Is *that* the problem?" said Dryden mildly. "She has a few delusions of grandeur, that's all. Goddamn it, she had just won a gold medal."

"It goes deeper than that," said Dr. Dalton. "I've been with her a good deal over the last few days, remember. For much of the time she is perfectly rational, a sweet-natured girl, almost an innocent, to use an old-fashioned word. Then there are quite different phases of behavior, when she becomes aggressive, domineering and disturbingly irrational. For example, till Sunday she was sharing a room in the Village with two other girls, Janie Canute and Mary-Lou Devine. Sunday morning she accused Janie quite unjustly of having taken her gold medal from its case and tried it on around her neck. Both the others insisted nothing like that had happened. Goldine said Janie was trying to take away her power, something like that, quite weird. She insisted they should call her Goldengirl in the future."

"She came to see me," put in McCorquodale, "and told me this story, demanding that I move her into a single room, which is one reason why she's now billeted here."

"She has also made complaints to the team manager that Dr. Nagel and I are not treating her with the respect due to a golden girl," said Dr. Dalton. "Apparently it offends her to be touched. At times she is highly abusive to us both, demanding a kind of servile approach."

"Which is what made me mention the incident with you," said Nagel.

"Yet, as I say, on other occasions she'll treat us normally, as if the hostile scenes had never happened," said Dalton. "Mr. Dryden, I'm no psychoanalyst, but I'm afraid this girl may be manifesting a split personality."

"Schizophrenia," said Nagel.

"Which is why we venture to question her statements about the origin of her diabetes," said Dalton.

"So you see why we want you to tell us some more about Goldine," said McCorquodale. "You've known her some time, I understand. We haven't, and we have the responsibility of deciding what to do about tomorrow. She is determined to run, but we can't put her in danger. What it comes down to is whether we can place any reliance on her statement that she has been diabetic for two years."

So Dryden felt another clamp tighten. There was no escape from involvement in this nightmare. "May I ask you a question? Who suggested you should talk to me about this?"

Dr. Dalton glanced toward McCorquodale. "Shall I answer this? Mr. Dryden, I questioned Goldine pretty closely. She said you would verify it. She doesn't know we're also consulting you about her mental state."

That was it, then. Goldine herself had put them on to him. The suggestion to mislead the doctors about the onset of the diabetes had come from him. She had returned the pass. "I don't know that I can comment on her behavior. Certainly it was strange the other afternoon after the one hundred meters, although the circumstances were exceptional." He flicked ash from the cigarette. "Goldine has been under tremendous pressure, with the kidnaping, all the interest of the media, the decision whether to compete. I was surprised, yes, but on reflection I can understand that the stress of that Final brought her to a mental crisis point. What you say is disturbing. I hope she can get over this. Looking at it as a nonspecialist, I'd say the important thing now is not to interfere any more with her expectations."

"To let her run?" said McCorquodale, beaming.

Dryden nodded.

Dalton said, "There's still the question of her diabetes."

McCorquodale turned to Dryden. "Well?"

"I can't say for sure when she contracted it, but it must have been established way back. If she says two years . . ."

"That's good enough for me," said McCorquodale firmly. "Gentlemen, Goldine runs tomorrow."

They had put Serafin in a high-backed armchair like a throne. He was pale under the arc lamps, but there was no trace of nervousness in his expression. Behind him was a blowup of Goldine winning the 100 meters. Facing him, unobtrusively, on a low chair, his interviewer, clipboard in hand.

First they had asked him to talk through the videotape of the gold-medal performance as they ran it through in slow motion. He had done it confidently, commenting with technical know-how on the minutiae of the start, pickup and sprint.

Then the interviewer had taken him over the salient events in Goldine's childhood: the accident on Huntington State Beach, her time in Tamarisk Lodge, the adoption. Clearly everything was on the clipboard. Stills were shown of Trudi in TWA uniform, Goldine at three, the Los Angeles *Times* report on the drowning.

The first indication that Serafin had his own ideas about the direction of the interview had come when the adoption was mentioned. He had insisted on outlining his research project. The interviewer had gone along with him for a short while, then put in a mild inquiry about the relevance of this to Goldine's track career, but Serafin had refused to be sidetracked. He had gone on for another half minute. Then he had brought it around to Goldine: "The research involved tracing people, you see. Goldine's mother was one of them. She had emigrated to California. When I tried to locate her, I learned about the accident. Out of compassion, my wife and I decided to adopt the child."

"Out of compassion," repeated the interviewer without emphasis.

"That was what I said."

"She had this exceptional physique, you said."

Serafin refused to be drawn. "That did not influence our decision."

They moved on to Goldine's upbringing.

"She went to school?"

"She was educated at home."

"Why was that, Dr. Serafin?"

"I wanted to be sure her physical potential was not neglected."

"It had, er, come to your notice by then?"

"As a physiologist, I recognized that she was exceptionally advanced in muscular and skeletal development."

"You figured she was a future sports star?"

"I suspected she could be, with the right encouragement."

"The right encouragement. That meant home schooling. Anything else?"

"Physical exercise. I fitted up a home gymnasium."

"Vaulting boxes, wall bars, weights—that kind of thing?"

"That kind of thing," Serafin repeated with a slight hesitation, as if uncertain whether he was being led into a trap.

A pause.

"Quite an outlay, I guess, Dr. Serafin—home tutors and all that apparatus?"

"It was worth it to me. As an investment."

The shot switched to the interviewer, his eyebrows lifted inquiringly. "You mean a profit-making venture?"

Serafin shifted in his chair. "No, no. I used the word in a figurative sense. By providing facilities I was investing in Goldine's health, her physical development. At the time we are talking about, when I installed the home gym, the Olympics were twelve or thirteen years ahead. Surely you must see that all those years ago I could not have been thinking in terms of financial reward." Sensing that in avoiding one snare, he was stepping into another, Serafin drew back. Too obviously. "Don't misunderstand me. I'm not suggesting athletes gain anything financially from winning the Olympics." Now the camera zoomed in to see how he was holding up. The sweat was beading on his forehead and his eyelids flickered as he stated, "Goldine is strictly an amateur. She runs for love of the sport."

The interviewer let that hang in the air a moment.

"Okay, let's get back to the time when you first learned she could run fast. How exactly did you discover she had this superlative speed?"

"Not merely speed. A superlative physique," said Serafin, riding that one smoothly. "That was obvious to me when she was a child."

"The running," gently pressed the interviewer. "When did the Olympic idea take root?"

"I wish you wouldn't single out the running as if that is the only manifestation of her ability," said Serafin, recouping some confidence. "She would excel in any sport involving agility, given time to acquire the necessary skill. On the Sheldon classification she rates as a mesomorph, despite her unusual height—"

The interviewer wasn't being bulldozed. "You hired one of the best track coaches in America to help Goldine acquire the necessary skill for Moscow. That was two years ago, wasn't it?"

"Where is this leading?" demanded Serafin, folding his arms defiantly. "You want me to admit I staked thousands of dollars to help Goldine win the Olympics? Well, I don't deny it. I provided every facility I could afford. Not for profit." He leaned forward in the chair. "I did it in the interest of science. Such is the stranglehold of the media that even scientists are compelled to resort to publicity to get their research noticed."

"Research? You mean she is running to publicize some theory of yours?"

"I mentioned the project just now," said Serafin with a click of impatience. "My investigations into human growth."

The interviewer looked puzzled. "I'm sorry, Dr. Serafin, I'm a little slow. Maybe it's the time of day. I just don't see where your theory of growth fits into this."

Serafin gripped the sides of the chair, plainly in some kind of mental turmoil. "Until this moment I fully intended to make this public only through the scientific press. I gave certain assurances . . . but now that you raise the matter so directly . . ." He raised his face suddenly, so that his spectacles flashed in the arc lights. "Goldine is the living answer to my critics, the people who said the human frame had somehow ossified into an immutable size. She is taller by ten centimeters—a full four inches—than conventional growth would have achieved." He spread his hands dramatically. "She is, in stature, a woman of the future, a century from now. There is no degeneration. She is not brittle-boned or misshapen." His voice had settled on a shrill monotone. "She has proved herself the fastest woman sprinter in the world. You may ask how this was achieved—"

"Okay," chipped in the interviewer. "How was it achieved?"

Serafin stopped and looked around the studio in a strange way, as if suddenly reminded that he was speaking not to one man, but millions. He had been on the point of admitting he had injected Goldine with the growth hormone. Now he drew back. "It is too technical to go into here, but I shall publish."

The interviewer shrugged. "For the present, let's admit Goldine is just one brilliant runner coached to perfection."

"No! That is a misrepresentation!" protested Serafin. "She is physiologically unique, a prototype of a generation as yet unborn. The mesomorphic characteristics—"

"You're so right, Doctor, it is a little technical," broke in the interviewer. "Maybe if we turned to the Cleveland kidnap incident—"

"So that's it!" Serafin said hysterically. "You won't give up until you have got me to admit Goldine is running for profit. If it isn't to increase my bank balance, it must be to pay back the ransom. Money is all you people are interested in. I tell you the kidnaping was of no importance. I've forgotten Cleveland, Goldine has forgotten it, and I suggest you do the same."

"I guess the gentlemen who put up the ransom haven't forgotten," commented the interviewer. "How much was it—a million? There must be a lot of pressure on Goldine to accept commercial offers after the Games are over."

"What happens after the Games is of no interest to me," said Serafin loftily. "As a scientist, my concern is with truth, not profit."

"Truth? Perhaps in that case you could verify something, Doctor. There's a story that a leading American merchandising agent is ready to launch your daughter on a commercial career as soon as she has finished running here in Moscow."

Serafin said in a spasm of viciousness, "I don't give a damn what happens to Goldine after the Games. Do you understand that?"

"I think so," the interviewer coolly answered. "You put it clearly."

An expression of pure fright crept over Serafin's features. He began to blurt out words. "Don't get the wrong impression. I was speaking of the girl's—of Goldine's—right to decide things for herself. I shan't interfere. That's all." It was unconvincing.

The interviewer levelly asked, "You would deny that you had conversations yourself with this agent?"

"Conversations?" repeated Serafin, stumbling over the word. In the last few minutes his dignity had been ripped away, leaving him old and incoherent. "A man can have conversations with anyone, can't he? As her father, I have a responsibility . . ." He took off his glasses and wiped them, as if that would produce more clarity in his responses. "What . . . what is this? Are you questioning my integrity? I'm a scientist. I live by facts, the truth." He replaced the glasses clumsily. "Goldine has proved my theory of growth. You can't shake that. That's what I stand by." He seemed to draw strength from his fixation. "You can say what you like about me. *She* can say what she likes, but the truth is secure." He was abstractedly examining the back of one of his hands. "I called her Goldine when she was a child, but she is Goldengirl now."

The interviewer made another try for a rational response. "You mean if she wins her other events she could become a legend, Doctor?"

"Fact," answered Serafin in a preoccupied way. "Not legend. A truth, secure for the rest of time."

What had shaped up as riveting television was becoming diffuse. The second camera caught the interviewer signaling to the control room.

"The truth is greater than Goldengirl," Serafin maundered on. "Science is greater than any individual. What are athletes but freaks and monsters? Give them a chance, and they will deform themselves to achieve success . . ." His words faded, but his lips still moved.

The shot switched to the interviewer, glancing up from his clipboard. "The, er, point that emerges is that in 1980 no athlete seriously pitching for gold medals can remain an amateur in the old-fashioned sense of the word. It just can't be done on weekends and evenings. You need long periods to train, specialized coaching. And for that you must have financial support, whether it comes in state aid or from private sources. In a free society such as ours it's up to individual athletes to get what assistance they can. You'd go along with that, Doctor?"

Serafin didn't look up. He was talking to himself.

The interviewer wrapped it up as fast as he decently could. "I'd like to underline that nobody condemns Goldine or her father for being realistic about the financial involvement necessary to Olympic success. We just like to face facts. Well, it's nearly 6 A.M. here in Moscow, and the city is waking up to what could be a great day for young Goldine Serafin in the Lenin Stadium. We've heard from her father. Now let's look in again on the press conference Goldine gave after her victory in the one-hundred-meter dash on Saturday . . ."

The schedule for Wednesday, August 20, was a repeat of the final day in Eugene, with the 200-meter Semi-Final, 200-meter Final and 400-meter Final packed into a single afternoon. The world press had crystallized it into a duel between two girls. They were pictured like contestants in a big fight, compared inch for inch, record for record. Only the special souvenir edition of *Sovietsky Sport* mentioned anyone else for honors, making Muratova one of the "Big Three" in the 200 meters, a compliment she justified by equaling her Olympic Record in the first Semi-Final, defeating Krüll by two meters. But it didn't require a deep knowledge of track to see that the East German was coasting, and had more in reserve for the Final than Muratova.

Goldine was equally undemonstrative in the second Semi-Final, easing into overdrive only in the last twenty meters to make sure of third place, then trotting straight through the competitors' tunnel and back to the medical unit.

Dryden could have gone down to get a progress report from Dalton and Nagel, but he decided against it. There was no more he could do to guarantee success; it was up to the doctors. Besides, he could not predict what effect his appearance in the room would have on Goldine. He dared not risk provoking an outburst at this stage of the game.

"Don't give yourself ulcers over this," cautioned Melody. "She has it all wrapped up. *This* isn't the crunch."

At 3:50 P.M. the phone rang in the U.S. Team Headquarters. McCorquodale took the call. He didn't say much, except to mutter "I see" a couple of times. When he put the phone down he was ashen.

"Jesus," he said. "That really does it. Goldine's old man is dead. Killed himself. Jumped out of his hotel window, twelve floors up. Bloody hell, why did he want to do a dumb thing like that?"

Nobody in the room had seen the TV interview. They learned about that from Klugman when they called him in. "Didn't see it myself, but I heard he took a mauling. You going to tell her?"

"Someone has to," said McCorquodale. "There's over an hour to the Finals. She's going to hear it someway before then. Yeah, she has to be told. We thought maybe . . ."

Klugman nodded. "I figured you would come to that."

"We thought she'd take it better from you, being her coach. This is going to shatter the kid. Too bad about those Finals. She'll be in no state to run after this . . . will she?"

Klugman shrugged. "Who knows?"

"Say now," said McCorquodale after a judicious pause, "you might try putting it to Goldine that the old man wouldn't have wanted her to cop out now. She could go in the Finals as a kind of tribute to his memory."

"It's a thought," said Klugman, looking at the ceiling.

He found Goldine limbering up in the covered area. He took her to sit on a bench.

"What is it?" she asked. "You know I should keep moving."

"Something has come up. Bad news."

"I drew inside lane in the two hundred?"

"No. It's Doc. He's dead, Goldine. Killed himself." She said nothing.

Tracksuited runners continued to jog around the circuit.

"They want me to say you should still run," said Klugman presently. "Don't let this throw you. He'd want you to run. You'll be doing it for him."

She caught her breath sharply, turned and spat hard in Klugman's face. "Punk! I'm doing *nothing* for him. I don't give a shit what he would want. Get this straight. I'm running for myself. No one else. Okay, Doc's dead. So what? I don't want to know how or why. I'm indifferent. This is *my* day, okay?"

Klugman took out a handkerchief and wiped his face. "You should keep moving, then."

The eight finalists for the 200 meters slipped into the arena at five-fifteen, while a men's track final was in progress. They walked as a group toward the start on the far side of the field, carrying their sports bags, not speaking, nor attempting communication, insulated from each other by the need to focus the mind. No group at all, really: eight lonely girls with eight dreams.

Dryden watched the limbering-up through his field glasses, calisthenics interspersed with frenetic bursts of running, apparently improvised, but familiar from earlier rounds as fixed, elaborate rituals. Krüll went in for repeated knee-raising, hopping and jumping in series, while Goldine favored lying and sitting exercises followed by short, swift dashes along the turf.

The starter ordered them to prepare.

They peeled off superfluous layers under the inspection of the TV cameras and moved onto the track.

When the crowd became quiet and the runners flexed from the hunkered position to the forward tilt ordered by *"Gotovo,"* Dryden's field glasses focused not on Goldine, but Ursula Krüll. That Cassandra-like pronouncement of Melody's—*"This* isn't the crunch"—had nagged at his brain, refusing to be subdued. Melody had always fatalistically accepted what Dryden had only dared by degrees to consider as a possibility: that Goldine would win her three gold medals. In Melody's mind the Games were a bore, a formality to be got through. Dryden had never been confident enough to think like that; each heat was a hazard, each final an ordeal. He had never projected his thoughts beyond Moscow in the way Melody had, because so much hinged on the achieving of those three victories. Now, two short races from realization, it came to him with paralyzing clarity what this was really going to achieve. He saw what Melody had seen from the start, and he recoiled. Goldine was poised to win her second gold, and if she beat Krüll now, the third would surely follow.

A defeat would sacrifice a fortune, undo the work of weeks, but what was the alternative?

Goldengirl.

He saw her as Melody had always seen her. Saw a monster. Saw himself.

He wanted Krüll to win.

The gun fired and they were moving, Krüll on the inner lane, Goldine out in 4, but Dryden kept the glasses on the German. She had got a smooth start and was running the bend, angled over the white curb, stride measured to take the strain without loss of power. Each time the back leg straightened, sharp lines defined the muscle tissue of thigh and calf, but it was unforced movement. He could see the soft side of her face ripple, her chest bob with the rhythm.

And she was overtaking other runners. Through the glasses he saw her reach and pass the Cuban girl in lane 2. Others successively came back to her as the bend unwound and the inequality of the staggered start was corrected. An Australian with the diagonal green stripe. Muratova, overstriding. The crowd roared its support, but Krüll went past.

Into the extreme right of Dryden's field of vision, level with Krüll's track shoes, came a blur of gold, the airborne mass of Goldine's hair. She was about a meter and a half clear, and because she was several lanes closer to the glasses it looked as if Krüll's shoes were reaching out to claw the shimmering hair. They *were* reaching it. Sheer strength was bringing the German level.

Ursula, come on!

The finish line couldn't be far away, and the blue of East Germany was edging ahead. Angles can be deceptive, but at the moment they passed level with the glasses, Krüll was decisively coming through. Her arms reached up in triumph as she crossed the line.

But this anticipation of success was miscalculated. Sensing victory in the last strides, she had imperceptibly eased. Goldine had galvanized, forced herself into contention again, and dipped for the tape. There was no question that she had won.

"Two up," said Melody indifferently. "Or two down, depending on your point of view."

"What do you mean?" said Dryden. He hadn't said a word to Melody about his support for Krüll.

"Down." She held out a hand toward the finish area. "Prostrate. Flat on the grass. Got it?"

Both girls were supine after their efforts, lying almost side by side, gasping to reclaim the oxygen, indifferent to the clamor around them.

The result was posted before they were on their feet.

200 METER FINAL

1 SERAFIN	USA	21.88 NWR
2 KRÜLL	GDR	21.89
3 MURATOVA	URS	22.45

"World record!" said Melody. "How about that?"

"Who cares?" said Dryden.

Melody simply raised her eyebrows.

Between the Finals of the 200 and 400 meters was a half-hour interval. When Goldine sat up and learned she had set a new world record, it pleased her, but she wasn't surprised. It had felt fast, and she had expected to run inside twenty-two seconds to defeat Ursula Krüll. She glanced across at the German, got to her feet and held out her hand to help her up.

"Come on. One more to go."

Krüll took the hand as if it was another challenge, and got up, rather red around the eyes, but straight-faced. "Congratulations. You surprised me."

"Surprised a lot of people, I guess," said Goldine. "Care to walk over to the other side with me?"

One of the U.S. team officials pushed through the cameramen and said he had come to escort Goldine to the medical unit.

"It's okay," she said. "I'll look after myself. I plan to spend some time out here."

"But Dr. Dalton instructed me——"

"Well, he won't instruct *me*," said Goldine petulantly. "So you can take a message right back to him. If he wants to send his musclemen to drag me over, they can try, but it won't look pretty, will it? Come on, Ursula."

They jogged together the long way around the track, receiving the crowd's applause. Several times children ran out with bunches of flowers. Goldine made sure Ursula had as many to hold as she. They couldn't speak much for the cheering. Other athletes kept running forward to shake her hand.

When they had reached their warm-up suits and put them on, it was time to join the other finalists warming up for the 400 meters. Goldine was confident. The physicians would think it was mean ignoring them after all they had done through the week, but she didn't need them any more. All she had to remember was to take the two glucose tablets in the pocket of her warm-ups. They would raise the bloodsugar level and prevent the risk of insulin reaction. That was what the doctors would have suggested anyway, for all their mumbo-jumbo. Two glucose tablets: that was all they ever prescribed.

Near the start, they were joined by Janie Canute.

"Hi," said Goldine.

"Hi, Goldengirl," said Janie with a smile.

That was good to hear. There had been some awkwardness earlier in the week about that. This was Janie's way of saying she was sorry.

"Got any tips for me, Janie?" Goldine magnanimously asked. "Last time, you told me about those two speedburners, remember? We let them scorch the first two hundred and they got clean away."

"No tips," said Janie. "You're the girl to beat."

"Ursula holds the record," Goldine pointed out.

Janie gave the right answer. "She's not Goldengirl, is she?"

The signal sounded to bring them under starter's

orders. Goldine unzipped the ankle fastenings of her warm-up suit without hurrying. This was her moment. She would be the last to go to her mark. She watched Krüll, making sure she went first. The German was taking her time, tucking her trackshirt into her shorts.

Just in time, Goldine remembered her tablets, picked up the sweat pants and felt in the pocket for them. No sweat, they were there, two of them in their paper wrapping. She took them out.

"Hey!"

Goldine turned. Janie Canute was behind her, wagging a finger.

"Uppers aren't allowed, Goldengirl."

Ursula Krüll had turned to see what was happening.

Goldine stood with the tablets in her palm. She could have said "Glucose" and swallowed them. Goddamn it, she was Goldengirl. She had been conditioned to function in disaster and finish in style.

The hell with tablets!

That was style. She dropped them on the ground, glanced over to see that Krüll was watching, and crushed them to powder under her spikes.

The others walked to their positions.

She eased her hair behind her ears, nodded to the starter and crossed sedately to lane 8, the outside position, 45 meters ahead of the innermost girl, with all that extra ground to cover on the bends. It meant running without anyone else in view, but that suited her. She could ignore the others, run without distraction. This wasn't a race, but an exhibition.

On the blocks it was so quiet she could have been back in the mountains training with Pete Klugman, knowing she would get volts up her arm if she was slow.

"*Gotovo.*"

If you come away slower, by Jesus, I'll step up the impulse.

The shot. She was into a perfect start, feeling the smoothness of the pickup, forgetting the technique because it was instinctive. Striding out in lane 8, hearing the buzz of wind on her eardrums, knowing that the first 200 could decide the race.

Get your ass moving!

Pete. He had said such mean things. It might have been different. What was it Sammy had said?

The relationship between a coach and an athlete has overtones neither may completely understand.

Something had gone wrong. She had wanted Pete, wanted him to treat her like she was one of the human race.

Off the bend already, into the backstretch.

Make it like you mean it. Give it everything.

Instead of Pete, she had made it with Jack Dryden. She had told herself she needed a man. A stud. It had been humiliating.

Am I so grotesque?

Past the 200-meter mark. Somewhere in the crowd, Pete would have taken the split. It should be fast. She still wanted to please him. She supposed she did.

When you mount the victory rostrum in Moscow, the glory will be yours. Little, if any, will reflect on anyone else.

Round the top bend, feeling the pain. If you didn't feel pain by now, something would be wrong. Why was she doing this? Not for Dean Hofmann. Not Goldine Serafin. They were finished, dead. For Goldengirl.

To be Goldengirl is to know that wherever you go there is warmth, admiration, affection.

Only the stretch now. Still alone. Concentrate on the tape, Goldengirl. Keep your eyes fixed on it. Let it draw you like a lodestone.

For those few days in Moscow, you will be the focus of more pride, more affection than any individual on this earth.

She didn't need Doc or Sammy, Pete or Jack Dryden. She was going to get her golds and give some meaning to her life, draw a line underneath and begin to find out who she really was.

The line. Keep watching the line.

She was moving, but she couldn't feel her limbs. A strange sensation, unlike anything before. Perhaps it had been a mistake destroying those tablets, but wasn't this one of the setbacks she had been conditioned to overcome?

The way you respond is vital to your success.

Success. Keep moving.

Winning in Moscow is fulfillment. Does that figure?

It figures.

She crossed the line.

A meter behind, Ursula Krüll crossed second.

Goldengirl didn't know. She had collapsed on the track.

[22]

THE crowd stood to watch the stretcher-bearers lift Goldine from where she had fallen. She remained immobile. Cameramen walked with the stretcher, recording each step to the tunnel.

"That's a crummy scenario," Melody commented. "Collapsing on the track. I don't go for that at all. I guess she already did the lap-of-honor bit, so she had to come up with something new. Maybe she's right. People could have gotten the idea it was easy winning three golds."

Dryden was sick with worry. "You're a cynical bitch," he rasped at Melody as he started for the exit.

"Thanks. Where are you going now?"

How could she be so dumb? "To the medical unit. See how she is."

"I'll come. Who knows—she may need me. She could have staged this to fit in a facial before she meets the press."

He pretended not to hear.

Below the stand, the area around the U.S. Team Headquarters had been sealed with mobile crowd-barriers. U.S. officials manned it at three-yard intervals. This was a security exercise worthy of the Russians. Half the international press were ranged around the barrier.

One official was arguing with a girl in a U.S. warm-up suit.

"Easy, buster," said a newsman. "You know who this

is? Janie Canute. She has just won a bronze medal for your country and mine."

It cut no ice with the official, but Dryden levered his way through the cameras to Janie's side. "Miss Canute, I'm Jack Dryden, a friend of Goldine's. Saw you first in Eugene."

"If you'll excuse me," she said, "I have to get inside that room." She tried another official. "Listen, I must see the doctors who are looking after Goldine. There's something they should know. If you won't let me in, would you take a message, please? It could be important."

"Sorry, sweetheart. With this crowd . . ."

"What is it?" asked Dryden. "What do you want to tell them?"

Resigned to making no headway with the men on the barrier, she turned to Dryden as second best. "Well, a few minutes ago I was in the dressing room untying my spikes when two women in U.S. team blazers came looking for the box containing Goldine's tracksuit. I pointed out which one, and they picked it up and went through the pockets. One of them said, "It's okay, nothing here," and they dropped the warm-up suit and walked off. It was only after they had gone I realized what they were talking about—a couple of tablets Goldine had with her before the race. They must have decided she had eaten them, only she didn't. She crushed them under her foot. I saw. I figure if the doctors sent two people to check on them, those tablets must be important."

Before Janie had finished speaking, Dryden had jumped the barrier. Two officials ran to tackle him, but he got to the door. One of the heavies on guard there recognized him.

"Must see Dr. Dalton," said Dryden, and to his relief the man stepped aside.

Inside, a huddle of doctors and officials surrounded Goldine's inert form. They had tugged up her trackshirt to her armpits and put a stethoscope against her heart.

Dalton glanced up at Dryden. "You?" he said angrily.

Dryden pitched into Janie's story.

"Of all the crazy things!" said Dalton. "That confirms hypoglycemia. We must give her another shot of epinephrine. Quick as you can." While the nurse prepared an injection, Dalton swabbed alcohol on Goldine's upper arm. "Oh boy, will they ever listen to you? I told her myself what would happen if she didn't take the glucose."

"It's a coma?" asked Dryden.

"Yeah. Insulin reaction." He took the syringe and injected a main vein. "It was bound to happen when she didn't take the glucose between races. The energy displacement lowers the blood-sugar level, which throws the balance of the insulin. I just hope we've caught it in time."

"What happens if . . .?"

"Brain damage. Maybe death," said Dalton. "I just don't understand why she did this. To forget to take the damned things I could believe, but to crush them like that is insane."

When Dryden came out, he had trouble convincing the newsmen he was making no statement of any kind. He was photographed, jostled and slanged before he eventually broke through. Two or three were still frowning asking questions when he found Melody on the fringe of the crowd. They photographed her as well.

"You're obviously the man of the hour," she said when they had finally shaken them off. "What's the news, then?"

"Coma."

"Bad?"

"Could be. Very bad."

"If the press get hold of it, you mean?" said Melody.

"No, damn it, I'm talking about Goldine."

"Sure you are," said Melody sarcastically. "I can see it's on account of her you're worried, like you have been all along, shaking your head each time you drew up another contract. Jack, I read you all wrong. I took you for a cynical, money-grabbing bastard. What do we do now—buy flowers?"

"I must cancel the TV linkup. She won't be fit to talk to the President."

"Too bad," said Melody.

"And arrange for McCorquodale to make some kind of holding statement to the press."

"Gee, that's sweet," said Melody. "Here you are, broken up with worry, and you can still go through the motions of straightening out the PR complications. Really touching."

At 7:15 P.M. Don McCorquodale made a brief statement to a crowded audience in the press center. Goldine Serafin had recovered consciousness, but on medical advice she wouldn't meet the press until she had rested. Routine tests were being carried out to determine the reason for her collapse. They were not ruling out the possibility that the shock news of her father's suicide had contributed to it. The team management wished to put on record that they had always been aware of heavy demands of Goldine's schedule, and had provided medical support from the beginning. Unfortunately, it had not been possible to check her condition in the short interval between the Finals of the 200 and 400 meters. They were hopeful she would be well enough to speak to the press sometime the following day.

At 9:20 P.M. Dryden got in to see McCorquodale in the Olympic Village. For two hours he had been trying to get more news of Goldine. The security had descended like steel shutters. Trying to see a doctor was impossible. The best he could get was Mc-Corquodale.

"I don't have a lot of time," he warned Dryden. "What a day! This problem over Goldine is just the end. I think we've succeeded in holding off the press till tomorrow, but it wasn't easy. I don't care for cover-ups as a rule, but, as I see it, Goldine's medical condition is her affair. No reason for the public to hear about it."

Dryden nodded and asked, "What's the latest? How is she now?"

"Fully conscious. We moved her back to the Embassy. Doctors are still with her."

"I suppose you wouldn't know . . ." Dryden took a long breath. "Do they expect her to recover—fully, I mean?"

McCorquodale scratched his ear. "They say the blood-sugar level is still erratic, which is making her a difficult patient." He regarded Dryden closely. "Hey, you really care about the kid. Do you have something going with her?"

"Just tell me what the doctors say," said Dryden in a tone that wasn't conversational.

"Dalton told me the diabetes has taken a much stronger grip. He describes it as severe now. Said it was mild the other day. That's the price of three gold medals. Still, I guess you'll be doing what you can to get some reparation for her in financial terms." McCorquodale winked. "This is worth a huge amount in endorsements, huh?"

Dryden lifted his shoulders slightly without saying anything.

"It's okay," went on McCorquodale. "You can trust me. I don't get disturbed about agents moving in on Olympic athletes. I'm a realist. You can do a lot to make young Goldine's life more tolerable. When I heard about Doc Serafin getting hammered on TV I figured you were the agent they mentioned. Bad business, that. You don't think it can hurt Goldine, do you? Seems to me any damage to her image is compensated by the sympathy she's gotten from the old man's death leap. Just think of her knowing about that as she went to the line for the last race! *Goldine's Agony*. That's going to go over big back home."

"Right now, I don't give a damn about the image," said Dryden. "I just want to see Goldine. Can you fix that, Mr. McCorquodale?"

"Don."

"Don."

"Confidentially, I'm a businessman myself," said McCorquodale. "This Olympic job is honorary, naturally. You get expenses, but hell . . . matter of fact, I'm in real estate. Wouldn't mind talking to you about it sometime. No hurry. After we get home, huh? I'm thinking about a scheme for the young executive buyer. Calling it the Golden Roof. You like it?"

"Yes," said Dryden. "I'm with you. It's a winner. Now, if I could get to see Goldine . . . ."

McCorquodale smiled broadly. "Why not? Dalton may kick up a bit. You know how medics are. He'll want to keep her on ice, but I can overrule him. We hired him to see Goldine through her track program, and that's complete. Let's say nine tomorrow morning at the Embassy. Christ, if we leave it to Dalton, she won't even get to the Stadium to collect her medals. That could really foul up her commercial prospects."

He arrived with Goldine's mail, a batch of it sent over from the Olympic Village. There must have been two hundred letters and cables. He offered to take them in to her. Behind them he tucked the flowers he was self-consciously carrying. Red roses, bought that morning in Kutozovsky Prospect.

Dryden had known plenty of women. Till now, he had managed that side of his life as efficiently as his business career. It was an extension of business entertainment: the contact, the meal, the wine, the transaction. Emotion had scarcely come into it, except

404

superficially. It did now. It was time to tell Goldine he loved her.

The door stood open, but he tapped before stepping inside.

The room was stacked with flowers, like a funeral parlor.

Goldine was sitting up in bed in a pink lace nightdress. Her gold medal for the 100 meters was around her neck. It looked bizarre.

"Oh, it's you," she said in a flat voice. "What's that you have with you? More mail? Put it with the rest."

A mass of unopened mail was heaped with the morning papers on a table behind the door. He added his delivery to it.

"Those can go in the washbasin," said Goldine, eyeing the roses. "There are no more vases."

He ran some water and dropped them in. "Looks as if the first thing you'll need is a secretary."

She was brushing her hair, not looking at him. "I've thought about that. I'll use Fryer."

"Melody?" said Dryden, surprised. "I thought you two didn't—"

"She can give me facials as well. Tint my hair. I want her to be around, see me living in style. You can fix that."

Her manner had caught him off guard. "I can try. I'm not sure if—"

"Fix it," she said with a glare. "And while Fryer works for me, I don't want you shacking up with her, understand? That's not what I employ you for."

He should have walked straight out. Instead, he clutched at the idea that this was an aberration. She was jealous of Melody. With that instinct women have for recognizing arousal in one of their own sex, she had seen what he had not considered till now: that Melody, cool, caustic Melody, was actually soft on him.

"Goldine," he said, moving closer, "you couldn't be more wrong. To me Melody is—"

"An easy lay," said Goldine casually. "Forget it."

"I want you to know how I feel about *you*," he insisted, seating himself on the bed. "I've got to tell you this—I love you, Goldine." He scanned her features for a flicker of interest. "Believe me, I'm crazy about you. Christ, I am!" He had moved his face to within inches of hers, impatient to end the tension.

She didn't move. She held his look with her wide blue eyes and said impassively, "You bore me out of my skull. Get your ass off my bed and get me a paper. I spend hours talking to goddamn newsmen and nobody gives me a paper to read."

Dryden drew back reeling, a pulse beating in his brain. She hadn't spoken in anger. She was calm and deliberate.

He had lost her. Something had been there once, but it was gone. Permanently. She didn't need love, not the kind he wanted to give.

Automatically, he picked up a Russian paper and handed it to her. "It's all there," he heard himself saying. "Pictures. Too soon for the American papers, but you'll be big news."

"And the TV?" she said, her eyes lighting up. "What did they say on TV?"

"I phoned New York. You were the lead story on every news bulletin."

"My running, you mean. They say anything about my collapse?"

He was answering mechanically. Like someone bereaved, he needed to be kept occupied while he adjusted to the overwhelming sense of loss. "They had it on film, of course, but they don't know the reason. The theory is that you ran yourself right out."

"I'll buy that," she said.

"How do you feel?"

She was looking at the paper. "Sore. How would you like an injection in your butt every morning for the rest of your life?"

"I'm sorry," said Dryden. "When we started this, none of us knew . . ."

"Skip it. What's done is over. Finished. I'm Goldengirl, like I was meant to be."

He looked at her, knowing she was right. Finished. For Goldengirl, love was the scrutiny of the media. Questions were caresses. She needed no other fulfillment.

He was left with himself, with loathing and disgust. He had helped to create her. Worse, he had been given the chance to preserve her from this. *You're in control now,* Serafin had told him. In control, he had sent her to her destruction. He was the monster.

Now the control was out of his hands. She knew that. She also knew he would not abandon her. He was not in control, but, by God, he was responsible.

She put down the paper. "Anything else?"

"Will you be collecting your medals in the Stadium this afternoon?"

"You bet."

"Dr. Dalton won't object?"

"Let him try stopping me. Let anyone try."

"I have some exciting news for you," he said, beginning to function again. "The TV people have arranged a linkup with Washington. The President wants to congratulate you personally."

"Exciting?" said Goldine. *"He* should be excited."

The crowds were four and five deep in Kropotkin Street when the white limousine with its police outriders carried Goldengirl, wearing her three gold medals, from the Lenin Stadium to the Kremlin. Their destination was the vast glass-and-aluminum Palace of Congresses, with seating for six thousand, the only building in Moscow capable of accommodating her press conference.

Dryden was seated with Melody at the back of the buzzing auditorium. Melody had spent the morning grooming Goldengirl for the occasion.

"How was she?" asked Dryden.

"Docile," said Melody. "If you indulge her, play up the fantasy, it's okay."

"It's no fantasy," said Dryden. "It happened. It's irreversible fact."

The conversation around them gathered in tempo and volume. Cameras were flashing somewhere. A group of people moved toward the forest of microphones at the center of the platform.

"Ladies and gentlemen," said a voice, "triple Olympic champion Miss Goldine Serafin."

Clapping put an end to conversation. It continued at least half a minute before she appeared, pausing for pictures. She was as lovely as when Dryden had first seen her in the simulation session in the mountains, exuberant, laughing, savoring the acclaim with unashamed delight. Flowers were heaped into her arms. The medals repeatedly caught the flashlight. It was impossible not to share her exhilaration.

"At this moment, she must be the most envied woman in the world," said Dryden.

Melody, usually so quick with a tart comment, remained silent.

The questions got under way, but Dryden hardly listened. He knew the replies would be witty, confident and apparently spontaneous. It would be a repeat of what he had heard before. Different in sequence, but essentially the same performance. The difference was in the performer.

Down on the platform, some question triggered a response. Goldengirl cupped the medals in her hand and said, "From now on, these are my charms."